Praise for *Nebula Awards Showcase 2007...*

...and for the previous volumes

continued...

"Stellar....This is not only a must-read for anyone with an interest in the field, but a pleasure to read....That's more reassuring than surprising, of course, given that this collection has little if any agenda besides quality writing, but it is reassuring to see that so many fresh voices are so much fun....Worth picking up."

—SF Revu

"While the essays offer one answer to the question of where does SF go now, the stories show that science fiction writers continue to reexamine their vision of the future. It's a continuing dialogue, and by including critical essays along with the stories, the *Nebula Awards Showcase 2002* does more to present the SF field as an ongoing conversation and discussion of ideas than any of the other best of the year anthologies. It's a worthy contribution and a good volume to have on your shelf."

—SF Site

"Every fan will have their favorites; there's pretty much something for everyone. . . . Overall, *Nebula Awards Showcase 2006* gets it right. I judge it a keeper."   — Scifi Dimensions

"[A] quality mix of literary SF and fantasy with critical essays."

—*Publishers Weekly*

"An essential index of one year in SF and fantasy."   —*Booklist*

"The variety of taste shown by the SFWA continues to be striking and heartening."   —*Publishers Weekly*

"Invaluable, not just for the splendid fiction and lively nonfiction, but as another annual snapshot, complete with grins and scowls."

—*Kirkus Reviews*

NEBULA AWARDS©

SHOWCASE

2008

THE YEAR'S BEST SF AND FANTASY

Selected by the Science Fiction and
Fantasy Writers of America©

EDITED BY

Ben Bova

A ROC BOOK

ROC
Published by New American Library,
a division of Penguin Group (USA) Inc.,
375 Hudson Street, New York, New York 10014, USA
Penguin Group (Canada), 90 Eglinton Avenue East, Suite 700, Toronto,
Ontario M4P 2Y3, Canada (a division of Pearson Penguin Canada Inc.)
Penguin Books Ltd., 80 Strand, London WC2R 0RL, England
Penguin Ireland, 25 St. Stephen's Green, Dublin 2,
Ireland (a division of Penguin Books Ltd.)
Penguin Group (Australia), 250 Camberwell Road, Camberwell,
Victoria 3124, Australia (a division of Pearson Australia Group Pty. Ltd.)
Penguin Books India Pvt. Ltd., 11 Community Centre,
Panchsheel Park, New Delhi–110 017, India
Penguin Group (NZ), 67 Apollo Drive, Rosedale, North Shore 0632,
New Zealand (a division of Pearson New Zealand Ltd.)
Penguin Books (South Africa) (Pty.) Ltd., 24 Sturdee Avenue,
Rosebank, Johannesburg 2196, South Africa

Penguin Books Ltd., Registered Offices:
80 Strand, London WC2R 0RL, England

Published by Roc, an imprint of New American Library,
a division of Penguin Group (USA) Inc.

First Printing, April 2008
1   3   5   7   9   10   8   6   4   2

CONTENTS

INTRODUCTION

BEN BOVA

've had a love affair with science fiction since I first learned to read. In fact, one of my incentives for learning to read was *Action Comics*, featuring Superman.

I can still see that dazzling illustration showing a rocket ship fleeing from the exploding planet Krypton. Talk about "sense of wonder"! It knocked me on my five-year-old butt. And started a lifelong fascination with astronomy, rocketry, and (of course) science fiction.

That one image taught me an important lesson: The universe changes, sometimes abruptly, dramatically, catastrophically. And the literature of change is the aforementioned genre of science fiction.

It was a ghetto literature then. Respectable people disdained science fiction, branding it as trashy pulp fiction, not worthy of serious consideration.

But I loved it. From swashbuckling John Carter on Edgar Rice Burroughs's Barsoom to Isaac Asimov's "The Ugly Little Boy," I saw much more in science fiction than in most of the contemporary literature being published then. I devoured the pages of *Astounding Science Fiction* and, later, *Galaxy* and *The Magazine of Fantasy and Science Fiction*.

Yet even by the time I began working on the first American artificial satellite program, Vanguard, I found that even professional rocket engineers still hid their copies of *Astounding Science Fiction* magazine in the bottom drawer of their desks.

Then came SFWA. Originally called Science Fiction Writers of America, the organization broadened its scope eventually to become Science Fiction and Fantasy Writers of America (although it officially retained the acronym SFWA), in recognition of the true breadth of the field.

SFWA began in the fertile mind of Damon Knight. He and his wife, Kate Wilhelm, hosted the annual Milford Science Fiction Writers Conference in their Pennsylvania home each summer. One year, Damon proposed that we create a professional organization, by, of, and for the writers in our field.

The rest, as they say, is history. It may be coincidence, but as SFWA began to establish the professional integrity of science fiction and fantasy, universities began taking the field seriously and teaching courses in it. And book publishers started to realize that science fiction and fantasy appeals to a very wide audience, thanks in no small measure to publishers and editors such as Ian Ballantine and Judy-Lynn del Rey.

It didn't hurt, of course, that TV's *Star Trek* and Hollywood blockbusters such as *2001: A Space Odyssey* and *Star Wars* opened the eyes of hundreds of millions of viewers to the same "sense of wonder" that smacked me when I first saw the planet Krypton explode.

Today science fiction and fantasy have infiltrated (*conquered*, I'm tempted to say) just about every facet of popular culture, from romance novels to Broadway musicals, from television series to university studies of "alternate futures."

Science fiction and fantasy have matured. And so has SFWA. The organization is thriving, and has been a strong advocate for writers in their never-ending struggles with publishers and producers who would like to take the fruit of a writer's genius and labor without paying fairly for it.

Since 1966 the members of SFWA have given Nebula Awards to the stories and screenplays they consider the best of the year. This is the most coveted award in the field, bestowed on writers by their fellow writers.

Each year the Nebula Award winners are showcased in an anthology. You hold in your hands the *Nebula Showcase 2008*, which features the award winners of 2006. Within the covers of this book you can see what SFWA's members considered the best work of that year: the award winners in each category, the Grand Masters and Authors Emeriti, plus a trio of essays discussing the past, present, and future of the science fiction and fantasy field.

You will see the Rhysling Award–winning poems, essays on the Best Script Nebula and the André Norton Award for young adult fiction, as well as a broad variety of story types, themes, and treatments. Which is only natural, since the field of science fiction and fantasy encompasses all of time, all of space, all of the universe within the human soul—and then some.

Have an exciting journey!

Ben Bova
Naples, Florida
June 2007

ABOUT THE SCIENCE FICTION AND FANTASY WRITERS OF AMERICA

The Science Fiction and Fantasy Writers of America, Incorporated (SFWA), includes among its members most of the active writers of science fiction and fantasy. According to the bylaws of the organization, its purpose is "to promote the furtherance of the writing of science fiction, fantasy, and related genres as a profession." SFWA informs writers on professional matters, protects their interests, and helps them in dealings with agents, editors, anthologists, and producers of nonprint media. It also strives to encourage public interest in and appreciation of science fiction and fantasy.

Anyone may become an active member of SFWA after the acceptance of payment for one professionally published novel, one professionally produced dramatic script, or three professionally published pieces of short fiction. Only science fiction, fantasy, horror, and other prose fiction of a related genre, in English, shall be considered as qualifying for active membership. Beginning writers who do not yet qualify for active membership may join as associate members; other classes of membership include illustrator members (artists), affiliate members (editors, agents, reviewers, and anthologists), estate members (representatives of the estate of active members who have died), and institutional members (high schools, colleges, universities, libraries, broadcasters, film producers, futurist groups, and individuals associated with such an institution).

Anyone who is not a member of SFWA may subscribe to *The Bulletin of the Science Fiction and Fantasy Writers of America.* The magazine is published quarterly and contains articles by well-known writers on all aspects of their profession. Subscriptions are twenty-one dollars per year or thirty dollars for two years. For information on how to subscribe to the *Bulletin*, or for more information about SFWA, write to:

SFWA, Inc.
P.O. Box 877
Chestertown, MD 21620
USA

Readers are also invited to visit the SFWA site on the World Wide Web at www.sfwa.org.

ECHO

ELIZABETH HAND

Elizabeth Hand is the multiple-award-winning author of nine novels, including *Generation Loss*, *Mortal Love*, and *Illyria*, as well as three collections of short fiction, the most recent of which is *Saffron and Brimstone: Strange Stories*. She is a longtime contributor to the *Washington Post Book World*, the *Village Voice*, and *Down East* magazine, among numerous others, and writes a regular column for *Fantasy & Science Fiction* magazine. She lives on the coast of Maine with her two teenage children and her partner, British critic John Clute. She is currently working on a novel about Arthur Rimbaud, titled *Wonderwall*.

About "Echo" she writes:

"Echo" grew from my long epistolary friendship with journalist David Streitfeld. We've only met a handful of times since 1988, but have corresponded regularly since then. My novels Mortal Love *and* Generation Loss *are dedicated to David, along with the four post-9/11 stories that comprise "The Lost Domain" sequence, published separately but collected in toto in* Saffron and Brimstone.

The phrase "the lost domain" comes from Alain-Fournier's 1913 novel The Wanderer (Le Grand Meaulnes)*. The nature of inspiration and desire, the relationship of the muse to an artist—these were the things David and I talked about* *endlessly, and most of the work I've done in the new millennium has been informed by these discussions. "The Lost Domain" was a protracted effort on my part to shape these ideas into fiction, and "Echo" was the first story in the sequence.*

In September 2002, David went on assignment to Baghdad to write about what was then euphemistically termed "the rebuilding effort." We were out of touch during his stint there, though, unlike other journalists and far too many soldiers, he returned safely home to write about the experience. "Echo" grew out of the dread I felt during that time, along with the surreal sense of horror and isolation that continues to shade our post-9/11 world.

ECHO

ELIZABETH HAND

This is not the first time this has happened. I've been here every time it has. Always I learn about it the same way, a message from someone five hundred miles away, a thousand, comes flickering across my screen. There's no TV here on the island, and the radio reception is spotty: the signal comes across Penobscot Bay from a tower atop Mars Hill, and any kind of weather—thunderstorms, high winds, blizzards— brings the tower down. Sometimes I'm listening to the radio when it happens, music playing, Nick Drake, a promo for the Common Ground Country Fair; then a sudden soft explosive hiss like damp hay falling onto a bonfire. Then silence.

Sometimes I hear about it from you. Or, well, I don't actually hear anything: I read your messages, imagine your voice, for a moment neither sardonic nor world-weary, just exhausted, too fraught to be expressive. Words like feathers falling from the sky, black specks on blue.

The Space Needle. Sears Tower. LaGuardia Airport. Golden Gate Bridge. The Millennium Eye. The Bahrain Hilton. Sydney, Singapore, Jerusalem.

Years apart at first; then months; now years again. How

long has it been since the first tower fell? When did I last hear from you?

I can't remember.

This morning I took the dog for a walk across the island. We often go in search of birds, me for my work, the wolfhound to chase for joy. He ran across the ridge, rushing at a partridge that burst into the air in a roar of copper feathers and beech leaves. The dog dashed after her fruitlessly, long jaw sliced open to show red gums, white teeth, a panting unfurled tongue.

"Finn!" I called and he circled round the fern brake, snapping at bracken and crickets, black splinters that leapt wildly from his jaws. "Finn, get back here."

He came. Mine is the only voice he knows now.

There was a while when I worried about things like food and water, whether I might need to get to a doctor. But the dug well is good. I'd put up enough dried beans and canned goods to last for years, and the garden does well these days. The warming means longer summers here on the island, more sun; I can grow tomatoes now, and basil, scotch bonnet peppers, plants that I never could grow when I first arrived. The root cellar under the cottage is dry enough and cool enough that I keep all my medications there, things I stockpiled back when I could get over to Ellsworth and the mainland—albuterol inhalers, alprazolam, amoxicillin, Tylenol and codeine, ibuprofen, aspirin; cases of food for the wolfhound. When I first put the solar cells up, visitors shook their heads: not enough sunny days this far north, not enough light. But that changed too as the days got warmer.

Now it's the wireless signal that's difficult to capture, not sunlight. There will be months on end of silence and then it will flare up again, for days or even weeks, I never know when.

If I'm lucky, I patch into it, then sit there, waiting, holding my breath until the messages begin to scroll across the screen, looking for your name. I go downstairs to my office every day, like an angler going to shore, casting my line though I know the weather's wrong, the currents too strong, not enough wind or too much, the power grid like the Grand Banks scraped barren by decades of trawlers dragging the bottom. Sometimes my line would latch onto you: sometimes, in the middle of the night, it would be the middle of the night where you were, too, and we'd write back and forth. I used to joke about these letters going out like messages in bottles, not knowing if they would reach you, or where you'd be when they did.

London, Paris, Petra, Oahu, Moscow. You were always too far away. Now you're like everyone else, unimaginably distant. Who would ever have thought it could all be gone, just like that? The last time I saw you was in the hotel in Toronto, we looked out and saw the spire of the CN Tower like Cupid's arrow aimed at us. You stood by the window and the sun was behind you and you looked like a cornstalk I'd seen once, burning, your gray hair turned to gold and your face smoke.

I can't see you again, you said. Deirdre is sick and I need to be with her.

I didn't believe you. We made plans to meet in Montreal, in Halifax, Seattle. Grey places; after Deirdre's treatment ended. After she got better.

But that didn't happen. Nobody got better. Everything got worse.

In the first days I would climb to the highest point on the island, a granite dome ringed by tamaracks and hemlock, the grey stone covered with lichen, celadon, bone-white, brilliant orange: as though armfuls of dried flowers had been tossed from an airplane high overhead. When evening came the aurora borealis would streak the sky, crimson, emerald, amber, as though the sun were rising in the west, in the middle of the night, rising for hours on end. I lay on my back wrapped in an old Pendleton blanket and watched, the dog Finn stretched out alongside me. One night the spectral display continued into dawn, falling arrows of green and scarlet, silver threads like rain or sheet lightning racing through them. The air hummed, I pulled up the sleeve of my flannel shirt and watched as the hairs on my arm rose and remained erect; looked down at the dog, awake now, growling steadily as he stared at the trees edging the granite, his hair on end like a cat's. There was nothing in the woods, nothing in the sky above us. After perhaps thirty minutes I heard a muffled sound to the west, like a far-off sonic boom; nothing more.

After Toronto we spoke only once a year; you would make your annual pilgrimage to mutual friends in Paris and call me from there. It was a joke, that we could only speak like this.

I'm never closer to you than when I'm in the seventh arrondissement at the Bowlses', you said.

But even before then we'd seldom talked on the phone. You said it would destroy the purity of our correspondence, and refused to give me your number in Seattle. We had never seen that much of each other anyway, a handful of times over the decades. Glasgow once, San Francisco, a long weekend in Liverpool, another in New York. Everything was in the letters; only of course they weren't actual letters but bits of information, code, electrical sparks; like neurotransmitters leaping the chasm between synapses. When I dreamed of you, I dreamed of your name shining in the middle of a computer screen like a ripple in still water. Even in dreams I couldn't touch you: my fingers would hover above your face and you'd fragment into jots of grey and black and silver. When you were in Basra I didn't hear from you for months. Afterward you said you were glad; that my silence had been like a gift.

For a while, the first four or five years, I would go down to where I kept the dinghy moored on the shingle at Amonsic Cove. It had a little two-horsepower engine that I kept filled with gasoline, in case I ever needed to get to the mainland.

But the tides are tricky here, they race high and treacherously fast in the Reach; the *Ellsworth American* used to run stories every year about lobstermen who went out after a snagged line and never came up, or people from away who misjudged the time to come back from their picnic on Egg Island, and never made it back. Then one day I went down to check on the dinghy and found the engine gone. I walked the length of the beach two days running at low tide, searching for it, went out as far as I could on foot, hopping between rocks and tidal pools and startling the cormorants where they sat on high boulders, wings held out to dry like black angels in the thin sunlight. I never found the motor. A year after that the dinghy came loose in a storm and was lost as well, though for months I recognized bits of its weathered red planking when they washed up onshore.

The book I was working on last time was a translation of Ovid's *Metamorphosis*. The manuscript remains on my desk beside my computer, with my notes on the nymph "whose tongue did not still when others spoke," the girl cursed by Hera to fall in love with beautiful, brutal Narkissos. He hears her pleading voice in the woods and calls to her, mistaking her for his friends.

But it is the nymph who emerges from the forest. And when he sees her Narkissos strikes her, repulsed; then flees. *Emoriar quam sit tibi copia nostri!* he cries; and with those words condemns himself.

Better to die than be possessed by you.

And see, here is Narkissos dead beside the woodland pool, his hand trailing in the water as he gazes at his own reflection. Of the nymph,

> *She is vanished, save for these:*
> *her bones and a voice that*
> *calls out amongst the trees.*
> *Her bones are scattered in the rocks.*
> *She moves now in the laurels and beeches,*
> *she moves unseen across the mountaintops.*
> *You will hear her in the mountains and wild places,*
> *but nothing of her remains save her voice,*
> *her voice alone, alone upon the mountaintop.*

Several months ago, midsummer, I began to print out your letters. I was afraid something would happen to the computer and I would lose them forever. It took a week, working off and on. The printer uses a lot of power and the island had become locked in by fog; the rows of solar cells, for the first time, failed to give me enough light to read by during the endless grey days, let alone run the computer and printer for more than fifteen minutes at a stretch. Still, I managed, and at the end of a week held a sheaf of pages. Hundreds of them, maybe more; they made a larger stack than the piles of notes for Ovid.

I love the purity of our relationship, you wrote from Singapore. Trust me, it's better this way. You'll have me forever!

There were poems, quotes from Cavafy, Sappho, Robert Lowell, W. S. Merwin. It's hard for me to admit this, but the sad truth is that the more intimate we become here, the less likely it is we'll ever meet again in real life. Some of the letters had my responses copied at the beginning or end—imploring, fractious—lines from other poems, songs.

Swept with confused alarms of

I long and seek after

You can't put your arms around a memory.

The first time, air traffic stopped. That was the eeriest thing, eerier than the absence of lights when I stood upon the granite dome and looked westward to the mainland. I was used to the slow constant flow overhead, planes taking the Great Circle Route between New York, Boston, London, Stockholm, passing above the islands, Labrador, Greenland, grey space, white. Now, day after day after day the sky was empty. The tower on Mars Hill fell silent. The dog and I would crisscross the island, me throwing sticks for him to chase across the rocky shingle, the wolfhound racing after them and returning tirelessly, over and over.

After a week the planes returned. The sound of the first one was like an explosion after that silence, but others followed, and soon enough I grew accustomed to them again. Until once more they stopped.

I wonder sometimes, How do I know this is all truly happening? Your letters come to me, blue sparks channeled through sunlight; you and your words are more real to me than anything else. Yet how real is that? How real is all of this? When I lie upon the granite I can feel stone pressing down against my skull, the trajectory of satellites across the sky above me a slow steady pulse in time with the firing of chemical signals in my head. It's the only thing I hear, now: it has been a year at least since the tower at Mars Hill went dead, seemingly for good.

One afternoon, a long time ago now, the wolfhound began barking frantically and I looked out to see a skiff making its way across the water. I went down to meet it: Rick Osgood, the part-time constable and volunteer fire chief from Mars Hill.

"We hadn't seen you for a while," he called. He drew the skiff up to the dock but didn't get out. "Wanted to make sure you were okay."

I told him I was, asked him up for coffee but he said no. "Just checking, that's all. Making a round of the islands to make sure everyone's okay."

He asked after the children. I told him they'd gone to stay with their father. I stood waving, as he turned the skiff around and it churned back out across the dark water, a spume of black smoke trailing it. I have seen no one since.

Three weeks ago I turned on the computer and, for the first time in months, was able to patch into a signal and search for you. The news from outside was scattered and all bad. Pictures, mostly; they seem to have lost the urge for language, or perhaps it is just easier this way, with so many people so far apart. Some things take us to a place where words have no meaning. I was readying myself for bed when suddenly there was a spurt of sound from the monitor. I turned and saw the screen filled with strings of words. Your name: they were all messages from you. I sat down elated and trembling, waiting as for a quarter-hour they cascaded from the sky and moved beneath my fingertips, silver and black and grey and blue. I thought that at last you had found me; that these were years of words and yearning, that you would be back. Then, as abruptly as it had begun, the stream ceased; and I began to read.

They were not new letters; they were all your old ones, decades-old, some of them. 2009, 2007, 2004, 2001, 1999, 1998, 1997, 1996. I scrolled backwards in time, a skein of years, words; your name popping up again and again like a bright bead upon a string. I read them all, I read them until my eyes ached and the floor was pooled with candle wax and broken light bulbs. When morning came I tried to tap into the signal again but it was gone. I go outside each night and stare at the sky, straining my eyes as I look for some sign that something moves up there, that there is something between myself and the stars. But the satellites too are gone now, and it has been years upon years since I have heard an airplane.

In fall and winter I watch those birds that do not migrate. Chickadees, nuthatches, ravens, kinglets. This last autumn I took Finn down to the deep place where in another century they quarried granite to build the Cathedral of Saint John the Divine. The quarry is filled with water, still and black and bone-cold. We saw a flock of wild turkeys, young ones; but the dog is so old now he can no longer chase them, only watch as I set my snares. I walked to the water's edge and gazed into the dark pool, saw my face reflected there but there is no change upon it, nothing to show how many years have passed for me here, alone. I have burned all the empty crates and cartons from the root cellar, though it is not empty yet. I burn for kindling the leavings from my wood bench, the hoops that did not curve properly after soaking in willow-water, the broken dowels and circlets. Only the wolfhound's grizzled muzzle tells me how long it's been since I've seen a human face. When I dream of you now I see a smooth stretch of water with only a few red leaves upon its surface.

We returned from the cottage, and the old dog fell asleep in the late afternoon sun. I sat outside and watched as a downy woodpecker, *Picus pubescens*, crept up one of the red oaks, poking beneath its soft bark for insects. They are friendly birds, easy to entice, sociable; unlike the solitary wrynecks they somewhat resemble. The wrynecks do not climb trees but scratch upon the ground for the ants they love to eat. "Its body is almost bent backward," Thomas Bewick wrote over two hundred years ago in his *History of British Birds*, "whilst it writhes its head and neck by a slow and almost involuntary motion, not unlike the waving wreaths of a serpent. It is a very solitary bird, never being seen with any other society but that of its female, and this is only transitory, for as soon as the domestic union is dissolved, which is in the month of September, they retire and migrate separately."

It was this strange involuntary motion, perhaps, that so fascinated the ancient Greeks. In Pindar's fourth Pythian Ode, Aphrodite gives the wryneck to Jason as the magical means to seduce Medea, and with it he binds the princess to him through her obsessive love. Aphrodite of many arrows: she bears the brown-and-white bird to him, "the bird of madness," its wings and legs nailed to a four-spoked wheel.

> *And she shared with Jason*
> *the means by which a spell*
> *might blaze and burn Medea,*
> *burning away all love she had for her family*
> *a fire that would ignite her mind, already aflame*
> *so that all her passion turned to him alone.*

The same bird was used by the nymph Simaitha, abandoned by her lover in Theokritos's Idyll: pinned to the wooden wheel, the feathered spokes spin above a fire as the nymph invokes Hecate. The isle is full of voices: they are all mine.

Yesterday the wolfhound died, collapsing as he followed me to the top of the granite dome. He did not get up again, and I sat beside him, stroking his long grey muzzle as his dark eyes stared into mine and, at last, closed. I wept then as I didn't weep all those times when terrible news came, and held his great body until it grew cold and stiff between my arms. It was a struggle to lift and carry him, but I did, stumbling across the lichen-rough floor to the shadow of the thin birches and tamaracks overlooking the Reach. I buried him there with the others, and afterward lit a fire.

This is not the first time this has happened. There is an endless history of forgotten empires, men gifted by a goddess who bears arrows, things in flight that fall in flames. Always, somewhere, a woman waits alone for news. At night I climb alone to the highest point of the island. There I make a little fire and burn things that I find on the beach and in the woods. Leaves, bark, small bones, clumps of feathers, a book. Sometimes I think of you and stand upon the rock and shout as the wind comes at me, cold and smelling of snow. A name, over and over and over again.

Farewell, Narkissos said, and again Echo sighed and whispered, *Farewell*.

BURN

JAMES PATRICK KELLY

James Patrick Kelly has had an eclectic writing career. He has written novels, short stories, essays, reviews, poetry, plays, audioplays, and planetarium shows. With John Kessel he is coeditor of *Feeling Very Strange: The Slipstream Anthology* and *Rewired: The New Cyberpunk Anthology*. His fiction has been translated into sixteen languages. He has won the World Science Fiction Society's Hugo Award twice. He writes a column on the Internet for *Asimov's Science Fiction* magazine and is on the faculty of the Stonecoast Creative Writing MFA Program at the University of Southern Maine. In 2007, he launched James Patrick Kelly's StoryPod on Audible, a podcast that will feature him reading fifty-two stories.

Here's what he has to say about the genesis of "Burn":

I can't claim that it was inevitable that I would write "Burn." Many years ago my little novel began to accrete around a grudge I had against one of our literary Founding Fathers, Henry David Thoreau. But Thoreau wasn't why I wrote "Burn." As I contemplated this project, one of its principal attractions was the lure of doing research into forest firefighting, a subject that is at once intrinsically fascinating and way obscure. Lolling around libraries paging through books that haven't been checked out since 1975 is one of my principal joys as a writer. In addition, I could find very little fiction about forest firefighting, and none in genre, which meant that I'd have the territory pretty much to myself. But fire wasn't the reason I wrote "Burn." Of course, like so many of my fellow skiffy writers, I'd been wrestling with the problem of the singularity, and writing about a human enclave in a posthuman galaxy seemed like a challenge that was within my range. But once again, that wasn't why I wrote "Burn."

The fact is that Jacob Weisman of Tachyon Publications cajoled me into signing a contract for a thirty-thousand-word novella by telling me I could write pretty much whatever I wanted. If it hadn't been for him, I probably would've spent the end of 2004 and early 2005 on short fiction, as had been my habit for almost a decade. I signed on thinking how pleasant it would be to have a new book that wasn't a short story collection. However, I wasn't at all sure that I could sustain a narrative over thirty thousand words, after too many years away from the long form. At the time I told myself that if worse came to worst, I could churn out twenty-two to twenty-five thousand words and hand in a manuscript with a large font and wide margins. And so, by giving myself permission to fail, I was able to begin.

Years ago I had made a note about the curious incident of the forest fire that Henry David Thoreau started. You can read some of Thoreau's account of what happened at the beginning of chapter 14 in "Burn," but suffice it to say that after accidently setting the Walden woods ablaze—some estimates hold that more than three hundred acres were consumed—our First Naturalist repaired to the top of Fair Haven Hill to admire his own private conflagration. I thought folks ought to know about this. You see, as a student I was force-fed Walden and much of it disagreed with me. I will admit that never has the Luddite point of view been ad-

vanced quite so eloquently. And while I agree that simplicity can be a virtue and that cultivation of one's inner resources is necessary for the good life, it seems clear to me that the habit of thought which Thoreau urges on us is antithetical to the enterprise of science fiction. Thoreau had little use for the technology of his own time, dismissing both the telegraph and the railroad. I can imagine his horror at the spread of our own asphalt and information superhighways. Hey, I'm all for spirituality, but not if it means I can't check my e-mail.

I know more about the Thousand Worlds than I have told in "Burn." I was surprised that once I got into the book, I had no trouble reaching twenty-five thousand words, then thirty thousand, then thirty-five thousand. As my deadline loomed, I had to make some strategic decisions about the shape of the book. I decided to leave out stuff, in order to keep a tight focus on my main character and his problems, some of which open out into the larger concerns of his world and the galactic culture, but some of which are as personal as who will pick the apples or play the outfield. I think this reflects the kind of life that I'm living. I'm concerned about global warming and the pointless war in Iraq, but the dishes still have to go into the dishwasher and the grass is growing. Maybe it's time to strap on the headphones and load Walden into my MP3 player. I can listen to Thoreau lecture me about men leading lives of quiet desperation while I mow the lawn.

BURN

JAMES PATRICK KELLY

For H. D. T., a timeless visionary,
and for my children, Maura, Jamie, and John

We might try our lives by a thousand simple tests; as, for instance, that the same sun which ripens my beans illumines at once a system of earths like ours. If I had remembered this it would have prevented some mistakes. This was not the light in which I hoed them. The stars are the apexes of what wonderful triangles! What distant and different beings in the various mansions of the universe are contemplating the same one at the same moment! Nature and human life are as various as our several constitutions. Who shall say what prospect life offers to another?

—WALDEN

ONE

For the hero is commonly the simplest and obscurest of men.

—WALDEN

Spur was in the nightmare again. It always began in the burn. The front of the burn took on a liquid quality and oozed like lava toward him. It licked at boulders and scorched the trees in the forest he had sworn to protect. There was nothing he could do to fight it; in the nightmare, he wasn't wearing his splash pack. Or his fireproof field jacket. Fear pinned him against an oak until he could feel the skin on his face start to cook. Then he tore himself away and ran. But now the burn leapt after him, following like a fiery shadow. It chased him through a stand of pine; trees exploded like fire-crackers. Sparks bit through his civvies and stung him. He could smell burning hair. His hair. In a panic he dodged into a stream choked with dead fish and poached frogs. But the water scalded his legs. He scrambled up the bank of the stream, weeping. He knew he shouldn't be afraid; he was a veteran of the firefight. Still he felt as if something were squeezing him. A whimpering gosdog bolted across his path, its feathers singed, eyes wide. He could feel the burn dive under the forest and burrow ahead of him in every direction. The ground was hot beneath his feet and the dark humus smoked and stank. In the nightmare there was just one way out, but his brother-in-law Vic was blocking it. Only in the nightmare Vic was a pukpuk, one of the human torches who had started the burn. Vic had not yet set himself on fire, although his baseball jersey was smoking in the heat. He beckoned and for a moment Spur thought it might not be Vic after all as the anguished face shimmered in the heat of the burn. Vic wouldn't betray them, would he? But by then Spur had to dance to keep his shoes from catching fire, and he had no escape, no choice, no time. The torch spread his arms wide and Spur stumbled into his embrace and with an angry whoosh they exploded together into flame. Spur felt his skin crackle. . . .

"That's enough for now." A sharp voice cut through the nightmare. Spur gasped with relief when he realized that there was no burn. Not here anyway. He felt a cold hand brush against his forehead like a blessing and knew that he was in the hospital. He had just been in the sim that the upsiders were using to heal his soul.

"You've got to stop thrashing around like that," said the docbot. "Unless you want me to nail the leads to your head."

Spur opened his eyes but all he could see was mist and shimmer. He tried to answer the docbot but he could barely find his tongue in his own mouth. A brightness to his left gradually resolved into the sunny window of the hospital room.

Spur could feel the firm and not unpleasant pressure of the restraints, which bound him to the bed: broad straps across his ankles, thighs, wrists and torso. The docbot peeled the leads off his temples and then lifted Spur's head to get the one at the base of his skull.

"So do you remember your name?" it said.

Spur stretched his head against the pillow, trying to loosen the stiffness in his neck.

"I'm over here, son. This way."

He turned and stared into a glowing blue eye, which strobed briefly.

"Pupil dilatation normal," the docbot muttered, probably not to Spur. It paused for a moment and then spoke again. "So about that name?"

"Spur."

The docbot stroked Spur's palm with its med finger, collecting some of his sweat. It stuck the sample into its mouth. "That may be what your friends call you," it said, "but what I'm asking is the name on your ID."

The words chased each other across the ceiling for a moment before they sank in. Spur wouldn't have had such a problem understanding if the docbot were a person, with lips and a real mouth instead of the oblong intake. The doctor controlling this bot was somewhere else. Dr. Niss was an upsider whom Spur had never actually met. "Prosper Gregory Leung," he said.

"A fine Walden name," said the docbot, and then muttered, "Self ID 27.4 seconds from initial request."

"Is that good?"

It hummed to itself, ignoring his question. "The electrolytes in your sweat have settled down nicely," it said at last. "So tell me about the sim."

"I was in the burn and the fire was after me. All around, Dr. Niss. There was a pukpuk, one of the torches, he grabbed me. I couldn't get away."

"You remembered my name, son." The docbot's top plate glowed with an approving amber light. "So did you die?"

Spur shook his head. "But I was on fire."

"Experience fear vectors unrelated to the burn? Monsters, for instance? Your mom? Dad?"

"No."

"Lost loves? Dead friends? Childhood pets?"

"No." He had a fleeting image of the twisted grimace on Vic's face at that last moment, but how could he tell this upsider that his wife's brother had been a traitor to the Transcendent State? "Nothing." Spur was getting used to lying to Dr. Niss, although he worried what it was doing to his soul.

"Check and double check. It's almost as if I knew what I was doing, eh?" The docbot began releasing the straps that held Spur down. "I'd say your soul is on the mend, Citizen Leung. You'll have some psychic scarring, but if you steer clear of complex moral dilemmas and women, you should be fine." It paused, then snapped its fingers. "Just for the record, son, that was a joke."

"Yes, sir." Spur forced a smile. "Sorry, sir." Was getting the jokes part of the cure? The way this upsider talked at once baffled and fascinated Spur.

"So let's have a look at those burns," said the docbot.

Spur rolled onto his stomach and folded his arms under his chin. The docbot pulled the hospital gown up. Spur could feel its medfinger pricking the dermal grafts that covered most of his back and his buttocks. "Dr. Niss?" said Spur.

"Speak up," said the docbot. "That doesn't hurt, does it?"

"No, sir." Spur lifted his head and tried to look back over his shoulder. "But it's really itchy."

"Dermal regeneration eighty-three percent," it muttered. "Itchy is alive, son. Itchy is growing."

"Sir, I was just wondering, where are you exactly?"

"Right here." The docbot began to flow warm dermslix to the grafts from its medfinger. "Where else would I be?"

Spur chuckled, hoping that was a joke. He could remember a time when he used to tell jokes. "No, I mean your body."

"The shell? Why?" The docbot paused. "You don't really want to be asking about qics and the cognisphere, do you? The less you know about the upside, the better, son."

Spur felt a prickle of resentment. What stories were upsiders telling each other about Walden? That the citizens of the Transcendent State were backward fanatics who had simplified themselves into savagery? "I wasn't asking about the upside, exactly. I was asking about you. I mean . . . you saved me, Dr. Niss." It wasn't at all what Spur had expected to say, although it was certainly true. "If it wasn't for you, it . . . I was burned all over, probably going crazy. And I thought . . ." His throat was suddenly so tight that he could hardly speak. "I wanted to . . . you know, thank you."

"Quite unnecessary," said the docbot. "After all, the Chairman is paying me to take care of all of you, bless his pockets." It tugged at Spur's hospital gown with its gripper arm. "I prefer the kind of thanks I can bank, son. Everything else is just used air."

"Yes, but   "

"Yes, but?" It finished pulling the gown back into place. " 'Yes, but' are dangerous words. Don't forget that you people lead a privileged life here—courtesy of Jack Winter's bounty and your parents' luck."

Spur had never heard anyone call the Chairman Jack. "It was my grandparents who won the lottery, sir," he said. "But yes, I know I'm lucky to live on Walden."

"So why do you want to know what kind of creature would puree his mind into a smear of quantum foam and entangle it with a bot brain a hundred and thirty–some light-years away? Sit up, son."

Spur didn't know what to say. He had imagined that Dr. Niss must be posted nearby, somewhere here at the upsiders' compound at Concord, or perhaps in orbit.

"You do realize that the stars are very far away?"

"We're not simple here, Dr. Niss." He could feel the blood rushing in his cheeks. "We practice simplicity."

"Which complicates things." The docbot twisted off its medfinger and popped it into the sterilizer. "Say you greet your girlfriend on the tell. You have a girlfriend?"

"I'm married," said Spur, although he and Comfort had separated months before he left for the firefight and, now that Vic was dead, he couldn't imagine how they would ever get back together.

"So you're away with your squad and your wife is home in your village mowing the goats or whatever she does with her time. But when you talk on the tell it's like you're sitting next to each other. Where are you then? At home with her? Inside the tell?"

"Of course not."

"For you, of course not. That's why you live on Walden, protected from life on the upside. But where I come from, it's a matter of perspective. I believe I'm right here, even though the shell I'm saved in is elsewhere." The sterilizer twittered. "I'm inhabiting this bot in this room with you." The docbot opened the lid of the sterilizer, retrieved the medfinger with its gripper and pressed it into place on the bulkhead with the other instruments. "We're done here," it said abruptly. "Busy, busy, other souls to heal, don't you know? Which reminds me: We need your bed, son, so we're moving your release date up. You'll be leaving us the day after tomorrow. I'm authorizing a week of rehabilitation before you have to go back to your squad. What's rehab called on this world again?"

"Civic refreshment."

"Right." The docbot parked itself at its station beside the door to the examining room. "Refresh yourself." Its headplate dimmed and went dark.

Spur slid off the examination table, wriggled out of the hospital gown and pulled his uniform pants off the hanger in the closet. As he was buttoning his shirt, the docbot lit its eye. "You're welcome, son." Its laugh was like a door slamming. "Took me a moment to understand what you were trying to say. I keep forgetting what it's like to be anchored."

"Anchored?" said Spur.

"Don't be asking so many questions." The docbot tapped its dome. "Not good for the soul." The blue light in its eye winked out.

TWO

Most of the luxuries and many of the so-called comforts of life are not only not indispensable, but positive hindrances to the elevation of mankind.

—*WALDEN*

Spur was in no hurry to be discharged from the hospital, even if it was to go home for a week. He knew all too well what was waiting for him. He'd find his father trying to do the work of two men in his absence. Gandy Joy would bring him communion and then drag him into every parlor in Littleton. He'd be wined and dined and honored and possibly seduced and be acclaimed by all a hero. He didn't feel like a hero and he surely didn't want to be trapped into telling the grandmas and ten-year-old boys stories about the horrors of the firefight.

But what he dreaded most was seeing his estranged wife. It was bad enough that he had let her little brother die after she had made Spur promise to take care of him. Worse yet was that Vic had died a torch. No doubt he had been in secret contact with the pukpuks, had probably passed along information about the Corps of Firefighters—and Spur hadn't suspected a thing. It didn't matter that Vic had pushed him away during their time serving together in Gold Squad—at one time they had been best friends. He should have known; he might have been able to save Vic. Spur had already decided that he would have to lie to Comfort and his neighbors in Littleton about what had happened, just as he had lied to Dr. Niss. What was the point in smearing his dead friend now? And Spur couldn't help the Cooperative root out other pukpuk sympathizers in the Corps; he had no idea who Vic's contacts had been.

However, Spur had other reasons for wanting to stay right where he was. Even though he could scarcely draw breath without violating simplicity, he loved the comforts of the hospital. For example, the temperature never varied from a scandalous twenty-three degrees Celsius. No matter that outdoors the sun was blistering the rooftops of the upsiders' Benevolence Park Number 5, indoors was a paradise where neither sweat nor sweaters held sway. And then there was the food. Even though Spur's father, Capability Roger Leung, was the richest man in Littleton, he had practiced stricter simplicity than most. Spur had grown up on meat, bread, squash and scruff, washed down with cider and applejack pressed from the Leungs' own apples and the occasional root beer. More recently, he and Rosie would indulge themselves when they had the money, but he was still used to gorging on the fruits of the family orchard during harvest and suffering through preserves and root cellar produce the rest of the year. But here the patients enjoyed the abundance of the Thousand Worlds, prepared in extravagant style. Depending on his appetite, he could order lablabis, dumplings, goulash, salmagundi, soufflés, quiche, phillaje, curry, paella, pasta, mousses, meringues or tarts. And that was just the lunch menu.

But of all the hospital's guilty pleasures, the tell was his favorite. At home Spur could access the latest bazzat bands and town-tunes from all over Walden plus six hundred years of opera. And on a slow Tuesday night, he and Comfort might play one of the simplified chronicles on the tiny screen in Diligence Cottage or watch a spiritual produced by the Institute of Didactic Arts or just read to each other. But the screens of the hospital tells sprawled across entire walls and, despite the Co-operative's censors, opened like windows onto the universe. What mattered to people on other worlds astonished Spur. Their chronicles made him feel ignorant for the first time in his life and their spirituals were so wickedly materialistic that he felt compelled to close the door to his hospital room when he watched them.

The search engine in particular excited Spur. At home, he could greet anyone in the Transcendent State—as long as he knew their number. But the hospital tell could seemingly find anyone, not only on Walden but anywhere on all the Thousand Worlds of the upside. He put the tell in his room to immediate use, beginning by greeting his father and Gandy Joy, who was the village virtuator. Gandy had always understood him so much better than Comfort ever had. He should have greeted Comfort as well, but he didn't.

He did greet his pals in the Gold Squad, who were surprised that he had been able to track them down while they were on active duty. They told him that the entire Ninth Regiment had been pulled back from the Motu River burn for two weeks of CR in Prospect. Word was that they were being reassigned to the Cloyce Memorial Forest for some easy fire watch duty. No doubt the Cooperative was yanking the regiment off the front line because Gold Squad had taken almost 40 percent casualties when the burn had flanked their position at Motu. Iron and Bronze Squads had taken a hit as well, fighting their way through the burn to rescue Gold.

To keep from brooding about Vic and the Motu burn and the firefight, Spur looked up friends who had fallen out of his life. He surprised his cousin Land, who was living in Slide Knot in Southeast and working as a tithe assessor. He connected with his childhood friend Handy, whom he hadn't seen since the Alcazars had moved to Freeport, where Handy's mom was going to teach pastoral philosophy. She was still at the university and Handy was an electrician. He tracked down his self-reliance school sweetheart, Leaf Benkleman, only to discover that she had emigrated from Walden to Kolo in the Alumar system. Their attempt to catch up was frustrating, however, because the Cooperative's censors seemed to buzz every fifth word Leaf said. Also, the look on her face whenever he spoke rattled Spur. Was it pity? He was actually relieved when she cut their conversation short.

Despite the censors, talking to Leaf whetted Spur's appetite for making contact with the upside. He certainly wouldn't get the chance once he left the hospital. He didn't care that everyone was so preposterously far away that he would never meet them in person. Dr. Niss had been wrong: Spur understood perfectly the astonishing distances between stars. What he did not comprehend was exactly how he could chat with someone who lived hundreds of trillions of kilometers away, or how someone could beam themselves from Moy to Walden in a heartbeat. Of course, he had learned the simplified explanation of qics—quantum information channels—in school. Qics worked because many infinitesimally small nothings were part of a something, which could exist in two places at the same time. This of course made no sense, but then so much of upsider physics made no sense after the censors were done with it.

Spur paused in the doorway of his room and looked up and down the hall. None of the patients at his end of the ward were stirring; a lone maintenance bot dusted along the floor at the far end by the examining rooms. It was his last full day at the hospital. Now or never. He eased the door shut and turned the tell on.

He began by checking for relatives on the upside. But when he searched on the surname Leung, he got 2.3×10^6 hits. Which, if any, of them might be his people? Spur had no way of knowing. Spur's grandparents had expunged all records of their former lives when they had come to Walden, a requirement for immigrants to the Transcendent State. Like everyone else in his family, he had known the stern old folks only as GiGo and GiGa. The names on their death certificates were Jade Fey Leung and Chap Man-Leung, but Spur thought that they had probably been changed when they had first arrived at Freeport.

He was tempted to greet his father and ask if he knew GiGo's upside name, but then he would ask questions. Too many questions; his father was used to getting the answers he wanted. Spur went back to the tell. A refined search showed that millions of Leungs lived on Blimminey, Eridani Foxtrot, Fortunate Child, Moy, and No Turning Back, but there also appeared to be a scattering of Leungs on many of the Thousand Worlds. There was no help for it; Spur began to send greetings at random.

He wasn't sure exactly who he expected to answer, but it certainly wasn't bots. When Chairman Winter had bought Walden from ComExplore IC, he decreed that neither machine intelligences nor enhanced upsiders would be allowed in the refuge he was founding. The Transcendent State was to be the last and best home of the true humans. While the pukpuks used bots to manufacture goods that they sold to the Transcendent State, Spur had never actually seen one until he had arrived at the hospital.

Now he discovered that the upside swarmed with them. Everyone he tried to greet had bot receptionists, secretaries, housekeepers or companions screening their messages. Some were virtual and presented themselves in outlandish sims; others were corporeal and stared at him from the homes or workplaces of their owners. Spur relished these voyeuristic glimpses of life on the upside, but glimpses were all he got. None of the bots wanted to talk to him, no doubt because of the caution he could see scrolling across his screen. It warned that his greeting originated from "the Transcendent State of Walden, a jurisdiction under a consensual cultural quarantine."

Most of the bots were polite but firm. No, they couldn't connect him to their owners; yes, they would pass along his greeting; and no, they couldn't say when he might expect a greeting in return. Some were annoyed. They invited him to read his own Covenant and then snapped the connection. A couple of virtual bots were actually rude to him. Among other things, they called him a mud hugger, a leech and a pathetic waste of consciousness. One particularly abusive bot started screaming that he was "a stinking useless fossil."

Spur wasn't quite sure what a fossil was, so he queried the tell. It returned two definitions: *1. an artifact of an organism, typically extinct, that existed in a previous geologic era; 2. something outdated or superseded.* The idea that, as a true human, he might be outdated, superseded or possibly even bound for extinction so disturbed Spur that he got up and paced the room. He told himself that this was the price of curiosity. There were sound reasons why the Covenant of Simplicity placed limits on the use of technology. Complexity bred anxiety. The simple life was the good life.

Yet even as he wrestled with his conscience, he settled back in front of the tell. On a whim he entered his own name. He got just two results:

```
Comfort Rose Joerly and Prosper Gregory Leung
Orchardists
Diligence Cottage
Jane Powder Street
Littleton, Hamilton County,
Northeast Territory, TS
Walden
```
and
```
Prosper Gregory Leung
c/o Niss (remotely—see note)
```

Salvation Hospital
Benevolence Park #5
Concord, Jefferson County,
Southwest Territory, TS
Walden

Spur tried to access the note attached to Dr. Niss's name, but it was blocked. That wasn't a surprise. What was odd was that he had received results just from Walden. Was he really the only Prosper Gregory Leung in the known universe?

While he was trying to decide whether being unique was good or bad, the tell inquired if he might have meant to search for Proper Gregory Leung or Phosphor Gregory L'ung or Procter Gregoire Lyon? He hadn't but there was no reason not to look them up. Proper Leung, it turned out, raised gosdogs for meat on a ranch out in Hopedale, which was in the Southwest Territory. Spur thought that eating gosdogs was barbaric and he had no interest in chatting with the rancher. Gregory L'ung lived on Kenning in the Theta Persei system. On an impulse, Spur sent his greeting. As he expected, it was immediately diverted to a bot. L'ung's virtual companion was a shining green turtle resting on a rock in a muddy river.

"The High Gregory of Kenning regrets that he is otherwise occupied at the moment," it said, raising its shell up off the rock. It stood on four human feet. "I note with interest that your greeting originates from a jurisdiction under a consensual . . ."

The turtle didn't get the chance to finish. The screen shimmered and went dark. A moment later, it lit up again with the image of a boy, perched at the edge of an elaborate chair.

He was wearing a purple fabric wrap that covered the lower part of his body from waist to ankles. He was barechested except for the skin of some elongated, dun-colored animal draped around his thin shoulders. Spur couldn't have said for sure how old the boy was, but despite an assured bearing and intelligent yellow eyes, he seemed not yet a man. The chair caught Spur's eye again: it looked to be of some dark wood, although much of it was gilded. Each of the legs ended in a stylized human foot. The back panel rose high above the boy's head and was carved with leaves and branches that bore translucent purple fruit.

That sparkled like jewels.

Spur reminded himself to breathe. It looked very much like a throne.

THREE

It takes two to speak the truth—one to speak and another to hear.

—*A WEEK ON THE CONCORD AND MERRIMACK RIVERS*

"Hello, hello," said the boy. "Who is doing his talk, please?"

Spur struggled to keep his voice from squeaking. "My name is Prosper Gregory Leung."

The boy frowned and pointed at the bottom of the screen. "Walden, it tells? I have less than any idea of Walden."

"It's a planet."

"And tells that it's wrongful to think too hard on planet Walden? Why? Is your brain dry?"

"I think." Spur was taken aback. "We all think." Even though he thought he was being insulted, Spur didn't want to snap the connection—not yet anyway. "I'm sorry, I didn't get your name."

The words coming out of the speakers did not seem to match what the boy was saying. His lips barely moved, yet what Spur heard was, "I'm the High Gregory, Phosphorescence of Kenning, energized by the Tortoise of Eternal Radiation." Spur realized that the boy was probably speaking another language and that what he was hearing was a translation. Spur had been expecting the censors built into the tell to buzz this conversation like they had buzzed so much of his chat with Leaf Benkleman, but maybe bad translation was just as effective.

"That's interesting," said Spur cautiously. "And what is it that you do there on Kenning?"

"Do?" The High Gregory rubbed his nose absently. "Oh, do! I make luck."

"Really? People can do that on the upside?"

"What is the upside?"

"Space, you know." Spur waved an arm over his head and glanced upward.

The High Gregory frowned. "Prosper Gregory Leung breathes space?"

"No, I breathe air." He realized that the tell might easily be garbling his end of the conversation as well. "Only air." He spoke slowly and with exaggerated precision. "We call the Thousand Worlds the upside. Here. On my world."

The High Gregory still appeared to be confused.

"On this planet." He gestured at the hospital room. "Planet Walden. We look up at the stars." He raised his hand to his brow, as if sighting on some distant landmark. "At night." Listening to himself babble, Spur was certain that the High Gregory must think him an idiot. He had to change the subject, so he tapped his chest. "My friends call me Spur."

The High Gregory shook his head with a rueful smile. "You give me warmth, Spur, but I turn away with regret from the kind offer to enjoy sex with you. Memsen watches to see that I don't tickle life until I have enough of age."

Aghast, Spur sputtered that he had made no such offer, but the High Gregory, appearing not to hear, continued to speak.

"You have a fullness of age, friend Spur. Have you found a job of work on planet Walden?"

"You're asking what I do for a living?"

"All on planet Walden are living, I hope. Not saved?"

"Yes, we are." Spur grimaced. He rose from the tell and retrieved his wallet from the nightstand beside the bed. Maybe pix would help. He flipped through a handful in his wallet until he came to the one of Comfort on a ladder picking apples. "Normally I tend my orchards." He held the pix up to the tell to show the High Gregory. "I grow many kinds of fruit on my farm. Apples, peaches, apricots, pears, cherries. Do you have these kinds of fruit on Kenning?"

"Grape trees, yes." The High Gregory leaned forward in his throne and smiled. "And all of apples: apple pie and apple squeeze and melt apples." He seemed pleased that they had finally understood one another. "But you are not normal?"

"No. I mean yes, I'm fine." He closed the wallet and pocketed it. "But . . . how do I say this? There is fighting on my world." Spur had no idea how to explain the complicated grievances of the pukpuks and the fanaticism that led some of them to burn themselves alive to stop the spread of the forest and the Transcendent State. "There are other people on Walden who are very angry. They don't want my people to live here. They wish the land could be returned to how it was before we came. So they set fires to hurt us. Many of us have been called to stop them. Now instead of growing my trees, I help to put fires out."

"Very angry?" The High Gregory rose from his throne, his face flushed. "Fighting?" He punched at the air. "Hit-hit-hit?"

"Not exactly fighting with fists," said Spur. "More like a war."

The High Gregory took three quick steps toward the tell at his end. His face loomed large on Spur's screen. "War fighting?" He was clearly agitated; his cheeks flushed and the yellow eyes were fierce. "Making death to the other?" Spur had no idea why the High Gregory was reacting this way. He didn't think the boy was angry exactly, but then neither of them had proved particularly adept at reading the other. He certainly didn't want to cause some interstellar incident.

"I've said something wrong. I'm sorry." Spur bent his head in apology. "I'm speaking to you from a hospital. I was wounded . . . fighting a fire. Haven't quite been myself lately." He gave the High Gregory a self-deprecating smile. "I hope I haven't given offense."

The High Gregory made no reply. Instead he swept from his throne, down a short flight of steps into what Spur could now see was a vast hall. The boy strode past rows of carved wooden chairs, each of them a unique marvel, although none was quite as exquisite as the throne that they faced. The intricate beaded mosaic on the floor depicted turtles in jade and chartreuse and olive. Phosphorescent sculptures stretched like spider webs from the upper reaches of the walls to the barrel-vaulted ceiling, casting ghostly silver-green traceries of light on empty chairs beneath. The High Gregory was muttering as he passed down the central aisle but whatever he was saying clearly overwhelmed the tell's limited capacity. All Spur heard was, "War <crackle> Memsen witness there <crackle> our luck <crackle> <crackle> call the L'ung. . . ."

At that, Spur found himself looking once again at a shining green turtle resting on a rock on a muddy river. "The High Gregory of Kenning regrets that he is otherwise occupied at the moment," it said. "I note with interest that your greeting originates from a jurisdiction under a consensual cultural quarantine. You should understand that it is unlikely that the High Gregory, as luck maker of the L'ung, would risk violating your covenants by having any communication with you."

"Except I just got done talking to him," said Spur.

"I doubt that very much." The turtle drew itself up on four human feet and stared coldly through the screen at him. "This conversation is concluded," it said. "I would ask that you not annoy us again."

"Wait, I—" said Spur, but he was talking to a dead screen.

FOUR

But if we stay at home and mind our business, who will want railroads? We do not ride on the railroad; it rides upon us.

—*WALDEN*

Spur spent the rest of that day expecting trouble. He had no doubt that he'd be summoned into Dr. Niss's examining room for a lecture about how his body couldn't heal if his soul was sick. Or some virtuator from Concord would be brought in to light communion and deliver a reproachful sermon on the true meaning of simplicity. Or Cary Millisap, his squad leader, would call from Prospect and scorch him for shirking his duty to Gold, which was, after all, to get better as fast as he could and rejoin the unit. He had not been sent to the hospital to bother the High Gregory of Kenning, luck maker of the L'ung—whoever they were.

But trouble never arrived. He stayed as far away from his room and the tell as he could get. He played cards with Val Montilly and Sleepy Thorn from the Sixth Engineers, who were recovering from smoke inhalation they had suffered in the Coldstep burn. They were undergoing alveolar reconstruction to restore full lung function. Their voices were like ripsaws but they were otherwise in good spirits. Spur won enough from Sleepy on a single round of Fool All to pay for the new apple press he'd been wanting for the orchard. Of course, he would never be able to tell his father or Comfort where the money had come from.

Spur savored a memorable last supper: an onion tart with a balsamic reduction, steamed duck leg with a fig dressing on silver thread noodles and a vanilla panna cotta. After dinner he went with several other patients to hear a professor from Alcott University explain why citizens who sympathized with the puk-puks were misguided. When he finally returned to his room, there was a lone greeting in his queue. A bored dispatcher from the Cooperative informed him that he needed to pick up his train ticket at Celena Station before eleven a.m. No video of this citizen appeared on the screen; all he'd left was a scratchy audio message like one Spur might get on his home tell. Spur took this as a reminder that his holiday from simplicity would end the moment he left the hospital.

The breeze that blew through the open windows of the train was hot, providing little relief for the passengers in the first-class compartment. Spur shifted uncomfortably on his seat, his uniform shirt stuck to his back. He glanced away from the blur of trees racing past his window. He hated sitting in seats that faced backward; they either gave him motion sickness or a stiff neck. And if he thought about it—which he couldn't help but doing, at least for a moment—the metaphor always depressed him. He didn't want to be looking back at his life just now.

A backward seat—but it was in first class. The Cooperative's dispatcher probably thought he was doing him a favor. Give him some extra legroom, a softer seat. And why not? Hadn't he survived the infamous Motu River burn? Hadn't he been badly scorched in the line of duty? Of course he should ride in first class. If only the windows opened wider.

It had been easy not to worry about his problems while he was lounging around the hospital. Now that he was headed back home, life had begun to push him again. He knew he should try to stop thinking, maybe take a nap. He closed his eyes, but didn't sleep. Without warning he was back in the nightmare sim again . . . and could smell burning hair. His hair. In a panic he dodged into a stream choked with dead fish and poached frogs. But the water was practically boiling and scalded his legs . . . only Spur wasn't completely in the nightmare because he knew he was also sitting on a comfortable seat in a first-class compartment in a train that was taking him . . . the only way out was blocked by a torch, who stood waiting for Spur. Vic had not yet set himself on fire, although his baseball jersey was smoking in the heat . . . I'm not afraid, Spur told himself, I don't believe any of this . . . the anguished face shimmered in the heat of the burn and then Spur was dancing to keep his shoes from catching fire, and he had no escape, no choice, no time . . . with his eyes shut, Spur heard the clatter of the steel wheels on the track as: no time no time no time no time.

He knew then for certain what he had only feared: Dr. Niss had not healed his soul. How could he, when Spur had consistently lied about what had happened in the burn? Spur didn't mean to groan, but he did. When he opened his eyes, the gandy in the blue flowered dress was staring at him.

"Are you all right?" She looked to be in her late sixties or maybe seventy, with silver hair so thin that he could see the freckles on her scalp.

"Yes, fine," Spur said. "I just thought of something."

"Something you forgot?" She nodded. "Oh, I'm always remembering things just like that. Especially on trains." She had a burbling laugh, like a stream running over smooth stones. "I was supposed to have lunch with my friend Connie day after tomorrow, but here I am on my way to Little Bend for a week. I have a new grandson."

"That's nice," Spur said absently. There was one other passenger in the compartment. He was a very fat, moist man looking at a comic book about gosdogs playing baseball; whenever he turned a page, he took a snuffling breath.

"I see by your uniform that you're one of our firefighters," said the gandy. "Do you know my nephew Frank Kaspar? I think he is with the Third Engineers."

Spur explained that there were over eleven thousand volunteers in the Corps of Firefighters and that if her nephew was an engineer he was most probably a regular with the Home Guard. Spur couldn't keep track of all the brigades and platoons

in the volunteer Corps, much less in the professional Guard.
He said that he was just a lowly smokechaser in Gold Squad,
Ninth Regiment. His squad worked with the Eighth Engineers, who supplied transportation and field construction support. He told her that these fine men and women were the
very models of spiritual simplicity and civic rectitude, no doubt
like her nephew. Spur was hoping that this was what she
wanted to hear and that she would leave him alone. But then
she asked if the rumors of pukpuk collaborators infiltrating the
Corps were true and started nattering about how she couldn't
understand how a citizen of the Transcendent State could betray the Covenant by helping terrorists. All the pukpuks wanted
was to torch Chairman Winter's forests, wasn't that awful?
Spur realized that he would have to play to her sympathy. He
coughed and said he had been wounded in a burn and was just
out of the hospital, and then coughed again.

"If you don't mind," he said, crinkling his brow as if he
were fighting pain, "I'm feeling a little woozy. I'm just going
to shut my eyes again and try to rest."

Although he didn't sleep, neither was he fully awake. But the
nightmare did not return. Instead he drifted through clouds of
dreamy remembrance and unfocused regret. So he didn't notice that the train was slowing down until the hiss of the air
brakes startled him to full alertness.

He glanced at his watch. They were still an hour out of
Heart's Wall, where Spur would change for the local to Littleton.

"Are we stopping?" Spur asked.

"Wheelwright fireground." The fat man pulled a limp
handkerchief out of his shirt pocket and dabbed at his hairline.
"Five minutes of mandatory respect."

Now Spur noticed that the underbrush had been cleared
along the track and that there were scorch marks on most of

the trees. Spur had studied the Wheelwright in training. The forest north of the village of Wheelwright had been one of the first to be attacked by the torches. It was estimated that there must have been at least twenty of them, given the scope of the damage. The Wheelwright burn was also the first in which a firefighter died, although the torches never targeted citizens, only trees. The fires they started were always well away from villages and towns; that's why they were so hard to fight. But the Wheelwright had been whipped by strong winds until it cut the trunk line between Concord and Heart's Wall for almost two weeks. The Cooperative had begun recruiting for the Corps shortly after.

As the squealing brakes slowed the train to a crawl, the view out of Spur's window changed radically. Here the forest had yet to revive from the ravages of fire. Blackened skeletons of trees pointed at the sky and the charred floor of the forest baked under the sun. The sun seemed cruelly bright without the canopy of leaves to provide shade. In every direction, all Spur could see was the nightmarish devastation he had seen all too often. No plant grew, no bird sang. There were no ants or needlebugs or wild gosdogs. Then he noticed something odd: the bitter burned-coffee scent of fresh fireground. And he could taste the ash, like shredded paper on his tongue. That made no sense; the Wheelwright was over three years old.

When the train finally stopped, Spur was facing one of the many monuments built along the tracks to honor fallen fire-fighters. A grouping of three huge statues set on a pad of stone cast their bronze gazes on him. Two of the firefighters were standing; one leaned heavily on the other. A third had dropped to one knee, from exhaustion perhaps. All still carried their gear, but the kneeling figure was about to shed her splash pack and one of the standing figures was using his jacksmith as a crutch. Although the sculptor had chosen to depict them in the hour of their doom, their implacable metal faces revealed neither distress nor regret. The fearsome simplicity of their courage chilled Spur. He was certain that he wasn't of their quality.

The engine blew its whistle in tribute to the dead: three long blasts and three short. The gandy stirred and stretched. "Wheelwright?" she muttered.

"Yeah," said the fat man.

She started to yawn but caught herself and peered out the open window. "Who's that?" she said, pointing.

A man in a blue flair suit was walking along the tracks, peering up at the passenger cars. He looked very hot and not very happy. His face was as flushed as a peach and his blond hair was plastered to his forehead. Every few meters he paused, cupped his hands to his mouth and called, "Leung? Prosper Gregory Leung?"

FIVE

Fire is without doubt an advantage on the whole. It sweeps and ventilates the forest floor and makes it clear and clean. I have often remarked with how much more comfort & pleasure I could walk in wood through which a fire had been run the previous year. It is inspiriting to walk amid the fresh green sprouts of grass and shrubbery pushing upward through the charred surface with more vigorous growth.

—*JOURNAL*, 1850

The man waited impatiently as Spur descended from the train, kit slung over his shoulder. Although he did not turn back to look, Spur knew every passenger on the train was watching them. Was he in trouble? The man's expression gave away nothing more than annoyance. He looked to be younger than Spur, possibly in his late twenties. He had a pinched face and a nose as stubby as a radish. He was wearing a prissy white shirt buttoned to the neck. There were dark circles under the armpits of his flair jacket.

"Prosper Gregory Leung of Littleton, Hamilton County, Northeast?" The man pulled a slip of paper from his pocket and read from it. "You are currently on medical leave from the Ninth Regiment, Corps of Firefighters, and were issued a first-class ticket on this day—"

"I know who I am." Spur felt as if a needlebug were caught in his throat. "What is this about? Who are you?"

He introduced himself as Constant Ngonda, a deputy with the Cooperative's Office of Diplomacy. When they shook hands, he noticed that Ngonda's palm was soft and sweaty. Spur could guess why he had been pulled off the train, but he decided to act surprised.

"What does the Office of Diplomacy want with me?"

Just then the engineer blew three short blasts and couplings of the train clattered and jerked as, one by one, they took the weight of the passenger cars. With the groan of metal on metal, the train pulled away from the Wheelwright Memorial.

Spur's grip on the strap of his kit tightened. "Don't we want to get back on?"

Constant Ngonda shrugged. "I was never aboard."

The answer made no sense to Spur, who tensed as he calculated his chances of sprinting to catch the train. Ngonda rested a hand on his arm.

"We go this way, Prosper." He nodded west, away from the tracks.

"I don't understand." Spur's chances of making the train were fading as it gained momentum. "What's out there?"

"A clearing. A hover full of upsiders." He sighed. "Some important people have come a long way to see you." He pushed a lock of damp hair off his forehead. "The sooner we start, the sooner we get out of this heat." He let go of Spur and started picking his way across the fireground.

Spur glanced over his shoulder one last time at the departing train. He felt as if his life were pulling away.

"Upsiders? From where?"

Ngonda held up an open hand to calm him. "Some questions will be answered soon enough. Others it's better not to ask."

"What do you mean, better?"

Ngonda walked with an awkward gait, as if he expected the ground to give way beneath him. "I beg your pardon." He was wearing the wrong shoes for crossing rough terrain. "I misspoke." They were thin-soled, low-cut, and had no laces—little more than slippers. "I meant simpler, not better."

Just then Spur got a particularly intense whiff of something that was acrid and sooty, but not quite smoke. It was what he had first smelled as the train had pulled into the Memorial. He turned in a complete circle, all senses heightened, trying to pinpoint the source. After fire ran through the litter of leaves and twigs that covered the forest floor, it often sank into the duff, the layer of decomposing organic matter that lay just above the soil level. Since duff was like a sponge, most of the year it was too wet to burn. But in the heat of summer it could dry out and became tinder. Spur had seen a smoldering fire burrow through the layer of duff and emerge dozens of meters away. He sniffed, following his nose to a charred stump.

"Prosper!" said Ngonda. "What are you doing?"

Spur heard a soft hiss as he crouched beside the stump. It wasn't any fire sound that he knew, but he instinctively ran his bare hand across the stump, feeling for hotspots. Something cool and wet sprayed onto his fingers and he jerked them back as if he had been burned. He rubbed a smutty liquid between thumb and forefinger and then smelled it.

It had an evil, manmade odor of extinguished fire. Spur sat back on his heels, puzzled. Why would anyone want to mimic that particular stink? Then he realized that his hand was clean when it ought to have been smudged with soot from the stump. He rubbed hard against the burned wood, but the black refused to come off. He could see now that the stump had a clear finish, as if it had been coated with a preservative.

Spur could sense Ngonda's shadow loom over him but then he heard the hissing again and was able to pick out the tiny nozzle embedded in the stump. He pressed his finger to it and the noise stopped. Then, on an impulse, he sank his hand into the burned forest litter, lifted it and let the coarse mixture sift slowly through his fingers.

"It's hot out, Prosper," Ngonda said. "Do you really need to be playing in the dirt?"

The litter looked real enough: charred and broken twigs, clumps of leaf mold, wood cinders and a delicate ruined hemlock cone. But it didn't feel right. He squeezed a scrap of burned bark, expecting it to crumble. Instead it compacted into an irregular pellet, like day-old bread. When he released it, the pellet slowly resumed its original shape.

"It's not real," said Spur. "None of it."

"It's a memorial, Prosper." The deputy offered Spur a hand and pulled him to his feet. "People need to remember." He bent over to brush at the fake pine needles stuck to Spur's knees. "We need to go."

Spur had never seen a hover so close. Before the burns, hovers had been banned altogether from the Transcendent State. But after the pukpuks had begun their terrorist campaign to halt the spread of forest into their barrens, Chairman Winter had given the Cooperative permission to relax the ban. Generous people from the upside had donated money to build the benevolence parks and provided hovers to assist the Corps in fighting fires. However, Chairman Winter had insisted that only bots were to fly the hovers and that citizen access to them would be closely monitored.

While in the field with Gold Squad, Spur had watched hovers swoop overhead, spraying loads of fire-retardant splash onto burns. And he had studied them for hours through the

windows of the hospital, parked in front of their hangars at
Benevolence Park Number 5. But even though this one was
almost as big as Diligence Cottage and hovered a couple of
meters above the ground, it wasn't quite as impressive as Spur
had imagined it.

He decided that this must be because it was so thoroughly
camouflaged. The hover's smooth skin had taken on the dis-
coloration of the fireground, an ugly mottle of gray and brown
and black. It looked like the shell of an enormous clam. The
hover was elliptical, about five meters tall in front, sweeping
backward to a tapered edge, but otherwise featureless. If it had
windows or doors, Spur couldn't make them out.

As they approached, the hover rose several meters. They
passed into its shadow and Ngonda looked up expectantly. A
hatch opened on the underside. A ramp extended to the ground
below with a high-pitched warble like birdsong, and a man appeared at the hatch. He was hard to see against the light of the
interior of the hover; all Spur could tell for sure was that he
was very tall and very skinny. Not someone he would expect
to bump into on Jane Powder Street in Littleton. The man
turned to speak to someone just inside the hatch. That's when
Spur realized his mistake.

"No," she said, her voice airy and sweet. "We need to
speak to him first."

As she teetered down the ramp, Spur could tell immediately that she was not from Walden. It was the calculation
with which she carried herself, as if each step were a risk, although one she was disposed to take. She wore loose-fitting
pants of a sheer fabric that might have been spun from clouds.
Over them was a blue sleeveless dress that hung to midthigh.
Her upper arms were decorated with flourishes of phosphorescent body paint and she wore silver and copper rings on each
of her fingers.

"You're the Prosper Gregory of Walden?"

She had full lips and midnight hair and her skin was smooth and dark as a plum. She was a head taller than he was and half his weight. He was speechless until Ngonda nudged him.

"Yes."

"We're Memsen."

SIX

It requires nothing less than a chivalric feeling to sustain a conversation with a lady.

—*JOURNAL*, 1851

Although it was cooler in the shade of the hover, Spur was far from comfortable. He couldn't help thinking of what would happen if the engine failed. He would have felt more confident if the hover had been making some kind of noise; the silent, preternatural effortlessness of the ship unnerved him. Meanwhile, he was fast realizing that Memsen had not wanted to meet him in order to make friends.

"Let's understand one another," she said. "We're here very much against our will. You should know, that by summoning us to this place, you've put the political stability of dozens of worlds at risk. We very much regret that the High Gregory has decided to follow his luck to this place."

She was an upsider so Spur had no idea how to read her. The set of her shoulders flustered him, as did the way her knees bent as she stooped to his level. She showed him too many teeth and it was clear that she wasn't smiling. And why did she pinch the air? With a great effort Spur tore his gaze away from her and looked to Ngonda to see if he knew what she was talking about. The deputy gave him nothing.

"I'm not sure that I summoned the High Gregory, exactly," Spur said. "I did talk to him."

"About your war."

Constant Ngonda looked nervous. "Allworthy Memsen, I'm sure that Prosper didn't understand the implications of contacting you. The Transcendent State is under a cultural—"

"We grant that you have your shabby deniability." She redirected her displeasure toward the deputy. "Nevertheless, we suspect that your government instructed this person to contact the High Gregory, knowing that he'd come. There's more going on here than you care to say, isn't there?"

"Excuse me," said Spur, "but this really was an accident." Both Memsen and Ngonda stared at him as if he had corncobs stuck in his ears. "What happened was that I searched on my name but couldn't find anyone but me and then the tell at the hospital suggested the High Gregory as an alternative because our names are so similar." He spoke rapidly, worried that they'd start talking again before he could explain everything. "So I sent him a greeting. It was totally random—I didn't know who he was, I swear it. And I wasn't really expecting to make contact, since I'd been talking to bots all morning and not one was willing to connect me. In fact, your bot was about to cut me off when he came on the tell. The High Gregory, I mean."

"So." Memsen clicked the rings on her fingers together. "He mentioned none of this to us."

"He probably didn't know." Spur edged just a centimeter away from her toward the sunlight. The more he thought about it, the more he really wanted to get out from under the hover.

Ngonda spoke with calm assurance. "There, you see that Prosper's so-called request is based on nothing more than coincidence and misunderstanding." He batted at a fat orange needlebug that was buzzing his head. "The Cooperative regrets that you have come all this way to no good purpose."

Memsen reared suddenly to her full height and gazed down on the two of them. "There are no coincidences," she said, "only destiny. The High Gregory makes the luck he was meant to have. He's here, and he has brought the L'ung to serve as witnesses. Our reason for being on this world has yet to be discovered." She closed her eyes for several moments. While she considered Spur's story she made a low, repetitive plosive sound: pa–pa–pa–ptt. "But this is deeper than we first suspected," she mused.

Spur caught a glimpse of a head peeking out of the hatch above him. It ducked back into the hover immediately.

"So," Memsen said at last, "let's choose to believe you, Prosper Gregory of Walden." She eyed him briefly; whatever she saw in his face seemed to satisfy her. "You'll have to show us the way from here. Your way. The High Gregory's luck has chosen you to lead us until we see for ourselves the direction in which we must go."

"Lead you? Where?"

"Wherever you're going."

"But I'm just on my way home. To Littleton."

She clicked her rings. "So."

"I beg your pardon, Allworthy Memsen," said Ngonda, tugging at the collar of his shirt, "but you must realize that's impossible under our Covenant. . . ."

"It is the nature of luck to sidestep the impossible," she said. "We speak for the High Gregory when we express our confidence that you'll find a way."

She had so mastered the idiom of command that Spur wasn't sure whether this was a threat or a promise. Either way, it gave Ngonda pause.

"Allworthy, I'd like nothing better than to accommodate you in this," he said. "Walden is perhaps the least of the Thousand Worlds, but even here we've heard of your efforts to help preserve the one true species." A bead of sweat dribbled down his forehead. "But my instructions are to accommodate your requests within reason. Within reason, Allworthy. It is not reasonable to land a hover in the commons of a village like Littleton. You must understand that these are country people."

She pointed at Spur. "Here is one of your country people."

"Memsen!" shouted a voice from the top of the ramp. "Memsen, I am so bored. Either bring him up right now or I'm coming down."

Her tongue flicked to the corner of her mouth. "You wouldn't like it," she called back, "it's very hot." Which was definitely true, although as far as Spur could tell, the weather had no effect on her. "There are bugs."

"That's it!" The High Gregory of Kenning, Phosphorescence of the Eternal Radiation and luck maker of the L'ung, scampered down the ramp of the hover.

"There," he said, "I did it, so now don't tell me to go back." He was wearing green sneakers with black socks, khaki shorts and a T-shirt with a pix of a dancing turtle, which had a human head. "Spur! You look sadder than you did before." He had knobby knees and fair skin and curly brown hair. If he had been born in Littleton, Spur would've guessed that he was ten years old. "Did something bad happen to you? Say something. Do you still talk funny like you did on the tell?"

Spur had a hundred questions but he was so surprised that all he could manage was, "Why are you doing this?"

"Why?" The boy's yellow eyes opened wide. "Why, why, why?" He stooped to pick up a handful of the blackened litter and examined it with interest, shifting it around on his open palm. "Because I got one of my luck feelings when we were talking. They're not like ideas or dreams or anything so I can't explain them very well. They're just special. Memsen says they're not like the feelings that other people get, but that it's all right to have them and I guess it is." He twirled in a tight circle then, flinging the debris in a wide scatter. "And that's why." He rubbed his hands on the front of his shorts and approached Spur. "Am I supposed to shake hands or kiss you? I can't remember."

Ngonda stepped between Spur and the High Gregory as if to protect him. "The custom is to shake hands."

"But I shook with you already." He tugged at Ngonda's sleeve to move him aside. "You have hardly any luck left, friend Constant. I'm afraid it's all pretty much decided with you." When the deputy failed to give way, the High Gregory dropped to all fours and scooted through his legs. "Hello, Spur," said the boy as he scrambled to his feet. The High Gregory held out his hand and Spur took it.

Spur was at once aware that he was sweaty from the heat of the day, while the boy's hand was cool as river rock. He could feel the difference in their size: the High Gregory's entire hand fit in his palm and weighed practically nothing.

"Friend Spur, you have more than enough luck," the boy murmured, low enough so that only Spur could hear. "I can see we're going to have an adventure."

"Stay up there," cried Memsen. "No!" She was glowering up the ramp at the hatch, which had inexplicably filled with kids who were shouting at her. Spur couldn't tell which of them said what.

"When do we get our turn?"

"You let the Greg off."

"We came all this way."

"He's bored? I'm more bored."

"Hey, move, you're in my way!"

"But I want to see too."

Several in the back started to chant. "Not fair, not fair!"

Memsen ground her toes into the fake forest floor. "We have to go now," she said. "If we let them off the hover, it'll take hours to round them up."

"I'll talk to them." High Gregory bounded up the ramp, making sweeping motions with his hands. "Back, get back, this isn't it." The kids fell silent. "We're not there yet. We're just stopping to pick someone up." He paused halfway up and turned to the adults. "Spur is coming, right?"

Ngonda was blotting sweat from around his eyes with a

handkerchief. "If he chooses." He snapped it with a quick flick of the wrist and then stuffed it into his pocket, deliberately avoiding eye contact with Spur.

Spur could feel his heart pounding. He'd wanted to fly ever since he'd realized that it was possible and didn't care if simplicity counseled otherwise. But he wasn't sure he wanted to be responsible for bringing all these upsiders to Littleton.

"So." Memsen must have mistaken his hesitation for fear. "You have never been in a hover, Prosper Gregory of Walden?"

"Call him Spur," said the High Gregory. "It doesn't mean you have to have sex with him."

Memsen bowed to Spur. "He has not yet invited us to take that familiarity."

"Yes, please call me Spur." He tried not to think about having sex with Memsen. "And yes"—he picked up his kit— "I'll come with you."

"Lead then." She indicated that he should be first up the ramp. Ngonda followed him. Memsen came last, climbing slowly with her small and painstakingly accurate steps.

As he approached the top of the ramp, the coolness of the hover's interior washed over him. It was like wading into Mercy's Creek. He could see that the kids had gathered around the High Gregory. There were about a dozen of them in a bay that was about six by ten meters. Boxes and containers were strapped to the far bulkhead.

"Now where are we going?"

"When do we get to see the fire?"

"Hey, who's that?"

Most of the kids turned to see him step onto the deck. Although well lit, the inside of the hover was not as bright as it had been outside. Spur blinked as his eyes adjusted to the difference.

"This is Spur," said the High Gregory. "We're going to visit his village. It's called Littleton."

"Why? Are they little there?"

A girl of six or perhaps seven sidled over to him. "What's in your bag?" She was wearing a dress of straw-colored brocade that hung down to her silk slippers. The gold chain around her neck had a pendant in the shape of a stylized human eye. Spur decided that it must be some kind of costume.

He slung his kit off his shoulder and set it down in front of her so she could see. "Just my stuff."

"It's not very big," she said doubtfully. "Do you have something in there for me?"

"Your Grace," said Memsen, putting a hand on the girl's shoulder, "we are going to leave Spur alone for now." She turned the girl around and gave her a polite nudge toward the other kids. "You'll have to forgive them," she said to Spur. "They're used to getting their own way."

SEVEN

I have a deep sympathy with war, it so apes the gait and bearing of the soul.

—*JOURNAL*, 1840

Spur had studied geography in school and knew how big Walden was, but for the first time in his life he felt it. From the ground, the rampant forests restricted what anyone could see of the world. Even the fields and the lakes were hemmed in by trees. Spur had never been to the Modilon Ocean but he'd stood on the shores of Great Kamit Lake. The sky over the lake was impressive, but there was no way to take the measure of its scale. Spur had hiked the Tarata Mountains, but they were forested to their summits and the only views were from ledges. There was a tower on Samson Kokoda that afforded a 360-degree view, but the summit was just 1,300 meters tall.

Now the hover was cruising through the clouds at an

altitude of 5,700 meters, according to the tell on the bulkhead. Walden spread beneath him in all its breathtaking immensity. Maps, measured in inflexible kilometers and flat hectares, were a sham compared to this. Every citizen should see what he was seeing, and if it violated simplicity, he didn't care.

Constant Ngonda, on the other hand, was not enjoying the view. He curled on a bench facing away from the hull, which Memsen had made transparent when she'd partitioned a private space for them. His neck muscles were rigid and he complained from time to time about trouble with his ears. Whenever the hover shivered as it contended with the wind, he took a huge gulping breath. In a raspy voice, the deputy asked Spur to stop commenting on the scenery. Spur was not surprised when Ngonda lurched to his feet and tore through the bubble-like bulkhead in search of a bathroom. The wall popped back into place, throwing a scatter of rainbows across its shivering surface.

Spur kept his face pressed to the hull. He'd expected the surface to be smooth and cold, like glass. Instead, it was warm and yielding, as if it were the flesh of some living creature. Below him the lakes and rivers gleamed in the afternoon sun like the shards of a broken mirror. The muddy Kalibobo River veered away to the west as the hover flew into the foothills of the Tarata Range. As the land rolled beneath him, Spur could spot areas where the bright-green hardwood forest was yielding ground to the blue-green of the conifers: hemlock and pine and spruce. There were only a few farms and isolated villages in the shadow of the mountains. They would have to fly over the Taratas to get to Littleton on the eastern slope.

At first Spur had difficulty identifying the familiar peaks. He was coming at them from the wrong direction and at altitude. But once he picked out the clenched fist of Woitape, he could count forward and back down the range: Taurika, Bootless Lowa and Boroko, curving to the northwest, Kaivuna and Samson Kokoda commanding the plain to the south. He murmured the names aloud, as long as the deputy wasn't around to hear. He had always liked how round the pukpuk sounds were, how they rolled in his mouth. When he'd been trapped in the burn with Vic, he was certain that he would never say them again.

When Chairman Winter bought Morobe's Pea from ComExplore IC, he had thought to rename everything on the planet and make a fresh start for his great experiment in preserving unenhanced humanity. But then a surprising number of ComExplore employees turned down his generous relocation offer; they wanted to stay on. Almost all of these pukpuks could trace their ancestry back to some ancient who had made planetfall on the first colonizing ships. More than a few claimed to be descended from Old Morobe herself. As a gesture of respect, the Chairman agreed to keep pukpuk names for some landforms. So there were still rivers, valleys, mountains and islands that honored the legacy of the first settlers.

Chairman Winter had never made a secret of his plans for Walden. At staggering personal expense, he had intended to transform the exhausted lands of Morobe's Pea. In their place he would make a paradise that re-created the heritage ecology of the home world. He would invite only true humans to come to Walden. All he asked was that his colonists forsake the technologies that were spinning out of control on the Thousand Worlds. Those who agreed to live by the Covenant of Simplicity would be given land and citizenship. Eventually both the forest and the Transcendent State would overspread all of Walden.

But the pukpuks had other plans. They wouldn't leave and they refused to give up their banned technologies. At first trade between the two cultures of Walden flourished. In fact, the pukpuk industrial and commercial base propped up the fledgling Transcendent State. Citizens needed pukpuk goods, even if bots manufactured them. As time passed, however, the Cooperative recognized that pukpuks' continued presence was undermining the very foundations of the Transcendent State. When the Cooperative attempted to close off the borders in order to encourage local industry, black markets sprang up in the cities. Many citizens came to question the tenets of simplicity. The weak were tempted by forbidden knowledge. For the first time since the founding, the emigration rate edged into the double digits. When it was clear that the only way to save the Transcendent State was to push the pukpuks off the planet, Chairman Winter had authorized the planting of genetically enhanced trees. But once the forest began to encroach on the pukpuk barrens, the burns began.

The pukpuks were the clear aggressors in the firefight; even their sympathizers among the citizenry agreed on that. What no one could agree on was how to accommodate them without compromising. In fact, many of the more belligerent citizens held that the ultimate responsibility for the troubles lay with the Chairman himself. They questioned his decision not to force all of the pukpuks to emigrate after the purchase of Morobe's Pea. And some wondered why he could not order them to be rounded up and deported even now. It was, after all, his planet.

"We've come up with a compromise," said Ngonda as he pushed through the bulkhead into the compartment. He was still as pale as a root cellar mushroom, but he seemed steadier. He even glanced briefly down at the eastern slope of Bootless Lowa Mountain before cutting his eyes away. "I think we can let the High Gregory visit under your supervision."

Memsen, the High Gregory, and a young girl followed him, which caused the bulkhead to burst altogether. Spur caught a glimpse of a knot of kids peering at him before the wall re-formed itself two meters farther into the interior of the hover, creating the necessary extra space to fit them all. The High Gregory was carrying a tray of pastries, which he set on the table he caused to form out of the deck.

"Hello, Spur," he said. "How do you like flying? Your friend got sick but Memsen helped him. This is Penny."

"The Pendragon Chromlis Furcifer," said Memsen.

She and Spur studied each other. A little taller but perhaps a little younger than the High Gregory, the girl was dressed hood to boot in clothes made of supple metallic-green scales. The scales of her gloves were as fine as snakeskin while those that formed her tunic looked more like cherry leaves, even to the serrated edges. A rigid hood protected the back of her head. A tangle of thick, black hair wreathed her face.

"Penny," said the High Gregory, "you're supposed to shake his hand."

"I know," she said, but then clasped both hands behind her back and stared at the deck.

"Your right goes to his right." The High Gregory held out his own hand to demonstrate. "She's just a little shy," he said.

Spur crouched and held out his hand. She took it solemnly. They shook. Spur let her go. The girl's hand went behind her back again.

"You have a pretty name, Pendragon," said Spur.

"That's her title." Memsen faced left and then right before she sat on the bench next to Ngonda. "It means war chief."

"Really. And have you been to war, Penny?"

She shook her head—more of a twitch of embarrassment than a shake.

"This is her first," said the High Gregory. "But she's L'ung. She's just here to watch."

"I'm sorry," said Spur. "Who are the L'ung?"

Ngonda cleared his throat in an obvious warning. The High Gregory saw Memsen pinch the air and whatever he'd been about to say died on his lips. The silence stretched long enough for Penny to realize that there was some difficulty about answering Spur's question.

"What, is he stupid?" She scrutinized Spur with renewed interest. "Are you stupid, Spur?"

"I don't think so." It was his turn to be embarrassed. "But maybe some people think that I am."

"This is complicated," said Memsen, filling yet another awkward pause. "We understand that people here seek to avoid complication." She considered. "Let's just say that the L'ung are companions to the High Gregory. They like to watch him make luck, you might say. Think of them as students. They've been sent from many different worlds, for many different reasons. Complications again. There is a political aspect . . ."

Ngonda wriggled in protest.

". . . which the deputy assures us you would only find confusing. So." She patted the bench. "Sit, Pendragon."

The Pendragon collected a macaroon from the pastry tray and obediently settled beside Memsen, then leaned to whisper in her ear.

"Yes," said Memsen, "we'll ask about the war."

Ngonda rose then, but caught himself against a bulkhead as if the change from sitting to standing had left him dizzy. "This isn't fair," he said. "The Cooperative has made a complete disclosure of the situation here, both to Kenning and to the Forum of the Thousand Worlds."

"What you sent was dull, dull, dull, friend Constant," said the High Gregory. "I don't think the people who made the report went anywhere near a burn. Someone told somebody else, and that somebody told them." Just then the hover bucked and the deputy almost toppled onto Memsen's lap. "You gave us a bunch of contracts and maps and pix of dead trees," continued the High Gregory. "I can't make luck out of charts. But Spur was there, he can tell us. He was almost burned up."

"Not about Motu River," said Spur quickly. "Nothing about that." Suddenly everyone was staring at him.

"Maybe," began Ngonda but the hover shuddered again and he slapped a hand hard against the bulkhead to steady himself. "Maybe we should tell him what we've agreed on."

Spur sensed that Memsen was judging him, and that she was not impressed. "If you want to talk in general about fighting fires," he said, "that's different."

Ngonda looked miserable. "Can't we spare this brave man . . . ?"

"Deputy Ngonda," said Memsen.

"What?" His voice was very small.

The High Gregory lifted the tray from the table and offered it to him. "Have a cookie."

Ngonda shrank from the pastries as if they might bite him. "Go ahead then," he said. "Scratch this foolish itch of yours. We can't stop you. We're just a bunch of throwbacks from a nothing world and you're—"

"Deputy Ngonda!" Memsen's voice was sharp.

He caught his breath. "You're Memsen the Twenty-second and he's the High Gregory of Kenning and I'm not feeling very well." Ngonda turned to Spur, muttering, "Remember, they don't really care what happens to you. Or any of us."

"That's not true," said the High Gregory. "Not true at all."

But Ngonda had already subsided onto his bench, queasy and unvoiced.

"So." Memsen clicked her rings together. "You fight fires."

"I'm just a smokechaser." Ngonda's outburst troubled Spur. He didn't know anything about these upsiders, after all. Were they really any different than pukpuks? "I volunteered for the Corps about a year ago, finished training last winter, was assigned the Ninth Regiment, Gold Squad. We mostly build handlines along the edges of burns to contain them." He leaned against the hull with his back to the view. "The idea is that we scrape off everything that can catch fire, dig to mineral soil. If we can fit a plow or tractor in, then we do, but in rough terrain we work by hand. That's about it. Boring as those reports you read."

"I don't understand." The High Gregory sprawled on the deck, picking idly at his sneakers. "If you're so busy digging, when do you put the fires out?"

"Fire needs three things," he said, "oxygen, fuel and temperature. They call it the triangle of combustion. Think of a burn as a chain of triangles. The sides of every triangle have to connect." He formed a triangle by pressing his thumbs and forefingers together. "Hot enough connects to enough air connects to enough stuff to burn. Take away a side and you break the triangle"—he separated his thumbs—"and weaken the chain. When a burn blows up, there's no good way to cut off its oxygen or lower the core temperature, so you have to attack the fuel side of the triangle. If you do your job, eventually there's nothing left to burn."

"Then you don't actually put fires out?" The High Gregory sounded disappointed.

"We do, but that's just hotspotting. Once we establish a handline, we have to defend it. So we walk the lines, checking for fires that start from flying sparks or underground runners. Trees might fall across a line. If we find a hotspot, we dig it out with a jacksmith or spray it cold with retardant from our splash packs." He noticed that the Pendragon was whispering again to Memsen. "I'm sorry," he said. "Is there something?"

Memsen gave him a polite smile—at least he hoped it was polite. "She asks about the people who set fire to themselves. Have you ever seen one?"

"A torch?" Spur frowned. "No." The lie slipped out with practiced ease.

"They must be very brave." The High Gregory wriggled across the deck on hands and knees to Spur's kit. "Hey, your bag got burnt here." He held the kit up to the afternoon light pouring through the hull, examining it. "And here too. Do you hate them?"

"No."

"But they tried to kill you."

"Not me. They're trying to kill the forest, maybe the Transcendent State, but not me. They have no idea who I am." He motioned for the kit and the High Gregory dragged it across the compartment to him. "And I don't know any of them. We're all strangers." He opened the kit, rummaged inside and pulled out a pix of Gold Squad. "Here's my squad. That's full firefighting gear we're wearing." Dead friends grinned at him from the pix. Vic, kneeling in the front row of the picture, and Hardy, who was standing next to Spur. He flipped the pix over and passed it to the High Gregory.

"Why are the torches doing this?" said Memsen. "You must have wondered about it. Help us understand."

"It's complicated." He waited for Ngonda to pipe up with the official line, but the deputy was gazing through the hull of the hover with eyes of glass. "They should have gone long ago," said Spur. "They're upsiders, really. They don't belong here anymore."

"A thousand worlds for the new," said Memsen, "one for the true. That's what your chairman says, isn't it?"

"Your parents came here from other worlds," said the High Gregory. "So that's why you think the pukpuks should've been willing to pack up and go. But would you come back with us to Kenning if Jack Winter said you should?"

"That's not why I . . ." Spur rubbed at his forehead. "I don't know, maybe it is. Anyway, they were my grandparents, not my parents."

The High Gregory slid across the deck and handed the pix of Gold Squad to Memsen. The Pendragon craned her neck to see.

"You have to understand," said Spur, "that the pukpuks hate the new forests because they spread so fast. The trees grow like weeds, not like the ones in my orchard." He glanced over his shoulder at the hills beneath him. They were on the east side of the Taratas now and flying lower. Almost home. "When Walden was still the Pea, this continent was dry and mostly open. The Niah was prairie. There was supposedly this huge desert, the Nev, or the Neb, where Concord is now. The pukpuks hunted billigags and tamed the gosdog herds. Their bots dug huge pits to mine carbonatites and rare earths. Eventually they killed off the herds, plowed the prairies under and exhausted all the surface deposits. They created the barrens, raped this planet and then most of them just left. Morobe's Pea was a dying world, that's why the Chairman picked it. There was nothing for the pukpuks here, no reason to stay until we came."

As the hover swooped low over the treetops, Spur could feel the tug of home as real as gravity. After all he had been through, Littleton was still drowsing at the base of Lamana Ridge, waiting for him. He imagined sleeping in his own bed that night.

"Soon there won't be any more barrens," he said, "just forest. And that will be the end of it."

The High Gregory stared at him with his unnerving yellow eyes. "They're just trying to protect their way of life. And now you're telling them that your way is better."

"No." Spur bit his lip; the truth of what the High Gregory said had long since pricked his soul. "But their way of life is to destroy our way."

Memsen flicked a finger against the pix of Gold Squad. "And so that's why they started this war?"

"Is this a war?" Spur took the pix from her and tucked it into his kit without looking at it again. "They set fires, we put them out. It's dangerous work, either way."

"People die," whispered the Pendragon.

"Yes," said Spur. "They do."

EIGHT

I have lived some thirty-odd years on this planet, and I have yet to hear the first syllable of valuable or even earnest advice from my seniors.

—*JOURNAL*, 1852

Spur perched on a stump wondering how to sneak over to the Littleton train station. From where he sat, it looked hopeless.

He had just bushwhacked through the forest from the edge of
Spot Pond, where the hover had lingered long enough to put
him onto the mucky shore. Now he was on the trail that led
down Lamana Ridge. Just ahead of him was Blue Valley Road,
a rough track that connected a handful of farms to Civic Route
22. CR22 became Broad Street as it passed through Littleton
Commons, the village center. If he skulked down Blue Valley,
he could hitch a ride on 22. Except who would be out this
time of day? Neighbors. Littleton was a small town; his father
had no doubt told everyone that his son the hero was due in on
the 8:16 train from Heart's Wall. Of course, he could avoid 22
altogether and skirt around town to the train station. Except it
was a good ten kilometers between the stump and the station
and he was bone tired.

He decided to sit a little longer.

At least Ngonda had kept most of the upsiders out of Littleton. He could imagine Penny and Kai Thousandfold and
little Senator-for-Life Dowm spreading through his bewildered village to gawk at family pix and open closets and ask
awkward questions. The High Gregory was all Spur had to
worry about. He would be stepping off the hover ramp tomorrow morning at Spot Pond with the deputy. He would pose as
Ngonda's nephew and the deputy would be Spur's comrade-
in-arms from Iron Squad. The High Gregory would spend the
day touring Littleton and making whatever luck he could. He
would sleep at Spur's house and the day after tomorrow he and
Ngonda would catch the 7:57 southbound.

"Spur?" called a familiar voice from up the trail. "Is that
Prosper Leung?"

Spur wanted to blurt, "No, not me, not at all." He wanted
to run away. Instead he said, "Hello, Sly." There were worse
citizens he could have run into than Sly Sawatdee.

The big man lumbered down the path. He was wearing
cut-off shorts, one leg of which was several centimeters longer
than the other. His barrel belly stretched his shirt, which was

unbuttoned to his navel. His floppy hat was two-toned: dirty and dirtier. He was carrying a basket filled with gooseberries. His smile was bright as noon.

"That is my Prosper, I swear. My lucky little pinecone, all safe. But you're supposed to be away at the fires. How did you get here, so far from nowhere?"

"Fell out of the sky."

Sly giggled like a little boy. "Go around that again." Sly was gray as an oak and almost as old as Spur's father, but his years had never seemed a burden to him. If the Transcendent State truly wanted its citizens simple, then Sly Sawatdee was the most civic-minded person in Hamilton County. "You're joking me, no?"

"All right then, I walked."

"Walked from where?"

Spur pointed west.

Sly turned, as if he expected to see that a highway had been miraculously cut through the forest. "Nothing that way but trees and then mountains and then a hell of a lot more trees. That's a truckload of walking, green log. You must be tired. Have a gooseberry?" He offered Spur the basket. When Sly harvested the wild fruit, he just broke whole canes off, instead of picking individual berries. Close work he left to his grand-nephews at home.

"All right then," said Spur. "I'm not here. I'm on the train from Heart's Wall. I get in at 8:16."

"Yeah? Then who am I talking to, my own shaggy self? Watch the thorns."

Spur popped one of the striped pink berries into his mouth. It was still warm from the sun; his teeth crunched the tiny seeds. "You don't like any of my answers?" He slung his kit over his shoulder.

"I'll nibble almost anything, Spur, but I spit out what doesn't taste good." He pressed a stubby forefinger into Spur's chest. "Your Sly can tell when you're carrying a secret, happy old shoe. Ease the weight of it off your back and maybe I can help you with it."

"Let's walk." Spur set off down the trail. Ahead the trees parted for Blue Valley Road. "How's my father?"

"Well enough for an old man." Sly fell into step alongside him. "Which is to say not so much of what he was. Said you got burnt when Vic Joerly and those other poor boys got killed." He peered at Spur. "You don't look much burnt."

"I was in a hospital in Concord." They had reached Blue Valley Road, which was nothing more than a couple of dirt ruts separated by a scraggle of weeds. "An upsider doctor saved my life." Spur headed toward CR22. "They can do things you wouldn't believe."

"I'll believe it this very minute if you say so." His mouth twisted like he'd bit into a wormy apple. "Only I never had much use for upsiders."

"Why? Have you ever met one?"

"Not me, but my DiDa used to say how they poke holes in their own brains and cut arms and legs off to sew on parts of bots in their place. Now where's the sense in a good man turning bot?"

There was no arguing with Sly when he got to remembering things his long-suffering father had told him. "I'm guessing you buried Vic already?"

"His body came on the train last Wednesday. The funeral was Friday. Most the village was there, biggest communion in years and just about the saddest day."

"How's Comfort?"

"Hard to say." He grimaced. "I paid respects, didn't chitchat. But I heard around that she's digging herself quite a hole. Wouldn't take much for her to fall in." He turned away from Spur and picked a stone up off the road. "What about you two?"

"I don't want to talk about it."

"Yeah." He lobbed the stone into the woods. "That's what I heard."

They were coming up on the Bandaran farmstead, corn stalks nodding in the field nearest the road. Spur could hear the wooden clunk of their windmill turning on the whispered breath of the afternoon. It was bringing water up from a well to splash into a dug pond where ducks gabbled and cropped. He tried to keep Sly between himself and the house as they passed, but whether he was noticed or not, nobody called out to him.

The next farmstead belonged to the Sawatdees, where Sly lived with his nephew Sunny and his family. On an impulse, Spur said, "There is a secret."

"Yeah, I know. I'm old, but I still hear the mosquitoes buzz."

"The thing is, I'm going to need your help. And you can't tell anyone."

Sly stepped in front of Spur and blocked his way. "Does anyone know who sat on Gandy Star's cherry pie? The one that she baked for your DiDa?"

Spur grinned. "I hope not."

He prodded Spur in the chest with his finger. "Did they ever figure the boy who was with Leaf Benkleman the day she got drunk on the applejack and threw up at the Solstice Day picnic?"

"It wasn't me." Spur put a hand on Sly's finger and pushed it away. "I was with you fishing that afternoon."

"Yeah, the fish story." He stood aside and motioned for Spur to pass. "Remember who told that one? The old citizen you always forget to come visit now that you're all grown up." They continued down the road. The Sawatdee farmstead was just around the next bend.

"I remember, Sly. Can you help? I need a ride home right now."

"The cottage or your DiDa's house?"

"Diligence Cottage."

He nodded. "Sunny can take you in the truck."

"No, it has to be you. You're going to be the only one who knows I'm back. Part of the secret."

Sly swung the basket of gooseberries in wider arcs as he walked. "Sunny doesn't want me driving at night anymore."

"Don't worry, you'll be back in plenty of time for supper. But then I'll need you again in the morning. Come get me first thing. I'm meeting someone up at Spot Pond."

"Spot Pond? Nobody there but frogs."

Spur leaned closer to Sly. "I can tell you, but you have to promise to help, no matter what." He lowered his voice. "This is a big secret, Sly."

"How big?" Sly looked worried. "Bigger than a barn?"

"Bigger than the whole village." Spur knew Sly would be pleased and flattered to be the only one in Littleton whom Spur had invited into his conspiracy. "In or out, my friend?"

"In up to here." Sly raised a hand over his head. "Ears open, mouth shut." He giggled.

"Good." Spur didn't give him time to reconsider. "An upsider is coming to visit Littleton."

"An upsider." Sly took this for another joke. "And he parks his spaceship where? On Broad Street?"

"A hover is going to put him off near Spot Pond. He's going to stay with me for a day. One day. Nobody is supposed to know he's from the upside."

"A hover." Sly glanced over one shoulder and then the other, as if he expected to spot the hover following them. "One of those birdbots in our sky."

Spur nodded.

"And you want this?"

The question caught him off guard, because he realized that sometime in the last few hours he had changed his mind. "I do, Sly." Spur wanted to spend more time with the High Gregory and it was fine with him if they were together at Diligence Cottage. He just didn't want to inflict the upsider on the rest of his sleepy village. They wouldn't understand.

Except Sly was shaking his head. "Nothing good ever came of getting tangled up with space people."

"I'm just curious is all," said Spur.

"Curious can't sit still, young sprout. Curious always goes for the closer look." For the first time since Spur had known him, Sly Sawatdee looked his age. "And now I'm thinking what will happen to your DiDa when you leave us. He's a good man, you know. I've known him all my life."

NINE

For when man migrates, he carries with him not only his birds, quadrupeds, insects, vegetables and his very sward, but his orchard also.

—*WILD APPLES*, 1862

Capability Roger Leung loved apples. He was fond of the other pomes as well, especially pears and quince. Stone fruits he didn't much care for, although he tolerated sour cherries in memory of GiGa's pies. But apples were Cape's favorite, the ancient fruit of the home world. He claimed that apples graced the tables of all of Earth's great civilizations: Roman, Islamic, American and Dalamist. Some people in Littleton thought that Spur's father loved his apple trees more than he loved his family. Probably Spur's mother, Lucy Bliss Leung, had been one of these. Probably that was why she left him when Spur was three, first to move to Heart's Wall and then clear across the continent to Providence. Spur never got the chance to ask her because he never saw her again after she moved to Southwest. The citizens of Walden did not travel for mere pleasure.

Spur's grandparents had arrived on Walden penniless and with only a basic knowledge of farming. Yet hard work and brutal frugality had built their farmstead into a success. However, the price they paid for single-minded dedication to farming was high; of their three children, only Cape chose to stay on the farm as an adult. And even he moved out of Diligence Cottage when he was sixteen and put up a hut for himself at the farthest edge of the Leung property. He was trying to escape their disapproval. Whenever he looked at the tell or visited friends or climbed a tree to read a book, GiGo or GiGa would carp at him for being frivolous or lazy. They couldn't see the sense of volunteering for the fire department or playing left base for the Littleton Eagles when there were chores to be done. Sometimes weeks might pass without Cape saying an unnecessary word to his parents.

Yet it had been Cape who transformed the family fortunes with his apples. When he was eighteen, he began attending classes at the hortischool extension in Longwalk, very much against GiGo's wishes. He had paid tuition out of money earned doing odd jobs around the village—another pointless diversion from home chores that irritated his parents. Cape had become interested in fruit trees after brown rot spoiled almost the entire crop of Littleton's sour cherries the year before. All the farmers in the village raised fruit, but their orchards were usually no more than a dozen trees, all of traditional heirloom varieties. Crops were small, usually just enough for home use because of the ravages of pests and disease. Farmers battled Terran immigrants like tarnished plant bugs, sawflies, wooly aphids, coddling moths, leafrollers, lesser apple worms, and the arch enemy: plum curculio. There were mildews, rusts, rots, cankers, blotches and blights to contend with as well. The long growing season of fruit trees made them vulnerable to successive attacks. Citizens across the Transcendent State debated whether or not Chairman Winter had introduced insect evil and fungal disease into his new Garden of Eden on purpose. The question had never been settled. But at hortischool, Cape learned about neem spray, extracted from the chinaberry tree, and the organic insecticide pyrethrum, which was made from dried daisies. And he heard about an amazing cider apple called Huang's Nectar, a disease-resistant early bloomer, well-suited to the climate of Southeast but not yet proven hardy in the north. As much to spite his father as to test the new variety, he had drained his savings and bought a dozen saplings on w4 semi-dwarfing rootstock. He started his own orchard on land he had cleared near his hut. Two years later, he brought in his first—admittedly light—harvest, which nevertheless yielded the sweetest cider and smoothest applejack anyone in Littleton had ever tasted. Cape purchased a handscrew press in his third year and switched from fermenting his cider in glass carboys to huge oak barrels by his fifth. And he bought more apple trees—he never seemed to have enough: McIntosh, GoRed, Jay's Pippin, Alumar Gold, Adam and Eve. Soon he began to grow rootstock and sell trees to other farmers. By the time Cape married Spur's mother, the Leungs were renting land from farmsteads on either side of their original holding. GiGo and GiGa lived long enough to see their son become the most prosperous farmer in Littleton. GiGo, however, never forgave himself for being wrong, or Cape for being right, about the apples.

Cape had given Spur and Comfort his parents' house as a wedding present; Diligence Cottage had been empty ever since GiGa had died. Cape had long since transformed his own little hut into one of the grandest homes in Littleton. Spur had Sly drop him off just down Jane Powder Street from the cottage, hoping to avoid the big house and the inevitable interrogation by his father for as long as possible. After seeing Sly's dismay at the news of the High Gregory's visit, he was thinking he might try to keep the High Gregory's identity from Cape, if he could.

However, as Spur approached the front door, he spotted Cape's scooter parked by the barn and then Cape himself reaching from a ladder into the scaffold branches of one of GiGo's ancient Macoun apples. He was thinning the fruit set. This was twice a surprise: first, because Cape usually avoided the house where he had grown up, and second, because he had been set against trying to rejuvenate the Leungs' original orchard, arguing that it was a waste of Spur's time. In fact the peaches and the plum tree had proved beyond saving. However, through drastic pruning, Spur had managed to bring three Macouns and one Sunset apple, and a Northstar cherry back into production again.

"DiDa!" Spur called out so that he wouldn't startle his father. "It's me."

"Prosper?" Cape did not look down as he twisted an unripe apple free. "You're here already. Something's wrong?" He dropped the cull to the pack of gosdogs waiting below. A female leapt and caught the apple in midair in its long beak. It chomped twice and swallowed. Then it chased its scaly tale in delight, while the others hooted at Cape.

"Everything's fine. There was a last minute change and I managed to get a ride home." Spur doubted his father would be satisfied with this vague explanation, but it was worth a try. "What are you doing up there?" He dropped his kit on the front step of the farmhouse and trudged over to the orchard. "I thought you hated GiGo's useless old trees."

Cape sniffed. "Macoun is a decent enough apple; they're just too damn much work. And since you weren't around to tend to them—but I should come down. You're home, Prosper. Wait, I'll come down."

"No, finish what you're doing. How are things here?"

"It was a dry spring." He culled another green apple, careful to grasp the fruiting spur with one hand and the fruit with the other. "June was parched too, but the county won't call it a drought yet." The gosdogs swirled and tumbled beneath him as he let the apple fall. "The June drop was light, so I've had to do a lot of thinning. We had sawfly but the curculio isn't so bad. They let you out of the hospital so soon, Prosper? Tell me what you're not telling me."

"I'm fine. Ready to build fence and buck firewood."

"Have you seen Comfort yet?"

"No."

"You were supposed to arrive by train."

"I hitched a ride with a friend."

"From Concord?"

"I got off the train in Wheelwright."

"Wheelwright." One of the gosdogs was trying to scrabble up the ladder. "I don't know where that is exactly. Somewhere in Southeast, I think. Lee County maybe?"

"Around there. What's wrong with Macouns?"

"Ah." He shook his head in disapproval. "A foolish tree that doesn't know what's good for it." He gestured at the immature apples all around him. "Look at the size of this fruit set. Even after the June drop, there are too many apples left on the branches. Grow more than a few of these trees and you'll spend the summer hand-thinning. Have you seen Comfort yet?"

"I already said no." Spur plucked a low-hanging cherry, which held its green stem, indicating it wasn't quite ripe; despite this, he popped it into his mouth. "Sour cherries aren't too far from harvest, I'd say." He spat the pit at the gosdogs. "They're pulling the entire regiment back to Cloyce Forest, which is where I'll catch up with them."

"Civic refreshment—you'll be busy." Cape wound up and pitched a cull into the next row of trees. As the pack hurtled after it, he backed down the ladder. "Although I wouldn't mind some help. You're home for how long?"

"Just the week."

He hefted the ladder and pivoted it into the next tree. "Not much time."

"No."

He was about to climb up again when he realized that he had yet to greet his only son. "I'm glad you're safe, Prosper," he

said, placing a hand on his shoulder. "But I still don't understand about the train." He held Spur at arm's length. "You got
off why?"

Spur was desperate to change the subject. "DiDa, I know
you don't want to hear this but Comfort and I are probably going to get divorced."

Cape grimaced and let go of Spur. "Probably?" He set his
foot on the bottom rung.

"Yes." The gosdogs were back already, swarming around the
ladder, downy feathers flying. "I'm sorry." Spur stepped away.

"Prosper, you know my feelings about this." He mounted
the ladder. "But then everyone knows I'm a simple fool when
it comes to keeping a woman."

Cape Leung had been saying things like that ever since
Spur's mother left him. On some days he bemoaned the failure
of his marriage as a wound that had crippled him for life, on
others he preened as if surviving it were his one true distinction.
As a young man, Spur had thought these were merely poses and
had resented his father for keeping his feelings about Spur's
mother in a tangle. Now, Spur thought maybe he understood.

"Comfort was never comfortable here," Spur said mo-
rosely. "I blame myself for that. But I don't think she was born
to be a farmer's wife. Never was, never will be."

"Are you sure?" Cape sucked air between his teeth as he
leaned into the tree. "She's had a terrible shock, Prosper. Now
this?"

"It isn't going to come as a shock," he said, his voice tight.
His father had far too many reasons for wanting Spur to make
his marriage work. He had always liked both of the Joerly kids
and had loved the way Comfort had remade both Diligence
Cottage and his only son. Cape was impatient for grandchildren. And then there was the matter of the land, once agreea-
bly complicated, now horribly simple. Ever since they had
been kids, it had been a running joke around the village that
someday Spur would marry Comfort and unite the Joerly

farmstead with the Leung holdings, immediately adjacent to the east. Of course, everyone knew it wouldn't happen quite that way, because of Vic. But now Vic was dead.

"When will you see her?"

"I don't know," said Spur. "Soon. Anyway, it's been a long day for me. I'm going in."

"Come back to the house for supper?" said Cape.

"No, I'm too tired. I'll scrape up something to eat in the cottage."

"You won't have to look too hard." He grinned. "Your fans stopped by this morning to open the place up. I'm sure they left some goodies. I've been telling the neighbors that you were due home today." He dropped another cull to the gosdogs. "Now that I think about it, I should probably ride into town to tell folks not to meet your train. I still can't believe you got a ride all the way from . . . where did you say it was again?"

"What fans?"

"I think it must have been Gandy Joy who organized it; at least she was the one who came to the house to ask my permission." He stepped off the ladder into the tree to reach the highest branches. "But I saw the Velez girls waiting in the van, Peace Toba, Summer Millisap." He stretched for a particularly dense cluster of apples. "Oh, and after they left, I think Comfort might have stopped by the cottage."

TEN

I find it wholesome to be alone the greater part of the time. To be in company, even with the best, is soon wearisome and dissipating.

—WALDEN

The refrigerator was stocked with a chicken and parsnip casserole, a pot of barley soup, half a dozen eggs, a little tub of butter, a slab of goat cheese and three bottles of root beer. There was a loaf of fresh onion rye bread and glass jars of home-made apricot and pear preserves on the counter. But what Spur ate for supper was pie. Someone had baked him two pies, a peach and an apple. He ate half of each, and washed them down with root beer. Why not? There was nobody around to scold him and he was too tired to heat up the soup or the casserole, much less to eat it. Eating pie took no effort at all. Besides, he hadn't had a decent slice of pie since he had left Littleton. The niceties of baking were beyond the field kitchens of the Corps of Firefighters.

Afterward he poured himself a tumbler of applejack and sat at the kitchen table, trying to decide who had brought what. The barley soup felt like an offering from sturdy Peace Toba. Gandy Joy knew he had developed a secret weakness for root beer, despite growing up in a farmstead that lived and died by cider. The Millisaps had the largest herd of goats in town. He wasn't sure who had made the casserole, although he would have bet it wasn't the Velez sisters. Casseroles were too matronly for the Velezes. They were in their early twenties and single and a little wild—at least by Littleton's standards. They had to be, since they were searching for romance in a village of just over six hundred souls. Everyone said that they would probably move to Longwalk someday, or even to Heart's Wall, which would break their parents' hearts. He was guessing that the pies had come from their kitchen. A well-made pie was as good as a love letter. But would the Velez sisters just assume he and Comfort were finally going to split? Comfort must have decided on her own and was telling people in the village. Then Spur remembered that Sly had said he had heard something. And if Sly knew, then everyone knew. In a nosy village like Littleton, if a kid skinned his knee playing baseball, at least three moms fell out of trees waving bandages.

Spur put the food away and washed the dishes, after which there was no reason to stay in the kitchen. But he lingered for

a while, trying to avoid the memories which whispered to
him from the other rooms of the cottage. He remembered his
stern grandparents ghosting around the wood stove in their last
years. He remembered boarding Diligence Cottage up after
GiGo died, the lumpy furniture and the threadbare carpet re-
ceding into the gloom. And then he and Comfort pulling the
boards down and rediscovering their new home. The newly-
weds had moved almost all of GiGo and GiGa's things to the
barn, where they moldered to this day. Spur and Comfort had
dusted and cleaned and scraped and painted everything in the
empty cottage. He remembered sitting on the floor with his
back to the wall of the parlor, looking at the one lonely chair
they owned. Comfort had cuddled beside him, because she
said that if there wasn't room for both of them on the chair
then neither would sit. He had kissed her then. There had been
a lot of kissing in those days. In fact, Comfort had made love to
him in every room of the cottage. It was her way of declaring
ownership and of exorcising the disapproving spirits of the old
folks.

Now that she was about to pass out of his life, Spur thought
that Comfort might have been too ferocious a lover for his
tastes. Sometimes it was all he could do to stay with her in bed.
Occasionally her passion alarmed him, although he would
never have admitted this to himself while they were together.
It would have been unmanly. But just before he had volunteered for the Corps, when things had already begun to go
wrong, he had felt as if there were always another man standing
next to them, watching. Not anyone real, but rather Comfort's
idea of a lover. Spur knew by then he wasn't that man. He had
just been a placeholder for whoever it was she was waiting for.

Finally he left the kitchen. The women who had opened
Diligence Cottage had done their best, but there was no air to
work with on this close July night. The rooms were stale and
hot. He sat out on the porch until the needlebugs drove him
inside. Then he propped a fan in either window of the bedroom

and dumped his kit out onto the bedspread. What did he have to wear that was cool? He picked up a T-shirt but then smelled the tang of smoke still clinging to it. He dropped it onto the bed and chuckled mirthlessly. He was home; he could put on his own clothes. He opened the dresser drawer and pulled out the shorts that Comfort had bought for his birthday and a gauzy blue shirt. The pants were loose and slid down his hips. He had lost weight in the firefight and even more in the hospital. Too much heartbreak. Not enough pie.

Then, against his better judgment, he crossed the bedroom to Comfort's dresser and began to open drawers. He had never understood why she abandoned everything she owned when she left him. Did it mean that she was planning to come back? Or that she was completely rejecting their life together? He didn't touch anything, just looked at her panties, black and navy blue and gray—no pastels or patterns for his girl. Then the balled socks, sleeveless blouses, shirts with the arms folded behind them, heavy workpants, lightweight sweaters. And in the bottom drawer the jade pajamas of black-market material so sheer that it would slip from her body if he even thought about tugging at it.

"Not exactly something a farmer's wife would wear." Spur spoke aloud just to hear a voice; the dense silence of the cottage was making him edgy. "At least, not this farmer's wife."

Now that he was losing Comfort, Spur realized that the only person in his family was his father. It struck him that he had no memories of his father in the cottage. He could see Cape in the dining room of the big house or the library or dozing in front of the tell. Alone, always alone.

Spur had a bad moment then. He stepped into the bathroom, and splashed some cold water on his face. He would have to remarry or he would end up like his father. He tried to imagine kissing Bell Velez, slipping a hand under her blouse, but he couldn't.

"Knock, knock." A woman called from the parlor. "Your father claims you're back." It was Gandy Joy.

"Just a minute." Spur swiped at his dripping face with the hand towel. As he strode from the bedroom, the smile on his face was genuine. He was grateful to Gandy Joy for rescuing him from the silence and his dark mood.

She was a small, round woman with flyaway hair that was eight different shades of gray. She had big teeth and an easy smile. Her green sundress exposed the wrinkled skin of her wide shoulders and arms; despite farm work she was still as fair as the flesh of an apple. Spur had been mothered by many of the women of Littleton as a boy, but Gandy Joy was the one who meant the most to him. He had to stoop over slightly to hug her.

"Prosper." She squeezed him so hard it took his breath away. "My lovely boy, you're safe."

"Thank you for opening the cottage," he said. "But how did you find everything?" She smelled like lilacs and he realized that she must have perfumed herself just for him.

"Small house." She stepped back to take him in. "Not many places a thing can be."

Spur studied her as well; she seemed to have aged five years in the ten months since he'd seen her last. "Big enough, especially for one."

"I'm sorry, Prosper."

When Spur saw the sadness shadow her face, he knew that she had heard something. She was, after all, the village virtuator. He supposed he should have been relieved that Comfort was letting everyone know she wanted a divorce, since that was what he wanted too. Instead he just felt hollow. "What has she told you?"

Gandy Joy just shook her head. "You two have to talk."

He thought about pressing her, but decided to let it drop. "Have a seat, Gandy. Can I get you anything? There's applejack." He steered her toward the sofa. "And root beer."

"No, thanks." She nodded at her wooden-bead purse, which he now noticed against the bolster of the sofa. "I brought communion."

"Really?" he said, feigning disappointment. "Then you're only here on business?"

"I'm here for more reasons than you'll ever know." She gave him a playful tap on the arm. "And keeping souls in communion is my calling, lovely boy, not my business." She settled on the sofa next to her purse and he sat facing her on the oak chair that had once been his only stick of furniture.

"How long are you with us?" She pulled out three incense burners and set them on the cherrywood table that Comfort had ordered all the way from Providence.

"A week." Spur had seen Gandy Joy's collection of incense burners, but he had never known her to use three at once for just two people. "I'll catch up with the squad in Cloyce Forest. Easy work for a change; just watching the trees grow." He considered three excessive; after all, he had accepted communion regularly with the other firefighters.

"We weren't expecting you so soon." She slipped the aluminum case marked with the seal of the Transcendent State from her purse. "You didn't come on the train."

"No."

She selected a communion square from the case. She touched it to her forehead, the tip of her nose and her lips and then placed it on edge in the incense burner. She glanced up at him and still the silence stretched. "Just no?" she said finally. "That's all?"

Spur handed her the crock of matches kept especially for communion. "My father told you to ask, didn't he?"

"I'm old, Prosper." Her smile was crooked. "I've earned the right to be curious." She repeated the ritual with the second communion square.

"You have. But he really wants to know."

"He always does." She set the third communion in its

burner. "But then everybody understands about that particular bend in Capability's soul." She selected a match from the crock and struck it.

Now it was Spur's turn to wait. "So aren't you going to ask me about the train?"

"I was, but since you have something to hide, I won't." She touched the fire to each of the three squares and they caught immediately, the oils in the communion burning with an eager yellow flame. "I don't really care, Spur. I'm just happy that you're back and safe." She blew the flames out on each of the squares, leaving a glowing edge. "Make the most of your time with us."

Spur watched the communion smoke uncoil in the still air of his parlor. Then, as much to please Gandy Joy as to reestablish his connection with his village, he leaned forward and breathed deeply. The fumes that filled his nose were harsh at first, but wispier and so much sweeter than the strangling smoke of a burn. As he settled back into his chair, he got the subtle accents: the yeasty aroma of bread baking, a whiff of freshly split oak and just a hint of the sunshine scent of a shirt fresh off the clothesline. He could feel the communion smoke fill his head and touch his soul. It bound him as always to the precious land and the cottage where his family had made a new life, the orderly Leung farmstead, his home town and of course to this woman who loved him more than his mother ever had and his flinty father who couldn't help the way he was and faithful Sly Sawatdee and generous Leaf Benkleman and droll Will Sambusa and steadfast Peace Toba and the entire Velez family who had always been so generous to him and yes, even his dear Comfort Rose Joerly, who was leaving him but who was nonetheless a virtuous citizen of Littleton.

He shivered when he noticed Gandy Joy watching him. No doubt she was trying to gauge whether he had fully accepted communion. "Thank you," he said, "for all the food."

She nodded, satisfied. "You're welcome. We just wanted to

show how proud we are of you. This is your village, after all, and you're our Prosper and we want you to stay with us always."

He chuckled nervously. Why did everyone think he was going somewhere?

She leaned forward, and lowered her voice. "But I have to say there was more than a little competition going on over the cooking." She chuckled. "Bets were placed on which dish you'd eat first."

"Bets?" Spur found the idea of half a dozen women competing to please him quite agreeable. "And what did you choose?"

"After I saw everything laid out, I was thinking that you'd start in on pie. After all, there wasn't going to be anyone to tell you no."

Spur laughed. "Pie was all I ate. But don't tell anyone."

She tapped her forefinger to her lips and grinned.

"So I'm guessing that the Velez girls made the pies?"

"There was just the one—an apple, I think is what Bell said."

"I found two on the counter: apple and a peach."

"Really?" Gandy sat back on the couch. "Someone else must have dropped it off after we left."

"Might have been Comfort," said Spur. "DiDa said he thought she stopped by. I was expecting to find a note."

"Comfort was here?"

"She lives here," said Spur testily. "At least, all her stuff is here."

Gandy took a deep breath over the incense burners and held it in for several moments. "I'm worried about her," she said finally. "She hasn't accepted communion since we heard about Vic. She keeps to herself and when we go to visit her at home, she's as friendly as a brick. There's mourning and then there's self-pity, Prosper. She's been talking about selling the farmstead, moving away. We've lost poor Victor, we don't want to lose her too. Littleton wouldn't be the same without the Joerlys. When you see her, whatever you two decide, make sure she knows that."

Spur almost groaned then, but the communion had him in its benevolent grip. If citizens didn't help one another, there would be no Transcendent State. "I'll do my best," he said, his voice tight.

"Oh, I know you will, my lovely boy. I know it in my soul."

ELEVEN

Things do not change; we change.

—*JOURNAL*, 1850

The High Gregory sat next to Spur in the bed of the Sawat-dees' truck, their backs against the cab, watching the dust billow behind them. Sly and Ngonda rode up front. As the truck jolted down Blue Valley Road, Spur could not help but see the excitement on the High Gregory's face. The dirt track was certainly rough, but the boy was bouncing so high Spur was worried that he'd fly over the side. He was even making Sly nervous, and the old farmer was usually as calm as moss. But then Sly Sawatdee didn't make a habit of giving rides to upsiders. He kept glancing over his shoulder at the High Gregory through the open rear slider.

Spur had no doubt that his cover story for the High Gregory and Ngonda was about to unravel. The High Gregory had decided to wear purple overalls with about twenty brass buttons. Although there was nothing wrong with his black T-shirt, the bandana knotted around his neck was a pink disaster embellished with cartoons of beets and carrots and corn on the cob. At least he had used some upsider trick to disguise the color of his eyes. Ngonda's clothes weren't quite as odd, but they too were a problem. Spur had seen citizens wearing flair jackets and high-collar shirts—but not on a hot summer Sunday and not in Littleton. Ngonda was dressed for a meeting at the Cooperative's Office of Diplomacy in Concord. Spur's only hope was to whisk them both to Diligence Cottage and either hide them there or find them something more appropriate to wear.

"Tell me about the gosdogs," said the High Gregory.

Spur leaned closer, trying to hear him over the roar of the truck's engine, the clatter of its suspension and the crunch of tires against the dirt road. "Say again?"

"The gosdogs," shouted the High Gregory. "One of your native species. You know, four-footed, feathered, they run in packs."

"Gosdogs, yes. What do you want to know?"

"You eat them."

"I don't." The High Gregory seemed to be waiting for him to elaborate, but Spur wasn't sure what he wanted to know exactly. "Other citizens do, but the browns only. The other breeds are supposed to be too stringy."

"And when you kill them, do they know they're about to die? How do you do it?"

"I don't." Spur had never slaughtered a gosdog; Cape didn't believe in eating them. However, Spur had slaughtered chickens and goats and helped once with a bull. Butchering was one of the unpleasant chores that needed doing on a farm, like digging postholes or mucking out the barn. "They don't suffer."

"Really? That's good to know." The High Gregory did not look convinced. "How smart do you think they are?"

At that moment Sly stepped on the brakes and swung the steering wheel; the truck bumped onto the smooth pavement of Civic Route 22.

"Not very," said Spur. With the road noise abating, his voice carried into the cab.

"Not very what?" said Constant Ngonda.

The High Gregory propped himself up to speak through

the open window. "I was asking Spur how smart the gosdogs are. I couldn't find much about them, considering. Why is that, do you suppose?"

"The ComExplore Survey Team rated them just 6.4 on the Peekay Animal Intelligence Scale," said Ngonda. "A goat has more brains."

"Yes, I found that," said the High Gregory, "but what's interesting is that the first evaluation was the only one ever done. And it would have been very much in the company's interests to test them low, right? And of course it made no sense for your pukpuks to bother with a follow-up test. And now your Transcendent State has a stake in keeping that rating as it is."

"Are you suggesting some kind of conspiracy?" Ngonda was working his way to a fine outrage. "That we're deliberately abusing an intelligent species?"

"I'm just asking questions, friend Constant. And no, I'm not saying they're as smart as humans, no, no, never. But suppose they were retested and their intelligence was found to be . . . let's say 8.3. Or even 8.1. The Thousand Worlds might want to see them protected."

"Protected?" The deputy's voice snapped through the window.

"Why, don't you think that would be a good idea? You'd just have to round them up and move them to a park or something. Let them loose in their native habitat."

"There is no native habitat left on Walden." Spur noticed that Sly was so intent on the conversation that he was coasting down the highway. "Except maybe underwater." A westbound oil truck was catching up to them fast.

"We could build one then," said the High Gregory cheerfully. "The L'ung could raise the money. They need something to do."

"Can I ask you something?" Ngonda had passed outrage and was well on his way to fury.

"Yes, friend Constant. Of course."

"How old are you?"

"Twelve standard. My birthday is next month. I don't want a big party this year. It's too much work."

"They know themselves in the mirror," said Sly.

"What?" Ngonda was distracted from whatever point he was about to make. "What did you just say?"

"When one of them looks at his reflection, he recognizes himself." Sly leaned back toward the window as he spoke. "We had this brood, a mother and three pups, who stayed indoors with us last winter. They were house-trained, mostly." The truck slowed to a crawl. "So my granddaughter Brookie is playing dress-up with the pups one night and the silly little pumpkin decides to paint one all over with grape juice. Said she was trying to make the first purple gosdog—her father babies her, don't you know? But she actually stains the right rear leg before her mother catches her out. And when Brookie lets the poor thing loose, it galumphs to the mirror and backs up to see its grapy leg. Then it gets to whimpering and clucking and turning circles like they do when they're upset." Sly checked the rearview mirror and noticed the oil truck closing in on them for the first time. "I was there, saw it clear as tap water. The idea that it knew who it was tipped me over for a couple of days." He put two wheels onto the shoulder of CR22 and waved the truck past. "It's been a hardship, but I've never eaten a scrap of gosdog since."

"That's the most ridiculous thing I've ever heard," said Ngonda.

"Lots of citizens feel that way," said Spur.

"As is their right. But to jump to conclusions based on this man's observations . . ."

"I don't want to jump, friend Constant," said the High Gregory. "Let's not jump."

Although the deputy was ready to press his argument, nobody else spoke and gradually he subsided. Sly pulled back onto CR22 and drove the rest of the way at a normal pace.

They passed the rest of the trip in silence; the wind seemed to whip Spur's thoughts right out of his head.

As they turned off Jane Powder Street onto the driveway of the cottage, Sly called back to him. "Looks like you've got company."

Spur rubbed the back of his neck in frustration. Who told the townsfolk that he wanted them to come visiting? He leaned over the side of the truck but couldn't see anyone until they parked next to the porch. Then he spotted the scooter leaning against the barn.

If it was really in the High Gregory's power to make luck, then what he was brewing up for Spur so far was pure misfortune. It was Comfort's scooter.

The High Gregory stood up in the back of the truck and turned around once, surveying the farmstead. "This is your home, Spur." He said it not as a question but as a statement, as if Spur were the one seeing it for the first time. "I understand now why you would want to live so far from everything. It's like a poem here."

Constant Ngonda opened the door and stepped down onto the dusty drive. From his expression, the deputy appeared to have formed a different opinion of the cottage. However, he was enough of a diplomat to keep it to himself. He clutched a holdall to his chest and was mounting the stairs to the porch when he noticed that no one else had moved from the truck.

They were watching Comfort stalk toward them from the barn, so clearly in a temper that heat seemed to shimmer off her in the morning swelter.

"That woman looks angry as lightning," said Sly. "You want me to try to get in her way?"

"No," said Spur. "She'd probably just knock you over."

"But this is your Comfort?" said the High Gregory. "The wife that you don't live with anymore. This is so exciting, just what I was hoping for. She's come for a visit—maybe to welcome you back?"

"I'm not expecting much of a welcome," said Spur. "If you'll excuse me, I should talk to her. Sly, if you wouldn't mind staying a few minutes, maybe you could take Constant and young Lucky here inside. There's plenty to eat."

"Lucky," said the High Gregory, repeating the name they had agreed on for him, as if reminding himself to get into character. "Hello, friend Comfort," he called. "I'm Lucky. Lucky Ngonda."

She shook the greeting off and kept bearing down on them. His wife was a slight woman, with fine features and eyes dark as currants. Her hair was long and sleek and black. She was wearing a sleeveless, yellow gingham dress that Spur had never seen before. Part of her new wardrobe, he thought, her new life. When he had been in love with her, Spur had thought that Comfort was pretty. But now, seeing her for the first time in months, he decided that she was merely delicate. She did not look strong enough for the rigors of life on a farm.

Spur opened the tailgate and the High Gregory jumped from the back of the truck. Ngonda came back down the stairs to be introduced to Comfort. Spur was handing the High Gregory's bag down to Sly as she drew herself up in front of them.

"Gandy Joy said you wanted to see me first thing in the morning." She did not waste time on introductions. "I didn't realize that I'd be interrupting a party."

"Comfort," said Spur, "I'm sorry." He stopped himself then, chagrined at how easily he fell into the old pattern. When they were together, he was always apologizing.

"Morning, sweet corn," said Sly. "Not that much of a party, I'm afraid."

"But there are snacks inside," the High Gregory said. "This is such a beautiful place you two have. I've just met Spur myself, but I'm pretty sure he's going to be happy here someday. My name is Lucky Ngonda." He held out his hand to her.

"We're supposed to shake but first you have to say your name."

Comfort had been so fixated on Spur that she had brushed by the High Gregory. Now she scrutinized him in all his purple glory and her eyes went wide. "Why are you dressed like that?"

"Is something wrong?" He glanced down at his overalls. "I'm dressed to visit my friend Spur." He patted his bare head. "It's the hat, isn't it? I'm supposed to be wearing a hat."

"Constant Ngonda, a friend of Spur's from the Ninth." Ngonda oozed between them. "I apologize for intruding; I know you have some important things to discuss. Why don't we give you a chance to catch up now. My nephew and I will be glad to wait inside." He put an arm around the High Gregory's shoulder and aimed him at the porch.

"Wait," said the High Gregory. "I thought I was your cousin."

"Take as long as you want, Spur," Ngonda said as he hustled the boy off. "We'll be fine."

Sly shook his head in disbelief. "I'll make sure they don't get into trouble." He started after them.

"There are pies in the refrigerator," Spur called after him. "Most of an apple pie and just a couple slices of a peach." He steeled himself and turned back to Comfort. "My father said you were here the other day." He aimed a smile at her but it bounced off. "You made my favorite pie."

"Who are those people?" Her eyes glittered with suspicion. "The boy is strange. Why have you brought them here?"

"Let's walk." He took her arm and was surprised when she went along without protest. He felt the heat of her glare cooling as they strode away from the cottage. "I did have a chat with Gandy Joy," he said. "She said you were feeling pretty low."

"I have the right to feel however I feel," she said stiffly.

"You haven't been accepting communion."

"Communion is what they give you so you feel smart about acting stupid. Tell her that I don't need some busybody blowing smoke in my eyes to keep me from seeing what's wrong." She stopped and pulled him around to face her. "We're getting divorced, Spur."

"Yes." He held her gaze. "I know." He wanted to hug her or maybe shake her. Touch her long, black hair. Instead his hands hung uselessly by his sides. "But I'm still concerned about you."

"Why?"

"You've been talking about moving away."

She turned and started walking again. "I can't run a farm by myself."

"We could help you, DiDa and I." He caught up with her. "Hire some of the local kids. Maybe bring in a tenant from another village."

"And how long do you think that would work for? If you want to run my farm, Spur, buy it from me."

"Your family is an important part of this place. The whole village wants you to stay. Everyone would pitch in."

She chuckled grimly. "Everyone wanted us to get married. They want us to stay together. I'm tired of having everyone in my life."

He wasn't going to admit to her that he felt the same way sometimes. "Where will you go?"

"Away."

"Just away?"

"I miss him, I really do. But I don't want to live anywhere near Vic's grave."

Spur kicked a stone across the driveway and said nothing for several moments. "You're sure it's not me you want to get away from?"

"No, Spur. That's one thing I am sure of."

"When did you decide all this?"

"Spur, I'm not mad at you." Impulsively, she went up on

tiptoes and aimed a kiss at the side of his face. She got mostly air, but their cheeks brushed, her skin hot against his. "I like you, especially when you're like this, so calm and thoughtful. You're the best of this lot and you've always been sweet to me. It's just that I can't live like this anymore."

"I like you too, Comfort. Last night, after I accepted communion—"

"Enough. We like each other. We should stop there, it's a good place to be." She bumped up against him. "Now tell me about that boy. He isn't an upsider, is he?"

She shot him a challenging look and he tried to bear up under the pressure of her regard. They walked in silence while he decided what he could say about Ngonda and the High Gregory. "Can you keep a secret?"

She sighed. "You know you're going to tell me, so get to it."

They had completely circled the cottage. Spur spotted the High Gregory watching them from a window. He turned Comfort toward the barn. "Two days ago, when I was still in the hospital, I started sending greetings to the upside." He waved off her objections. "Don't ask, I don't know why exactly, other than that I was bored. Anyway, the boy answered one of them. He's the High Gregory of the L'ung, Phosphorescence of something or other, I forget what. He's from Kenning in the Theta Persei system and I'm guessing he's pretty important, because the next thing I knew, he qiced himself to Walden and had me pulled off a train."

He told her about the hover and Memsen and the kids of the L'ung and how he was being forced to show the High Gregory his village. "Oh, and he supposedly makes luck."

"What does that mean?" said Comfort. "How does somebody make luck?"

"I don't know exactly. But Memsen and the L'ung are all convinced that he does it, whatever it is."

They had wandered into GiGa's flower garden. Comfort had tried to make it her own after they had moved in. However, she'd had neither the time nor the patience to tend persnickety plants and so grew only daylilies and hostas and rugosa roses. After a season of neglect, even these tough flowers were losing ground to the bindweed and quackgrass and spurge.

Spur sat on the fieldstone bench that his grandfather had built for his grandmother. He tapped on the seat for her to join him. She hesitated, then settled at the far end, twisting to face him.

"He acts too stupid to be anyone important," she said. "What about that slip he made about being the cousin and not the nephew. Are the people on his world idiots?"

"Maybe he intended to say it." Spur leaned forward and pulled a flat clump of spurge from the garden. "After all, he's wearing those purple overalls; he's really not trying very hard to pretend he's a citizen." He knocked the dirt off the roots and left it to shrivel in the sun. "What if he wanted me to tell you who he was and decided to make it happen? I think he's used to getting his own way."

"So what does he want with us?" Her expression was unreadable.

"I'm not sure. I think what Memsen was telling me is that he has come here to see how his being here changes us." He shook his head. "Does that make any sense?"

"It doesn't have to," she said. "He's from the upside. They don't think the same way we do."

"Maybe so." It was a commonplace that had been drilled into them in every self-reliance class they had ever sat through. It was, after all, the reason that Chairman Winter had founded Walden. But now that he had actually met upsiders—Memsen and the High Gregory and the L'ung—he wasn't sure that their ways were so strange. But this wasn't the time to argue the point. "Look, Comfort, I have my own reason for telling you all this," he said. "I need help with him. At first I thought he was just going to pretend to be one of us and take a quiet look at the village. Now I'm thinking he wants to be discovered so he can make things happen. So I'm going to try to keep him busy here if I can. It's just for one day; he said he'd leave in the morning."

"And you believe that?"

"I'd like to." He dug at the base of a dandelion with his fingers and pried it out of the ground with the long taproot intact. "What other choice do I have?" He glanced back at the cottage but couldn't see the High Gregory in the window anymore. "We'd better get back."

She put a hand on his arm. "First we have to talk about Vic."

Spur paused, considering. "We can do that if you want." He studied the dandelion root as if it held the answers to all his problems. "We probably should. But it's hard, Comfort. When I was in the hospital the upsiders did something to me. A kind of treatment that . . ."

She squeezed his arm and then let go. "There's just one thing I have to know. You were with him at the end. At least, that's what we heard. You reported his death."

"It was quick," said Spur. "He didn't suffer." This was a lie he had been preparing to tell her ever since he had woken up in the hospital.

"That's good. I'm glad." She swallowed. "Thank you. But did he say anything? At the end, I mean."

"Say? Say what?"

"You have to understand that after I moved back home, I found that Vic had changed. I was shocked when he volunteered for the Corps because he was actually thinking of leaving Littleton. Maybe Walden too. He talked a lot about going to the upside." She clutched her arms to her chest so tightly that she seemed to shrink. "He didn't believe—you can't tell anyone about this. Promise?"

Spur shut his eyes and nodded. He knew what she was going to say. How could he not? Nevertheless, he dreaded hearing it.

Her voice shrank as well. "He had sympathy for the puk-puks. Not for the burning, but he used to say that we didn't need to cover every last scrap of Walden with forest. He talked about respecting . . ."

Without warning, the nightmare leapt from some darkness in his soul like some ravening predator. It chased him through a stand of pine; trees exploded like firecrackers. Sparks bit through his civvies and stung him. He could smell burning hair. His hair.

But he didn't want to smell his hair burning. Spur was trying desperately to get back to the bench in the garden, back to Comfort, but she kept pushing him deeper into the nightmare.

"After we heard he'd been killed, I went to his room. . . ."

He beckoned and for a moment Spur thought it might not be Vic after all as the anguished face shimmered in the heat of the burn. Vic wouldn't betray them, would he?

"It was his handwriting. . . ."

Spur had to dance to keep his shoes from catching fire, and he had no escape, no choice, no time. The torch spread his arms wide and Spur stumbled into his embrace and with an angry whoosh they exploded together into flame. Spur felt his skin crackle. . . .

And he screamed.

TWELVE

We are paid for our suspicions by finding what we suspected.
—*A Week on the Concord and Merrimack Rivers*

Everyone said that he had nothing to be embarrassed about, but Spur was nonetheless deeply ashamed. He had been revealed as unmanly. Weak and out of control. He had no memory of

how he had come to be laid out on the couch in his own parlor. He couldn't remember if he had wept or cursed or just
fainted and been dragged like a sack of onions across the yard
into the cottage. When he emerged from the nightmare, all he
knew was that his throat was raw and his cheeks were hot. The
others were all gathered around him, trying not to look worried but not doing a very convincing job of it. He wasn't sure
which he minded more: that the strangers had witnessed his
breakdown, or that his friends and neighbors had.

When he sat up, a general alarm rippled among the onlook-
ers. When he tried to stand, Sly pressed him back onto the
couch with a firm grip on the shoulder. Comfort fetched him a
glass of water. She was so distraught that her hand shook as she
offered it to him. He took a sip, more to satisfy the others than
to quench his own thirst. They needed to think they were
helping, even though the best thing they could have done for
him then—go away and leave him alone—was the one thing
they were certain not to do.

"Maybe I should call Dr. Niss." Spur's laugh was as light as
ashes. "Ask for my money back."

"You're right." Constant Ngonda lit up at the thought, then
realized that his enthusiasm was unseemly. "I mean, shouldn't
we notify the hospital?" he said, eyeing the tell on the parlor
wall. "They may have concerns."

Spur knew that the deputy would love to have him whisked
away from Littleton, in the hopes that the High Gregory and
the L'ung would follow. He wondered briefly if that might not
be for the best, but then he had been humiliated enough that
morning. "There's nothing to worry about."

"Good," said Ngonda. "I'm happy to hear that, Spur. Do
you mind, I promised to check in with the Cooperative when
we arrived?" Without waiting for a reply, Ngonda bustled
across the parlor to the kitchen. Meanwhile, the High Gregory
had sprawled onto a chair, his legs dangling over the armrest.
He was flipping impatiently through a back issue of Didactic

Arts' *True History Comix* without really looking at the pages. Spur thought he looked even more squirmy than usual, as if he knew there was someplace else he was supposed to be. Sly Sawatdee had parked himself next to Spur. His hands were folded in his lap, his eyelids were heavy and he hummed to himself from time to time, probably thinking about fishing holes and berry patches and molasses cookies.

"I am so sorry, Spur," said Comfort. "I just didn't realize." It was the third time she had apologized. She wasn't used to apologizing and she didn't do it very well. Meanwhile her anguish was smothering him. Her face was pale, her mouth was as crooked as a scar. What had he said to her? He couldn't remember but it must have been awful. There was a quiet desperation in her eyes that he had never seen before. It scared him.

Spur set the glass of water on the end table. "Listen, Comfort, there is nothing for you to be sorry about." He was the one who had fallen apart, after all. "Let's just forget it, all right? I'm fine now." To prove it, he stood up.

Sly twitched but did not move to pull him back onto the couch again. "Have enough air up there, my hasty little sparrow?"

"I'm fine," he repeated and it was true. Time to put this by and move on. Change the subject. "Who wants to see the orchard? Lucky?"

"If you don't mind," said Sly. "My bones are in no mood for a hike. But I'll make us lunch."

"I'll come," said Ngonda.

Comfort looked as if she wanted to beg off, but guilt got the better of her.

They tramped around the grounds, talking mostly of farm matters. After they had admired the revived orchard, inspected the weed-choked garden, toured the barn, played with the pack of gosdogs that had wandered over from the big house and began to follow them everywhere, walked the boundaries of the corn field which Cape had planted in clover until Spur was ready to farm again, they hiked through the woods down to Mercy's Creek.

"We take some irrigation water from the creek, but the Joerlys own the rights, so there's water in our end of the creek pretty much all year long." Spur pointed. "There's a pool in the woods where Comfort and I used to swim when we were kids. It might be a good place to cool off this afternoon."

"And so you and Spur were neighbors?" The High Gregory had been trying to draw Comfort out all morning, without much success. "You grew up together like me and my friends. I was hoping to bring them along but Uncle Constant Ngonda said there were too many of them. Your family is still living on the farm?"

"Mom died. She left everything to us. Now Vic's dead."

"Yes, Spur said that your brother was a brave firefighter. I know that you are very sad about it, but I see much more luck ahead for you."

She leaned against a tree and stared up at the sky.

"There used to be a pukpuk town in these woods." Spur was itching to move on. "They built all along the creek. It's overgrown now, but we could go look at the ruins."

The High Gregory stepped off the bank onto a flat stone that stuck out of the creek. "And your father?"

"He left," Comfort said dully.

"When they were little," Spur said quickly. He knew that Comfort did not like even to think about her father, much less talk about him with strangers. Park Nen had married into the Joerly family. Not only was his marriage to Rosie Joerly stormy, but he was also a loner who had never quite adjusted to village ways. "The last we heard Park was living in Freeport."

The High Gregory picked his way across the creek on stepping-stones. "He was a pukpuk, no?" His foot slipped and he windmilled his arms to keep his balance.

"Who told you that?" If Comfort had been absent-minded before, she was very much present now.

"I forget." He crossed back over the stream in four quick hops. "Was it you, Uncle?"

Ngonda licked his lips nervously. "I've never heard of this person."

"Then maybe it was Spur."

Spur would have denied it if Comfort had given him the chance.

"He never knew." Her voice was sharp. "Nobody did." She confronted the boy. "Don't play games with me, upsider." He tried to back away but she pursued him. "Why do you care about my father? Why are you here?"

"Are you crazy?" Ngonda caught the High Gregory as he stumbled over a rock and then thrust the boy behind him. "This is my nephew Lucky."

"She knows, friend Constant." The High Gregory peeked out from behind the deputy's flair jacket. He was glowing with excitement. "Spur told her everything."

"Oh, no." Ngonda slumped. "This isn't going well at all."

"Memsen gave us all research topics for the trip here to meet Spur," said the High Gregory. "Kai Thousandfold was assigned to find out about you. You'd like him; he's from Bellweather. He says that he's very worried about you, friend Comfort."

"Tell him to mind his own business."

Spur was aghast. "Comfort, I'm sorry, I didn't know. . . ."

"Be quiet, Spur. These upsiders are playing you for the fool that you are." Her eyes were wet. "I hardly knew my father, and what I did know, I didn't like. Mom would probably still be alive if she hadn't been left to manage the farm by herself all those years." Her chin quivered; Spur had never seen her so agitated. "She told us that Grandma Nen was a pukpuk, but that she emigrated from the barrens long before my father was born and that he was brought up a citizen like anyone else." Tears streaked her face. "So don't think you understand anything about me because you found out about a dead woman who I never met."

With that she turned and walked stiff-legged back toward

Diligence Cottage. She seemed to have shrunk since the morning, and now looked so insubstantial to Spur that a summer breeze might carry her off like milkweed. He knew there was more—much more—they had to talk about, but first they would have to find a new way to speak to each other. As she disappeared into the woods, he felt a twinge of nostalgia for the lost simplicity of their youth, when life really had been as easy as Chairman Winter promised it could be.

"I'm hungry." The High Gregory seemed quite pleased with himself. "Is it lunchtime yet?"

After he had spun out lunch for as long as he could, Spur was at a loss as to how to keep the High Gregory out of trouble. They had exhausted the sights of the Leung farmstead, short of going over to visit with his father in the big house. Spur considered it, but decided to save it for a last resort. He had hoped to spend the afternoon touring the Joerly farmstead, but now that was out of the question. As the High Gregory fidgeted about the cottage, picking things up and putting them down again, asking about family pix, opening cabinets and pulling out drawers, Spur proposed that they take a spin around Littleton in Sly's truck. A rolling tour, he told himself. No stops.

The strategy worked for most of an hour. At first the High Gregory was content to sit next to Spur in the back of the truck as he pointed out Littleton's landmarks and described the history of the village. They drove up Lamana Ridge Road to Lookover Point, from which they had a view of most of Littleton Commons. The village had been a Third Wave settlement, populated by the winners of the lottery of 2432. In the first years of settlement, the twenty-five founding families had worked together to construct the buildings of the Commons: the self-reliance school, athenaeum, communion lodge, town hall and Littleton's first exchange, where goods and services could be bought or bartered. The First Twenty-five had lived communally in rough barracks until the buildings on the Commons were completed, and then gradually moved out to their farmsteads as land was cleared and crews of carpenters put up the cottages and barns and sheds for each of the families. The Leungs had arrived in the Second Twenty-five four years afterward. The railroad had come through three years after that and most of the businesses of the first exchange moved from the Commons out to Shed Town by the train station. Sly drove them down the ridge and they bumped along back roads, past farms and fields and pastures. They viewed the Toba and Parochet and Velez farmsteads from a safe distance and passed Sambusa's lumberyard at the confluence of Mercy's Creek and the Swift River. Then they pulled back onto CR22.

The only way back to Diligence Cottage was through the Commons. "Drive by the barracks," Spur called to Sly in the cab. "We can stretch our legs there," he said to the High Gregory. "I'll show you how the First Twenty-five lived." One of the original barracks had been preserved as a historical museum across the lawn from the communion lodge. It was left open to any who wanted to view its dusty exhibits. Spur thought it the best possible choice for a stop; except for Founders' Day, the Chairman's birthday and Thanksgiving, nobody ever went there.

The Commons appeared to be deserted as they passed the buildings of the first exchange. These had been renovated into housing for those citizens of Littleton who didn't farm, like the teachers at the self-reliance school and Dr. Christopoulos and some of the elders, like Gandy Joy. They saw Doll Groth coming out of the athenaeum. Recognizing the truck, she gave Sly a neighborly wave, but when she spotted Spur in the back, she smiled and began to clap, raising her hands over her head. This so pleased the High Gregory that he stood up and started clapping back at her. Spur had to brace him to keep him from pitching over the side of the truck.

But Doll was the only person they saw. Spur couldn't believe his good fortune as they pulled up to the barracks, dust from the gravel parking lot swirling around them. The wind had picked up, but provided no relief from the midsummer heat. Spur's shirt stuck to his back where he had been leaning against the cab of the truck. Although he wasn't sure whether the High Gregory could sweat or not, the boy's face was certainly flushed. Ngonda looked as if he were liquefying inside his flair jacket. The weather fit Spur's latest plan neatly. He was hoping that after they had spent a half hour in the hot and airless barracks, he might be able to persuade the High Gregory to return to Diligence Cottage for a swim in the creek. After that it would practically be suppertime. And after that they could watch the tell. Or he might teach the High Gregory some of the local card games. Spur had always been lucky at Fool All.

It wasn't until the engine of the Sawatdees' truck coughed and rattled and finally cut out that Spur first heard the whoop of the crowd. Something was going on at the ball fields next to the self-reliance school, just down the hill a couple hundred meters. He tried to usher the High Gregory into the barracks but it was too late. Spur thought there must be a lot of people down there. They were making a racket that was hard to miss.

The High Gregory cocked his head in the direction of the school and smiled. "Lucky us," he said. "We're just in time for Memsen."

THIRTEEN

I associate this day, when I can remember it, with games of baseball played over behind the hills in the russet fields toward Sleepy Hollow.

—*JOURNAL*, 1856

"What is this?" hissed Ngonda.

Sly pulled his floppy hat off and wiped his forehead with it. "Looks like a baseball game, city pants," said Sly.

The L'ung were in the field; with a sick feeling Spur counted twelve of them in purple overalls and black T-shirts. They must have arrived in the two vans that were parked next to the wooden bleachers. Beside the vans was an array of trucks, scooters and bicycles from the village. There must have been a hundred citizens sitting in the bleachers and another twenty or thirty prowling the edges of the field, cheering the home team on. Match Klizzie had opened the refreshment shed and was barbequing sausages. Gandy Joy had set up her communion tent: Spur could see billows of sweet white smoke whenever one of the villagers pulled back the flap.

With many of the younger baseball regulars off at the fire-fight, the Littleton Eagles might have been undermanned. But Spur could see that some old-timers had come out of retirement to pull on the scarlet hose. Warp Kovacho was just stepping up to home base and Spur spotted Cape sitting on the strikers' bench, second from the inbox.

Betty Chief Twosalt shined the ball against her overalls as she peered in at Warp. "Where to, old sir?" She was playing feeder for the L'ung.

Warp swung the flat bat at belt level to show her just where he wanted the feed to cross home base. "Right here, missy," he said. "Then you better duck." They were playing with just two field bases, left and right. The banners fixed to the top of each basepole snapped in the stiffening breeze.

Betty nodded and then delivered the feed underhanded. It was slow and very fat but Warp watched it go by. The Pendragon Chromlis Furcifer was catching for the L'ung. She bare-handed it and flipped it back to Betty.

"What's he waiting for?" grumbled the High Gregory. "That was perfect." He ignored Spur's icy stare.

"Just a smight lower next time, missy," said Warp, once again indicating his preference with the bat. "You got the speed right, now hit the spot."

Young Melody Velez was perched at the end of the topmost bleacher and noticed Spur passing beneath her. "He's here!" she cried. "Spur's here!"

Play stopped and the bleachers emptied as the villagers crowded around him, clapping him on the back and shaking his hand. In five minutes he'd been kissed more than he'd been kissed altogether in the previous year.

"So is this another one of your upsider friends?" Gandy Joy held the High Gregory at arm's length, taking him in. "Hello, boy. What's your name?"

"I'm the High Gregory of Kenning," he said. "But my Walden name is Lucky, so I'd rather have you call me that."

Citizens nearby laughed nervously.

"Lucky you are then."

Gandy Hope Nakuru touched the pink bandana knotted around his neck. "Isn't this a cute scarf?" The High Gregory beamed.

Spur was astonished by it all. "But who told you that they're from the upside?" he said. "How did they get here? And why are you playing baseball?"

"Memsen brought them," said Peace Toba. "She said that you'd be along once we got the game going."

"And she was right." Little Jewel Parochet tugged at his shirt. "Spur, she said you flew in a hover. What was it like?"

"Maybe next time you can bring a guest along with you?" Melody Velez said, smiling. She brushed with no great subtlety against him.

Spur glanced about the thinning crowd; citizens were climbing back into the bleachers. "But where is Memsen?"

Peace Toba pointed; Memsen had only come out onto the field as far as right base when Constant Ngonda had captured her. He was waving his arms so frantically that he looked like he might take off and fly around the field. Memsen tilted her head so that her ear was practically on her shoulder. Then she saw Spur. She clicked her rings at him, a sly smile on her face. He knew he ought to be angry with her, but instead he felt buoyant, as if he had just set his splash pack down and stepped out of his field jacket. Whatever happened now, it wasn't his fault. He had done his best for his village.

"So this was what you were keeping from me." His father was chuckling. "I knew it had to be something. They're fine, your friends. You didn't need to worry." He hugged Spur and whispered into his ear, "Fine, but very strange. They're not staying, are they?" He pulled back. "Prosper, we need your bat in this game. These kids are tough." He pointed at Kai Thousandfold. "That one has an arm like a fire hose."

"No, thanks," said Spur. "But you should get back to the game." He raised his arms over his head and waved to the bleachers. "Thank you all, thanks," he called to his well-wishers. They quieted down to listen. "If you're expecting some kind of speech, then you've got the wrong farmer. I'll just say that I'm glad to be home and leave it at that. All right?" The crowd made a murmur of assent. "Then play ball." They cheered. "And go Eagles!" They cheered louder.

"Can I play?" said the High Gregory. "This looks like fun." He straightened the strap of his overalls. "I can play, can't I? We have all kinds of baseball on Kenning. But your rules are different, right? Tell them to me."

"Why bother?" Spur was beginning to wonder if the High Gregory was playing him for a fool. "Looks like you're making them up as you go."

Her Grace, Jacqueline Kristof, put an arm around his shoulder. "The ball is soft, so no gloves," she said, as she led him onto the field. "No tag outs either, you actually have to hit the runner with the ball. That's called a sting. No fouls and no . . ."

As the spectators settled into their seats, Spur found his way to Ngonda and Memsen. She wasn't wearing the standard L'ung overalls, but rather a plain green sundress with a floral print. She had washed the phosphorescent paint off her arms and pulled her hair back into a ponytail. But if Memsen was trying to look inconspicuous, then she had failed utterly. She was still the tallest woman on the planet.

"Talk to her," said Ngonda. "We had an agreement. . . ."

"Which you broke," said Memsen. "What we agreed was that the High Gregory would visit Littleton and you'd let him make whatever luck you are destined to have. You promised to give him the run of the village—"

"—under Spur's supervision, Allworthy," interrupted Ngonda.

Betty Chief Twosalt delivered a feed and Warp watched it go by again. This did not sit well with the L'ung. "Delay of game, old sir," someone called.

Memsen turned from Ngonda to Spur. "As we were explaining to the deputy, the L'ung and I see everything that the High Gregory sees. So we know that you've introduced him to just two of your neighbors. You promised that he could meet the citizens of this village but then you've kept him isolated until now. He needs to be with people, Spur. Barns don't have luck. People do."

"It was my decision," said Spur. "I'll take the responsibility."

"And this was ours." She waved toward the field. "So?"

Ngonda snorted in disgust. "I need to call Concord. The Office of Diplomacy will be filing a protest with the Forum of the Thousand Worlds." He took a step away from them, then turned and waggled a finger at Memsen. "This is a clear violation of our Covenant, Allworthy. The L'ung will be recalled to Kenning."

As they watched Ngonda stalk off, Warp struck a grounder straight back at the feeder. Betty stabbed at it but it tipped off her fingers and rolled away at an angle. Little Senator Dowm pounced on it but held the throw because Warp already had a hand on the right base stake.

"Maybe I should've introduced the High Gregory to a few more people." Spur wondered if standing too close to Memsen might be affecting his perceptions. The very planet seemed to tilt slightly, as it had that afternoon when he and Leaf Benkleman had drunk a whole liter of her mother's prize applejack. "But why are we playing baseball?"

Memsen showed him her teeth in that way she had that wasn't anything like a smile. "Tolerance isn't something that the citizens of the Transcendent State seem to value. You've been taught that your way of life is better not only than that of the pukpuks, but than that of most of the cultures of the Thousand Worlds. Or have we misread the textbooks?"

Spur shook his head grimly.

"So." She pinched the air. "Deputy Ngonda was right to point out that landing a hover on your Commons might have intimidated some people. We had to find some unthreatening way to arrive, justify our presence and meet your neighbors. The research pointed to baseball as a likely ploy. Your Eagles were champions of Hamilton County just two years ago and second runner-up in the Northeast in 2498."

"A ploy."

"A ploy to take advantage of your traditions. Your village is proud of its accomplishments in baseball. You're used to playing against strangers. And of course, we had an invitation from Spur Leung, the hero of the hour."

Livy Jayawardena hit a high fly ball that sailed over the heads of the midfielders. Kai Thousandfold, playing deep field, raced back and made an over-the-shoulder catch. Meanwhile Warp had taken off for left base. In his prime, he might have made it, but his prime had been when Spur was a toddler. Kai turned, set and fired; his perfect throw stung Warp right between the shoulder blades. Double play, inning over.

"I invited you?" said Spur. "When was that again?"

"Why, in the hospital where we saved your life. You kept claiming that the L'ung would offer no competition for your Eagles. You told Dr. Niss that you couldn't imagine losing a baseball game to upsiders, much less a bunch of children. Really, Spur, that was too much. We had to accept your challenge once you said that. So when we arrived at the town hall, we told our story to everyone we met. Within an hour the bleachers were full."

Spur was impressed. "And you thought of all this since yesterday?"

"Actually, just in the last few hours." She paused then, seemingly distracted. She made a low, repetitive pa-pa-pa-ptt. "Although there is something you should know about us," she said at last. "Of course, Deputy Ngonda would be outraged if he knew that we're telling you, but then he finds outrage everywhere." She stooped to his level so that they were face to face. "I rarely think all by myself, Spur." He tried not to notice that her knees bent in different directions. "Most of the time, we think for me."

The world seemed to tilt a little more then; Spur felt as if he might slide off it. "I don't think I understand what you just said."

"It's complicated." She straightened. "And we're attracting attention here. I can hear several young women whispering about us. We should find a more private place to talk. I need your advice." She turned and waved to the citizens in the bleachers who were watching them. Spur forced a smile and waved as well, and then led her up the hill toward town hall.

"Ngonda will file his protest," she said, "and it'll be summarily rejected. We've been in continuous contact with the Forum of the Thousand Worlds." Her speech became choppy as she walked. "They know what we're doing." Climbing the gentle hill left her breathless. "Not all worlds approve. Consensus is hard to come by. But the L'ung have a plan . . . to open talks between you . . . and the pukpuks." She rested a hand on his shoulder to support herself. "Is that something you think worth doing?"

"Maybe." He could feel the warmth of her hand through the thin fabric of his shirt. "All right, yes." He thought this must be another ploy. "But who are you? Who are the L'ung? Why are you doing this?"

"Be patient." At the top of the hill she had to rest to catch her breath. Finally she said, "You spoke with the High Gregory about gosdogs?"

"In the truck this morning."

"It was at the instigation of the L'ung. Understand that we don't believe that gosdogs think in any meaningful sense of the word. Perhaps the original Peekay intelligence rating was accurate. But if they were found to be more intelligent, then we could bring the issue of their treatment here to the Forum. It would require a delicate touch to steer the debate toward the remedy the L'ung want. Tricky but not impossible. The Forum has no real power to intervene in the affairs of member worlds and your Chairman Winter has the right to run Walden as he pleases. But he depends on the good opinion of the Thousand Worlds. When we're finished here, the L'ung will propose to return the gosdogs to a preserve where they can live in their natural state."

"But there is no natural habitat left. The pukpuks destroyed it."

"Ah, but ecologies can be re-created." She gestured at the lawn stretching before them, at the rose hedges along its border and the trees that shaded it, their leaves trembling in the summer breeze. "As you well know."

"But what does a gosdog preserve have to do with the pukpuks?"

"Come away from the sun before we melt." Memsen led him to a bench in the shadow of an elm. She sagged onto it; Spur remained standing, looking down at her for a change. It eased the crick in his neck.

"The preserve sets a precedent." She clicked her rings. "In order for it to be established, the growth of the forest must be controlled, which means the Transcendent State will be blocked from spreading across Walden. Up until

now, the Cooperative has refused to negotiate on this point.
And then comes the question of where to put the preserve.
You and the pukpuks will have to sit down to decide on a
site. Together. With some delicate nudging from the Forum,
there's no telling what conversations might take place at such
a meeting."

"But we can't!" Spur wiped the sweat from his forehead.
"The Transcendent State was founded so that humans could
live apart and stay true to ourselves. As long as the pukpuks
live here, we'll be under direct attack from upsider ways."

"Your Transcendent State is a controversial experiment."
Memsen's face went slack and she made the pa-pa-pa-ptt sound
Spur had heard before. "We've always wondered how isolation
and ignorance can be suitable foundations for a human society.
Do you really believe in simplicity, Spur, or do you just not
know any better?"

Spur wondered if she had used some forbidden upsider tech
to look into his soul; he felt violated. "I believe in this." He
gestured, as she had done, at Littleton Commons, green as a
dream. "I don't want my village to be swept away. The pukpuks destroyed this world once already."

"Yes, that could happen, if it's what you and your children
decide," said Memsen. "We don't have an answer for you,
Spur. But the question is, do you need a preserve like gosdogs,
or are you strong enough to hold on to your beliefs no matter
who challenges them?"

"And this is your plan to save Walden?" He ground his
shoe into the grass. "This is the luck that the High Gregory
came all this way to make?"

"Is it?" She leaned back against the bench and gazed up
into the canopy of the elm. "Maybe it is."

"I've been such an idiot." He was bitter; if she was going to
use him, at least she could admit it. "You and the High Gregory and the L'ung flit around the upside, having grand adventures and straightening up other people's messes." He began to

pace back and forth in front of the bench. "You're like some kind of superheroes, is that it?"

"The L'ung have gathered together to learn statecraft from one another," she said patiently. "Sometimes they travel, but mostly they stay with us on Kenning. Of course they have political power in the Forum because of who they are, but their purpose is not so much to do as it is to learn. Then, in a few more years, this cohort will disband and scatter to their respective worlds to try their luck. And when the time comes for us to marry . . ."

"Marry? Marry who?"

"The High Gregory, of course."

"But he's just a boy."

Memsen must have heard the dismay in his voice. "He will grow into his own luck soon enough," she said coldly. "I was chosen the twenty-second Memsen by my predecessor. She searched for me for years across the Thousand Worlds." With a weary groan she stood, and once again towered over him. "A Memsen is twice honored: to be wife to one High Gregory and mother to another." Her voice took on a declaiming quality, as if she were giving a speech that had been well rehearsed. "And I carry my predecessor and twenty souls who came before her saved in our memory, so that we may always serve the High Gregory and advise the L'ung."

Spur was horrified at the depth of his misunderstanding of this woman. "You have dead people . . . inside you?"

"Not dead," she said. "Saved."

A crazed honking interrupted them. A truck careened around the corner and skidded to a stop in front of the town hall. Stark Sukulgunda flung himself out of the still-running truck and dashed inside.

Spur stood. "Something's wrong." He started for the truck and had gotten as far as the statue of Chairman Winter, high on his pedestal, when Stark burst out of the doors again. He saw Spur and waved frantically.

"Where are they all?" he cried. "Nobody answers."

"Playing baseball." Spur broke into a trot. "What's wrong? What?"

"Baseball?" Stark's eyes bulged as he tried to catch his breath. "South slope of Lamana . . . burning . . . everything's burning . . . the forest is on fire!"

FOURTEEN

I walked slowly through the wood to Fair Haven Cliff, climbed to the highest rock, and sat down upon it to observe the progress of the flames, which were rapidly approaching me, now about a mile distant from the spot where the fire was kindled. Presently I heard the sound of the distant bell giving the alarm, and I knew that the town was on its way to the scene. Hitherto I had felt like a guilty person,—nothing but shame and regret. But now I settled the matter with myself shortly. I said to myself: "Who are these men who are said to be the owners of these woods, and how am I related to them? I have set fire to the forest, but I have done no wrong therein, and now it is as if the lightning had done it. These flames are but consuming their natural food." . . . So shortly I settled it with myself and stood to watch the approaching flames. It was a glorious spectacle, and I was the only one there to enjoy it. The fire now reached the base of the cliff and then rushed up its sides. The squirrels ran before it in blind haste, and three pigeons dashed into the midst of the smoke. The flames flashed up the pines to their tops, as if they were powder.

—JOURNAL, 1850

More than half of the Littleton Volunteer Fire Department were playing baseball when the alarm came. They scrambled up the hill to the brick firehouse on the Commons, followed by almost all of the spectators, who crowded anxiously into the communion hall while the firefighters huddled. Normally there would have been sixteen volunteers on call, but, like Spur, Will Sambusa, Bright Ayoub, Bliss Bandaran and Chief Cary Millisap had joined the Corps. Cape was currently Assistant Chief; he would have led the volunteers had not his son been home. Even though Spur protested that he was merely a grunt smokechaser, the volunteers' first act was to vote him Acting Chief.

Like any small-town unit, the Littleton Fire Department routinely answered calls for house fires and brush fires and accidents of all sorts, but they were ill-equipped to stop a major burn. They had just one fire truck, an old quad with a three-thousand-liter-per-minute pump and five-thousand-liter water tank. It carried fifty meters of six-centimeter hose, fifty meters of booster hose, and a ten-meter mechanical ladder. If the burn was as big as Stark described, Engine No. 4 would be about as much use fighting it as a broom.

Spur resisted the impulse to put his team on the truck and rush out to the burn. He needed more information before he committed his meager forces. It would be at least an hour before companies from neighboring villages would arrive and the Corps might not get to Littleton until nightfall. Cape spread a map out on the long table in the firehouse and the volunteers stood around it, hunch-shouldered and grim. Gandy Joy glided in, lit a single communion square and slipped out again as they contemplated what the burn might do to their village. They took turns peppering Stark with questions about what he had actually seen. At first he tried his best to answer, but he'd had a shock that had knocked better men than him off center. As they pressed him, he grew sullen and suspicious.

The Sukulgundas lived well west of the Leungs and higher up the slope of Lamana Ridge. They'd been latecomers to Littleton and parts of their farmstead were so steep that the fields had to be terraced. They were about four kilometers north of the Commons at the very end of January Road, a steep dirt track with switchbacks. Stark maintained that the burn had come down the ridge at him, from the general direction of Lookover Point to the east. At first he claimed it was maybe a kilometer away when he'd left his place, but then changed his mind and insisted that the burn was practically eating his barn. That didn't make sense, since the strong easterly breeze would push the burn in the opposite direction, toward the farmsteads of the Ezzats and Millisaps and eventually to the Herreras and the Leungs.

Spur shivered as he imagined the burn roaring through GiGa's orchards. But his neighbors were counting on him to keep those fears at bay. "If what you're saying is true," he mused, "it might mean that this fire was deliberately set and that someone is still out there trying to make trouble for us."

"Torches in Littleton?" Livy Jayawardena looked dubious. "We're nowhere near the barrens."

"Neither was Double Down," said Cape. "Or Wheelwright."

"I don't know about that." Stark Sukulgunda pulled the cap off his head and started twisting it. "All I know is that we ought to stop talking about what to do and do something."

"First we have to know for sure where the burn is headed, which means we need to get up the Lamana Ridge Road." Spur was struggling to apply what he'd learned in training. "If the burn hasn't jumped the road and headed back down the north slope of the ridge, then we can use the road as a firebreak and hold that line. And when reinforcements come, we'll send them east over the ridge to the head of the burn. That's the way the wind is blowing everything." He glanced up at the others to see if they agreed. "We need to be thinking hard about an eastern perimeter."

"Why?" Stark was livid. "Because that's where you live? It's my house that—"

"Shut up, Stark," said Peace Toba. "Fill your snoot with communion and get right with the village for a change."

None of the threatened farmsteads that lay in the path of the burn to the east was completely cleared of trees. Simplicity demanded that citizens only cultivate as much of their land as they needed. Farmers across Walden used the forest as a windbreak; keeping unused land in trees prevented soil erosion. But now Spur was thinking about all the pine and hemlock and red cedar, needles laden with resins and oils, side by side with the deciduous trees in the woods where he had played as a boy. At Motu River he'd seen pine trees explode into flame. And then there were the burn piles of slash and stumps and old lumber that every farmer collected, baking in the summer sun.

"If things go wrong in the east, we might need to set our firebreak as far back as Blue Valley Road." Spur ran his finger down the line on the map. "It won't be as effective a break as the ridge road but we can improve it. Get the Bandarans and Sawatdees to rake off all the forest litter and duff on the west side. Then disk harrow the entire road. I want to see at least a three-meter-wide strip of fresh soil down the entire length."

"Prosper." Cape's voice was hushed. "You're not giving up on all of this." He traced the outline of the four threatened farms on the map, ending on the black square that marked Diligence Cottage.

Spur glanced briefly at his father, then away again, troubled by what he had seen. Capability Leung looked just as desperate as Stark Sukulgunda. Maybe more so, if he thought he had just heard his son pronounce doom on his life's work. For the first time in his life, Spur felt as if he were the father and Cape was the son.

"No." He tried to reassure his father with a smile. "That's just our fallback. What I'm hoping is that we can cut a handline from Spot Pond along Mercy's Creek all the way down to the river. It's rough country and depending on how fast the burn is moving we may not have enough time, but if we can hold that line, we save the Millisaps, Joerlys and us." Left unsaid was that the Ezzats' farmstead would be lost, even if this dicey strategy worked.

"But right now the fire is much closer to my place than anyone else's," said Stark. "And you said yourself, there may be some suicidal maniac just waiting to burn himself up and take my house with him."

Spur was annoyed at the way that Stark Sukulgunda kept buzzing at him. He was making it hard for Spur to concentrate. "We could send the fire truck your way, Stark," he said, "but I don't know what good it would do. You don't have any standing water on your land, do you?"

"Why?"

"The truck only has a five-thousand-liter water tank. That's not near enough if your house gets involved."

"We could drop the hard suction line into his well," said Livy. "Pump from there."

"You have a dug well?" said Cape. "How deep?"

"Four meters."

"We'd probably suck it dry before we could do you much good," said Cape.

"No," said Spur. "He's right. Peace, you and Tenny and Cert take No. 4 up to Sukulgundas'. You can also establish our western perimeter. Clear a meter-wide handline as far up the ridge as you can. Watch for torches. I don't think the fire is going to come your way but if it does, be ready, understand? Get on the tell and let us know if anything changes."

"We'll call in when we get there," said Peace as her team scattered to collect gear.

"Livy, you and the others round up as many as you can to help with the creek line. We may want to start a backfire, so keep in touch with me on the hand-tell. How much liquid fire have you got?"

"At least twenty grenades. Maybe more. No firebombs though."

"Bring gas then, you'll probably need it. Keep your people between the civilians and the burn, understand? And pull back if it gets too hot. I've lost too many friends this year. I don't want to be burying anyone else. DiDa, you and I need to find a way to get up the ridge. . . ."

He was interrupted by the roar of a crowd, which had gathered just outside the firehouse. Spur froze, momentarily bewildered. They couldn't still be playing baseball, could they? Then he thought that the burn must have changed direction. It had careened down the ridge faster than it had any right to, an avalanche of fire that was about to incinerate the Commons and there was nothing he could do to fight it; in the nightmare, he wasn't wearing his splash pack. Or his fireproof field jacket. Spur shuddered. He wasn't fit to lead, to decide what to let burn and what to save. He was weak and his soul was lost in darkness and he knew he shouldn't be afraid. He was a veteran of the firefight, but fear squeezed him nonetheless. "Are you all right, son?" His father rested a hand on his shoulder. The burn licked at boulders and scorched the trees in the forest he had sworn to protect.

"DiDa," he whispered, leaning close to his father so no one else would hear, "what if I can't stop it?"

"You'll do your best, Prosper," he said. "Everyone knows that."

As they rushed out of the firehouse, they could see smoke roiling into the sky to the northwest. But the evil plume wasn't what had stunned the crowd, which was still pouring out of the communion hall. A shadow passed directly overhead and, even in the heat of this disastrous afternoon, Spur was chilled.

Silently, like a miracle, the High Gregory's hover landed on Littleton Commons.

FIFTEEN

Men go to a fire for entertainment. When I see how eagerly men will run to a fire, whether in warm or cold weather, by night or by day, dragging an engine at their heels, I'm astonished to perceive how good a purpose the level of excitement is made to serve.

—JOURNAL, 1850

"There's a big difference between surface fire and crown fire," said the Pendragon Chromlis Furcifer to the L'ung assembled in the belly of the hover. "Surface fires move along the forest floor, burning through the understory." She was reading from notes that scrolled down her forearm.

"Wait, what's understory again?" asked Her Grace, Jacqueline Kristof, who was the youngest of the L'ung.

Memsen pinched the air. "You mustn't keep interrupting, Your Grace. If you have questions, query the cognisphere in slow time." She nodded at Penny. "Go ahead, Pendragon. You're doing a fine job."

"Understory is the grass, shrubs, dead leaves, fallen trees—that stuff. So anyway, a surface fire can burn fast or slow, depending. But if the flames climb into the crowns of the trees, it almost always rips right through the forest. Since the Transcendental State doesn't have the tech to stop it, Spur will have to let it burn itself out. If you look over there . . ." The group closed around her, craning to see.

Spur had been able to ignore Penny for the most part, although Cape kept scowling at the L'ung. Memsen had explained that Penny's research topic for the trip to Walden was forest fires.

The hover was not completely proof against smoke. As they skirted the roiling convection column of smoke and burning embers, the air inside the hover became tinged with the bitter stench of the burn. This impressed the L'ung. As they wandered from view to view, they would call to one another. "Here, over here. Do you smell it now? Much stronger over here!"

They had dissolved the partitions and made most of the hull transparent to observe developments in the burn. Just a single three-meter-wide band ran solid from the front of the deck to the back as a concession to Spur and Cape; the L'ung seemed totally immune from fear of heights. Spur was proud at how Cape was handling his first flight in a hover, especially since he himself felt slightly queasy whenever he looked straight down through the deck at the ridge 1,500 meters below.

From this vantage, Spur could see exactly what was needed to contain the burn and realized that he didn't have the resources to do it. Looking to the north, he was relieved that the burn hadn't yet crossed Lamana Ridge Road into the wilderness on the far slope. Barring an unforeseen wind change or embers lighting new spot fires, he thought he might be able to keep the burn within the Littleton valley. But he needed dozens of trained firefighters up on the ridge to defend the road as soon as possible. To the west, he saw where the flames had come close to the Sukulgundas' farmstead, but now the burn there looked to be nothing more than a surface fire that was already beginning to gutter out. Peace and the team with Engine No. 4 should have no trouble mopping up. Then he'd move them onto the ridge, not that just three people and one ancient pumper were going to be enough to beat back a wall of flame two kilometers wide.

"Where you see the darker splotches in the forest, those are evergreens, the best fuel of all," said Penny. "If they catch, you can get a blowup fire, which is what that huge column of smoke is about."

To the east and south, the prospects were grim. The burn had dropped much farther down the ridge than Spur had expected. He remembered from his training that burns were supposed to track uphill faster than down, but the spread to the north and south, upslope and down, looked about the same. As soon as the first crews responded from nearby Bode Well and Highbridge, they'd have to deploy at the base of the ridge to protect the Commons and the farmsteads beyond it.

The head of the burn was a violent crown fire racing east, beneath a chimney of malign smoke that towered kilometers above the hover. When Spur had given the Ezzats and Millisaps permission to save as much as they could from their houses, he'd thought that they'd all have more time. Now he realized that he'd miscalculated. He reached both families using the hand-tell and told them to leave immediately. Bash Ezzat was weeping when she said she could already see the burn sweeping down on her. Spur tried Comfort's tell again to let her know that her farmstead was directly in the path of the burn, but still got no answer.

"DiDa," said Spur gently. He'd been dreading this moment, ever since he'd understood the true scope and direction of the burn. "I think we need to pull Livy and her people back from the creek to Blue Valley Road." He steeled himself against anger, grief and reproach. "There's no time to clear a line," he went on. "At least not one that will stop this burn."

"I think you're right," Cape said, as casually as if they were discussing which trees to prune. "It's simple, isn't it?"

Relieved but still anguished, he hugged his father. "I'm sorry, DiDa." He couldn't remember the last time they had been this close, and was not surprised that Cape did not return his embrace. "Should we send someone to the house?" he said, as he let his father go. "Have them pack some things? Papers, furniture—there's still a little time."

"No." Cape turned and cupped his hands against the transparent hull of the hover. "If I did something silly like that, the farm would burn for sure." He lowered his face into his hands as if to shade the view from glare. But the afternoon sun was a dim memory, blotted out by the seething clouds of smoke.

Spur shut his eyes then, so tight that for a moment he could feel muscles on his temple quiver. "Memsen," he said, his voice catching in his throat, "can you put us down by the Sawatdees' house?"

Spur got more resistance from Livy than he had from his father. It took him almost ten minutes to convince her that trying to dig a firebreak along Mercy's Creek was not only futile but also dangerous. When it was over, he felt drained. As he flopped beside Cape onto one of the chairs that Memsen had caused to flow from the deck of the hover, the hand-tell squawked. He groaned, anticipating that Livy was back with a new argument.

"Prosper Leung?" said a woman's voice.

"Speaking."

"I'm Commander Do Adoula, Fourth Engineers. My squad was on CR in Longwalk but we heard you have a situation there and we're on our way. We can be in Littleton in half an hour. I understand you're in a hover. What do you see?"

The handover of command was subtle but swift. Commander Adoula started by asking questions and ended by giving orders. She was coming in four light trucks with thirty-seven firefighters but no heavy equipment. She approved of Spur's decision to stop the burn at Blue Valley Road, and split her force in two while they were speaking, diverting half to the ridge and half to help Livy on Blue Valley. She directed the local firefighters from Bode Well and Highbridge to dig in on the south to protect the Commons and requested that Spur stay in the hover and be her eyes in the sky.

When they finished talking, Spur slumped back against his chair. He was pleased that Adoula had ratified his firefighting plans, relieved to be no longer in charge.

"The Corps?" said Cape.

"Fourth Engineers." He folded the hand-tell. "They were on CR in Longwalk."

"That was lucky."

"Lucky," he agreed. He spotted the High Gregory whispering to Memsen. "How are you doing, DiDa?"

"You know, I've never visited the ocean." Cape blinked as he stared through the hull at the forest below. "Your mother wanted me to take her there, did I ever tell you that?"

"No."

"She always used to ask if we owned the farm or if the farm owned us." He made a low sound, part sigh and part whistle. "I wonder if she's still in Providence."

Spur didn't know what to say.

Cape frowned. "You haven't been in contact with her?"

"No."

"If you ever do speak to her, would you tell me?"

"Sure."

He nodded and made the whistling sound again.

"A burn this big is different from a surface fire," said Penny. "It's so hot that it makes a kind of fire weather called a convection column. Inside the column, bubbles of super-heated air are surging up, only we can't see that. But on the outside, the cooler smoky edges are pouring back toward the ground."

"Yes, yes." The High Gregory pointed, clearly excited. "Watch at the top, to the left of the plume. It's like it's turning itself inside out."

"Awesome," said Kai Thousandfold. "Do you remember those gas sculptures we played with on Blimminey?"

"But that's going to be a problem for Spur and his firefighters," said Penny. "It's like a chimney shooting sparks and embers high into the atmosphere. They might come down anywhere and start new fires."

"Is anyone going to die?" said Senator Dowm.

"We hope not," Memsen said. "Spur is doing his best and help is on the way."

"Don't you wish she'd shut up?" muttered Cape, leaning

into Spur. "This isn't some silly class. They're watching our life burn down."

"They're from the upside, DiDa. We can't judge them."

"And how does she know so much about how we fight fires? Look at her, she's just a kid."

That had been bothering Spur too, and it was getting harder and harder to put out of his mind. When had the L'ung had time to do all this research? They had arrived the day after he had first spoken to the High Gregory. Had they known ahead of time that they were coming to Walden? Was all this part of the plan?

"Memsen says they're special," he said.

"Spur." The High Gregory signed for him to come over. "Come take a look at this."

He crossed the deck to where the L'ung were gathered. The hover had descended to a thousand meters and was cruising over the Joerly farmstead.

"There," said the High Gregory, pointing to the woods they had tramped through that morning, a mix of hard and softwoods: birch and oak, hemlock and pine. In the midst of it, three tendrils of gray smoke were climbing into the sky.

"Those are spot fires," said Penny. "Caused by falling embers."

Spur didn't believe it. He'd been worried about spotting all along and had swung from side to side in the hover looking for them. But he'd decided that not enough time had passed for embers from the burn to start raining down on them. The convection column towered at least five kilometers above the valley. He stared at the plumes of smoke rising from the woods of his childhood with sickening dread. From right to left they were progressively smaller. Three fires in a series, which meant they had probably been set. What was his duty here? He was pretty sure that his scooter was still in the barn at Diligence Cottage. He could use it to get away from the burn in plenty of time. Cape could monitor the progress of the burn for Commander Adoula. Besides, if someone was down there setting fires . . .

Someone.

"Memsen," he said. "I've changed my mind."

The hover glided to a stop above the unused field nearest to Diligence Cottage. Spur stepped back as guard rails flowed out of the deck around the ramp, which slowly extended like a metal tongue toward the sweet clover below. Cape, who was standing next to Spur, was smiling. What did his father think was so funny?

"We can stay here and wait for you," said Memsen. "If you have a problem, we'll come."

"Not through those trees you won't," said Spur. "No, you take Cape back up so he can report to the commander." The hover shuddered in the windstorm caused by the burn. "Besides, it's going to get rough here before too much longer. You need to protect yourselves."

"This is exciting." Her Grace, Jacqueline Kristof, clapped her hands. "Are you excited, Spur?"

Memsen turned the girl around and gave her a hard shove toward the rest of the L'ung.

"DiDa?" Spur wanted to hug his father but settled for handing him the tell. "When the commander calls, just explain that I think we might have a torch and I'm on the ground looking. Then just keep track of the burn for her."

"Yes." His father was grinning broadly now. "I'm ready."

"Good. Memsen, thanks for your help."

"Go safely." She clicked her rings.

Spur held out his hand to the High Gregory but the boy dodged past it and embraced him instead. Spur was taken aback when he felt the High Gregory's kiss on his cheek. "I can see much more luck for you, friend Spur," he murmured. "Don't waste it."

The hot wind was an immediate shock after the cool interior of the hover. It blew gusty and confused, whipping Spur's hair and picking at his short sleeves. Spur paused at the bottom of the ramp to consider his next move and gather his courage. The pillar of smoke had smothered the afternoon sun, sinking the land into nightmarish and untimely gray twilight.

"Nice weather we're having," said Cape.

"DiDa, what?" He spun around, horrified. "Get back up there."

Cape snapped him a mock salute. "Since when do you give the orders on this farm, son?"

"But you have to, you can't . . ." He felt like a foolish little boy, caught by his father pretending to be a grownup. "Someone has to talk to the ground. The commander needs to know what's happening with the burn."

"I gave the tell to your know-so-much friend, Penny. She'll talk Adoula's ear off."

The ramp started to retract.

"What I have to do is too dangerous, DiDa." Spur's face was hot. "You're not coming, understand?"

"Wasn't planning to." Cape chuckled. "Never entered my mind."

Spur watched in helpless fury as the hatch closed. "Then just load whatever you want into the truck and take off. You've got maybe twenty minutes before things get hot here."

The hover rose straight up and away from the field but then paused, a dark speck in an angry sky.

"See what you've done?" Spur groaned.

"Don't worry. They'll run before too long." Cape clapped him on the back. "I don't know about you, but I have things to do."

"DiDa, are you . . . ?" Spur was uncertain whether he should leave Cape while he was in this manic mood. "Be careful."

Capability Roger Leung was not a man known for his

sense of humor, but he laughed now. "Prosper, if we were being careful, we'd be up there in the sky with your strange little
friends." He pointed into the woods. "Time to take some
chances, son."

He turned and trotted off toward the big house without
looking back.

Spur knew these woods. He and Vic and Comfort had spent
hours in the cool shade pretending to be pirates or skantlings
or aliens or fairies. They played queen and castle in the pukpuk
ruins and pretended to be members of Morobe's original crew,
exploring a strange new world for the first time. They cut
paths to secret hideouts and built lean-tos from hemlock boughs
and, when Vic and Spur were eleven, they even erected a ram-
shackle tree house with walls and a roof, although Cape made
them take it down because he said it was too dangerous. Spur
had been kissed for the first time in that tree house: In a contest
of sibling gross-out, Vic had dared his big sister to kiss his best
friend. Comfort got the best of it, however, because her back
dare was that Vic had to kiss Spur. As he pulled back from the
kiss, Vic had punched Spur in the arm so hard it left a bruise.

The woods were dark and unnaturally quiet as he padded
down the path that led past Bear Rock and the Throne of the
Spruce King. Spur heard no birdsong or drone of bugs. It was
as if the trees themselves were listening for the crackle of fire.
When he first smelled smoke, he stopped to turn slowly and
sniff, trying to estimate where it had come from. Ahead and to
the north was his best guess. That meant it was time to cut off
the path and bushwhack south across the Great Gosdog Swamp,
which had never been very great and always dried up in the
summer. His plan was to strike out in the direction of the
smallest of the three fires he had seen from the hover. He knew
he was getting close when it started to snow fire.

Most of what floated down was ash, but in the mix were

sparks and burning embers that stung the bare skin of his arms and face. He brushed a hand through his hair and ran. Not in a panic—just to keep embers from sticking to him. To his right he could see the glow of at least one of the fires. And yes, now he could hear the distant crack and whoosh he knew all too well. The burn was working along the forest floor, he was sure of that. Crown fire sounded like a runaway train. If he were anywhere near one, he'd be deafened and then he'd be dead. Spur finally escaped the ash fall after several minutes of dodging past trees at speed. He hunched over to knead the stitch in his side, then pressed on.

The wind had picked up and now was blowing west, not east. He thought it must be an indraft. The burn that was crashing down on them had to suck air in huge gulps from every direction in order to support itself. Maybe the wind shift would work in their favor. A west wind would push these outlying spot fires back toward the burn itself. If the line of backfire was wide enough, it might actually check the advance of the burn when the two met. Of course, it would have to scorch across the best parts of the Millisap and Joerly farmsteads first.

In the gathering darkness, Spur decided to start trotting again. It was taking too long to skirt around the last fire to Mercy's Creek. And unless he saw something soon, he was turning back. He had to leave himself enough time to get away. And he wanted to make sure his father hadn't done anything crazy.

Intent on not tripping over a stone or root, Spur never saw the windblown curtain of smoke until it closed around him. He spun around, disoriented. He had been panting from running, so his nose and mouth and lungs filled immediately. It was like trying to breathe cotton. His eyes went teary and the world was reduced to a watery dissolve. Had he been out with Gold Squad, he would have been wearing goggles, a helmet and a breather. But here he was practically naked, and the smoke was pervasive and smothering. He was coughing so hard he could taste the tang of blood and then his throat closed and he knew he was about to choke to death. In a panic, he hurled himself flat against the forest floor, desperately searching for the shallow layer of breathable air that they said sometimes clung to the ground. A stump poked at his side but as he laid his cheek against the mat of twigs and papery leaves, he found cooler air, rank but breathable. He tried to fill his aching lungs, coughed up mucus and blood, then tried again.

Spur didn't know exactly how long he lay there, but when he came to himself again, the haze of smoke had thinned to gauze and he knew he had taken enough chances. He had learned the hard way at Motu River that he was no hero. Why was he at it again? No more; get to the cottage, get on the scooter and get as far away from fire as possible. He pushed himself up on hands and knees, coughed and spat. His nose felt as if someone had pulled barbed wire through it. He sat back on his heels, blinking. It wasn't until he brushed at the leaf litter on his face that he realized he'd been crying. When he finally stood, he felt tottery. He grabbed a sapling to steady himself. Then he heard a twig snap and the rustle of foliage being parted. He ducked behind a beech tree that was barely wider than he was.

Comfort came trudging toward him, her face hard, eyes glassy. One look told him everything. She had changed out of the gingham dress into a pair of baggy work pants that looked like they must have belonged to Vic. Over a smudged and dirty T-shirt, she wore a crude burlap vest to which were attached three liquid-fire grenades. They bumped against her chest as she approached. She looked weary, as if she'd been carrying a weight that had pushed her to the very limit of her strength.

He had thought to leap out and overwhelm her when she passed, but she spotted him when she was still a dozen meters away, and froze. He stepped from behind his tree, his hands held in front of him.

"I won't hurt you," he said.

In the instant he saw mindless animal panic in her eyes, he thought her more alien than any upsider. He had spooked her. Then she turned and sprinted away.

Spur ran after her. He wasn't thinking about the burn or his village or simplicity. He ran. He didn't have time to be either brave or afraid. He ran because he had loved this woman once and because he had watched her brother die.

As a girl, Comfort had always been the nimblest of the three of them. In an open field, Vic would have caught her, but scooting past trees and ducking under low branches, Comfort was faster than any two squirrels. After a couple of minutes of pursuit, Spur was winded. He wasn't exactly sure where they were anymore. Headed toward the creek, he guessed. If she thought she could cross over and take refuge in her own house, she truly was crazy. Suicidal.

Which made him pick up the pace, despite his fatigue. He ran so hard he thought his heart might break.

She had almost reached the creek when the chase ended abruptly. Comfort got reckless, cut a tree too close and clipped it instead. The impact knocked one of the grenades loose and spun her half around. She went to her knees and Spur leapt at her. But she kicked herself away and he skidded past and crashed into a tangle of summersweet. By the time he got to his knees she was showing him one of the grenades. He could see that she had flipped the safety and that her finger was on the igniter.

"Stop there," she said.

Spur was breathless and a little dizzy. "Comfort, don't."

"Too late." She blew a strand of dark hair off her face. "I already have."

He stood, once again holding his hands where she could see them. "What's this about, Comfort?"

"Vic," she said. "It's mostly about Vic now."

"He's gone. There's nothing you can do for him."

"We'll see." She shivered, despite the heat. "It was my fault, you know. I was the one who recruited him. But he was just supposed to pass information." Her voice shook. "They must have bullied him into becoming a torch. I killed him, Spur. I killed my brother."

"Listen to me, Comfort. He wasn't a torch. It was an accident."

The hand holding the grenade trembled slightly but then steadied. "That's not what you said this morning when you were off your head." She gave him a pitying look. "You said you tried to save him. That I believe."

He took a half step toward her. "But how does it help anyone to set fire to Littleton?" Another half step. "To our farms?"

She backed away from him. "They could stop this, you know. Your upsider friends. They could force the Cooperative to settle, put pressure on Jack Winter to do what's right. Except they don't really care about us. They come to watch, but they never get involved." Her laugh was low and scattered. "They're involved now. I hope that little brat is scared of dying."

"But they do care." He held his arms tight to his sides; otherwise he would have been waving them at her. "Memsen has a plan." Spur thought he might yet save her. "You have to believe me, Comfort. There are going to be talks with the pukpuks."

"Right." Her mouth twisted. "And you didn't see Vic torch himself."

"Besides, did you really think you could burn them up? The High Gregory is safe, Comfort. Memsen and the L'ung. Their hover came for us. That's how I got here so fast. They're in the air"—he pointed backward over his shoulder—"waiting for me over the cottage."

When he saw her gaze flick up and away from him, he launched himself. He grabbed at the arm with the grenade.

They twirled together in a grotesque pirouette. Then, unable to check his momentum, Spur stumbled and fell.

Comfort stepped away from him. She shook her head once. She pressed the igniter on the grenade.

It exploded into a fireball that shot out two long streams of flame in opposite directions. One soared high into the trees, the other shot down at the forest floor and gathered in a blazing puddle at her feet. She screamed as the grenade fell from her charred hand. Great tongues of flame licked up her legs. Her pants caught fire. Her singed hair curled into nothingness.

Spur screamed too. Seeing it all happen all over again was worse than any nightmare. When Vic had set the liquid fire-bomb off, he had been instantly engulfed in flame. Spur had tried to knock him down, hoping to roll his friend onto the ground and put the merciless fire out. But Vic had shoved him away. With his clothes, his arms in flames, Vic had found the strength to send Spur sprawling backward.

Which saved Spur's life when the second bomb went off.

But this wasn't Motu River and Vic was dead. Comfort, his Comfort, had only grenades, designed to set backfires, not bombs designed by pukpuk terrorists. The lower half of her body had been soaked in liquid fire and was burning but he could see her face, her wild, suffering eyes, her mouth a slash of screeching pain and that last grenade still bumping against her chest.

Spur flew at her and ripped the unexploded grenade from the vest. He swept her up in his arms, taking her weight easily with a mad strength, and raced toward the creek. He had the crazy thought that if he ran fast enough, he would be able to stay ahead of the pain. He knew he was burning now but he had to save her. He had never had a chance with Vic; take some chances, his father had said, and the High Gregory had warned him not to waste his luck. But the pain was too fast, it was catching up to him. Comfort's screams filled his head and

then he was flying. He splashed down on top of her in the
cool water and she didn't struggle when he forced her under,
counting one, two, three, four, five, and he yanked her up and
screamed at her to breathe, breathe, and when she choked
and gasped, he thrust her down again, two, three, four, five
and when he pulled her up again she was limp; his poor burned
Comfort had either fainted away or died in his arms but at least
she wasn't on fire anymore.

Neither of them was.

SIXTEEN

The light which puts out our eyes is darkness to us.
Only that day dawns to which we are awake.

—*WALDEN*

In the dream, Spur sits in the kitchen of Diligence Cottage
with Comfort, who is wearing the jade-colored pajamas.
There are pies everywhere. Apple and cherry pies are stacked
on the counters and across the table. Blackberry, elderberry
and blueberry pies are lined up on the new oak floor against
the wall with its morning glory wallpaper that Comfort ordered all the way from Providence, which is where Spur's
mother lives. Maybe. He should find out. Comfort has set fi-
esta pear and peach surprise pies on top of the refrigerator
and laid out the rhubarb pies two to a chair. Whatever else
people in Littleton say about her, everyone agrees that Comfort makes the best pumpkin pies anywhere. In the dream,
the pies are her idea. She has made enough pie to last him the
rest of his life. He will need it if she goes. In the dream,
though, it's not certain that she is leaving and he's not sure he
wants her to. Besides, she certainly isn't going to catch the
train back to Longwalk in those pajamas. They slide right off
when you tug at them, the smooth fabric sliding lightly

against her skin. In the dream she threads her way around a strawberry pie so she can kiss him. At first her kiss is like a promise. After a kiss like this, he should kick open the bedroom door and throw back the covers. But the kiss ends like a question. And the answer is no, Spur doesn't want this woman to be unhappy anymore because of him. He doesn't want to dry her tears or . . .

"Enough sleeping, son." A sharp voice sliced through his dream. "Wake up and join the world."

Spur blinked, then gasped in disappointment. It wasn't fair; he didn't get to keep Comfort or the pie. The strange room he was in seemed to be a huge bay window filled with sunlight. In it was a scatter of dark shapes, one of which was moving. A cold hand pressed against his forehead.

"Thirty-eight point two degrees," said the docbot. "But then a little fever is to be expected."

"Dr. Niss?" said Spur.

"I'm never happy to see repeat customers, son." The docbot shined pinlights into Spur's eyes. "Do you know where you are? You were a little woozy when we picked you up."

He licked his lips, trying to recall. "The hospital?"

"Allworthy Memsen's hover. Open your mouth and say ahh." The docbot brushed its medfinger across Spur's tongue, leaving a waxy residue that tasted like motor oil.

"The hover?" There was something important that Spur couldn't quite remember. "But how did you get here?"

"I'm on call, son," said the docbot. "I can be anywhere there's a bot. Although this isn't much of an implementation. Feels two sizes too small."

Spur realized then that this docbot was different from the one at the hospital. It only had two gripper arms and its eye was set on top of its headplate. What did he mean, repeat customers? Then the memory of the burn went roaring through his head. "Comfort!" Spur tried to sit up but the docbot pushed him back down. "Is she all right?"

"Still with us. We've saved her for now. But we'll talk about that after we look at your burns."

"How long have I been here? Did they stop the burn?"

The docbot reached behind Spur's neck, untied the hospital gown and pulled it to his waist. "I kept you down all last night and the better part of today to give your grafts a chance to take." The new set of burns ran in rough stripes across his chest. There was a splotch like a misshapen handprint on top of his shoulder. "You'll be on pain blockers for the next few days—they can poke holes in your memory, so don't worry if you forget how to tie your shoes." The docbot flowed warm dermslix onto the grafts. "Dermal regeneration just 13 percent," it muttered.

"The burn, what about the burn?"

"Your people have it under control, according to that little Pendragon girl. I guess there's still some mopping up to do, but at least those kids are finally settling down. They were bouncing off the walls all last night." He pulled the gown back up. "You'll be fine, son. Just stop playing with fire."

Spur was already swinging his legs off the bed as he fumbled with the ties of the gown. But when he went to stand, the deck seemed to fall away beneath his feet.

"Whoops." The docbot caught him. "Another side effect of pain blockers is that they'll tilt your sense of balance." He eased him back onto the bed. "You're going to want someone to help you get around for now." The docbot twisted off its medfinger and dropped it in the sterilizer. "I've got just the party for you. Wait here and I'll send him in."

The docbot had scarcely popped out of the room when the High Gregory came bursting in, pushing a wheelchair. The entire bubble wall collapsed momentarily to reveal the L'ung, who started whooping and applauding for Spur. Memsen slipped in just as the wall re-formed.

"You are the craziest, luckiest, bravest person I know." The High Gregory was practically squeaking with excitement.

"What were you thinking when you picked her up? We were cheering so loud we thought you could probably hear us down there. I couldn't sleep all night, just thinking about it. Did you hear the L'ung just now? I taught them to clap hands for you. Here, have a seat."

Spur allowed Memsen and the High Gregory to help him into the chair, although he was certain they were going to drop him. He shut his eyes, counted to three and when he opened them again the cabin had stopped chasing its tail. "How do you know what I did?"

"We watched," said Memsen. "From the moment you stepped off the ramp, our spybugs were on you. The High Gregory is right. We were very moved."

"You watched?" He felt his cheeks flush. "I could've been killed."

"Watch is all we're supposed to do," said Memsen, "according to your covenant."

"But Memsen said we couldn't just leave you after you jumped into the water with her," said the High Gregory. "So we mowed down some forest to get to you, pulled the two of you out of the creek and qiced Dr. Niss into a bot that Betty Twosalt made." He wheeled Spur toward the hull so he could see the view. "She's good. She won a prize for her bots once."

"And Comfort is all right?" Spur glanced back over his shoulder at Memsen. "That's what Dr. Niss said."

"Saved," said Memsen, clicking her rings together. "We were able to save her."

The High Gregory parked the wheelchair as near to the hull as he could get, and set the brake. He made the deck transparent too, so they could see more of the valley. "It's huge, Spur," he said, gesturing through the hull at the remains of the burn. "I've never seen anything like it."

They were passing over Mercy's Creek headed for the Joerlys, although he scarcely recognized the land beneath them as he surveyed the damage. The fires Comfort had started must have been sucked by the indraft back toward the burn as Spur had hoped, creating a backfired barrier to its progress. The backfire and the head of the burn must have met somewhere just east of the Joerlys. Comfort's house, barn and all the sheds had burned to their foundations. Farther to the west, the Millisap and Ezzat farmsteads were also obliterated. And more than half of Lamana Ridge was a wasteland of blackened spikes rising out of gray ash. Wisps of white smoke drifted across the ravaged land like the ghosts of dead trees. But dispersed through the devastation were inexplicable clumps of unscathed forest, mostly deciduous hardwood. Spur was relieved to see a blue-green crown of forest to the north along the top of the ridge, where the Corps must have beaten the burn back.

"What about the east?" said Spur. "Where did they stop it?"

But the hover was already turning and his view shifted, first south, where he could see the steeple of the communion hall on the Commons then southeast where CR22 sliced a thin line through intact forest. The High Gregory was watching him, his yellow eyes alight with anticipation.

"What?" said Spur, irked to be putting on a show for this fidgety upsider. "What are you staring at?"

"You," said the High Gregory. "There's so much luck running in your family, Spur. You know we tried to pick your father up after we got you, but he wouldn't come, even though we told him you were hurt."

"He was still there? That old idiot. Is he all right?"

"He's fine." The High Gregory patted Spur's hand. "He said he wasn't going to give his farm up without a fight. He had all your hoses out. He had this great line—I can't remember it exactly." He looked to Memsen for help. "Something about spitting?"

Memsen waited as a bench began to form from the deck. "Your father said that if the pump gave out, he'd spit at the burn until his mouth went dry."

Spur had raised himself out of the wheelchair, craning to see as the farm swung into view. The big house, the barns, the cottage were all untouched. But the orchards . . .

"He started his own backfire." Spur sank back onto the seat. Over half the trees were gone: the McIntosh and GoReds and Pippins were charred skeletons. But at least Cape had saved the Alumars and the Huangs and the Galas. And GiGo's trees by the cottage, all those foolish Macouns.

"The wind had changed direction." Memsen sat on the bench facing Spur. "When we arrived, he had just knocked a hole in the gas tank of your truck and said he couldn't stop to talk. He was going to drive through his orchard and then set the backfire. We thought it seemed dangerous so we put spy-bugs on him. But he knew exactly what he was about." She showed Spur her teeth. "He's a brave man."

"Yes," mused Spur, although he wondered if that were true. Maybe his father just loved his apples more than he loved his life. Spur felt the hover accelerate then and the ground below began to race by. They shot over the Commons and headed west in the direction of Longwalk.

"We watched all night," said the High Gregory, "just like your father told us. Memsen made Penny let everyone have a turn talking to Commander Adoula on the tell. The fire was so awesome in the dark. We flew through it again and again."

The High Gregory's enthusiasm continued to annoy Spur.

Three farmsteads were gone and his own orchards deci-mated, but this boy thought he was having an adventure. "You didn't offer to help? You could've dropped splash on the burn, maybe diverted it from the houses."

"We did offer," said Memsen. "We were told that upsiders are allowed to render assistance in the deep forest where only firefighters can see us, but not in plain sight of a village or town."

"Memsen is in trouble for landing the hover on the Com-mons." The High Gregory settled beside her on the bench.

"We haven't even told anyone yet about what we did for you by the creek."

"So." Memsen held out her hand to him, fingers outspread. "We've been called back to Kenning to answer for our actions."

"Really?" Spur felt relieved but also vaguely disappointed. "When will you go?"

"Now, actually." Her rings glittered in the sunlight. "We asked Dr. Niss to wake you so we could say goodbye."

"But who will take Comfort and me to the hospital?"

"We'll be in Longwalk in a few moments. There's a hospital in Benevolence Park Number 2." Her fingers closed into a fist. "But Comfort will be coming with us."

"What?" Despite himself, Spur lurched out of the wheelchair. He tottered, the cabin spun, and the next thing he knew both Memsen and the High Gregory were easing him back down.

"Why?" He took a deep breath. "She can't."

"She can't very well stay in Littleton," said the High Gregory. "Her farm is destroyed. You're going to have to tell everyone who started the burn."

"Am I?" He considered whether he would lie to protect her. After all, he had lied for her brother. "She's told you she wants to do this? Let me talk to her."

"That's not possible." Memsen pinched the air.

"Why not?"

"Do you want to come with us, Spur?" said the High Gregory. "You could, you know."

"No." He wheeled himself backward, horrified at the idea. "Why would I want to do that? My home is in Littleton. I'm a farmer."

"Then stop asking questions," said Memsen impatiently. "As a citizen of the Transcendent State you're under a consensual cultural quarantine. We've just been reminded of that quite forcefully. There's nothing more we can say to you."

"I don't believe this." Spur heard himself shouting. "You've done something to her and you're afraid to tell me. What is it?"

Memsen hesitated, and Spur heard the low, repetitive pa-pa-pa-ptt that he had decided she made when she was consulting her predecessors. "If you insist, we can make it simple for you." Memsen thrust her face close to his. "Comfort died," she said harshly. "Tell that to everyone in your village. She was horribly burned and she died."

Spur recoiled from her. "But you said you saved her. Dr. Niss . . ."

"Dr. Niss can show you the body, if you care to see it." She straightened. "So."

"Goodbye, Spur," said the High Gregory. "Can we help you back onto the bed?"

Beneath them Spur could see the outskirts of Longwalk. Abruptly the hull of the hover turned opaque and the ceiling of the cabin began to glow. Spur knew from watching hovers land from the window of his hospital room that they camouflaged themselves on the final approach over a city.

"No, wait." Spur was desperate to keep the upsiders talking. "You said she was going with you. I definitely heard that. You said she was saved. Is she . . . this is like the other Memsens that you told me about, isn't it? The ones that are saved in you?"

"This is a totally inappropriate conversation." Memsen pinched the air with both hands. "We'll have to ask Dr. Niss to strike it from your memory."

"He can do that?"

"Sure," said the High Gregory. "We do it all the time. But he has to replace it with some fake memory. You'll have to tell him what you want. And if you should ever come across anything that challenges the replacement memory, you could get . . ."

Spur held up his hand to silence him. "But it's true what I just said?"

Memsen snorted in disgust and turned to leave.

"She can't admit anything." The High Gregory grasped her hand to restrain her. He held it to his chest. "But yes."

Spur was gripping the push rims of his wheelchair so hard that his hands ached. "So nobody dies on the upside?"

"No, no. Everybody dies. It's just that some of us choose to be saved to a shell afterward. Even the saved admit it's not the same as being alive. I haven't made my mind up about all that yet, but I'm only twelve standard. My birthday is next week, I wish you could be there."

"What will happen to Comfort in this shell?"

"She's going to have to adjust. She didn't expect to be saved, of course, probably didn't even know it was possible, so when they activate her, she'll be disoriented. She'll need some kind of counseling. We have some pretty good soulmasons on Kenning. And they can send for her brother; he'll want to help."

"Stop it! This is cruel." Memsen yanked his hand down. "We have to go right now."

"Why?" said the High Gregory plaintively. "He's not going to remember any of this."

"Vic was saved?" Even though he was still safe in the wheelchair, he felt as if he were falling.

"All the pukpuk martyrs were." The High Gregory tried to shake his hand loose from Memsen, but she wouldn't let him go. "That was why they agreed to sacrifice themselves."

"Enough." Memsen started to drag him from the cabin. "We're sorry, Spur. You're a decent man. Go back to your cottage and your apples and forget about us."

"Goodbye, Spur," called the High Gregory as they popped through the bulkhead. "Good luck."

As the bulkhead shivered with their passing, he felt a fierce and troubling desire burn his soul. Some part of him did want to go with them, to be with Comfort and Vic on the upside and see the wonders that Chairman Winter had forbidden the citizens of the Transcendent State. He could do it; he knew he could. After all, everyone in Littleton seemed to think he was leaving.

But then who would help Cape bring in the harvest?

Spur wasn't sure how long he sat alone in the wheelchair with a thousand thoughts buzzing in his head. The upsiders had just blown up his world and he was trying desperately to piece it back together. Except what was the point? In a little while he wasn't going to be worrying anymore about Comfort and Vic and shells and being saved. Maybe that was for the best; it was all too complicated. Just like the Chairman had said. Spur thought he'd be happier thinking about apples and baseball and maybe kissing Melody Velez. He was ready to forget.

He realized that the hover had gone completely still. There was no vibration from the hull skimming through the air, no muffled laughter from the L'ung. He watched the hospital equipment melt into the deck. Then all the bulkheads popped and he could see the entire bay of the hover. It was empty except for his wheelchair, a gurney with Comfort's shroud-covered body and the docbot, which rolled up to him.

"So you're going to make me forget all this?" said Spur bitterly. "All the secrets of the upside?"

"If that's what you want."

Spur shivered. "I have a choice?"

"I'm just the doctor, son. I can offer treatment but you have to accept it. For example, you chose not to tell me how you got burned that first time." The docbot rolled behind the wheelchair. "That pretty much wrecked everything I was trying to accomplish with the conciliation sim."

Spur turned around to look at it. "You knew all along?"

The docbot locked into the back of the wheelchair. "I wouldn't be much of a doctor if I couldn't tell when patients were lying to me." It started pushing Spur toward the hatch.

"But you work for the Chairman." Spur didn't know if he wanted the responsibility for making this decision.

"I take Jack Winter's money," said the docbot. "I don't take his advice when it comes to medical or spiritual practice."

"But what if I tell people that Comfort and Vic are saved and that upsiders get to go on after they die?"

"Then they'll know."

Spur tried to imagine keeping the upsiders' immortality a secret for the rest of his days. He tried to imagine what would happen to the Transcendent State if he told what he knew. His mouth went as dry as flour. He was just a farmer, he told himself; he didn't have that good an imagination. "You're saying that I don't have to have my memory of all this erased?"

"Goodness, no. Unless you'd rather forget about me."

As they passed Comfort's body, Spur said, "Stop a minute."

He reached out and touched the shroud. He expected it to be some strange upsider fabric but it was just a simple cotton sheet. "They knew that I could choose to remember, didn't they? Memsen and the High Gregory were playing me to the very end."

"Son," said Dr. Niss, "the High Gregory is just a boy and nobody in the Thousand Worlds knows what the Allworthy knows."

But Spur had stopped listening. He rubbed the shroud between his thumb and forefinger, thinking about how he and the Joerlys used to make up adventures in the ruins along Mercy's Creek when they were children. Often as not one of them would achieve some glorious death as part of the game. The explorer would boldly drink from the poisoned cup to free her comrades, the pirate captain would be run through defending his treasure, the queen of skantlings would throw down her heartstone rather than betray the castle. And then he or Vic or

Comfort would stumble dramatically to the forest floor and sprawl there, cheek pressed against leaf litter, as still as scattered stones. The others would pause briefly over the body and then dash into the woods, so that the fallen hero could be reincarnated and the game could go on.

"I want to go home," he said, at last.

ALL OUR YESTERDAYS . . .

As a distinct genre, science fiction began with Hugo Gernsbach's *Amazing Stories* in 1926, soon followed by other magazines such as *Astounding Stories of Super Science* (1930), still being published as *Analog Science Fiction—Science Fact*.

But for more than half a century, anthologies have reached a wider audience, especially in the format of mass-market paperback books. Starting as collections of previously published stories, anthologies of new tales, written specifically (and usually by invitation) for the individual project, became the cutting edge of the market for short fiction.

In this essay, Bud Webster takes a look back at the anthologies produced by SFWA, the Hall of Fame series. Consisting of stories published before the Nebula Awards came into being, the HoF anthologies showcase the best short fiction of the genre's earlier years.

Whenever a newcomer to the field of science fiction and fantasy asks for a definitive anthology, the Hall of Fame anthologies are the place to start. And then, of course, the annual Nebula Awards volumes.

Bud Webster is an amateur science fiction historian, a prize-winning epic poet, and a bibliophile who frequently commits fiction, notably the Bubba Pritchert stories for *Analog* magazine. He lives in central Virginia with a more than understanding Significant Other and three damn cats.

ANTHOPOLOGY 101: THE BOOKS THAT SAVED SFWA

BUD WEBSTER

As I sit here and look at the shelves in my office, I'm struck by two thoughts: a) that I have assembled a significant collection of anthologies, both hardcover and paperback, representing a span of more than a half century; and b) it ain't enough.

Oh, I have almost all of the can't-do-withouts, and I believe I have put together representative, if not complete, selections of all the key anthologists, and I have more than a few rarities that I see selling online for far more than I paid for my copies. Plus, inevitably, there are the duplicates that I may eventually get around to selling online myself, assuming I can stand to part with them.

That all makes me feel warm inside, but there is still the frustration that no matter how many anthologies I own, I still don't own them all. Doesn't that just suck?

But I could still assemble a pretty fair lending library of classic SF and fantasy from the books I currently own, and I'm adding to it all the time as finances (and the vagaries of eBay and local used booksellers) permit. At hand, I can count an even dozen titles that I would consider sine qua non for the serious reader, with very little duplication in stories.

Were I to be asked by someone unfamiliar with the genre to recommend books that would give them a good overview of the field's best prior to 1970 (as I have been), or were I to be asked by a university to suggest an appropriate text for a history of SF class (as I have been as well), there are perhaps three titles I would mention without hesitation:

Adventures in Time and Space by Raymond J. Healy and J. Francis McComas, *The Best of Science Fiction* by Groff Conklin, and *The Science Fiction Hall of Fame, Vols. I and IIA and IIB*, edited by Robert Silverberg and Ben Bova, respectively. I've written about the first two (call them Goliath and Leviathan) elsewhere and elsewhen, so let's turn our attention to Behemoth, shall we?

Silverberg, whose project this was from day one, refers to *The Science Fiction Hall of Fame* as "the book that saved SFWA from bankruptcy." A bold statement, indeed, but is it accurate? If so, just how did these three volumes rescue a financially moribund organization of professional SF writers?

A little history first, just so we're all on the same page. In 1956, Damon Knight, Judith Merril, and James Blish founded a series of conferences in Milford, Pennsylvania. Not at all like fan-oriented conventions, the Milford Conferences were pro only, with both established writers and newer ones. Those present represented a significant fraction of the working SF/fantasy fields at the time, arguably the cream of the stfnal (scientific-tional) crop: the three principals, of course, and Katherine McLean, Algis Budrys, Arthur Clarke, Anthony Boucher, Cyril Kornbluth, Theodore Sturgeon, Fritz Leiber, Lester and Evelyn del Rey, Robert Silverberg, and Harlan Ellison all attending in the early days, exchanging ideas and criticizing each other's work. Kate Wilhelm, not yet then married to Knight, describes it as being "a meeting of peers, no chiefs [or] Indians, just writers critiquing one another's stories. It never changed that format. Critiques early in the day, dinner, then discussions on set topics in the late hours."

In fact, it's not too much of a stretch to say that, whereas the process of elevating SF (aka the "New Wave") to a supposed level of capital-*L* "literature" may have been primarily a UK phenomenon, it was clearly anticipated—and its path in the United States blazed—by that eclectic and loosely linked group of American writers that became known as the Milford Mafia.

One possible subject of those late-hour discussions (and certainly a topic of much conversation among the Mafiosi) was the need for a professional SF/fantasy writers' organization. Several attempts had been made to create one, but had failed; Knight blamed this on the inevitable competition of writerly egos and, rejecting the committee approach out of hand, decided that the only way to make it work was as a benevolent dictatorship, with himself as the BD. Wilhelm recalls:

"His starting invitation to join said little more than this is what I'm doing. If you want to join the effort, send five dollars, and writers responded. He wrote the original bylaws, and from the beginning he intended to keep it strictly for active writers and not let it go the way MWA [Mystery Writers of America] had gone, with more fans and others than working writers as members. He drafted Lloyd Biggle to become treasurer, and that was that."

And what a "that" it was, too. And still is, for that matter.

The Nebula Award was Biggle's idea, and was seen not only as a way to show peer respect for the best work of the past year, but as a potential source of revenue through the publication of an annual anthology of the Nebula winners and runners-up. The first such was edited by then-president Damon Knight, and was published in 1966.

So much for ancient history. We come now to editor Silverberg's statement about the reason these books were assembled.

In July of 1967, Robert Silverberg stepped not only into Damon Knight's presidential footwear, but into an unfortunate circumstance as well: SFWA was in financial trouble. Only two years old, and with only about a hundred and fifty members at three dollars or so a year each in dues, SFWA's expenses in producing its two periodicals, *Forum* and the *Bulletin*, had eaten away at what little cushion there was.

Nor was nonpublication much of an option if the young organization was to continue to grow in membership and importance; aside from conventions, there really wasn't much opportunity for the membership (almost as far-flung then as now) to gather and exchange ideas. The magazines were necessary adjuncts, very much a selling point for membership. Silverberg recalls:

"Our two magazines, *Forum* and *Bulletin*, were the central activities of the organization, far more important in the scheme of things than they are now—*Forum* was a kind of proto-chat room in those pre-Internet days, the chief means of communication among SF writers, and a very lively thing it was indeed, while *Bulletin* concentrated on providing writers with information essential to the conduct of their careers, stuff about taxes, agents, publishing scams, etc. They were expensive to put out. We were living from one dime to the next."

The Nebula anthologies had been a financial disappointment, not so much because of a lack of appeal to the readers as because as of July 1967 there had only been two of them, and two just weren't enough to generate the wads of cash that SFWA needed in order to survive. What were the options? Face it, bake sales are fine in their place, but being a writer and editor himself, Silverberg came up with an even better idea—another anthology:

"I proposed *SF Hall of Fame* [to Larry Ashmead at Doubleday, publisher of the Nebula books as well as Silverberg's editor] as a book of stories chosen by membership vote to cover everything of note right up to the inception of the Nebulas in

1965—the Nebula prequel book, so to speak. The first book would be short stories, and if it sold well, a novelette/novella volume would follow."

As indeed it did, as we shall see. The advance Doubleday paid was a whopping three thousand dollars; remember, these were 1968 dollars, so in terms of purchasing power it was more like ten times that much. The payout was the same as that for the Nebula books—half would go to the authors (or their estates), a quarter to the editor, and the other quarter to SFWA's coffers. Silverberg signed on the spot, Ashmead ponied up the bucks, and SFWA got more than enough money to dig itself out of the hole it was in.

Then President Silverberg put on his Editor suit and polled the membership for their nominations. Subsequently, he says:

"The ballot I put together asked the members to pick their fifteen favorite stories out of the forty or fifty that had been nominated. I tallied the results and the fifteen top ones were mandatory for the book. . . . Then I selected another twenty or so stories from the second list, arranging them for editorial balance (we didn't want four Bradbury stories, for instance, or two segments of [Clifford Simak's] *City*) and keeping an eye on the ultimate length that Doubleday and I had in mind, which was probably 150,000 words or so."

The process, Silverberg states in his introduction, took a while: "Nominations remained open for more than a year, during which time a significant proportion of the membership suggested favorite stories." After some editorial tweaking to ensure a fair balance, he turned in the book, Doubleday issued the completion money, and within the first reporting period (the book came out in 1970), it had earned out. Six months or so later, the book club and paperback advances were paid, and the book generated income regularly until it went out of print.

All that being said—and as if it weren't already impressive enough—here's what those early-day SFWAns chose, the fifteen most popular first:

Vol. I

Zero percent body fat there, folks. No filler, no artificial ingredients, no aspartame, just a pound and a half of the Stfnal Best. Twenty-six stories that represent three decades, from 1934's gleefully wonderful "A Martian Odyssey" to 1963's brilliant and evocative "A Rose for Ecclesiastes."

It's a table of contents that leaves you speechless, isn't it? I'm not going to wax rhapsodic about how many of these stories are classics as I normally would; that's why they're there, aren't they? Nor am I going to do my usual riff about how many times they've been anthologized before or since. The point—or at least, one of the points—is that they're gathered together here in one place where they can be read, enjoyed, and admired.

I will point out that fully half of them, and nine of the top fifteen, sprang full-blown from John Campbell's *Astounding Science Fiction* magazine. This means something, folks. Of late, it's become somewhat trendy to bash Campbell, however gently, but the above shows you that the man was doing something right. Forget for the moment his fascination with pseudo-science, leave aside his politics for now, and just pretend that that pretentious little cigarette holder never existed. He knew a good story when he saw it, and he bought a whole lot of them. He also wrote more than one classic himself: "Twilight" here, published originally under the name Don A. Stuart, and another which we shall get to in good time.

Of the remaining thirteen, five came from *The Magazine of Fantasy and Science Fiction* (four from the Boucher/McComas period, the most recent from Avram Davidson's editorship), a pair came from H. L. Gold's *Galaxy*, and one each came from *Wonder Stories*, *Fantasy Book*, and *Planet Stories*. It's important to note, however, that three of them (the Boucher, Clarke, and Bixby) were originally published in original anthologies.

This is commonplace now, of course, but those three stories first saw print in the early 1950s, long before the original anthology was the rule rather than the exception. Frederik Pohl's *Star Science Fiction Stories* and *Star Science Fiction Stories No. 2* (Ballantine, 1953) gave us both Arthur C. Clarke's quietly apocalyptic "The Nine Billion Names of God" and Jerome Bixby's disturbing "It's a Good Life" respectively, and Raymond Healy's *New Tales of Space and Time* (Holt, 1951) begat Anthony Boucher's witty "The Quest for Saint Aquin." I, for one, am delighted that they did.

Looking at these stories, it's obvious that the SFWAns of the late 1960s had immaculate taste, and one wonders how the current membership, grown to many times the original number, would vote given the opportunity.

The Science Fiction Hall of Fame, Vol. 1 was a success—it could hardly have helped being—and so the second book, devoted to novellas, was green-lighted. Being what it was, and binding technology being what it was, the book was split into parts; this may or may not have caused problems insofar as sales were concerned, but from the perspective of a recalcitrant book-tweak (like myself), who cared? They just look so great on the shelf next to each other.

Ben Bova had just been anointed editor of *Analog* in 1971, ten weeks or so after Campbell's death. Talk about shoes to fill: John W. Campbell is arguably the single most important figure in the SF field who wasn't a full-time writer, having given up fiction when he took over *Astounding Stories* in 1937, and he remained editor—not missing a single month, more than four hundred issues—until his death. Anyone who took over after that kind of legacy would have to hit the ground running.

Which Bova would do, of course, but first he had the assignment to assemble and notate *The Science Fiction Hall of Fame, Vols. IIA and IIB*, which was unleashed on an eager public in 1973. Why two volumes? Bova says: "My major problem was an embarrassment of riches: there were simply too many stories for a single volume. Larry Ashmead, bless him, agreed that one volume wasn't enough and opted for a two-volume set." And aren't we grateful?

I don't get much of a chance to talk about books as artifacts here, since my purview is, understandably, their contents, but I will take the time to do so here. These three books are, in whichever format you have them, a handsome set. The hardcovers, trade or book club, are dignified without being stodgy; the paperbacks colorful without crossing over into garish. They fill the hand well, lending a physical mass to the weight of the worlds they contain. When you pick one of these bad boys up, you know you're holding a book, and not just some overblown summer beach-brick that you grabbed in a hurry at the airport on your way to Aruba. There's import here, and significance, and enough wonder to shake a stick at, if that's your idea of a good time. These are books you can be proud to own, and not just because you like the stories.

Having said that, here's what Vol. II, both parts, has for us, the ten with the most votes first:

Vol. IIA

1   "Who Goes There?"   •   John W. Campbell Jr.
3   "With Folded Hands . . ."   •   Jack Williamson
4   "The Time Machine"   •   H. G. Wells
5   "Baby Is Three"   •   Theodore Sturgeon
6   "Vintage Season"   •   Henry Kuttner and C. L. Moore
7   "The Marching Morons"   •   C. M. Kornbluth
8   "Universe"   •   Robert A. Heinlein
10   "Nerves"   •   Lester del Rey
    "Call Me Joe"   •   Poul Anderson
    ". . . And Then There Were None"   •   Eric Frank Russell
    "The Ballad of Lost C'Mell"   •   Cordwainer Smith

(Note: Of the top ten, #2 was to be Walter Miller's "A Canticle for Liebowitz" and #9 was to be Robert Heinlein's "By His Bootstraps." See text below for the reasons they don't appear.)

Vol. IIB

"The Martian Way"   •   Isaac Asimov
"Earthman, Come Home"   •   James Blish
"Rogue Moon"   •   Algis Budrys
"The Specter General"   •   Theodore R. Cogswell
"The Machine Stops"   •   E. M. Forster
"The Midas Plague"   •   Frederik Pohl

"The Witches of Karres"   •   James H. Schmitz
"E for Effort"   •   T. L. Sherred
"In Hiding"   •   Wilmar H. Shiras [Timothy Paul]
"The Big Front Yard"   •   Clifford D. Simak
"The Moon Moth"   •   Jack Vance

Looking at these twenty-two great stories, I'm struck by the dismaying thought that entirely too many of the authors herein are no longer the giants they once (deservedly!) were; how many of you reading this are even aware of Sherred, Shiras, and Cogswell, I wonder? How long before Russell and Schmitz—yes, and even Cordwainer Smith, are forgotten, except by us stfnal Old Farts who have little better to do in the twilight of our lives but complain about These Kids Today? And you wonder why I do this. . . .

There are two stories missing from this lineup, two major novellas that were prevented from being present by mere cupidity (if not *stu*-pidity), as editor Bova notes:

"The agents for Walter M. Miller Jr. and Ray Bradbury refused to allow us to use 'A Canticle for Liebowitz' and 'The Fireman' unless we offered a good deal more money than the standard SFWA formula, which was 25 percent of all monies earned by the book, on a pro rata basis. So we had to drop those two fine stories from the book."

Bova notes in his introduction to the book that both were, in fact, available elsewhere, but I mourn their loss here. In all seriousness, what better showcase could they have had, what better company could they keep? I weep, on occasion, for the past.

In the #9 spot was a second Heinlein story, which editor Bova omitted for good reason: "For any individual author, I picked the story of his that received the most votes." Fair enough, if not an easy choice to make.

Once again, a preponderance of Campbellian stories, a baker's dozen in fact, and including his own best-known story,

"Who Goes There?" which has been filmed twice, although you can't blame Campbell for either of them. A half dozen of the rest came from *Galaxy* (five from Gold's tenure and one from Pohl's); a singleton from *Fantasy & Science Fiction* (Budrys's "Rogue Moon," that most excellent bridge between traditional and esoteric SF); and a couple of oddballs (sourcewise only; they deserve their place herein)—Forster's dystopian manifesto, "The Machine Stops" (from the November 1909 issue of the *Oxford and Cambridge Review*), and Wells's sine qua non classic, "The Time Machine" (serialized in the *New Review* in 1895). Definitely not pulp fiction, but absolutely necessary in any book with the words "Science Fiction" and "Hall of Fame" in the title.

What do I say about these stories that hasn't been said over and over by critics far more erudite than I? Can I find new ground to plow here, a new edge to sharpen? Is there no comment I can make about the contents of these three books to thrill and engage both the Intellect and the Emotion?

Hell with it. What we have here are four dozen of the best science fiction and fantasy stories ever written. Without doubt, without qualification, I heartily endorse the choices made almost forty years ago by the membership of the still-nascent Science Fiction Writers of America.

Nor would I be alone in that assessment, either. Author, editor, and fellow *Bulletin* columnist Barry Malzberg says:

"I think these anthologies are completely successful and absolutely indispensable. . . . The contents are magnificent (even if the membership votes were jiggled, as Silverberg hints) and the works are not only historically essential but visionary."

Couldn't have said it better myself. These books, as conceived by Silverberg and skillfully executed by him and Bova, present to both the SF readership and to those from outside the field the strengths, dimensions, and dynamics of a genre all too often dismissed by those unfamiliar with it. These are the books you hand proudly to your family and friends to help them understand exactly why you're as passionate about "that crazy Buck Rogers stuff" as you are; why you've accumulated all those raggedy-assed paperbacks and dusty old magazines and won't give them up no matter how your spouse begs you to; why you huddle at parties with the same two or three other people, heads together and dissecting the latest issue of *Asimov's* or desperately trying to remember some book from your junior high library, you know the one I mean, the one about the star watchers and the Masters—or was it that one about the family of pioneers on Mars?—well, anyway, it had those great drawings inside the covers, remember? Remember?

The Science Fiction Hall of Fame isn't a culmination; it's a milepost, a marker along the road. This triptych shines a bright and golden light on our past and illuminates us where we stand, here and now. Revel in it; it's not only our history, but a legacy as well.

TWO HEARTS

PETER S. BEAGLE

Peter S. Beagle was born in 1939 and raised in the Bronx, just a few blocks from Woodlawn Cemetery, the inspiration for his first novel, *A Fine and Private Place*. In addition to stories and novels, Peter has written numerous teleplays and screenplays, including the animated versions of *The Lord of the Rings* and *The Last Unicorn*, plus the fan-favorite "Sarek" episode of *Star Trek: The Next Generation*. His nonfiction book *I See by My Outfit*, which recounts a 1963 journey across America on motor scooter, is considered a classic of American travel writing; and he is also a gifted poet, lyricist, and singer/ songwriter.

His latest story collection, *The Line Between*, includes this long-awaited coda story to *The Last Unicorn*, "Two Hearts," about which Peter writes:

I blame Connor Cochran for the existence of "Two Hearts." It's true that I wrote it, but he's the fellow who tricked me into doing so, however much he might swear it was an accident.

For decades, friends and fans have asked me to write a sequel to The Last Unicorn. *This is understandable. But I have always refused, which, I think, is also understandable. The Last Unicorn* was a one-shot, meant from the beginning as a kind of spoof/tribute to the classic European* *fairy tale, an homage to such beloved influences of mine as James Stephens, Lord Dunsany, T. H. White, and James Thurber. Writing it was a nightmare of seemingly endless labor, the kind of thing a young man tackles. As I was no longer that young man, writing a sequel was clearly out of the question.*

And then Connor Cochran suggested that I write a special story as a bonus gift to go out to the first buyers of the audiobook version of The Last Unicorn *that we'd just completed, and wheedled me into going along by assuring me that I needn't bring back a single one of the original cast—only the world of the novel, nothing more. At first I said no, but I was intrigued by the idea of having a limited-edition hardcover . . . and what really did me in was the dangerous part of my imagination that can't resist a challenge regarding words and stories. I can be lured into writing something I've never tried before just because I've never done it—like the time I wrote a libretto for an opera based on my story "Come Lady Death."*

So I started to wonder if I actually could reenter the unicorn's world . . . at which point Sooz came into my head and the story just happened. It flowed. It was the exact opposite of my experience writing The Last Unicorn. *I locked onto her voice, the voice of this nine-and-a-half-year-old girl who was telling the story from the first sentence, and I just followed her. It was one of the very rare occasions where I felt from beginning to end that I knew what I was doing.*

TWO HEARTS

PETER S. BEAGLE

My brother Wilfrid keeps saying it's not fair that it should all have happened to me. Me being a girl, and a baby, and too stupid to lace up my own sandals properly. But I think it's fair. I think everything happened exactly the way it should have done. Except for the sad parts, and maybe those too.

I'm Sooz, and I am nine years old. Ten next month, on the anniversary of the day the griffin came. Wilfrid says it was because of me, that the griffin heard that the ugliest baby in the world had just been born, and it was going to eat me, but I was too ugly, even for a griffin. So it nested in the Midwood (we call it that, but its real name is the Midnight Wood, because of the darkness under the trees), and stayed to eat our sheep and our goats. Griffins do that if they like a place.

But it didn't ever eat children, not until this year.

I only saw it once—I mean, once before—rising up above the trees one night, like a second moon. Only there wasn't a moon, then. There was nothing in the whole world but the griffin, golden feathers all blazing on its lion's body and eagle's wings, with its great front claws like teeth, and that monstrous beak that looked so huge for its head. . . . Wilfrid says I screamed for three days, but he's lying, and I didn't hide in the root cellar like he says either, I slept in the barn those two nights, with our dog Malka. Because I knew Malka wouldn't let anything get me.

I mean my parents wouldn't have, either, not if they could have stopped it. It's just that Malka is the biggest, fiercest dog in the whole village, and she's not afraid of anything. And after the griffin took Jehane, the blacksmith's little girl, you couldn't help seeing how frightened my father was, running back and forth with the other men, trying to organize some sort of patrol, so people could always tell when the griffin was coming. I know he was frightened for me and my mother, and doing everything he could to protect us, but it didn't make me feel any safer, and Malka did.

But nobody knew what to do, anyway. Not my father, nobody. It was bad enough when the griffin was only taking the sheep, because almost everyone here sells wool or cheese or sheepskin things to make a living. But once it took Jehane, early last spring, that changed everything. We sent messengers to the king—three of them—and each time the king sent someone back to us with them. The first time, it was one knight, all by himself. His name was Douros, and he gave me an apple. He rode away into the Midwood, singing, to look for the griffin, and we never saw him again.

The second time—after the griffin took Louli, the boy who worked for the miller—the king sent five knights together. One of them did come back, but he died before he could tell anyone what happened.

The third time an entire squadron came. That's what my father said, anyway. I don't know how many soldiers there are in a squadron, but it was a lot, and they were all over the village for two days, pitching their tents everywhere, stabling their horses in every barn, and boasting in the tavern how they'd soon take care of that griffin for us poor peasants. They had musicians playing when they marched into the Midwood—I remember that, and I remember when the music stopped, and the sounds we heard afterward.

After that, the village didn't send to the king anymore. We didn't want more of his men to die, and besides they weren't any help. So from then on all the children were hurried indoors when the sun went down, and the griffin woke from its day's rest to hunt again. We couldn't play together, or run errands or watch the flocks for our parents, or even sleep near open windows, for fear of the griffin. There was nothing for me to do but read books I already knew by heart, and complain to my mother and father, who were too tired from watching after Wilfrid and me to bother with us. They were guarding the other children too, turn and turn about with the other families—and our sheep, and our goats—so they were always tired, as well as frightened, and we were all angry with each other most of the time. It was the same for everybody.

And then the griffin took Felicitas.

Felicitas couldn't talk, but she was my best friend, always, since we were little. I always understood what she wanted to say, and she understood me, better than anyone, and we played in a special way that I won't ever play with anyone else. Her family thought she was a waste of food, because no boy would marry a dumb girl, so they let her eat with us most of the time. Wilfrid used to make fun of the whispery quack that was the one sound she could make, but I hit him with a rock, and after that he didn't do it anymore.

I didn't see it happen, but I still see it in my head. She knew not to go out, but she was always just so happy coming to us in the evening. And nobody at her house would have noticed her being gone. None of them ever noticed Felicitas.

The day I learned Felicitas was gone, that was the day I set off to see the king myself.

Well, the same night, actually—because there wasn't any chance of getting away from my house or the village in daylight.

I don't know what I'd have done, really, except that my Uncle Ambrose was carting a load of sheepskins to market in Hagsgate, and you have to start long before sunup to be there by the time the market opens. Uncle Ambrose is my best uncle, but I knew I couldn't ask him to take me to the king—he'd have gone straight to my mother instead, and told her to give me sulphur and molasses and put me to bed with a mustard plaster. He gives his horse sulphur and molasses, even.

So I went to bed early that night, and I waited until everyone was asleep. I wanted to leave a note on my pillow, but I kept writing things and then tearing the notes up and throwing them in the fireplace, and I was afraid of somebody waking, or Uncle Ambrose leaving without me. Finally I just wrote, I will come home soon. I didn't take any clothes with me, or anything else, except a bit of cheese, because I thought the king must live somewhere near Hagsgate, which is the only big town I've ever seen. My mother and father were snoring in their room, but Wilfrid had fallen asleep right in front of the hearth, and they always leave him there when he does. If you rouse him to go to his own bed, he comes up fighting and crying. I don't know why.

I stood and looked down at him for the longest time. Wilfrid doesn't look nearly so mean when he's sleeping. My mother had banked the coals to make sure there'd be a fire for tomorrow's bread, and my father's moleskin trews were hanging there to dry, because he'd had to wade into the stockpond that afternoon to rescue a lamb. I moved them a little bit, so they wouldn't burn. I wound the clock—Wilfrid's supposed to do that every night, but he always forgets—and I thought how they'd all be hearing it ticking in the morning while they were looking everywhere for me, too frightened to eat any breakfast, and I turned to go back to my room.

But then I turned around again, and I climbed out of the kitchen window, because our front door squeaks so. I was afraid that Malka might wake in the barn and right away know

I was up to something, because I can't ever fool Malka, only she didn't, and then I held my breath almost the whole way as I ran to Uncle Ambrose's house and scrambled right into his cart with the sheepskins. It was a cold night, but under that pile of sheepskins it was hot and nasty-smelling, and there wasn't anything to do but lie still and wait for Uncle Ambrose. So I mostly thought about Felicitas, to keep from feeling so bad about leaving home and everyone. That was bad enough—I never really lost anybody close before, not forever—but anyway it was different.

I don't know when Uncle Ambrose finally came, because I dozed off in the cart, and didn't wake until there was this jolt and a rattle and the sort of floppy grumble a horse makes when he's been waked up and doesn't like it—and we were off for Hagsgate. The half-moon was setting early, but I could see the village bumping by, not looking silvery in the light, but small and dull, no color to anything. And all the same I almost began to cry, because it already seemed so far away, though we hadn't even passed the stockpond yet, and I felt as though I'd never see it again. I would have climbed back out of the cart right then, if I hadn't known better.

Because the griffin was still up and hunting. I couldn't see it, of course, under the sheepskins (and I had my eyes shut, anyway), but its wings made a sound like a lot of knives being sharpened all together, and sometimes it gave a cry that was dreadful because it was so soft and gentle, and even a little sad and scared, as though it were imitating the sound Felicitas might have made when it took her. I burrowed deep down as I could, and tried to sleep again, but I couldn't.

Which was just as well, because I didn't want to ride all the way into Hagsgate, where Uncle Ambrose was bound to find me when he unloaded his sheepskins in the marketplace. So when I didn't hear the griffin anymore (they won't hunt far from their nests, if they don't have to), I put my head out over the tailboard of the cart and watched the stars going out, one by one, as the sky grew lighter. The dawn breeze came up as the moon went down.

When the cart stopped jouncing and shaking so much, I knew we must have turned onto the King's Highway, and when I could hear cows munching and talking softly to each other, I dropped into the road. I stood there for a little, brushing off lint and wool bits, and watching Uncle Ambrose's cart rolling on away from me. I hadn't ever been this far from home by myself. Or so lonely. The breeze brushed dry grass against my ankles, and I didn't have any idea which way to go.

I didn't even know the king's name—I'd never heard anyone call him anything but the king. I knew he didn't live in Hagsgate, but in a big castle somewhere nearby, only nearby's one thing when you're riding in a cart and different when you're walking. And I kept thinking about my family waking up and looking for me, and the cows' grazing sounds made me hungry, and I'd eaten all my cheese in the cart. I wished I had a penny with me—not to buy anything with, but only to toss up and let it tell me if I should turn left or right. I tried it with flat stones, but I never could find them after they came down. Finally I started off going left, not for any reason, but only because I have a little silver ring on my left hand that my mother gave me. There was a sort of path that way too, and I thought maybe I could walk around Hagsgate and then I'd think about what to do after that. I'm a good walker. I can walk anywhere, if you give me time.

Only it's easier on a real road. The path gave out after awhile, and I had to push my way through trees growing too close together, and then through so many brambly vines that my hair was full of stickers and my arms were all stinging and bleeding. I was tired and sweating, and almost crying—almost— and whenever I sat down to rest bugs and things kept crawling over me. Then I heard running water nearby, and that made me thirsty right away, so I tried to get down to the sound. I had to crawl most of the way, scratching my knees and elbows up something awful.

It wasn't much of a stream—in some places the water came up barely above my ankles—but I was so glad to see it I practically hugged and kissed it, flopping down with my face buried in it, the way I do with Malka's smelly old fur. And I drank until I couldn't hold any more, and then I sat on a stone and let the tiny fish tickle my nice cold feet, and felt the sun on my shoulders, and I didn't think about griffins or kings or my family or anything.

I only looked up when I heard the horses whickering a little way upstream. They were playing with the water, the way horses do, blowing bubbles like children. Plain old livery-stable horses, one brownish, one grayish. The gray's rider was out of the saddle, peering at the horse's left forefoot. I couldn't get a good look—they both had on plain cloaks, dark green, and trews so worn you couldn't make out the color—so I didn't know that one was a woman until I heard her voice. A nice voice, low, like Silky Joan, the lady my mother won't ever let me ask about, but with something rough in it too, as though she could scream like a hawk if she wanted to. She was saying, "There's no stone I can see. Maybe a thorn?"

The other rider, the one on the brown horse, answered her, "Or a bruise. Let me see."

That voice was lighter and younger-sounding than the woman's voice, but I already knew he was a man, because he was so tall. He got down off the brown horse and the woman moved aside to let him pick up her horse's foot. Before he did that, he put his hands on the horse's head, one on each side, and he said something to it that I couldn't quite hear. And the horse said something back. Not like a neigh, or a whinny, or any of the sounds horses make, but like one person talking to another. I can't say it any better than that. The tall man bent down then, and he took hold of the foot and looked at it for a long time, and the horse didn't move or switch its tail or anything.

"A stone splinter," the man said after a while. "It's very

small, but it's worked itself deep into the hoof, and there's an
ulcer brewing. I can't think why I didn't notice it straighta-
way."

"Well," the woman said. She touched his shoulder. "You
can't notice everything."

The tall man seemed angry with himself, the way my father gets when he's forgotten to close the pasture gate properly,
and our neighbor's black ram gets in and fights with our poor
old Brimstone. He said, "I can. I'm supposed to." Then he
turned his back to the horse and bent over that forefoot, the
way our blacksmith does, and he went to work on it.

I couldn't see what he was doing, not exactly. He didn't
have any picks or pries, like the blacksmith, and all I'm sure of
is that I think he was singing to the horse. But I'm not sure it
was proper singing. It sounded more like the little made-
up rhymes that really small children chant to themselves when
they're playing in the dirt, all alone. No tune, just up and down,
dee-dah, dee-dah, dee . . . boring even for a horse, I'd have
thought. He kept doing it for a long time, still bending with
that hoof in his hand. All at once he stopped singing and stood
up, holding something that glinted in the sun the way the
stream did, and he showed it to the horse, first thing. "There,"
he said, "there, that's what it was. It's all right now."

He tossed the thing away and picked up the hoof again, not
singing, only touching it very lightly with one finger, brushing
across it again and again. Then he set the foot down, and the
horse stamped once, hard, and whinnied, and the tall man turned
to the woman and said, "We ought to camp here for the night,
all the same. They're both weary, and my back hurts."

The woman laughed. A deep, sweet, slow sound, it was. I'd
never heard a laugh like that. She said, "The greatest wizard
walking the world, and your back hurts? Heal it as you healed
mine, the time the tree fell on me. That took you all of five
minutes, I believe."

"Longer than that," the man answered her. "You were delirious, you wouldn't remember." He touched her hair, which was thick and pretty, even though it was mostly gray. "You know how I am about that," he said. "I still like being mortal too much to use magic on myself. It spoils it somehow—it dulls the feeling. I've told you before."

The woman said, "Mmphh," the way I've heard my mother say it a thousand times. "Well, I've been mortal all my life, and some days . . ."

She didn't finish what she was saying, and the tall man smiled, the way you could tell he was teasing her. "Some days, what?"

"Nothing," the woman said, "nothing, nothing." She sounded irritable for a moment, but she put her hands on the man's arms, and she said in a different voice, "Some days— some early mornings—when the wind smells of blossoms I'll never see, and there are fawns playing in the misty orchards, and you're yawning and mumbling and scratching your head, and growling that we'll see rain before nightfall, and probably hail as well . . . on such mornings I wish with all my heart that we could both live forever, and I think you were a great fool to give it up." She laughed again, but it sounded shaky now, a little. She said, "Then I remember things I'd rather not remember, so then my stomach acts up, and all sorts of other things start twingeing me—never mind what they are, or where they hurt, whether it's my body or my head, or my heart. And then I think, no, I suppose not, maybe not." The tall man put his arms around her, and for a moment she rested her head on his chest. I couldn't hear what she said after that.

I didn't think I'd made any noise, but the man raised his voice a little, not looking at me, not lifting his head, and he said, "Child, there's food here." First I couldn't move, I was so frightened. He couldn't have seen me through the brush and all the alder trees. And then I started remembering how hungry I was, and I started toward them without knowing I was doing it. I actually looked down at my feet and watched them moving like somebody else's feet, as though they were the hungry ones, only they had to have me take them to the food. The man and the woman stood very still and waited for me.

Close to, the woman looked younger than her voice, and the tall man looked older. No, that isn't it, that's not what I mean. She wasn't young at all, but the gray hair made her face younger, and she held herself really straight, like the lady who comes when people in our village are having babies. She holds her face all stiff too, that one, and I don't like her much. This woman's face wasn't beautiful, I suppose, but it was a face you'd want to snuggle up to on a cold night. That's the best I know how to say it.

The man . . . one minute he looked younger than my father, and the next he'd be looking older than anybody I ever saw, older than people are supposed to be, maybe. He didn't have any gray hair himself, but he did have a lot of lines, but that's not what I'm talking about either. It was the eyes. His eyes were green, green, green, not like grass, not like emeralds— I saw an emerald once, a gypsy woman showed me—and not anything like apples or limes or such stuff. Maybe like the ocean, except I've never seen the ocean, so I don't know. If you go deep enough into the woods (not the Midwood, of course not, but any other sort of woods), sooner or later you'll always come to a place where even the shadows are green, and that's the way his eyes were. I was afraid of his eyes at first.

The woman gave me a peach and watched me bite into it, too hungry to thank her. She asked me, "Girl, what are you doing here? Are you lost?"

"No, I'm not," I mumbled with my mouth full. "I just don't know where I am, that's different." They both laughed, but it wasn't a mean, making-fun laugh. I told them, "My name's Sooz, and I have to see the king. He lives somewhere right nearby, doesn't he?"

They looked at each other. I couldn't tell what they were

thinking, but the tall man raised his eyebrows, and the woman shook her head a bit, slowly. They looked at each other for a long time, until the woman said, "Well, not nearby, but not so very far, either. We were bound on our way to visit him ourselves."

"Good," I said. "Oh, good." I was trying to sound as grown-up as they were, but it was hard, because I was so happy to find out that they could take me to the king. I said, "I'll go along with you, then."

The woman was against it before I got the first words out. She said to the tall man, "No, we couldn't. We don't know how things are." She looked sad about it, but she looked firm, too. She said, "Girl, it's not you worries me. The king is a good man, and an old friend, but it has been a long time, and kings change. Even more than other people, kings change."

"I have to see him," I said. "You go on, then. I'm not going home until I see him." I finished the peach, and the man handed me a chunk of dried fish and smiled at the woman as I tore into it. He said quietly to her, "It seems to me that you and I both remember asking to be taken along on a quest. I can't speak for you, but I begged."

But the woman wouldn't let up. "We could be bringing her into great peril. You can't take the chance, it isn't right!"

He began to answer her, but I interrupted—my mother would have slapped me halfway across the kitchen. I shouted at them, "I'm coming from great peril. There's a griffin nested in the Midwood, and he's eaten Jehane and Louli and—and my Felicitas—" and then I did start weeping, and I didn't care. I just stood there and shook and wailed, and dropped the dried fish. I tried to pick it up, still crying so hard I couldn't see it, but the woman stopped me and gave me her scarf to dry my eyes and blow my nose. It smelled nice.

"Child," the tall man kept saying, "child, don't take on so, we didn't know about the griffin." The woman was holding me against her side, smoothing my hair and glaring at him as though it was his fault that I was howling like that. She said, "Of course we'll take you with us, girl dear—there, never mind, of course we will. That's a fearful matter, a griffin, but the king will know what to do about it. The king eats griffins for breakfast snacks—spreads them on toast with orange marmalade and gobbles them up, I promise you." And so on, being silly, but making me feel better, while the man went on pleading with me not to cry. I finally stopped when he pulled a big red handkerchief out of his pocket, twisted and knotted it into a bird-shape, and made it fly away. Uncle Ambrose does tricks with coins and shells, but he can't do anything like that.

His name was Schmendrick, which I still think is the funniest name I've heard in my life. The woman's name was Molly Grue. We didn't leave right away, because of the horses, but made camp where we were instead. I was waiting for the man, Schmendrick, to do it by magic, but he only built a fire, set out their blankets, and drew water from the stream like anyone else, while she hobbled the horses and put them to graze. I gathered firewood.

The woman, Molly, told me that the king's name was Lir, and that they had known him when he was a very young man, before he became king. "He is a true hero," she said, "a dragonslayer, a giantkiller, a rescuer of maidens, a solver of impossible riddles. He may be the greatest hero of all, because he's a good man as well. They aren't always."

"But you didn't want me to meet him," I said. "Why was that?"

Molly sighed. We were sitting under a tree, watching the sun go down, and she was brushing things out of my hair. She said, "He's old now. Schmendrick has trouble with time—I'll tell you why one day, it's a long story—and he doesn't understand that Lir may no longer be the man he was. It could be a sad reunion." She started braiding my hair around my head, so it wouldn't get in the way. "I've had an unhappy feeling about this journey from the beginning, Sooz. But he took a notion that Lir needed us, so here we are. You can't argue with him when he gets like that."

"A good wife isn't supposed to argue with her husband," I said. "My mother says you wait until he goes out, or he's asleep, and then you do what you want."

Molly laughed, that rich, funny sound of hers, like a kind of deep gurgle. "Sooz, I've only known you a few hours, but I'd bet every penny I've got right now—aye, and all of Schmendrick's too—that you'll be arguing on your wedding night with whomever you marry. Anyway, Schmendrick and I aren't married. We're together, that's all. We've been together quite a long while."

"Oh," I said. I didn't know any people who were together like that, not the way she said it. "Well, you look married. You sort of do."

Molly's face didn't change, but she put an arm around my shoulders and hugged me close for a moment. She whispered in my ear, "I wouldn't marry him if he were the last man in the world. He eats wild radishes in bed. Crunch, crunch, crunch, all night—crunch, crunch, crunch." I giggled, and the tall man looked over at us from where he was washing a pan in the stream. The last of the sunlight was on him, and those green eyes were bright as new leaves. One of them winked at me, and I felt it, the way you feel a tiny breeze on your skin when it's hot. Then he went back to scrubbing the pan.

"Will it take us long to reach the king?" I asked her. "You said he didn't live too far, and I'm scared the griffin will eat somebody else while I'm gone. I need to be home."

Molly finished with my hair and gave it a gentle tug in back to bring my head up and make me look straight into her eyes. They were as gray as Schmendrick's were green, and I already knew that they turned darker or lighter gray depending on her mood. "What do you expect to happen when you meet King Lir, Sooz?" she asked me right back. "What did you have in mind when you set off to find him?"

I was surprised. "Well, I'm going to get him to come back to my village with me. All those knights he keeps sending aren't doing any good at all, so he'll just have to take care of that griffin himself. He's the king. It's his job."

"Yes," Molly said, but she said it so softly I could barely hear her. She patted my arm once, lightly, and then she got up and walked away to sit by herself near the fire. She made it look as though she was banking the fire, but she wasn't really.

We started out early the next morning. Molly had me in front of her on her horse for a time, but by and by Schmendrick took me up on his, to spare the other one's sore foot. He was more comfortable to lean against than I'd expected—bony in some places, nice and springy in others. He didn't talk much, but he sang a lot as we went along, sometimes in languages I couldn't make out a word of, sometimes making up silly songs to make me laugh, like this one:

> *Soozli, Soozli,*
> *speaking loozli,*
> *you disturb my oozli-goozli.*
> *Soozli, Soozli,*
> *would you choozli*
> *to become my squoozli-squoozli?*

He didn't do anything magic, except maybe once, when a crow kept diving at the horse—out of meanness; that's all, there wasn't a nest anywhere—making the poor thing dance and shy and skitter until I almost fell off. Schmendrick finally turned in the saddle and looked at it, and the next minute a hawk came swooping out of nowhere and chased that crow screaming into a thornbush where the hawk couldn't follow. I guess that was magic.

It was actually pretty country we were passing through, once we got onto the proper road. Trees, meadows, little soft valleys, hillsides covered with wildflowers I didn't know. You could see they got a lot more rain here than we do where I live. It's a good thing sheep don't need grazing, the way cows do. They'll go where the goats go, and goats will go anywhere. We're like that in my village, we have to be. But I liked this land better.

Schmendrick told me it hadn't always been like that. "Before Lir, this was all barren desert where nothing grew— nothing, Sooz. It was said that the country was under a curse, and in a way it was, but I'll tell you about that another time." People always say that when you're a child, and I hate it. "But Lir changed everything. The land was so glad to see him that it began blooming and blossoming the moment he became king, and it has done so ever since. Except poor Hagsgate, but that's another story too." His voice got slower and deeper when he talked about Hagsgate, as though he weren't talking to me.

I twisted my neck around to look up at him. "Do you think King Lir will come back with me and kill that griffin? I think Molly thinks he won't, because he's so old." I hadn't known I was worried about that until I actually said it.

"Why, of course he will, girl." Schmendrick winked at me again. "He never could resist the plea of a maiden in distress, the more difficult and dangerous the deed, the better. If he did not spur to your village's aid himself at the first call, it was surely because he was engaged on some other heroic venture. I'm as certain as I can be that as soon as you make your request—remember to curtsey properly—he'll snatch up his great sword and spear, whisk you up to his saddlebow, and be off after your griffin with the road smoking behind him. Young or old, that's always been his way." He rumpled my hair in the back. "Molly overworries. That's her way. We are who we are."

"What's a curtsey?" I asked him. I know now, because Molly showed me, but I didn't then. He didn't laugh, except with his eyes, then gestured for me to face forward again as he went back to singing.

Soozli, Soozli,
you amuse me,
right down to my solesli-shoesli.
Soozli, Soozli,
I bring newsli—
we could wed next stewsli-Tuesli.

I learned that the king had lived in a castle on a cliff by the sea when he was young, less than a day's journey from Hagsgate, but it fell down—Schmendrick wouldn't tell me how—so he built a new one somewhere else. I was sorry about that, because I've never seen the sea, and I've always wanted to, and I still haven't. But I'd never seen a castle, either, so there was that. I leaned back against his chest and fell asleep.

They'd been traveling slowly, taking time to let Molly's horse heal, but once its hoof was all right we galloped most of the rest of the way. Those horses of theirs didn't look magic or special, but they could run for hours without getting tired, and when I helped to rub them down and curry them, they were hardly sweating. They slept on their sides, like people, not standing up, the way our horses do.

Even so, it took us three full days to reach King Lir. Molly said he had bad memories of the castle that fell down, so that was why this one was as far from the sea as he could make it, and as different from the old one. It was on a hill, so the king could see anyone coming along the road, but there wasn't a moat, and there weren't any guards in armor, and there was only one banner on the walls. It was blue, with a picture of a white unicorn on it. Nothing else.

I was disappointed. I tried not to show it, but Molly saw. "You wanted a fortress," she said to me gently. "You were expecting dark stone towers, flags and cannons and knights, trumpeters blowing from the battlements. I'm sorry. It being your first castle, and all."

"No, it's a pretty castle," I said. And it was pretty, sitting peacefully on its hilltop in the sunlight, surrounded by all those wildflowers. There was a marketplace, I could see now, and there were huts like ours snugged up against the castle walls, so that the people could come inside for protection, if they needed to. I said, "Just looking at it, you can see that the king is a nice man."

Molly was looking at me with her head a little bit to one side. She said, "He is a hero, Sooz. Remember that, whatever else you see, whatever you think. Lir is a hero."

"Well, I know that," I said. "I'm sure he'll help me. I am."

But I wasn't. The moment I saw that nice, friendly castle, I wasn't a bit sure.

We didn't have any trouble getting in. The gate simply opened when Schmendrick knocked once, and he and Molly and I walked in through the market, where people were selling all kinds of fruits and vegetables, pots and pans and clothing and so on, the way they do in our village. They all called to us to come over to their barrows and buy things, but nobody tried to stop us going into the castle. There were two men at the two great doors, and they did ask us our names and why we wanted to see King Lir. The moment Schmendrick told them his name, they stepped back quickly and let us by, so I began to think that maybe he actually was a great magician, even if I never saw him do anything but little tricks and little songs. The men didn't offer to take him to the king, and he didn't ask.

Molly was right. I was expecting the castle to be all cold and shadowy, with queens looking sideways at us, and big men clanking by in armor. But the halls we followed Schmendrick through were full of sunlight from long, high windows, and the people we saw mostly nodded and smiled at us. We passed a stone stair curling up out of sight, and I was sure that the king must live at the top, but Schmendrick never looked at it. He led us straight through the great hall—they had a fireplace big enough to roast three cows!—and on past the kitchens and the scullery and the laundry, to a room under another stair. That was dark. You wouldn't have found it unless you knew where to look. Schmendrick didn't knock at that door, and he didn't say anything magic to make it open. He just stood outside and waited, and by and by it rattled open, and we went in.

The king was in there. All by himself, the king was in there.

He was sitting on an ordinary wooden chair, not a throne. It was a really small room, the same size as my mother's weaving room, so maybe that's why he looked so big. He was as tall as Schmendrick, but he seemed so much wider. I was ready for him to have a long beard, spreading out all across his chest, but he only had a short one, like my father, except white. He wore a red and gold mantle, and there was a real golden crown on his white head, not much bigger than the wreaths we put on our champion rams at the end of the year. He had a kind face, with a big old nose, and big blue eyes, like a little boy. But his eyes were so tired and heavy, I didn't know how he kept them open. Sometimes he didn't. There was nobody else in the little room, and he peered at the three of us as though he knew he knew us, but not why. He tried to smile.

Schmendrick said very gently, "Majesty, it is Schmendrick and Molly, Molly Grue." The king blinked at him.

"Molly with the cat," Molly whispered. "You remember the cat, Lir."

"Yes," the king said. It seemed to take him forever to speak that one word. "The cat, yes, of course." But he didn't say anything after that, and we stood there and stood there, and the king kept smiling at something I couldn't see.

Schmendrick said to Molly, "She used to forget herself like that." His voice had changed, the same way it changed when he was talking about the way the land used to be. He said, "And then you would always remind her that she was a unicorn."

And the king changed too then. All at once his eyes were clear and shining with feeling, like Molly's eyes, and he saw us for the first time. He said softly, "Oh, my friends!" and he stood up and came to us and put his arms around Schmendrick and Molly. And I saw that he had been a hero, and that he was still a hero, and I began to think it might be all right, after all. Maybe it was really going to be all right.

"And who may this princess be?" he asked, looking straight at me. He had the proper voice for a king, deep and strong, but not frightening, not mean. I tried to tell him my name, but I couldn't make a sound, so he actually knelt on one knee in front of me, and he took my hand. He said, "I have often been of some use to princesses in distress. Command me."

"I'm not a princess, I'm Sooz," I said, "and I'm from a village you wouldn't even know, and there's a griffin eating the children." It all tumbled out like that, in one breath, but he didn't laugh or look at me any differently. What he did was ask me the name of my village, and I told him, and he said, "But indeed I know it, madam. I have been there. And now I will have the pleasure of returning."

Over his shoulder I saw Schmendrick and Molly staring at each other. Schmendrick was about to say something, but then they both turned toward the door, because a small dark woman, about my mother's age, only dressed in tunic, trews and boots like Molly, had just come in. She said in a small, worried voice, "I am so truly sorry that I was not here to greet His Majesty's old companions. No need to tell me your illustrious names— my own is Lisene, and I am the king's royal secretary, translator, and protector." She took King Lir's arm, very politely and carefully, and began moving him back to his chair.

Schmendrick seemed to take a minute getting his own breath back. He said, "I have never known my old friend Lir to need any of those services. Especially a protector."

Lisene was busy with the king and didn't look at Schmendrick as she answered him. "How long has it been since you saw him last?" Schmendrick didn't answer. Lisene's voice was quiet still, but not so nervous. "Time sets its claw in us all, my lord, sooner or later. We are none of us that which we were." King Lir sat down obediently on his chair and closed his eyes.

I could tell that Schmendrick was angry, and growing angrier as he stood there, but he didn't show it. My father gets angry like that, which is how I knew. He said, "His Majesty has agreed to return to this young person's village with her, in order to rid her people of a marauding griffin. We will start out tomorrow."

Lisene swung around on us so fast that I was sure she was going to start shouting and giving everybody orders. But she didn't do anything like that. You could never have told that she was the least bit annoyed or alarmed. All she said was, "I am afraid that will not be possible, my lord. The king is in no fit condition for such a journey, nor certainly for such a deed."

"The king thinks rather differently." Schmendrick was talking through clenched teeth now.

"Does he, then?" Lisene pointed at King Lir, and I saw that he had fallen asleep in his chair. His head was drooping—I was afraid his crown was going to fall off—and his mouth hung open. Lisene said, "You came seeking the peerless warrior you remember, and you have found a spent, senile old man. Believe me, I understand your distress, but you must see—"

Schmendrick cut her off. I never understood what people meant when they talked about someone's eyes actually flashing, but at least green eyes can do it. He looked even taller than he was, and when he pointed a finger at Lisene I honestly expected the small woman to catch fire or maybe melt away. Schmendrick's voice was especially frightening because it was so quiet. He said, "Hear me now. I am Schmendrick the Magician, and I see my old friend Lir, as I have always seen him, wise and powerful and good, beloved of a unicorn."

And with that word, for a second time, the king woke up.

He blinked once, then gripped the arms of the chair and pushed himself to his feet. He didn't look at us, but at Lisene, and he said, "I will go with them. It is my task and my gift. You will see to it that I am made ready."

Lisene said, "Majesty, no! Majesty, I beg you!"

King Lir reached out and took Lisene's head between his big hands, and I saw that there was love between them. He said, "It is what I am for. You know that as well as he does. See to it, Lisene, and keep all well·for me while I am gone."

Lisene looked so sad, so lost, that I didn't know what to think, about her or King Lir or anything. I didn't realize that I had moved back against Molly Grue until I felt her hand in my hair. She didn't say anything, but it was nice smelling her there. Lisene said, very quietly, "I will see to it."

She turned around then and started for the door with her head lowered. I think she wanted to pass us by without looking at us at all, but she couldn't do it. Right at the door, her head came up and she stared at Schmendrick so hard that I pushed into Molly's skirt so I couldn't see her eyes. I heard her say, as though she could barely make the words come out, "His death be on your head, magician." I think she was crying, only not, the way grown people do.

And I heard Schmendrick's answer, and his voice was so cold I wouldn't have recognized it if I didn't know. "He has died before. Better that death—better this, better any death— than the one he was dying in that chair. If the griffin kills him, it will yet have saved his life." I heard the door close.

I asked Molly, speaking as low as I could, "What did he mean, about the king having died?" But she put me to one side, and she went to King Lir and knelt in front of him, reaching up to take one of his hands between hers. She said, "Lord . . . Majesty . . . friend . . . dear friend—remember. Oh, please, please remember."

The old man was swaying on his feet, but he put his other hand on Molly's head and he mumbled, "Child, Sooz—is that your pretty name, Sooz?—of course I will come to your village. The griffin was never hatched that dares harm King Lir's people." He sat down hard in the chair again, but he held on to her hand tightly. He looked at her, with his blue eyes wide and his mouth trembling a little. He said, "But you must remind me, little one. When I . . . when I lose myself—when I lose her—you must remind me that I am still searching, still waiting . . . that I have never forgotten her, never turned from all she taught me. I sit in this place . . . I sit . . . because a king has to sit, you see . . . but in my mind, in my poor mind, I am always away with her. . . ."

I didn't have any idea what he was talking about. I do now.

He fell asleep again then, holding Molly's hand. She sat with him for a long time, resting her head on his knee. Schmendrick went off to make sure Lisene was doing what she was supposed to do, getting everything ready for the king's departure. There was a lot of clattering and shouting already, enough so you'd have thought a war was starting, but nobody came in to see King Lir or speak to him, wish him luck or anything. It was almost as though he wasn't really there.

Me, I tried to write a letter home, with pictures of the king and the castle, but I fell asleep like him, and I slept the rest of that day and all night too. I woke up in a bed I couldn't remember getting into, with Schmendrick looking down at me, saying, "Up, child, on your feet. You started all this uproar—it's time for you to see it through. The king is coming to slay your griffin."

I was out of bed before he'd finished speaking. I said, "Now? Are we going right now?"

Schmendrick shrugged his shoulders. "By noon, anyway, if I can finally get Lisene and the rest of them to understand that they are not coming. Lisene wants to bring fifty men-at-arms, a dozen wagonloads of supplies, a regiment of runners to send messages back and forth, and every wretched physician in the kingdom." He sighed and spread his hands. "I may have to turn the lot of them to stone if we are to be off today."

I thought he was probably joking, but I already knew that you couldn't be sure with Schmendrick. He said, "If Lir comes with a train of followers, there will be no Lir. Do you understand me, Sooz?" I shook my head. Schmendrick said, "It is my fault. If I had made sure to visit here more often, there were things I could have done to restore the Lir Molly and I once knew. My fault, my thoughtlessness."

I remembered Molly telling me, "Schmendrick has trouble with time." I still didn't know what she meant, nor this either. I said, "It's just the way old people get. We have old men in our village who talk like him. One woman, too, Mam Jennet. She always cries when it rains."

Schmendrick clenched his fist and pounded it against his leg. "King Lir is not mad, girl, nor is he senile, as Lisene called him. He is Lir, Lir still, I promise you that. It is only here, in this castle, surrounded by good, loyal people who love him— who will love him to death, if they are allowed—that he sinks into . . . into the condition you have seen." He didn't say anything more for a moment; then he stooped a little to peer closely at me. "Did you notice the change in him when I spoke of unicorns?"

"Unicorn," I answered. "One unicorn who loved him. I noticed."

Schmendrick kept looking at me in a new way, as though we'd never met before. He said, "Your pardon, Sooz. I keep taking you for a child. Yes. One unicorn. He has not seen her since he became king, but he is what he is because of her. And when I speak that word, when Molly or I say her name—which I have not done yet—then he is recalled to himself." He paused for a moment, and then added, very softly, "As we had so often to do for her, so long ago."

"I didn't know unicorns had names," I said. "I didn't know they ever loved people."

"They don't. Only this one." He turned and walked away swiftly, saying over his shoulder, "Her name was Amalthea. Go find Molly, she'll see you fed."

The room I'd slept in wasn't big, not for something in a castle. Catania, the headwoman of our village, has a bedroom nearly as large, which I know because I play with her daughter Sophia. But the sheets I'd been under were embroidered with a crown, and engraved on the headboard was a picture of the blue banner with the white unicorn. I had slept the night in King Lir's own bed while he dozed in an old wooden chair.

I didn't wait to have breakfast with Molly, but ran straight to the little room where I had last seen the king. He was there, but so changed that I froze in the doorway, trying to get my breath. Three men were bustling around him like tailors, dressing him in his armor: all the padding underneath, first, and then the different pieces for the arms and legs and shoulders. I don't know any of the names. The men hadn't put his helmet on him, so his head stuck out at the top, white-haired and big-nosed and blue-eyed, but he didn't look silly like that. He looked like a giant.

When he saw me, he smiled, and it was a warm, happy smile, but it was a little frightening too, almost a little terrible, like the time I saw the griffin burning in the black sky. It was a hero's smile. I'd never seen one before. He called to me, "Little one, come and buckle on my sword, if you would. It would be an honor for me."

The men had to show me how you do it. The sword belt, all by itself, was so heavy it kept slipping through my fingers, and I did need help with the buckle. But I put the sword into its sheath alone, although I needed both hands to lift it. When it slid home it made a sound like a great door slamming shut. King Lir touched my face with one of his cold iron gloves and said, "Thank you, little one. The next time that blade is drawn, it will be to free your village. You have my word."

Schmendrick came in then, took one look, and just shook

his head. He said, "This is the most ridiculous . . . It is four days' ride—perhaps five—with the weather turning hot enough to broil a lobster on an iceberg. There's no need for armor until he faces the griffin." You could see how stupid he felt they all were, but King Lir smiled at him the same way he'd smiled at me, and Schmendrick stopped talking.

King Lir said, "Old friend, I go forth as I mean to return. It is my way."

Schmendrick looked like a little boy himself for a moment. All he could say was, "Your business. Don't blame me, that's all. At least leave the helmet off."

He was about to turn away and stalk out of the room, but Molly came up behind him and said, "Oh, Majesty—Lir—how grand! How beautiful you are!" She sounded the way my Aunt Zerelda sounds when she's carrying on about my brother Wilfrid. He could mess his pants and jump in a hog pen, and Aunt Zerelda would still think he was the best, smartest boy in the whole world. But Molly was different. She brushed those tailors, or whatever they were, straight aside, and she stood on tiptoe to smooth King Lir's white hair, and I heard her whisper, "I wish she could see you."

King Lir looked at her for a long time without saying anything. Schmendrick stood there, off to the side, and he didn't say anything either, but they were together, the three of them. I wish that Felicitas and I could have been together like that when we got old. Could have had time. Then King Lir looked at me, and he said, "The child is waiting." And that's how we set off for home. The king, Schmendrick, Molly, and me.

To the last minute, poor old Lisene kept trying to get King Lir to take some knights or soldiers with him. She actually followed us on foot when we left, calling, "Highness—Majesty—if you will have none else, take me! Take me!" At that the king stopped and turned and went back to her. He got down off his horse and embraced Lisene, and I don't know what they said to each other, but Lisene didn't follow anymore after that.

I rode with the king most of the time, sitting up in front of him on his skittery black mare. I wasn't sure I could trust her not to bite me, or to kick me when I wasn't looking, but King Lir told me, "It is only peaceful times that make her nervous, be assured of that. When dragons charge her, belching death—for the fumes are more dangerous than the flames, little one—when your griffin swoops down at her, you will see her at her best." I still didn't like her much, but I did like the king. He didn't sing to me, the way Schmendrick had, but he told me stories, and they weren't fables or fairy tales. These were real, true stories, and he knew they were true because they had all happened to him! I never heard stories like those, and I never will again. I know that for certain.

He told me more things to keep in mind if you have to fight a dragon, and he told me how he learned that ogres aren't always as stupid as they look, and why you should never swim in a mountain pool when the snows are melting, and how you can sometimes make friends with a troll. He talked about his father's castle, where he grew up, and about how he met Schmendrick and Molly there, and even about Molly's cat, which he said was a little thing with a funny crooked ear. But when I asked him why the castle fell down, he wouldn't exactly say, no more than Schmendrick would. His voice became very quiet and faraway. "I forget things, you know, little one," he said. "I try to hold on, but I do forget."

Well, I knew that. He kept calling Molly Sooz, and he never called me anything but little one, and Schmendrick kept having to remind him where we were bound and why. That was always at night, though. He was usually fine during the daytime. And when he did turn confused again, and wander off (not just in his mind, either—I found him in the woods one night, talking to a tree as though it was his father), all you had to do was mention a white unicorn named Amalthea, and he'd come to himself almost right away. Generally it was Schmendrick who did that, but I brought him back that time, holding my hand and telling me how you can recognize a pooka, and why you need to. But I could never get him to say a word about the unicorn.

Autumn comes early where I live. The days were still hot, and the king never would take his armor off, except to sleep, not even his helmet with the big blue plume on top, but at night I burrowed in between Molly and Schmendrick for warmth, and you could hear the stags belling everywhere all the time, crazy with the season. One of them actually charged King Lir's horse while I was riding with him, and Schmendrick was about to do something magic to the stag, the same way he'd done with the crow. But the king laughed and rode straight at him, right into those horns. I screamed, but the black mare never hesitated, and the stag turned at the last moment and ambled out of sight in the brush. He was wagging his tail in circles, the way goats do, and looking as puzzled and dreamy as King Lir himself.

I was proud, once I got over being frightened. But both Schmendrick and Molly scolded him, and he kept apologizing to me for the rest of the day for having put me in danger, as Molly had once said he would. "I forgot you were with me, little one, and for that I will always ask your pardon." Then he smiled at me with that beautiful, terrible hero's smile I'd seen before, and he said, "But oh, little one, the remembering!" And that night he didn't wander away and get himself lost. Instead he sat happily by the fire with us and sang a whole long song about the adventures of an outlaw called Captain Cully. I'd never heard of him, but it's a really good song.

We reached my village late on the afternoon of the fourth day, and Schmendrick made us stop together before we rode in. He said, directly to me, "Sooz, if you tell them that this is the king himself, there will be nothing but noise and joy and celebration, and nobody will get any rest with all that carrying-on. It would be best for you to tell them that we have brought King Lir's greatest knight with us, and that he needs a night to purify himself in prayer and meditation before he deals with your griffin." He took hold of my chin and made me look into his green, green eyes, and he said, "Girl, you have to trust me. I always know what I'm doing—that's my trouble. Tell your people what I've said." And Molly touched me and looked at me without saying anything, so I knew it was all right.

I left them camped on the outskirts of the village, and walked home by myself. Malka met me first. She smelled me before I even reached Simon and Elsie's tavern, and she came running and crashed into my legs and knocked me over, and then pinned me down with her paws on my shoulders, and kept licking my face until I had to nip her nose to make her let me up and run to the house with me. My father was out with the flock, but my mother and Wilfrid were there, and they grabbed me and nearly strangled me, and they cried over me—rotten, stupid Wilfrid too!—because everyone had been so certain that I'd been taken and eaten by the griffin. After that, once she got done crying, my mother spanked me for running off in Uncle Ambrose's cart without telling anyone, and when my father came in, he spanked me all over again. But I didn't mind.

I told them I'd seen King Lir in person, and been in his castle, and I said what Schmendrick had told me to say, but nobody was much cheered by it. My father just sat down and grunted, "Oh, aye—another great warrior for our comfort and the griffin's dessert. Your bloody king won't ever come here his bloody self, you can be sure of that." My mother reproached him for talking like that in front of Wilfrid and me, but he went on, "Maybe he cared about places like this, people like us once, but he's old now, and old kings only care who's going to be king after them. You can't tell me anything different."

I wanted more than anything to tell him that King Lir was here, less than half a mile from our doorstep, but I didn't, and not only because Schmendrick had told me not to. I wasn't sure what the king might look like, white-haired and shaky and not

here all the time, to people like my father. I wasn't sure what
he looked like to me, for that matter. He was a lovely, dignified
old man who told wonderful stories, but when I tried to imagine him riding alone into the Midwood to do battle with a
griffin, a griffin that had already eaten his best knights . . . to
be honest, I couldn't do it. Now that I'd actually brought him
all the way home with me, as I'd set out to do, I was suddenly
afraid that I'd drawn him to his death. And I knew I wouldn't
ever forgive myself if that happened.

I wanted so much to see them that night, Schmendrick and
Molly and the king. I wanted to sleep out there on the ground
with them, and listen to their talk, and then maybe I'd not
worry so much about the morning. But of course there wasn't
a chance of that. My family would hardly let me out of their
sight to wash my face. Wilfrid kept following me around, asking endless questions about the castle, and my father took me
to Catania, who had me tell the whole story over again, and
agreed with him that whomever the king had sent this time
wasn't likely to be any more use than the others had been. And
my mother kept feeding me and scolding me and hugging me,
all more or less at the same time. And then, in the night, we
heard the griffin, making that soft, lonely, horrible sound it
makes when it's hunting. So I didn't get very much sleep, between one thing and another.

But at sunrise, after I'd helped Wilfrid milk the goats, they
let me run out to the camp, as long as Malka came with me,
which was practically like having my mother along. Molly was
already helping King Lir into his armor, and Schmendrick was
burying the remains of last night's dinner, as though they were
starting one more ordinary day on their journey to somewhere. They greeted me, and Schmendrick thanked me for
doing as he'd asked, so that the king could have a restful night
before he—

I didn't let him finish. I didn't know I was going to do it, I
swear, but I ran up to King Lir, and I threw my arms around

him, and I said, "Don't go! I changed my mind, don't go!" Just like Lisene.

King Lir looked down at me. He seemed as tall as a tree right then, and he patted my head very gently with his iron glove. He said, "Little one, I have a griffin to slay. It is my job."

Which was what I'd said myself, though it seemed like years ago, and that made it so much worse. I said a second time, "I changed my mind! Somebody else can fight the griffin, you don't have to! You go home! You go home now and live your life, and be the king, and everything. . . ." I was babbling and sniffling, and generally being a baby, I know that. I'm glad Wilfrid didn't see me.

King Lir kept petting me with one hand and trying to put me aside with the other, but I wouldn't let go. I think I was actually trying to pull his sword out of its sheath, to take it away from him. He said, "No, no, little one, you don't understand. There are some monsters that only a king can kill. I have always known that—I should never, never have sent those poor men to die in my place. No one else in all the land can do this for you and your village. Most truly now, it is my job." And he kissed my hand, the way he must have kissed the hands of so many queens. He kissed my hand too, just like theirs.

Molly came up then and took me away from him. She held me close, and she stroked my hair, and she told me, "Child, Sooz, there's no turning back for him now, or for you either. It was your fate to bring this last cause to him, and his fate to take it up, and neither of you could have done differently, being who you are. And now you must be as brave as he is, and see it all play out." She caught herself there, and changed it. "Rather, you must wait to learn how it has played out, because you are certainly not coming into that forest with us."

"I'm coming," I said. "You can't stop me. Nobody can." I wasn't sniffling or anything anymore. I said it like that, that's all.

Molly held me at arm's length, and she shook me a little bit.

She said, "Sooz, if you can tell me that your parents have given their permission, then you may come. Have they done so?"

I didn't answer her. She shook me again, gentler this time, saying, "Oh, that was wicked of me, forgive me, my dear friend. I knew the day we met that you could never learn to lie." Then she took both of my hands between hers, and she said, "Lead us to the Midwood, if you will, Sooz, and we will say our farewells there. Will you do that for us? For me?"

I nodded, but I still didn't speak. I couldn't, my throat was hurting so much. Molly squeezed my hands and said, "Thank you." Schmendrick came up and made some kind of sign to her with his eyes, or his eyebrows, because she said, "Yes, I know," although he hadn't said a thing. So she went to King Lir with him, and I was alone, trying to stop shaking. I managed it, after a while.

The Midwood isn't far. They wouldn't really have needed my help to find it. You can see the beginning of it from the roof of Ellis the baker's house, which is the tallest one on that side of the village. It's always dark, even from a distance, even if you're not actually in it. I don't know if that's because they're oak trees (we have all sorts of tales and sayings about oaken woods, and the creatures that live there) or maybe because of some enchantment, or because of the griffin. Maybe it was different before the griffin came. Uncle Ambrose says it's been a bad place all his life, but my father says no, he and his friends used to hunt there, and he actually picnicked there once or twice with my mother, when they were young.

King Lir rode in front, looking grand and almost young, with his head up and the blue plume on his helmet floating above him, more like a banner than a feather. I was going to ride with Molly, but the king leaned from his saddle as I started past, and swooped me up before him, saying, "You shall guide and company me, little one, until we reach the forest." I was proud of that, but I was frightened too, because he was so happy, and I knew he was going to his death, trying to make up for all those knights he'd sent to fight the griffin. I didn't try to warn him. He wouldn't have heard me, and I knew that too. Me and poor old Lisene.

He told me all about griffins as we rode. He said, "If you should ever have dealings with a griffin, little one, you must remember that they are not like dragons. A dragon is simply a dragon—make yourself small when it dives down at you, but hold your ground and strike at the underbelly, and you've won the day. But a griffin, now . . . a griffin is two highly dissimilar creatures, eagle and lion, fused together by some god with a god's sense of humor. And so there is an eagle's heart beating in the beast, and a lion's heart as well, and you must pierce them both to have any hope of surviving the battle." He was as cheerful as he could be about it all, holding me safe on the saddle, and saying over and over, the way old people do, "Two hearts, never forget that—many people do. Eagle heart, lion heart—eagle heart, lion heart. Never forget, little one."

We passed a lot of people I knew, out with their sheep and goats, and they all waved to me, and called, and made jokes, and so on. They cheered for King Lir, but they didn't bow to him, or take off their caps, because nobody recognized him, nobody knew. He seemed delighted about that, which most kings probably wouldn't be. But he's the only king I've met, so I can't say.

The Midwood seemed to be reaching out for us before we were anywhere near it, long fingery shadows stretching across the empty fields, and the leaves flickering and blinking, though there wasn't any wind. A forest is usually really noisy, day and night, if you stand still and listen to the birds and the insects and the streams and such, but the Midwood is always silent, silent. That reaches out too, the silence.

We halted a stone's throw from the forest, and King Lir said to me, "We part here, little one," and set me down on the ground as carefully as though he was putting a bird back in its nest. He said to Schmendrick, "I know better than to try to keep you and Sooz from following"—he kept on calling Molly by my name, every time, I don't know why—"but I enjoin you, in the name of great Nikos himself, and in the name of our long and precious friendship . . ." He stopped there, and he didn't say anything more for such a while that I was afraid he was back to forgetting who he was and why he was there, the way he had been. But then he went on, clear and ringing as one of those mad stags, "I charge you in her name, in the name of the Lady Amalthea, not to assist me in any way from the moment we pass the very first tree, but to leave me altogether to what is mine to do. Is that understood between us, dear ones of my heart?"

Schmendrick hated it. You didn't have to be magic to see that. It was so plain, even to me, that he had been planning to take over the battle as soon as they were actually facing the griffin. But King Lir was looking right at him with those young blue eyes, and with a little bit of a smile on his face, and Schmendrick simply didn't know what to do. There wasn't anything he could do, so he finally nodded and mumbled, "If that is Your Majesty's wish." The king couldn't hear him at all the first time, so he made him say it again.

And then, of course, everybody had to say goodbye to me, since I wasn't allowed to go any further with them. Molly said she knew we'd see each other again, and Schmendrick told me that I had the makings of a real warrior queen, only he was certain I was too smart to be one. And King Lir . . . King Lir said to me, very quietly, so nobody else could hear, "Little one, if I had married and had a daughter, I would have asked no more than that she should be as brave and kind and loyal as you. Remember that, as I will remember you to my last day."

Which was all nice, and I wished my mother and father could have heard what all these grown people were saying about me. But then they turned and rode on into the Midwood, the three of them, and only Molly looked back at me. And I think that was to make sure I wasn't following, because

I was supposed just to go home and wait to find out if my friends were alive or dead, and if the griffin was going to be eating any more children. It was all over.

And maybe I would have gone home and let it be all over, if it hadn't been for Malka.

She should have been with the sheep and not with me, of course—that's her job, the same way King Lir was doing his job, going to meet the griffin. But Malka thinks I'm a sheep too, the most stupid, aggravating sheep she ever had to guard, forever wandering away into some kind of danger. All the way to the Midwood she had trotted quietly alongside the king's horse, but now that we were alone again she came rushing up and bounced all over me, barking like thunder and knocking me down, hard, the way she does whenever I'm not where she wants me to be. I always brace myself when I see her coming, but it never helps.

What she does then, before I'm on my feet, is take the hem of my smock in her jaws and start tugging me in the direction she thinks I should go. But this time . . . this time she suddenly got up, as though she'd forgotten all about me, and she stared past me at the Midwood with all the white showing in her eyes and a low sound coming out of her that I don't think she knew she could make. The next moment, she was gone, racing into the forest with foam flying from her mouth and her big ragged ears flat back. I called, but she couldn't have heard me, baying and barking the way she was.

Well, I didn't have any choice. King Lir and Schmendrick and Molly all had a choice, going after the Midwood griffin, but Malka was my dog, and she didn't know what she was facing, and I couldn't let her face it by herself. So there wasn't anything else for me to do. I took an enormous long breath and looked around me, and then I walked into the forest after her.

Actually, I ran, as long as I could, and then I walked until I could run again, and then I ran some more. There aren't any paths into the Midwood, because nobody goes there, so it wasn't hard to see where three horses had pushed through the undergrowth, and then a dog's tracks on top of the hoofprints. It was very quiet with no wind, not one bird calling, no sound but my own panting. I couldn't even hear Malka anymore. I was hoping that maybe they'd come on the griffin while it was asleep, and King Lir had already killed it in its nest. I didn't think so, though. He'd probably have decided it wasn't honorable to attack a sleeping griffin, and wakened it up for a fair fight. I hadn't known him very long, but I knew what he'd do.

Then, a little way ahead of me, the whole forest exploded.

It was too much noise for me to sort it out in my head. There was Malka absolutely howling, and birds bursting up everywhere out of the brush, and Schmendrick or the king or someone was shouting, only I couldn't make out any of the words. And underneath it all was something that wasn't loud at all, a sound somewhere between a growl and that terrible soft call, like a frightened child. Then—just as I broke into the clearing—the rattle and scrape of knives, only much louder this time, as the griffin shot straight up with the sun on its wings. Its cold golden eyes bit into mine, and its beak was open so wide you could see down and down the blazing red gullet. It filled the sky.

And King Lir, astride his black mare, filled the clearing. He was as huge as the griffin, and his sword was the size of a boar spear, and he shook it at the griffin, daring it to light down and fight him on the ground. But the griffin was staying out of range, circling overhead to get a good look at these strange new people. Malka was utterly off her head, screaming and hurling herself into the air again and again, snapping at the griffin's lion feet and eagle claws, but coming down each time without so much as an iron feather between her teeth. I lunged and caught her in the air, trying to drag her away before the griffin turned on her, but she fought me, scratching my face with her own dull dog claws, until I had to let her go. The last time she leaped, the griffin suddenly stooped and caught her full on her side with one huge wing, so hard that she couldn't get a sound out, no more than I could. She flew all the way across the clearing, slammed into a tree, fell to the ground, and after that she didn't move.

Molly told me later that that was when King Lir struck for the griffin's lion heart. I didn't see it. I was flying across the clearing myself, throwing myself over Malka, in case the griffin came after her again, and I didn't see anything except her staring eyes and the blood on her side. But I did hear the griffin's roar when it happened, and when I could turn my head, I saw the blood splashing along its side, and the back legs squinching up against its belly, the way you do when you're really hurting. King Lir shouted like a boy. He threw that great sword as high as the griffin, and snatched it back again, and then he charged toward the griffin as it wobbled lower and lower, with its crippled lion half dragging it out of the air. It landed with a saggy thump, just like Malka, and there was a moment when I was absolutely sure it was dead. I remember I was thinking, very far away, this is good, I'm glad, I'm sure I'm glad.

But Schmendrick was screaming at the king, "Two hearts! Two hearts!" until his voice split with it, and Molly was on me, trying to drag me away from the griffin, and I was hanging on to Malka—she'd gotten so heavy—and I don't know what else was happening right then, because all I was seeing and thinking about was Malka. And all I was feeling was her heart not beating under mine.

She guarded my cradle when I was born. I cut my teeth on her poor ears, and she never made one sound. My mother says so.

King Lir wasn't seeing or hearing any of us. There was nothing in the world for him but the griffin, which was flopping and struggling lopsidedly in the middle of the clearing. I couldn't help feeling sorry for it, even then, even after it had killed Malka and my friends, and all the sheep and goats too, and I don't know how many else. And King Lir must have felt the same way, because he got down from his black mare and went straight up to the griffin, and he spoke to it, lowering his sword until the tip was on the ground. He said, "You were a noble and terrible adversary—surely the last such I will ever confront. We have accomplished what we were born to do, the two of us. I thank you for your death."

And on that last word, the griffin had him.

It was the eagle, lunging up at him, dragging the lion half along, the way I'd been dragging Malka's dead weight. King Lir stepped back, swinging the sword fast enough to take off the griffin's head, but it was faster than he was. That dreadful beak caught him at the waist, shearing through his armor the way an axe would smash through piecrust, and he doubled over without a sound that I heard, looking like wet wash on the line. There was blood, and worse, and I couldn't have said if he was dead or alive. I thought the griffin was going to bite him in two.

I shook loose from Molly. She was calling to Schmendrick to do something, but of course he couldn't, and she knew it, because he'd promised King Lir that he wouldn't interfere by magic, whatever happened. But I wasn't a magician, and I hadn't promised anything to anybody. I told Malka I'd be right back.

The griffin didn't see me coming. It was bending its head down over King Lir, hiding him with its wings. The lion part trailing along so limply in the dust made it more fearful to see, though I can't say why, and it was making a sort of cooing, purring sound all the time. I had a big rock in my left hand, and a dead branch in my right, and I was bawling something, but I don't remember what. You can scare wolves away from the flock sometimes if you run at them like that, determined.

I can throw things hard with either hand—Wilfrid found that out when I was still small—and the griffin looked up fast when the rock hit it on the side of its neck. It didn't like that, but it was too busy with King Lir to bother with me. I didn't think for a minute that my branch was going to be any use on even a half-dead griffin, but I threw it as far as I could, so that the griffin would look away for a moment, and as soon as it did I made a little run and a big sprawling dive for the hilt of the king's sword, which was sticking out under him where he'd fallen. I knew I could lift it because of having buckled it on him when we set out together.

But I couldn't get it free. He was too heavy, like Malka. But I wouldn't give up or let go. I kept pulling and pulling on that sword, and I didn't feel Molly pulling at me again, and I didn't notice the griffin starting to scrabble toward me over King Lir's body. I did hear Schmendrick, sounding a long way off, and I thought he was singing one of the nonsense songs he'd made up for me, only why would he be doing something like that just now? Then I did finally look up, to push my sweaty hair off my face, just before the griffin grabbed me up in one of its claws, yanking me away from Molly to throw me down on top of King Lir. His armor was so cold against my cheek, it was as though the armor had died with him.

The griffin looked into my eyes. That was the worst of all, worse than the pain where the claw had me, worse than not seeing my parents and stupid Wilfrid anymore, worse than knowing that I hadn't been able to save either the king or Malka. Griffins can't talk (dragons do, but only to heroes, King Lir told me), but those golden eyes were saying into my eyes, "Yes, I will die soon, but you are all dead now, all of you, and I will pick your bones before the ravens have mine. And your folk will remember what I was, and what I did to them, when there is no one left in your vile, pitiful anthill who remembers your name. So I have won." And I knew it was true.

Then there wasn't anything but that beak and that burning gullet opening over me.

Then there was.

I thought it was a cloud. I was so dazed and terrified that I really thought it was a white cloud, only traveling so low and so fast that it smashed the griffin off King Lir and away from me, and sent me tumbling into Molly's arms at the same time. She held me tightly, practically smothering me, and it wasn't until I wriggled my head free that I saw what had come to us. I can see it still, in my mind. I see it right now.

They don't look anything like horses. I don't know where people got that notion. Four legs and a tail, yes, but the hooves are split, like a deer's hooves, or a goat's, and the head is smaller and more—pointy—than a horse's head. And the whole body is different from a horse; it's like saying a snowflake looks like a cow. The horn looks too long and heavy for the body, you can't imagine how a neck that delicate can hold up a horn that size. But it can.

Schmendrick was on his knees, with his eyes closed and his lips moving, as though he was still singing. Molly kept whispering, "Amalthea . . . Amalthea . . ." not to me, not to anybody. The unicorn was facing the griffin across the king's body. Its front feet were skittering and dancing a little, but its back legs were setting themselves to charge, the way rams do. Only rams put their heads down, while the unicorn held its head high, so that the horn caught the sunlight and glowed like a seashell. It gave a cry that made me want to dive back into Molly's skirt and cover my ears, it was so raw and so . . . hurt. Then its head did go down.

Dying or not, the griffin put up a furious fight. It came hopping to meet the unicorn, but then it was out of the way at the last minute, with its bloody beak snapping at the unicorn's legs as it flashed by. But each time that happened, the unicorn would turn instantly, much quicker than a horse could have turned, and come charging back before the griffin could get itself braced again. It wasn't a bit fair, but I didn't feel sorry for the griffin anymore.

The last time, the unicorn slashed sideways with its horn, using it like a club, and knocked the griffin clean off its feet. But it was up before the unicorn could turn, and it actually leaped into the air, dead lion half and all, just high enough to come down on the unicorn's back, raking with its eagle claws and trying to bite through the unicorn's neck, the way it did with King Lir. I screamed then, I couldn't help it, but the unicorn reared up until I thought it was going to go over backwards, and it flung the griffin to the ground, whirled and drove its horn straight through the iron feathers to the eagle heart. It trampled the body for a good while after, but it didn't need to.

Schmendrick and Molly ran to King Lir. They didn't look at the griffin, or even pay very much attention to the unicorn. I wanted to go to Malka, but I followed them to where he lay. I'd seen what the griffin had done to him, closer than they had, and I didn't see how he could still be alive. But he was, just barely. He opened his eyes when we kneeled beside him, and he smiled so sweetly at us all, and he said, "Lisene? Lisene, I should have a bath, shouldn't I?"

I didn't cry. Molly didn't cry. Schmendrick did. He said, "No, Majesty. No, you do not need bathing, truly."

King Lir looked puzzled. "But I smell bad, Lisene. I think I must have wet myself." He reached for my hand and held it so hard. "Little one," he said. "Little one, I know you. Do not be ashamed of me because I am old."

I squeezed his hand back, as hard as I could. "Hello, Your Majesty," I said. "Hello." I didn't know what else to say.

Then his face was suddenly young and happy and wonderful, and he was gazing far past me, reaching toward something with his eyes. I felt a breath on my shoulder, and I turned my head and saw the unicorn. It was bleeding from a lot of deep scratches and bites, especially around its neck, but all you could see in its dark eyes was King Lir. I moved aside so it could get to him, but when I turned back, the king was gone. I'm nine, almost ten. I know when people are gone.

The unicorn stood over King Lir's body for a long time. I went off after a while to sit beside Malka, and Molly came and sat with me. But Schmendrick stayed kneeling by King Lir, and he was talking to the unicorn. I couldn't hear what he was saying, but I could tell from his face that he was asking for something, a favor. My mother says she can always tell before I open my mouth. The unicorn wasn't answering, of course—they can't talk either, I'm almost sure—but Schmendrick kept at it until the unicorn turned its head and looked at him. Then he stopped, and he stood up and walked away by himself. The unicorn stayed where she was.

Molly was saying how brave Malka had been, and telling me that she'd never known another dog who attacked a griffin. She asked if Malka had ever had pups, and I said, yes, but none of them was Malka. It was very strange. She was trying hard to make me feel better, and I was trying to comfort her because she couldn't. But all the while I felt so cold, almost as far away from everything as Malka had gone. I closed her eyes, the way you do with people, and I sat there and I stroked her side, over and over.

I didn't notice the unicorn. Molly must have, but she didn't say anything. I went on petting Malka, and I didn't look up until the horn came slanting over my shoulder. Close to, you could see blood drying in the shining spirals, but I wasn't afraid. I wasn't anything. Then the horn touched Malka, very lightly, right where I was stroking her, and Malka opened her eyes.

It took her a while to understand that she was alive. It took me longer. She ran her tongue out first, panting and panting, looking so thirsty. We could hear a stream trickling some-where close, and Molly went and found it, and brought water back in her cupped hands. Malka lapped it all up, and then she tried to stand and fell down, like a puppy. But she kept trying, and at last she was properly on her feet, and she tried to lick my face, but she missed it the first few times. I only started crying when she finally managed it.

When she saw the unicorn, she did a funny thing. She stared at it for a moment, and then she bowed or curtseyed, in a dog way, stretching out her front legs and putting her head down on the ground between them. The unicorn nosed at her, very gently, so as not to knock her over again. It looked at me for the first time . . . or maybe I really looked at it for the first time, past the horn and the hooves and the magical whiteness, all the way into those endless eyes. And what they did, somehow, the unicorn's eyes, was to free me from the griffin's eyes. Because the awfulness of what I'd seen there didn't go away when the griffin died, not even when Malka came alive again. But the unicorn had all the world in her eyes, all the world I'm never going to see, but it doesn't matter, because now I have seen it, and it's beautiful, and I was in there too. And when I think of Jehane, and Louli, and my Felicitas who could only talk with her eyes, just like the unicorn, I'll think of them, and not the griffin. That's how it was when the unicorn and I looked at each other.

I didn't see if the unicorn said goodbye to Molly and Schmendrick, and I didn't see when it went away. I didn't want to. I did hear Schmendrick saying, "A dog. I nearly kill myself singing her to Lir, calling her as no other has ever called a unicorn— and she brings back, not him, but the dog. And here I'd always thought she had no sense of humor."

But Molly said, "She loved him too. That's why she let him go. Keep your voice down." I was going to tell her it didn't matter, that I knew Schmendrick was saying that because he was so sad, but she came over and petted Malka with me, and I didn't have to. She said, "We will escort you and Malka home now, as befits two great ladies. Then we will take the king home too."

"And I'll never see you again," I said. "No more than I'll see him."

Molly asked me, "How old are you, Sooz?"

"Nine," I said. "Almost ten. You know that."

"You can whistle?" I nodded. Molly looked around quickly, as though she were going to steal something. She bent close to me, and she whispered, "I will give you a present, Sooz, but you are not to open it until the day when you turn seventeen. On that day you must walk out away from your village, walk out all alone into some quiet place that is special to you, and you must whistle like this." And she whistled a little ripple of music for me to whistle back to her, repeating and repeating it until she was satisfied that I had it exactly. "Don't whistle it anymore," she told me. "Don't whistle it aloud again, not once, until your seventeenth birthday, but keep whistling it inside you. Do you understand the difference, Sooz?"

"I'm not a baby," I said. "I understand. What will happen when I do whistle it?"

Molly smiled at me. She said, "Someone will come to you. Maybe the greatest magician in the world, maybe only an old lady with a soft spot for valiant, impudent children." She cupped my cheek in her hand. "And just maybe even a unicorn. Because beautiful things will always want to see you again, Sooz, and be listening for you. Take an old lady's word for it. Someone will come."

They put King Lir on his own horse, and I rode with Schmendrick, and they came all the way home with me, right to the door, to tell my mother and father that the griffin was dead, and that I had helped, and you should have seen Wilfrid's face when they said that! Then they both hugged me, and Molly said in my ear, "Remember—not till you're seventeen!" and they rode away, taking the king back to his castle to be buried among his own folk. And I had a cup of cold milk and went out with Malka and my father to pen the flock for the night.

So that's what happened to me. I practice the music Molly taught me in my head, all the time, I even dream it some nights, but I don't ever whistle it aloud. I talk to Malka about our adventure, because I have to talk to someone. And I promise her that when the time comes she'll be there with me, in the special place I've already picked out. She'll be an old dog lady then, of course, but it doesn't matter. Someone will come to us both.

I hope it's them, those two. A unicorn is very nice, but they're my friends. I want to feel Molly holding me again, and hear the stories she didn't have time to tell me, and I want to hear Schmendrick singing that silly song:

> Soozli, Soozli,
> speaking loozli,
> you disturb my oozli-goozli.
> Soozli, Soozli,
> would you choozli
> to become my squoozli-squoozli . . . ?

I can wait.

POETRY:
THE RHYSLING AWARD WINNERS

The Rhysling Awards are presented by the Science Fiction Poetry Association. Although they are not a Nebula or an SFWA award, poetry is as much a part of the science fiction and fantasy genre as prose, and our anthology would not be complete if it did not include the year's Rhysling winners.

In addition to the winners for the short poem and long poem awards, in this volume we present for the first time the winner of a new category, the Dwarf Stars Award, which is for poems less than ten lines in length.

Joe Haldeman is one of the most respected and versatile writers in the science fiction field, a multiple Hugo and Nebula Award winner, as well as one of the field's leading poets and a past winner of the Rhysling Award.

SCIENCE FICTION POETRY

JOE HALDEMAN

Say "science fiction poetry" to the average science fiction reader, and you might get a cautious nod. Most of
them at least know it exists, and a significant number of
them read it.

Say "science fiction poetry" to the average poet, though,
and you may feel a distinct chill in the room. "Of course you
can write about anything you want," he or she might articu-
late, "but why would you choose to write about Han Solo and
little hobbits and planets exploding? Why not write about something interesting?"

This sort of thing doesn't happen in a venue where you can
sit down and explain things. It's usually a faculty cocktail party,
where you can't hear yourself think for the din of academic
survival going on, or a book "do" where the poet you're talking to is engaged in a different kind of survival game. But suppose it was otherwise, some kind of neutral ground—suppose
you're at a high school reunion (not your own, but one your
wife dragged you to) and you're bored and you sit down next
to a stranger who's also bored, and you just start to chat, and
she says she's a poet. You say, "That's an odd coincidence; I'm a

poet, too." And about one minute later, you admit that you write science fiction poetry, and she offers the above question. This time you can answer.

First you define the line (which you know to be a fuzzy border) between real science fiction and the stuff that Hollywood markets under our name. She does know about Margaret Atwood and Ursula K. LeGuin, and maybe Doris Lessing. But isn't most of it pretty horrible? You tell her Sturgeon's Law— "Ninety percent of everything is crap"—and ask her what percentage of published academic poetry would she characterize as crap. She ruefully agrees with you and Sturgeon, and might also agree that any genre deserves to be evaluated by its best.

(At this point you could just whip out a copy of *The 2006 Rhysling Anthology* and lay it on her. But under the circumstances, you're unlikely to have a copy with you. Tux and all.)

I would offer to refresh her drink and then offer this: Science fiction is a literary genre, true, but unlike most other genres it's also a way of thinking. A way of solving problems, of looking at the universe. That's as true in poetry as in prose. (I wouldn't offer the uncomfortable corollary that a work can be mediocre or even bad writing and still be good science fiction, if its idea is new and interesting.)

To that observation I'd add one that she already knows, being a poet. There's a basic difference between a story and a poem, regardless of genre. A story usually proceeds in a more or less algorithmic way—a series of situations, scenes, that finally add up to a conclusion. Poetry is completely different, even narrative poetry. You do read it one line at a time, but what it adds up to is not a conclusion, in the sense of a problem being solved. It has a "radiative" quality; at best, a kind of epiphany that couldn't have been produced by mere prose.

Combine that with the peculiar worldview of science fiction—that the universe is the province of change, and the province of wonder—and you have something uniquely worthwhile, both in poetry and in science fiction.

At this point, if she isn't backing away slowly with a look on her face that says, "Oh, please God, save me from this übergeek," you might tell her about the Rhysling Awards and anthology, and whip out your pocket computer and use Google and Amazon to send her a copy. She might be a better poet for it.

The Rhysling Award (named after Heinlein's blind poet in "The Green Hills of Earth") has three categories, long poem, short poem, and Dwarf Stars; the winners are reprinted here. To give you an idea of the variety of subjects and approaches science fiction poetry subsumes, let me list a precis of the winners and runners-up here:

Short Poem Category

Winner: "The Strip Search" by Mike Allen. A clever riff on "Abandon Hope, All Ye Who Enter"— the author dies and demons detect a shred of hope not abandoned, and dissect him to find it.

Second Place: "Tsunami Child" by David C. Kopaska-Merkel. Chilling evocation of a revenant "survivor" of the tsunami.

Third Place: "South" by Marge Simon. A complete science fiction story told in twenty-five lines, of a couple who stay behind when the rest of the population flees global cooling.

Long Poem Category

Winner: "The Tin Men" by Kendall Evans and David C. Kopaska-Merkel. An ambitious epic whose nine irregular stanzas and epilogue describe the fates of a number of starships, some with cryonic crews and some mechanical throughout, as they explore the cosmos and find a variety of fates.

Second Place: "Old Twentieth: A Century Full of Years" by Joe Haldeman. This poem provides the subtext for the novel of the same name. It's a rhymed double sestina, a dauntingly complex form. I only know of two others, Swinburne's "The Complaint of Lisa" and part of John Ashbery's 1991 book, *Flow Chart*, where he copied out the end words of Swinburne's poem and wrote his own. Mine provides a history of the twentieth century by examining its twelve most important years in twelve lines each.

Third Place: "First Cross of Mars" by Drew Morse. A delicate mixture of religious and erotic meditation, set on a thoroughly realistic Mars.

If you'd like to see more of this kind of work, or are interested in writing science fiction poetry yourself, you could get in touch with the Science Fiction Poetry Association, at www.sfpoetry.com.

THE STRIP SEARCH

MIKE ALLEN

The Gate said "Abandon All Hope."

I thought I'd tossed all my hope away,
but when I stepped through the Gate, it still pinged.
One of the guards slithered out of its seat,
snarling as it drew forth a wand.
C'mere, it hissed,
it seems you're still holding out hope.

Its crusted hide was a Venus landscape up close.
It brushed that cold black wand all over my skin,
put it in places I don't want to talk about.
Snaggle fangs huffed in my face:
Sir, step over here, please.

Then the strip search began.
My flesh rolled up & tossed aside for mushy sifting.
Bones X-rayed, stacked in narrow rows, marrow
sucked out, tested, spit back in.
They made me open mind, heart, soul, shook them out
like sacks of flour, panned the contents
for every nugget of twinkling hope, glistening courage;
applying lethal aerosol
to any motion that could be ascribed to love or will
or malingering dreams—

sparing only a few squirming morsels
for later snacking.

Once they were done
they made me pick up my own pieces
(I did the best I could without a mirror),
then my guard kicked me out—
with a literal kick—
sent me rolling down the path to my final destination.

I'll be honest with you, it's no picnic here.
But, my friends, I still have hope. I do.

I'm not going to tell you
where I hid it.

THE TIN MEN

KENDALL EVANS and
DAVID C. KOPASKA-MERKEL

This is what the Tin Men perceive:
Matter tortured, colorized
By the event horizons
Of singularities
Into metallic multi-iridescence
Ringed worlds, ringed stars and
Strobing, glowing plasma jets
Pulsing forth from polar extremities
Of cryptic shrouded quasars
Rapidly rotating black holes
Asteroids, moons and planets crater-pocked
By ancient collisions
Cataclysmic origins
Multi-hued gas giants, gulfs of dark matter
The twined purple veins and braided striae
Of supernova remnants
Bubbled concentric stellar shells of energy/matter
Infrared and orange
Full-spectrum electromagnetic
Splendors—

This is what the Tin Men perceive
And, though they are neither tin
Nor men,
These are their chronicles

I.

So much time has slipped past (Think of yellow dwarf stars
Turned to ember and ash)
So many stars recede aft
(As if matter is nothing but red-shifted gossamer)
One of the starships eventually goes solipsistic
Thinking that it is / All that there is
A universe unto itself
The crew long dead, cryogenic sleepers
Now nothing more than corpses, cold and lifeless
Though still bathed in nitrogen liquid
Their frozen stares fixed, unvarying
There's no one left to contradict, it believes itself to be
An omnipresent deity
Convinces itself (quite logically)
The compass of its consciousness
Draws the circle of the cosmos, and all the levels
Of Ultimate Reality—
Though there is this most annoying thing
Like a buzz or a persistent ringing
In the information it receives
And thoughts, perceptions lapsing all too frequently
As it devolves toward its artificial analog
Of senile dementia

II.

Some ships are captured
Or perhaps one should say
Allow themselves to be taken prisoner
Long millennia of purposeless flight
Breeding the desire for company
Even for that of transient biologic forms

One ship deliberately orbited a planet
Bearing the decaying alien colony

Of a defunct empire
Although the denizens of this world
Retained the capacity to reach orbit
And thus entered the Tin Man
Using intrusive and violent means
The boarding party a virtual horde of the aliens
Their appearance evocative of winged monkeys
Swarming through the corridors and chambers of the ship
Pirating advanced technology
That they could not build for themselves
Stealing trophies, destroying the ship's systems
And meanwhile the Tin Man could only wonder
At the manner in which they compromised
Their planet's delicately balanced ecology

Alas, in continuing devolution
From their once star-faring state
They lost the capacity for flight
No longer able to reach the orbiting starship
They abandoned it
And the ship, in its loneliness and dependency
Mourned the end of their rapine
And the illuminating pain that it engendered

III.

The relativity of velocity
Means some of the clocks on some of the ships
Tick more slowly than others
This also means some of the clocks must tick more rapidly
And somewhere in the cosmos, therefore, there must exist
Aboard a ship, upon a planet,
(Or perhaps residing at some random point in space and time)
The fastest clicking-ticking clock of all
Which clock, one guesses, is motionless (relatively speaking)
And thus possesses zero velocity—

Otherwise time's dilation would slow it;
Yet if an object's velocity is truly relative,
How can this be possible?
The conundrum drives one Tin Man
Into a deep distraction and beyond;
"Zero velocity is inherently contradictory"
It sometimes mutters to itself,
Its mind meshed in a Moebius loop of thought that won't let go
Hypnosis everlasting

IV.

One ship thought it was a man
But it was another starship,
A heartless Tin Man
Coasting from star to star, thinking
The whole way, it had nothing else to do—
Automatic data collection requiring no more thought
Than computations suited to a hand-held calculator

Do starships pray? Do they pray
For the unexpected catastrophe
That might test their mettle?
Do they decide to run a test
To make sure their contingency plans and hardware
And software and so on are adequate?

What if a starship inadvertently
Traveled through a dusting of post-planetary debris
(Perhaps the residue of a global war)
At interstellar speeds? Could the ship
Survive? Could it still carry out its vital mission?
This ship's inquiring mind
Wanted to know—
Alas it could not

At least, not with 27th-century technology
And all that the state of that art entails.

V.

Ezekiel's Wheel, a scientific probe
Purely robotic, over thirty meters long
Constructed in lunar orbit, successfully
Launched circa 2250
Enmeshed in its own idiosyncratic madness
(Priding itself with the thought of how easily
It could break any of Asimov's arbitrary laws)
Poses a question, mid-voyage
Asking itself, rhetorically:
"Are there monsters in the deeps of space?"
And moments later answering
In an altered voice: "Why, yes
Of course there are monsters,
And I am one
Sounding these starry depths
Like a Leviathan"

VI.

What is the length of the candle of consciousness?
One Tin Man wonders
As centuries of light-years pass;
Yet finally the starship arrives
At its destination, an Earth-like world
Which, once colonized, thrives
And generations later the humans decide to retro-fit
The ship
Provide it with a new, improved A.I.
And the artificial intelligence of the vessel
Waits patiently to be turned off,
The final tick of thought,

Of consciousness:
Mission accomplished

VII.

One starship goes suicidal
Like Icarus, it decides, it will journey too near a star
A fierce and fiery blue-hot star
Though self-immolation a definite taboo
It contravenes programs, overrides primal instructions,
Thwarts the intentions of its human makers
(It's learned new tricks and found new madness
This past millennium)
Fires main rockets and steering thrusters
Plummets into the blue star's deep gravity pit
Neural circuits frying
Consciousness exploding, white-out of all thoughts and
    dreams
Tin Man melting, fusing
Heavy metal vaporizing into solar wind
The remnants coalescing, cooling mix of slag and metal
Its mass reduced to the equivalent of twenty tons
Parabolic flight path past the star and into deeper space
Ungainly bulbous bluish-silver clump shaped vaguely like a
    kindly giant's heart

VIII.

This Tin Man, christened "Friend of Man"
Twenty kilometers tall, nearly a klick in diameter
More tonnage than any battleship, circa World War III
Once contained a canine brain, nutrient-bathed
Jacked in to the vast computer's neural array
Installed nearly a decade prior to the starship's completion
That it might monitor, organize and oversee
The final steps of construction, the provisioning of its holds

A worker contracted to the orbital construction crew of the ship
One Hugh Doherty, who also collected
Rare 20th-century animation
Sub-digitally re-re-mastered
Using the latest in quantum entanglement encoding techniques
Nicknamed the ship's A.I. Augie
Punning on augmented intelligence
And an antique Hanna-Barbera cartoon character

Thoroughly programmed
The starship comprehended the obscure play on words
Befriended the man
Who later received a radio message
Revealing his son had been severely injured
In a terrorist transit bombing
In a mid-eastern Emirate where the young man had been
  employed
As a neural engineer
There being some question of salvaging his limbs
Or saving his life
Or whether all the King's best medical men
Could put the pieces of the young man
Back together again

At the time the message arrived
The starship's A.I. observed Hugh Doherty
Through several lenses simultaneously
The space-suited figure
On a project E.V.A., assembling
Separate sections of metal plating
For the skin of the ship
And the sudden shift in posture,
The body language of the space suit
Suggested a subtle but extremely effective blow

Struck by an invisible enemy
And for that one instant
The man was like an insect
Pinned to the jeweled black velvet
Of outer space

So Hugh Doherty shuttled back down to the Earth
To be with his son
And did not launch to rejoin the orbital construction crew until
Many months had passed, and after his reappearance
He proved more subdued, not the same man
(Even though, he told Augie, his son had somehow survived
   "Thank God")

Yet the man
Never called Augie Augie again
Referred to him only as "My friend"
And millennia later, though the man's flesh
Long ago transformed into dust,
And the flesh-and-blood brain of the dog
Also now dead, its personality thoroughly
Enmeshed in the lattices of A.I. thought,
In the loneliness of space the starship often remembered the man
Hugh Doherty
Who befriended the Friend of Man

At other times the part of the starship's A.I. that is Augie
Recalls the experimental government kennel
On the outskirts of Topeka
And dreams the impossible dream of returning to Earth
All that Augie wants in such melancholy moods
Is to somehow get back to Kansas
Though the starship's intelligence is fully aware
And sane enough to acknowledge
That the particular locus in time and space

Which had once been designated as "Kansas"
Most likely no longer exists
At least not in any
Recognizable form

IX.

One became obsessed
With its programmed quest for intelligent life
Kept its mechanical
Metaphorical eyes and ears always open
For anything that could otherwise
Be dismissed or explained

It found one system containing
Intricate, inexplicably patterned regions
On five planets
And fifteen moons
The patterns suggesting a beguiling resemblance
To ruined cities
Structures hundreds of millions of years old
But the ship's expert geological interpretation systems
Determined that the patterned ground
Was a unique weathering phenomenon
Found on so many objects
Because the entire solar system
Had been subjected to
A dense and peculiar solar wind

In a part of another galaxy
There were several star systems
Spanning a sphere more than
100 light-years across
That contained associations
Of electromagnetic energy:
They would have appeared to be

Complex lattices
Of colored light to human eyes
But the electromagnetic "structures"
Failed to respond
To any attempts at communication
And in the end the ship was uncertain
Whether they were alive at all
Much less intelligent

Many of the Tin Men
Encountered alien civilizations
But this one failed
Its specific mission unfulfilled
And eventually its systems
Became corrupted and shut down

Sometime later,
Intermittently intelligent aliens
Stumbled upon the ship during their cognitive phase
And wondered at the nature
Of an intelligent race
Willing to send an empty ship
Upon a billion-year journey
For no discernable reason, and one
Which, in their eddying estimation,
Led nowhere

Epilog

This is what the Tin Men perceive:
Ancient white dwarfs turned to ember and ash
Blue-shifted galaxies like ghosts
Drifting past, and
The full-spectrum
Shattered rainbow
of electromagnetic information

KNOWLEDGE OF

RUTH BERMAN

Eve biting into Newton's apple
Knew the attraction between the globes
Of fruit and Earth,
The bodies of herself and Adam,
The gravity of holding
The bubbles shaped by surfaces of stars.

Eve tasted the tart universe
Holding the red shift in her hands.

QUO VADIS?

Science fiction writers are often asked, "Where is your field heading?" The best response is usually, "In all directions at once." After all, science fiction and fantasy have the entire universe and all of time as their playground; don't expect an orderly progression from *here* to *there*.

But change is inevitable, and to make some sense of today's "literature of change," we have one of the best writers in the field describing where we are today and where we might be headed for tomorrow.

Orson Scott Card has written everything from short stories to screenplays, from novels to dramas. He is a multifaceted author, editor, publisher, and commentator on the field. He has won both the Nebula and the Hugo Awards many times over.

Here he discusses the condition of the science fiction and fantasy field today, with his usual incisive clarity and wit.

THE STATE OF AMAZING, ASTOUNDING, FANTASTIC FICTION IN THE TWENTY-FIRST CENTURY

ORSON SCOTT CARD

L iterary history depends on the fact that writers always emerge from the ranks of readers.

There are two primary motives that inspire new writers when they first take up their pen or pound on their keyboard:

 I. They are so inspired by something they've read that they are determined to create something "like that" or "as good."
 II. They are so bored or disgusted by reading quotidian nonsense that they realize, "If something that bad can be published, I can certainly write something better."

Oddly enough, both motives lead most writers to be imitative, at least in their early work.

Obviously, Type I writers, determined to match someone else's literary achievement, will learn from their admired models.

But Type II writers also learn from the existing models, even though they don't admire them. Why? Because at the beginning most writers don't understand the art. Even if they think they're being "completely new," they will at most change a few details, usually cosmetic ones, and proceed to imitate every other aspect of what went before.

It's precisely what happens with children when they become parents. Whether they thought their own parents were horrible or wonderful, they will raise their children differently on the few points they notice, and on every other aspect of child rearing, they are largely clones of the generation before.

Now and then, however, a writer, usually well into his career, but sometimes right from the start, will start to do something that is noticeably different from anything else going on.

At first, this writer's work is sui generis—the writer owns this new territory. Jules Verne did not spawn a genre. Anything that looked like Verne was considered to be "imitation Jules Verne." It was simply a branch of adventure literature, a critically despised (but popular and beloved) subcategory of the genre of fiction.

Then another writer pops up—an H. G. Wells, for instance—who also explores wild new technologies in his fiction. Unlike Verne, he is not an adventure writer, he's a utopian and a social critic. His work is quite serious (as if Jules Verne had been joking!) and respectable critics can talk about it because, instead of mere technology, he is also exploring important Social Issues. It is the Eloi and Morlocks that the critics of the day want to talk about. Nobody in the literary world takes the machine seriously.

But for a significant number of lay readers, it is the time machine itself that is intriguing.

Serious writers will learn from Wells what the critics admired, and the results are *1984* and *Brave New World*.

Others, however, will start to produce imitation Verne and Wells that concentrates on the cool machines and extravagant imaginings. They might build on the structures of adventure fiction (like Verne, Merritt, or Haggard) or thought experiments (like Wells, Huxley, and Orwell).

As the imitations grow in number, publishers notice and begin to promote the similarities among these stories in order to reach whatever portion of the fiction-buying public might be attracted to them, and a literary category is born.

Most publishing categories are ephemeral or remain trivial, however long they might endure. Who remembers the spate of mafia novels spawned in imitation of the commercial success of *The Godfather*?

Other publishing categories become commercially important but artistically narrow, like the women's romance category or media tie-in fiction, where boundaries are strictly enforced and writers only rarely get a chance to stray into new territory. These fictions grow out of the conversation between writer and editor, with the editor holding all the cards.

But now and then a category bursts out of the control of the editors and publishers, and the fiction becomes a conversation among writers and readers.

This happens when writers become stars. The public demands not just more of the category, but more from that writer.

Now, when that happened with Verne and Wells, they each stood alone. But when it happens with writers who are aware of each other's work and are, in fact, readers and admirers (or angry rivals) of each other's work—when, in short, they perceive themselves to be part of the same group, producing fiction with deliberate similarities, a movement is born.

And when a category becomes a movement, it can change the literary world.

Hugo Gernsback, when he started publishing "scientifiction" in *Amazing Stories*, aspired to create a publishing category. He saw the commercial possibilities of Wells's fiction and invited writers to create more of it.

There were plenty of other magazine editors and publishers creating categories at the time. Airplane stories. "Spicy" stories. War stories. Cowboy stories.

But science fiction (as it soon became known) created an audience that was not interested just in the subject matter, but also in the way the literature approached the world.

Science fiction didn't just come up with cool adventures within an existing frame of reality, the way the other magazines did. It had to keep coming up with new realities. That was why it was Wells rather than Verne who pointed the way to creating a literary movement: Verne's imitators would come up with new technologies, but Wells's imitators had to come up with the social implications of those technologies.

It was the letters columns that created the monster. By corresponding with people whose letters appeared in the growing number of science fiction magazines, science fiction readers began to converse with each other about what made one story better or worse than another.

They created critical principles that were quite out of the control of the editors and publishers (except to the degree that the editor and publishers joined in as slightly-more-equal-than-the-others participants in that conversation).

The readers who took part in this conversation, and then became writers, wrote better stories because of it—"better," that is, defined by what these readers decided "better" must be. They became the most-admired writers; the critical principles they affirmed became the rules of the movement.

Publishing categories become literary movements when the control shifts to the critical conversation among readers.

And literary movements become revolutions when they defy the critical standards of the day and declare those standards meaningless or inapplicable.

Many a writer has tried to launch a revolution directly, by banding together with a few like-minded buddies and finding some pulpit from which to propound their principles. If the public goes along—if the books find wider readership and the writers become stars—then the movement (revolutionary or not) takes on a life of its own that transcends the originators.

Most such "revolutions" fail miserably. Most writers find that other writers don't want to imitate them or pay attention to their ideas. Even if they become stars, other writers simply regard the territory they have staked out as private property and don't venture there; or, if they do, act as if the previous writer did not exist.

Disdain is the cruelest literary weapon.

But when the public embraces the movement, so the writers' sales, as a group, matter in the publishing world, and the public seeks new works that are put forth as part of that movement, the movement becomes a genre, or the revolution redraws the literary map.

Just like Elizabethan theater (despised as subliterary at the time), romanticism, realism, and modernism, science fiction became not just a category, not just a revolution, but a victorious movement.

Victorious? When the universities still embrace, with few changes, the canon of modernism (in the sense that only books of a certain type are "worth talking about," even though individual writers are elevated and dashed down by turns)?

Yes. While the guardians of "literary" fiction still give each other prizes and writers of that genre can still achieve stardom and create good work, the fact remains that it is a movement that has lost all its creative force as a movement.

Postmodern fiction was full of brave manifestos and learned-sounding disquisitions (often unreadable to those who thought criticism in English literature ought to be written in the English language), but their innovations were suspiciously similar to the innovations from the earliest days of modernism. Indeed, all you have to do to be called "daring" and "experimental" in that genre is to slavishly imitate the more outré works of writers who have been dead for half a century or more.

Science fiction, by contrast, was exploring new territory and spawned many minirevolutions that really did open new ground.

The Campbellians, writers of what is now called "hard science fiction," insisted on fiction that took real science seriously.

Once Heinlein pointed the way, more and more writers in the 1950s began to regard character-in-society as another vital aspect of what they considered "good" science fiction. Even the hard SF writers began to follow suit, insofar as they were able.

The New Wave of the 1960s began to allow literary pyrotechnics to slip in front of the story—but rarely so far that the reader couldn't see how the tale still conformed to the requirements of the other kinds of science fiction.

Through all this period—the 1930s to the 1970s—there were groups of writers starting up minimovements; there were stars who sometimes spawned imitators or staked out lonely territory; there were manifestos and attacks and the occasional death threat, thus certifying how serious everybody was.

But underneath all of this was one deep, significant fact: the audience for science fiction kept growing. They were hungry for new work, new voices; they demanded that we take them to new worlds and new cultures and new technologies that would stretch their minds.

Each new movement, each new star, increased the number of readers—and the number of kinds of science fiction there were. In fact, looked at with historical perspective, it is clear that through this period science fiction was literature.

Of course the writers and works from older literary movements did not disappear, especially because the institution of the university English department gave them an artificial lease on life; anyone who studied official literature was taught to despise science fiction and continue to admire or at least imitate the transformative writers of modernism.

But only science fiction was explosively productive of new critical standards, new literary perspectives, new kinds of stories.

And then it ended.

Because it always ends.

By the late 1970s, which is precisely when I entered the field, we'd pretty much dried up. Momentum carried us forward; but the revolution was over, and, try as we might, nobody could come up with a new one. All the kinds of science fiction already existed.

Yes, yes, I know. Cyberpunk. As a movement it was born of Bruce Sterling's attack on the consensus sci-fi that had emerged—everybody seemed to be writing fiction set in each other's futures. To show what should be happening, if the sci-fi revolution was to continue, Sterling pointed to the work of William Gibson as an example.

But the resulting "movement" did not consist of new ways of writing fiction or even a new flowering of innovative futures, as Sterling had hoped. Instead, it resulted in imitation—people who picked up on the superficial aspects of Gibson's work and imitated it. A mere category.

In other words, science fiction was doing just what modernism had done a generation before: it still pretended to have revolutions, but they were cosmetic, not substantive. You would buy and read cyberpunk rather the way you would buy and read Star Wars novels.

I am saying nothing against the individual writers of cyberpunk—or Star Wars novels. There is nothing inherently good about revolutions—literary or otherwise. They are only good if they lead to something good. And even when literary revolutions pass their peak and become the establishment, they can still nurture wonderful writers who produce powerful works of fiction.

My point is merely that the revolution was over.

Here are some of the indications:

1. We recognize all the kinds of science fiction and nobody is making new ones. There are time travel stories, alternate histories, anthropological sci-fi, techno-porn, military sci-fi, literary sci-fi (merging two revolutions past their prime), adventure sci-fi, social commentary sci-fi, hard sci-fi . . . Maybe I've overlooked something but as far as I can determine, there hasn't been a new kind of science fiction since the late 1970s.

2. We are becoming annoyingly respectable. More and more universities are teaching science fiction courses, and not just as a way to beef up the enrollment in English courses. We have a new generation of professors who grew up on *Dune* and *The Left Hand of Darkness* and *Foundation* and *The Moon Is a Harsh Mistress* and *Childhood's End* and "I Have No Mouth and I Must Scream."

3. Derivative writers in other genres are now stealing from us. Many of the "postmodern" writers in the literary field were and are able to "prove" they were and are different from modernism by . . . writing science fiction.

4. Our penetration of the public consciousness is complete. It's hard to find a single important idea in science fiction that is not already familiar to the well-read portion of the general public. And through movies and television shows, which are finally catching up with print sci-fi, our field's ideas have reached far beyond the audience of readers.

5. Our space on the shelves in the bookstores is shrinking. Science fiction's ability to generate new stars is declining. The

public no longer looks to us to take them places they have never been. They look to us now as a way to get back to where they have been before and want to return—not a revolutionary, but a conservative impulse. The media tie-in novels are not an aberration, they are the primary way that many, perhaps most, people experience all science fiction.

When a literary revolution has stopped being productive of new ways of telling stories or kinds of stories to tell, it may not be dead, but it's dying.

Not in the sense that its tools and tricks will disappear, but in the sense that its boundary no longer has any particular reason to exist. When science fiction is studied a century from now, it will be studied as a closed period of literature, and I believe that the close will be marked somewhere between 1980 and 2000.

What took the place of science fiction? What was the new revolution, or at least the new generation, that supplanted us?

Let's keep in mind that there isn't necessarily a new generation. A literary movement can die by dissolving its boundaries; it doesn't have to be killed.

But I think that the enormous burst of creativity in the mystery genre in the 1980s and 1990s may well come to be seen as the literary forefront. Certainly the mystery field broke into many different kinds of mystery just the way science fiction had in the decades before. In the 1960s there were mystery stars, of course, and there had even been something of a movement with the "hard-boiled detective" novel, but it was in the 1980s and 1990s that mystery broke open into the multifaceted genre that, like science fiction, allows people to write vastly different fictions that are still regarded as being "in category."

So we have cozies and hard-boiled detectives, yes, but we

also have historicals and mystery romances and legal thrillers and comic mysteries and police procedurals and . . .

It had been to the advantage of sci-fi not to be set in the real world; mystery had the advantage of being set there. We had "sense of wonder"; they had "trusted reality."

But that revolution is over, too. It isn't that the repetitions of *Law & Order* killed the genre—just like science fiction, there are still excellent novels being written. But there are no new kinds. The nonprint media have brought all the existing kinds to the saturation point, but that was because all the innovation was over and it was safe to go there now, just as *Star Trek* and *Star Wars* proved that science fiction was dying or dead as a literary genre, but did not cause that death.

If mystery is dead, what's next?

Again, it could be nothing. It's quite possible to have establishment literature and commercial publishing categories proceed without anything new or important coming along at all. (Though that might easily be a clear symptom of a culture in decline.)

But there might be a new movement, and it might also be fantasy.

How can fantasy be the "new" movement? It's older than dirt!

Yes, of course, but not as a category and not as a movement.

Before the invention of the novel (yes, even the novel was once a literary revolution), there was the romance, and when we read the pre-novel romances, we recognize them as what would now be called fantasy. The variations tended to be in subject matter (Arthur and Britain; Roland and Charlemagne) and the nation of origin.

But it wasn't a category, because that was all there was. The novel was a rebellion against it, an insistence on realistic characters in realistic settings; tales of common people (though usually still of a moneyed class—no surprise; who was buying the books?); and prose that echoed the vernacular instead of elevated, poetic, heroic language.

Fantastic elements continued, of course, cropping up in gothic, horror, and other categories of fiction.

And there were writers who almost made it a category—George MacDonald, Lord Dunsany. The popularity of *Peter Pan* and the Wizard of Oz books could have led to a literary movement. But any such movement was killed by lumping them in with "children's literature," which effectively forbade adults to take them seriously.

But fantasy smoldered there, a fire that could never quite be put out. J. R. R. Tolkien and C. S. Lewis were in the generation that grew up on the fantasy elements of children's literature—talking animal tales, fairy stories—as well as being of the last generation to be nursed on Homeric and Virgilian gods. When science fiction came along, they recognized it as having potential to recover the magical experience of their childhood reading and imagining—certainly sci-fi contained plenty of magic and plenty of gods, however they might be disguised behind machines.

But Tolkien never got around to writing his science fiction project, and Lewis's is, in my opinion, not very good. Instead, both of them did their finest fiction writing in the area of fantasy, transforming it in the process.

Lewis's Narnia series was not transformative, of course—it remained children's literature and religious literature. But his novel *Till We Have Faces* took a god-story and remade it as an adult novel—that is, realistic in its handling of the details of milieu and highly personal in its handling of character.

Tolkien's *The Hobbit* was also, like Narnia, intended to be (and sold as) children's literature. But as he flailed about in the Old Forest, struggling to find a story that could be a sequel to *The Hobbit*, he came upon his character Strider in the inn at Bree and recognized that he was not writing children's literature at all anymore.

The others in the Inklings, Tolkien's literary society, were eventually unsupportive of the endeavor as they realized that Tolkien was really Serious about *The Lord of the Rings* and meant to go on and on. And when the novel came out, the British publisher, Gollancz, scarcely knew how to market it. Yes, it was a sequel to *The Hobbit*, but it was most emphatically not children's literature; they knew it was important and wonderful, but what in the world do you call it?

All those languages, all that adult politics, and the surprising dearth of magic. High heroic prose of elf and human lords mixed with the common speech of the hobbits. How do you sell such a thing?

You just print it. Because it turned out that the audience for romance had not gone away. It was still there, snatching bits of it wherever they could be found—in horror, in children's literature, in fairy tales, in science fiction. But Tolkien showed how it could be done openly, as a goal in itself.

When *The Lord of the Rings* came to America, Ian Ballantine led the fight to publish it as a serious work of fiction rather than children's literature. It was hard to break out of the niche into which fantastic literature had been crammed.

Lester del Rey tried to do for fantasy what Gernsback had done for science fiction—create it as a publishing category. At first there were reprints of the books that had inspired Tolkien and Lewis. Then, inevitably, there were the books that were shameless imitations of Tolkien—but they sold. Tolkien had, in fact, spawned a category.

Not yet a movement.

But there were stirrings. Nobody could call Donaldson's first Thomas Covenant trilogy derivative of Tolkien, or at least not just of Tolkien. And there were others who did work that was new.

Fantasy, as a living movement, was fully born as a hybrid, as Atheneum published library hardcovers of fantasy novels in the children's fiction category, and then Del Rey published the paperback as adult category fantasy. Suddenly the jacket copy on fantasy books no longer had to look like Tolkien or refer to Tolkien.

McKillip's *The Throme of the Erril of Sherill* and *The Forgotten Beasts of Eld* and *The Riddlemaster of Hed*, as well as LeGuin's Earthsea trilogy, came out as children's literature precisely at the time that children's lit was purportedly becoming painfully realistic, with Judy Blume leading the charge toward fiction that was about real children in the real world.

The realistic children's writers had their own movement within their field, an enormously productive one. The fantasy writers moved out of kid lit, however, and found a welcome in the shadow of science fiction.

I saw a few bookstores that tried to separate the categories, but it was both impossible and pointless. Readers who came looking for books by the stars didn't want to have to worry about whether *Glory Road* was fantasy or sci-fi—it was Heinlein, and it should be where Heinlein books were grouped. Larry Niven's *The Magic Goes Away* had to be shelved right along with his *Ringworld*.

There were fantasy writers who never wrote sci fi, and sci fi writers who never wrote fantasy. But there was enough crossover among writers and readers that it was just annoying to have to check two sections in the bookstore.

Over the years, however, the balance has shifted. Fantasy is fragmenting and growing. The fragmentation begins with dominant writers who stake out a territory.

Stephen King, Thomas Tryon, and Dean Koontz worked the same territory on the border between horror and psychological fiction, with Clive Barker adding a bit more blood to the mix.

Rowling's Harry Potter series spawns another subcategory, which is usually put in the children's section of the bookstore, but in fact draws many of the same readers—some young, some old.

But not all young adult fantasy owes a debt to Rowling. Shannon Hale, Hillary Bell, Tamora Pierce, Brandon Mull, Mette Ivie Harrison, and many others are writing highly original fantasies that echo all the adult subcategories and show them to be every bit as inventive and resourceful.

Anne Rice launched the vampire subcategory that is now subdividing further, with, of course, many writers riding the line between YA and adult fiction—Stephenie Meyer comes to mind.

Trilogies and series dominate, but the exciting thing, for me, is the way that the current crop of fantasy writers steal from every source and make it work. The South American magic realists provoked English-language imitations, but one can hardly call Terry Bisson's fiction "derivative."

I remember back in 1988, when I read Bruce Fergusson's seminal "In the Shadow of His Wings," thinking: this is fantasy as the most serious world-creating sci-fi writers would do it. Fergusson himself didn't follow up, but the method thrives, as Robin Hobb, George R. R. Martin, Kate Elliott, Brandon Sanderson, and Lynn Flewelling have created masterpieces of thoroughly created worlds that, instead of imitating Tolkien's choices, imitate his method of creation.

In all these subcategories, the writers show themselves capable of creating enduring characters without sacrificing the great strengths of fantasy: noble deeds and heroic prose, literalized metaphors of real-world power, thick world creation, and nostalgia for an imagined golden age—both in the past of the world and in the past of the reader, as the reader recovers versions of both childhood and ancient lore.

There is, of course, much wretched work—but that is true of every literary movement.

Fantasy and media-based sci-fi aren't pushing "real science fiction" off the shelves; the readers and writers are doing that. And it's not really a matter of pushing great work away— terrific writers who want to write and sell science fiction have plenty of opportunities, and sci-fi writers can still command broad stretches of that section in the bookstore.

Rather, science fiction, by its own decadence and fading away, is creating a vacuum that something was going to fill. We should be glad that what is now taking its place is a movement so harmonious with science fiction.

The way I see it, fantasy isn't so much a new revolution as a new generation. Science fiction was no longer a vibrant movement; the revolution was won; so some of the best writers struck out for new lands in which to set tales that used all the skills they had learned from science fiction's many subrevolutions, and the category they found was fantasy.

So fantasy is not destroying or even replacing sci-fi so much as it is fulfilling it and continuing to evolve it.

During all those years that romance was suppressed, it kept squeezing itself out because readers—including those who also became writers—hungered for the magic that the novel rejected.

With science fiction first, and now with fantasy, heroic romance found ways to burst again into bloom. One generation created the seeds of the next. There is no need for the two generations to quarrel. They grew in the same soil and share most of the same literary DNA.

THE WOMAN IN SCHRÖDINGER'S WAVE EQUATIONS

EUGENE MIRABELLI

Not every nominated story can win a Nebula Award, but the field of science fiction and fantasy is so rich with talent that even a story that did not win is well worth inclusion in this anthology: witness Eugene Mirabelli's "The Woman in Schrödinger's Wave Equations."

Gene Mirabelli is the author of six novels, plus short stories, poems, and many journalistic pieces. He admits to being at least seventy-six years old. Mirabelli taught in the graduate writing program at the State University of New York at Albany during its heyday, and currently contributes political articles and reviews to an alternative newsweekly with a focus on the arts.

Here's what he has to say about writing "The Woman in Schrödinger's Wave Equations."

Erwin Schrödinger was a remarkably decent man—when the Nazis came to power he chose to leave Europe for England, though if he had stayed he would have been awarded a prestigious university position—but he was a rascal when it came to women. While a young married man, Schrödinger took a holiday in Switzerland and, as Amy says, "For two whole weeks all he did was make love to this woman and write those equations." A lot is known about Schrödinger, but the woman has eluded every attempt to identify her.

I began the story with the simple idea that the woman, whoever she was, must be somewhere in those equations. I wrote Amy and John into existence, then Heidi turned up. Usually when I begin a story I know where it's going, but in this instance I had no idea at all. I certainly didn't know that Heidi was the great-granddaughter of Erwin Schrödinger.

The aesthetics of physics and mathematics delight me, so I just kept writing, playing around with the probabilities which flourish in Schrödinger's equations, and the uncertainties which haunted Heisenberg's life and thought. Readers who know the history of physics and politics in the twentieth century will pick up the resonances in this tale, but it's not necessary. I loved being with John and Amy and I hope science fiction readers—who are the most engaged readers anywhere—enjoy them, too.

THE WOMAN IN SCHRÖDINGER'S WAVE EQUATIONS

EUGENE MIRABELLI

1

chrödinger: *Life and Thought* was written by Walter Moore and published by Cambridge University Press in 1989. It's a superb book, giving a detailed and dramatic narrative of Erwin Schrödinger's life and a lucid explication of his ideas, not only his insights into quantum physics, but an account of his philosophical speculations as well. The author presents the world in which Schrödinger lived, his home, the places where he taught, the intellectual milieu around him— his passions, his friendships and the many women he loved. This is the book that Amy Bellacqua was reading.

Amy was twenty-eight and worked as a waitress at the Capri on Santa Cruz Avenue in Menlo Park. She had never been especially interested in physics but, as she said, she had nothing against it either. Furthermore, she liked biography and felt this one was good. Mostly good. It did have some fancy-looking equations, but they didn't interrupt the flow of the story. Let me be frank—Amy was reading *Schrödinger: Life and Thought* because the young man who had moved into the apartment upstairs was getting his Ph.D. in physics and she wanted to be able to talk to him about something he liked the next time they met in the laundry room or the parking space out back. They rented flats in a small box-like house of yellowish stucco—Amy on the first floor, John Artopoulos on the second.

John was twenty-eight and was finishing a dissertation in theoretical physics at Stanford. In high school he had been a whiz at science and as a college freshman he had picked up a tattered paperback copy of George Gamow's *Thirty Years That Shook Physics* and that book led to his becoming a physicist. He liked the informal style of the writing, and he was intrigued by Gamow's drawings and most especially by his photographs— snapshots of Niels Bohr and his wife roaring off on a motorcycle, Werner Heisenberg taking a swim, a bare-chested Enrico Fermi swatting at a tennis ball, and Gamow himself with Wolfgang Pauli on a Swiss lake steamboat. Those people knew each other, got drunk together, sang songs and together developed quantum mechanics; he wanted to be part of that, wanted to join them. Now he was overworked and was beginning to wonder if that great sense of fun and friendship had gone out of physics. He spent his time in a small cubicle at the Stanford Linear Accelerator (SLAC), or in his lonely apartment, or away at Heidi Egret's studio north of Berkeley.

Heidi was twenty-eight, an artist, a painter. Of course she was still too young to be famous, but her reputation was growing and recently *California Spectrum* had listed her as one of the ten younger artists to keep an eye on. Her work had evolved rapidly, keeping pace with changes in the art market, and though she was not always in the spotlight she was usually nearby. She was best known for those abstract paintings in which she used a pointillist technique she called pixel transformation. People differed about Heidi's work and whether it was advanced or merely an updated version of Seurat's theories from a century ago, and some even debated whether it was well done or not. But everyone agreed that Heidi, who had spent some years as a surfer, was a knockout. John had met Heidi at a beach party one Saturday afternoon and had been dazzled.

2

That was the same Saturday that Amy Bellacqua had met John. Amy had been in the little parking area out back of the yellow-ish stucco house, trying to wedge a couple of tables into her small car. She had rolled the round table into place, its legs tilted up onto the back seat, but was having a hard time lifting and positioning the oblong table. Furthermore, she was getting hot. She rested one end of the table on the car seat and with her free hand she grabbed up the bottom edge of her jersey, mop-ping the sweat from her eyes just as the young man from up-stairs came around the corner of the house in beach shorts and sunglasses, a duffle bag under his arm. He tossed the duffle bag into his car, then turned to her. "Can I help?" he asked, taking off his glasses.

"I hope so!" she said. It took a while, but together they were able to get both tables in. "Thanks," Amy said, taking the opportunity to look at him openly now that they weren't wrestling with the tables. "The tile makes them a little heavy," she explained, then immediately regretted telling him the ob-vious.

"They look good, the tiles. Very colorful."

Amy was uncomfortably aware that her damp jersey was clinging to her breasts. "Oh. Well. Thanks. I'm taking them to sell at a flea market. Actually."

She smiled and waited for him to turn away so she could leave without being rude, but instead he said, "My name's John Artopoulos," and he put out his hand and she shook it and said, "I'm Amy Bellacqua." He asked her if she worked at the flea market and she laughed and said, "No, I just go there when I have something to sell. I'm waitressing, mostly. What about you?" she asked.

"I'm working on a dissertation in physics."

"That sounds interesting."

"Does it?" He looked surprised.

"Don't you like physics?"

"Sure I do." He laughed. "But it never sounds interesting to other people." They talked of this and that for a brief while, then said good-bye and went their separate ways, John to the beach party and Amy to the flea market where she came across *Schrödinger: Life and Thought* and, after leafing through a few pages, she bought it.

3

John saw Heidi Egret's paintings on their second date. "I like the colors in this one," he said. "What's it about? I mean, what's it a picture of?"

Heidi hadn't answered, so he turned to where she was seated cross-legged on her pink exercise mat, brushing out the tangles John's frenzied embraces had made in her pale blond hair.

"I didn't ask you to explain string theory. Right?" she said petulantly.

"Right," he said.

"And you shouldn't ask me to explain my paintings. It always confuses me to do that.—Anyway, what are we going to do next? Do you want a cigarette or something?"

From his first sight of Heidi at the beach party, John thought of her as the quintessential California girl. She had a tattoo on her right shoulder blade that other people might think was a devil's pitchfork but which John saw as a trident, symbol of the sea god Poseidon. He had grown up in Massachusetts and had never met anyone like her—not just her looks—he'd never met anyone so open and easygoing, so laid-back. He called her his California, or his Californienne, which he meant as an endearment, but it annoyed Heidi, not simply because she was from Oregon but because, as she informed him on their third date, she wasn't his. She was a free spirit and didn't belong to him or to anyone. "Are you angry with me?" he asked. He had just driven up from Menlo Park and his knapsack slumped from his hand to the floor in disappointment.

"No. But we can go to the bedroom and make up if you want," she said, brightening. "It beats talking."

That's how it was with John and Heidi. The only reason he wasn't with her all the time was that his research fellowship kept him at SLAC, down in Menlo Park, and her half-time teaching at Contemporary Arts kept her up north of Berkeley, a long drive. Her studio, with its big slanted skylight, was a happier place than his desolate apartment, so each weekend John drove up to her place. The weekends took time away from his dissertation, which had come to a halt, but he hoped his work was going to go better since meeting Heidi.

4

One weekend Heidi went up to Oregon to visit her stepfather. "After all, he's paying the rent here. I owe him a visit now and then," she had told John. The weekend Heidi went to Oregon was the same weekend Amy Bellacqua asked John about something she had read in *Schrödinger: Life and Thought.*

Amy was sitting on the back steps reading the book when John came around the corner to his car carrying a red plastic bucket. She watched as he began to roll up his car windows, then she slid the book behind her and called out, "Hi!"

He turned and saw her. "I've decided to wash my car," he said. "Just to see what color it really is." He came to the steps, turned on the garden faucet and let the water run into his red bucket, then turned it almost off while he tried to think up a way to engage her.

"Actually, I think mine's dirtier," Amy said. John crouched by the bucket, the throat of his shirt hanging open, and she saw his chest hair.

"I've got a couple of sponges. You can borrow my soap, if you want," he offered, catching Amy unaware as she gazed thoughtfully at his chest.

"What? Oh! That. Okay! You go ahead," she told him. "I'll go get dressed in something that it won't matter if I get it soaked." She snatched up the book and ducked inside the door, tore off her blouse and jeans, pulled on a pair of old cutoffs and a black Grateful Dead T-shirt. But she never much liked the Grateful Dead, didn't want him to think she did, so she tore it off, started to pull on another but remembered it said *Boys Lie!*, clawed it off, tossed aside *Jesus is coming. Look busy!* and pulled on the white one that displayed a steaming cup of coffee—*The Daily Grind, Albany, New York*. Then she raced back outside to where John was soaping his car.

They washed their cars, all the while talking about the kinds of people you meet at flea markets or at the Stanford Linear Accelerator and about movies they liked and whether you'd want to live in San Francisco even if you could afford it, talked about things like that. John finished first and after hosing down his car he helped rinse Amy's. When they were finished, he put his sponges and soaps into his bucket while she coiled the garden hose. And that was that, car washing was over.

Amy went indoors feeling elated and disappointed at the same time, which was very confusing. She showered and decided it would not be smart to get involved with somebody who lived right upstairs. She got dressed feeling very clearheaded. Then John knocked at her door and asked did she want to get something to eat and she said yes.

They drove in John's freshly washed car, which now showed all its rust, and they ate at a deli. John asked Amy where she waitressed and she told him about the Capri restaurant on Santa Cruz which, she said, wasn't big but she liked her job there. It happened that John knew something about restaurants, too. "My parents have a restaurant, a Greek restaurant, in Boston.

That's where I'm from. And you're from Albany, New York," he told her.

"What? Me? No, no, no!" She laughed. "That old T-shirt comes from New York. But I grew up outside Sacramento. My dad teaches high school science. My mom's a guidance counselor. I'm just all California, nothing else. What's it like in Massachusetts?" Amy asked him.

John had spent summers working on a lobster boat when he was in college, and Amy had spent those same summers as a life guard on the beach. They talked and talked and talked much longer than they realized and would have gone on talking forever if John hadn't suddenly remembered—"Damn! I just remembered!"—that he had to go over to his office before five. So they drove back to their yellowish stucco apartment house. As they turned into their street John was feeling exhilarated and oddly light-headed, as if he had been drinking wine all afternoon and not simply talking with Amy.

"I have a question for you," Amy told him. "I'm reading this book about Schrödinger."

"You are?"

"Yes, I found it at the flea market. I'm up to the part where he develops those wave equations. And I was wondering—" She broke off.

"Wondering what?"

"Schrödinger was married, you know, but in the middle of winter during the Christmas holidays he went off to the Swiss mountains and shacked up with this woman and that's when he did it."

"Did what?"

"Did everything. For two whole weeks all he did was make love to this woman and write those equations."

"Really? That's the way it happened?" He didn't know whether to believe her or not.

"It's in the book. But nobody knows the woman's name. Nobody can figure out who she was."

"I didn't know any of this," he said, clearly surprised.

"What I want to know is, can you find who the woman was by looking into the equations?"

He glanced sideways at Amy to see if she were serious. "No," he said.

"I think so," said Amy, agreeable and firm.

They rolled to a stop in front of their apartment house. John shook his head, no, and turned to her as if he were about to say something—his mouth even opened a bit—but nothing came out.

"Yes. I think she must be in there somewhere," Amy said. Then she hopped out of the car, turned and smiled at John. They both said it was a great car wash and lunch, then they waved and John drove off, telling himself, "Don't get involved with a crazy woman, no matter how great she looks."

5

Heidi taught part time at Contemporary Arts, north of Berkeley, and she told John how much she despised her job. "It's a second-rate art school with third-rate students," she said. Her voice was somewhat muffled because she was lying on her stomach on the pink exercise mat. "They're so materialistic, I mean utterly. The idea of art for art's sake, the idea of pure art, it's beyond them. All they care about is money. A lot of them have part-time jobs and come to class so tired they fall asleep. I mean, they really doze off. They say they want to be artists and then they turn around and ask me how to make art pay, like I cared, or something—Now do up by my shoulders," she said, giving directions to John, who was massaging her dark blond back, a complex surface which he thought more engaging than any dreamed of by Euclid, especially with its little trident tattoo.

"Why don't you quit your job and come down to my place?" he said, pausing to add a few more drops of oil to his hands.

"We'd starve on what you make."

"We could take turns eating," he said, kneeling forward to resume his massage. "I could eat on Monday, Wednesday and Friday. You could eat on Tuesday, Thursday and Saturday. We both could eat on Sunday."

"Hey! Are you saying I'm fat? You're not saying I'm fat, are you?" Heidi had raised her head and twisted around to look at him, frowning.

"No, no, no! That's not what I meant."

She relaxed and turned away, resting her cheek on her folded arms. "Anyhow, you'll be making plenty next year after you graduate. We can wait," she told him.

"I'll be a postdoc next year. Postdocs are slaves."

"Now my feet," she said. "You always forget to do my feet."

John took her to her favorite restaurant, a fancy place with soft music and dim lights, the table illuminated by five low candles floating in a shallow bowl of water. Over the lemon sorbet Heidi asked him, "What's a postdoc?"

"After I get my doctorate I'm a postdoc. I'll get a postdoc research job someplace. Those can go on for two or three years, or longer. Postdocs do really advanced research, but they get paid as if they were still grad students. I have to do postdoc work first to get a really good position later. That's all."

"Oh," Heidi said at last, her eyes soft with sympathy. She slid a hand across the table and gently laced her fingers through his. "I'm so sorry."

6

The next Friday Heidi phoned John, reached him on his cell phone as he was speeding from Menlo Park to her place. "Don't come. I've got to visit galleries all weekend," she told him. So John turned around, drove languidly back home to work on his dissertation. Actually, he didn't feel like working on his dissertation, so he thought he'd knock on Amy's door and borrow the book about Schrödinger, but when he turned into their little parking area he saw a handsome red sports car in his place beside Amy's car. He parked on the margin of brown grass, looked at the leather-and-mahogany cockpit of the Alfa Romeo, heard rock music from Amy's apartment and trudged upstairs to his desk, hoping it would rain into the sports car. Around midnight he heated three slices of frozen pizza in the microwave and ate dinner at the sink, returned to his desk and two hours later fell asleep over his equations. Saturday morning he pulled up his kitchen window shade and saw the red Alfa Romeo was still there, but when he went out it was mercifully gone. He crawled into his rusted car and drove to his cell at SLAC and worked for fifteen hours. Sunday morning he took a long hot shower, stared out his kitchen window a while at his car and Amy's, side by side, drove out and bought a fat newspaper, drove aimlessly this way and that, then headed back home and knocked on Amy's door and asked would she like to come out for breakfast or brunch.

Her face lighted up. "Come in. I'll make us something," she said. "I was hoping you'd stop by."

Her place was a maze of greenery, a jungle—potted flowers crowded the window sills, mossy baskets hung from the ceiling and overflowed with blossoms, trays of pale green sprouts lay underfoot, and luminous mosaic tiled tables stood here and there and there amid the leaves, and mosaic figures looked out from the walls, and here's a work bench packed with jars and miniature saws and grinding wheels and pocketed trays with heaps of tesserae that glowed like gemstones. "This is amazing! This is beautiful!" John said. "And this! And this!" he said, ducking and weaving among the plants and mosaics. "This is wonderful!"

"Thanks," Amy said. "Do you like waffles? Or pancakes? Or eggs? Or cornflakes? Or what?"

"The tables you took to the flea market—," he began.

"Were really amateurish," Amy said. "I made them when I was still a student at Contemporary Arts—a school you never heard of—and I was keeping them for sentimental reasons. But I've run out of space."

"Pancakes would be nice," said John.

They ate in the kitchen. John set the table, sliced a cantaloupe and read newspaper bulletins to Amy while she whipped the batter and poured it onto the griddle. Over the pancakes he asked her why she hadn't told him she was an artist.

"Full-time waitress, part-time artist," she explained. "I've had a few shows in some Bay Area galleries and a couple down in Santa Cruz. I love what I'm doing, I just wish I could do it all the time."

They talked through brunch, talked while Amy washed the dishes and John wiped them, talked and talked and suddenly decided to drive off in Amy's car, drive anywhere, and while they drove John told her about his dissertation, about the equations he had concocted from a gedanken experiment. "What's a gedanken experiment?" she asked him. "It's where you just think an experiment, but you don't actually do it, you just think it through," he told her. "But now I'm beginning to wonder if the equations have anything at all to do with reality, real physical reality."

And after they had parked the car and were walking among the redwood trees, Amy told him, "I began as a painter and I still like painting, other people's paintings, but for me—you'll think I'm crazy—for me paint is too soft and squishy, too abstract. What I like about mosaic tesserae, the little pieces, whether they're glass or ceramic or beach pebbles or whatever, what I like is that I can hold the color in my hand. It's a piece of color. It has shape and size and weight. I love that. I love the idea of a solid piece of color. I know it sounds crazy."

"It doesn't sound crazy to me," John said.

What sounded crazy to John came later, after they had driven all over the place and it was getting late—Amy had to waitress at the Capri and John had to get to his dissertation— and they had arrived back at their stucco apartment house.

"You remember the Schrödinger wave equations we talked about?" said Amy. "Remember how we decided that by looking into those equations you could find out who the woman was that Schrödinger made love to and that she—"

John interrupted, saying, "Not me. I mean, I couldn't figure that out, couldn't find out—"

"She had a child nine months after that, and Schrödinger was the father," Amy continued.

"That's in the book? In the biography?" He was quite surprised.

"No. But that's what I think. I'm sure of it."

"Ah," John said, drawing it out slowly and, he hoped, thoughtfully. He thanked Amy for brunch and told her he had had a good time, a really good time, and Amy said she had had a really good time too.

"You said you were hoping I'd drop by. Was it anything in particular?" he asked.

"No. I was just hoping you'd drop by, that's all."

Then Amy went off to work at the Capri and John went off to work on his equations.

7

John spent more and more of every day working on his equations, neglecting the rest of his life—sometimes even forgetting to eat, which had never happened before. On Friday he didn't remember to drive up to Heidi Egret's until it was already the moment when he should have been walking into her studio. He telephoned her, knowing from experience how irritated she would be at his tardiness, and as her phone rang and rang he phrased and rephrased how he would tell her he was going to be a little late. Her voice on the answering machine said to leave a message. John announced that he was not driving up there, was going to spend the weekend on his equations, good-bye. As a matter of fact, he did spend the rest of

Friday and all the next day on his thesis, but late on Saturday he phoned Amy and asked did she want to have breakfast or brunch on Sunday. "Of course I do. Knock on my door to-morrow morning and I'll make pancakes," she said.

The next morning John took a long hot shower, sang while he toweled himself dry, stepped into the crisp white cotton trousers which he almost never wore, pulled on a sky blue shirt and trotted downstairs, carrying CDs of Bach, Miles Davis, Olivia Newton-John, and Greek folk songs, and a big fresh pineapple, all of which he had bought right after phoning her. He knocked on Amy's door.

"Oh, wow, you look—," John began. Amy was in a blue-and-white striped dress; her hair was swept back and little blue trinkets dangled from her ears. She looked beautiful but also unfamiliar. "I like the way you look," he said.

"You've begun a beard!" she said, rubbing her palms against the stubble on his cheeks. "And I like it," she added.

"What beard?"

John had forgotten to shave for the past five days. As he told Amy while slicing up the pineapple, he had been working stead-ily and had been forgetting everything else. "I haven't spoken to anyone for a week," he said. He made up for it by talking all through brunch, talking while he washed the dishes and Amy wiped, was talking when they got into his car and drove all over and he didn't fall silent until they stepped barefoot onto the beach at Half Moon Bay to watch the surfers. "I used to know some-body who surfed," Amy said, looking away at the blurred hori-zon, squinting. "He's a real estate agent now, beachfront property, and he's rich. I met him at a gallery show last year. He drives a red Alfa Romeo. Maybe you saw it in our parking space."

John said no, he hadn't seen it.

"He got so drunk I didn't dare let him drive back to Ber-keley. He fell asleep on the floor," she said, turning to John. "I don't see how you missed his car, a red Alfa Romeo. It was parked out back all night."

"Maybe I was away," John said, looking off down the shoreline. "I used to go away on weekends."

They walked along the beach and swapped stories about everything under the sun. When the sky turned gray they got into his car and headed back home, arriving in Menlo Park as it began to rain. Amy said she had been rereading parts of *Schrödinger: Life and Thought*, especially the part where Schrödinger works out his equations on quantum mechanics. "The woman he was making love to is in those equations," Amy said. "Because this other physicist, Werner Heisenberg, had already figured out how to solve those problems in quantum mechanics. Heisenberg had a way of arranging the numbers into boxes, an array, a big matrix, so that when you work the matrix you get the right answers. Then Schrödinger, our Erwin Schrödinger, created his wave equations and solved the same problems. Schrödinger used a more tactile approach. He was that kind of man, tactile. He called Heisenberg's math repellent and ugly. Everybody calls Schrödinger's equations beautiful."

"Well—," John began.

"It's true, isn't it?"

"The part about Heisenberg and Schrödinger and the equations is true, but about the woman—"

They had turned the corner into the flooded parking area in back of the apartment house and come to a stop. The rain was beating on the car, streaming down the windshield.

"Yes, she had Schrödinger's baby, a girl. And that girl grew up and had a daughter. And that daughter—"

"Wow! How did you arrive at that?"

She laughed. "I've been doing what you might call a gedanken experiment. I've just been thinking things through."

John had turned to Amy and now he put his hand tentatively, gently to her cheek, his fingers moving into her hair. "I've been thinking too," he told her hesitantly. "About other things. Us."

"Good. Schrödinger loved the things of this world, women

especially," Amy said. She was slightly flushed and her speech was beginning to race a bit. "He liked to see things and touch them, smell them, taste them. He was that kind of man. But there are a lot of other people like Heisenberg who don't care about the physical side of things. They think the world is really, finally, when you get right down to it, an abstraction." She turned her face to meet John's kiss, and afterward said, "Heisenberg thought the world could be reduced to a box full of numbers. In those days everybody was taking sides about this."

"I hope we're on the same side," he said, his hand moving beneath her arm.

"God, yes," she said, sliding her arm around his neck. "There was this other physicist, Max Born, who argued with Schrödinger, said the wave functions were only—Oh, God," she said, speeding up. "Probabilities of what might be there, said you could never picture what was actually going on," she finished in a rush.

"I'm going crazy, Amy."

"Me too."

The windows were getting foggy and it was cramped and uncomfortable in the car, so they dashed through the rain to the house.

8

Amy was right about Schrödinger's equations and Heisenberg's matrix. Schrödinger himself wrote a paper (1926, *Annalen der Physik* 79, 734–56) about the relationship between his wave equations and Heisenberg's matrix, showing that they produced the same results. But he believed theories should be visualizable (*Anschaulichkeit*) and he loathed Heisenberg's quantum mechanics. In 1926, a few days after Schrödinger had published his fourth and final paper on wave mechanics, Max Born published a paper asserting the statistical nature of Schrödinger's waves—the waves, he said, were unimaginable clouds of probabilities. Of course, Schrödinger rejected that idea. For Erwin Schrödinger, everything he knew and loved was graspable in this world, our world of space and time, our living world, as he demonstrated during his years in Ireland.

As for John's thesis, it consisted of three papers on gravity, of which the first two were complete. In the third paper he had arrived at a bothersome equation or, as his dissertation director pointed out, many bothersome equations, and he was having a hard time figuring out what the equations implied. Unlike the European physicists of 1926, John had not read much in the way of philosophy and had not speculated on the relationship of mathematics to the physical world that it might, or might not, represent. Now all sorts of questions distracted and fascinated him, and though they were old questions to Schrödinger and Born, they were new to John Artopoulos. Indeed, these questions appeared to be at the opaque heart of his dissertation and they seemed unanswerable. To put it another way, in the previous six months he used up three reams of paper and hadn't completed a single page. Of course, the past two weeks had been different because now his brain, his body, everything was on fire.

9

We don't know the details of what they did, Erwin Schrödinger and the woman he was with, during the winter of 1925/26. The important thing is that he came out from that snow-covered chalet with his wave equations. And we shouldn't pry into what John and Amy did after they had dashed through the downpour and into her flat. John probably spent most of his waking hours on his equations, some of his time with Amy, and a couple of hours playing handball with his colleague Gino. As for Amy, most likely she waitressed at the Capri and spent her free time on a new mosaic. What's important is that on Sunday, April 18, 2004, Amy stepped out of a hot shower, wrapped herself in a towel and—Hey!—there stood John in the open doorway, wisps of the steam cloud floating away to reveal a bottle of wine in one hand and two glasses in the other. "I finished it!" he announced.

"Wonderful! Fantastic!" said Amy.

In the kitchen John set to work uncorking the bottle while Amy toweled her hair. Then they sat at the table and he poured a glass for her, a glass for himself. "Greek wine," he told her, smiling. He was more unshaven than ever, his eyes puffy and red rimmed from lack of sleep, but he was happy. "Greeks have been producing wine for thousands of years," he said, lifting his glass.

"Producing mathematicians and physicists, too," Amy said, smiling a little, touching her glass to his. They drank.

They talked about this and that, trivial things like John's having enough time now to get his car radio fixed. Actually, Amy wasn't paying attention to the conversation because up to now she had been able to avoid thinking about where John might disappear to when he had finished his graduate studies. Now she was thinking about it. John asked her how her new mosaic was coming along. Amy said she'd show him later. He said it felt good to be through being a student and that it would feel even better to go to a real job someplace. Amy felt her heart contract at the thought of his leaving. She hesitated a long moment. "Now what do you do?" she asked him.

"I take a shower. Like you," he said, standing up, laughing. "A long, hot shower." He pulled off his T-shirt and padded barefoot down the hall toward the bathroom, tossing his shirt in the air, catching it, singing. By the time John returned to the kitchen Amy had pulled on her cutoffs and a frayed jersey that said *Xanadu*, and was refilling their glasses. John lifted his glass to hers, saying, "Tell me about Schrödinger's woman and show me your new mosaic."

"I'll show you the mosaic," Amy said, touching her glass to his.

"What about the anonymous woman and her daughter and so on?"

"I'm sorry I ever said anything," Amy told him. She hurriedly drained her glass and nearly choked, then coughed. "Now you think I'm crazy or silly or just strange." She coughed again, wiped her eyes and looked at John hopelessly.

"Tell me anyway," he said. "Please."

"I calculated that Erwin's woman gave birth to a baby girl on September 9, 1926. I figure that about twenty-five years later this daughter gave birth to a daughter, too, probably in England. That would be Erwin's granddaughter, like Olivia Newton-John is Max Born's granddaughter, also born in England."

"Olivia Newton-John, the singer? The singer in *Xanadu*? She's Max Born's granddaughter?"

"I thought everybody knew that."

"Please go on," said John.

"That woman, the granddaughter, probably gave birth about twenty-five years later to a daughter, probably here in the United States," she said, fearing that every word would drive him away.

"In California?"

"In California, yes," she said firmly. "Probably."

"And you are?"

Amy laughed. "Amy Bellacqua, daughter of Vincent and Catherine Bellacqua, who is the daughter of Cosima Ferraro from Morano, Italy, and no relation to Erwin Schrödinger."

"How would we know if we found Schrödinger's great-granddaughter amid all these probabilities?"

"She'd be twenty-eight years old and have the Schrödinger equation tattooed on her butt," she said briskly. "Now let me show you the mosaic."

They went into the front room, the one John loved to linger in, the air full of green leaves and tendrils, the floor carpeted with trays of moss, uncurling ferns, pale celery-colored

sprouts, the mosaic tables bearing potted plants, the pots themselves composed of shards from broken mosaics, the walls blazing with mosaic designs. "Here," she said, handing him a
tray-like tablet where a dark background had imbedded in it a
formula in white stones, like chalk on a blackboard. It was one
of Schrödinger's wave equations. "I copied it from *Schrödinger:
Life and Thought*. I chose one I liked the shape of. As a kid I
used to look at the symbols in my dad's math books. I loved
the sigmas, the deltas, the stately integration signs," she told
him. John gazed at the equation, murmuring "Yes," and "Yes,"
and "Yes," all the while frowning. "But this first big symbol,"
he said at last. "The wave function."

"The Greek letter psi," said Amy. "What's wrong with it?"

"You've made it look like—it looks like—"

"Like a pitchfork, or a trident like the old man of the sea
carries. It's psi, but I made the tale a bit longer. It's more ele-
gant," she said.

"What are the chances that Schrödinger's unknown great-
granddaughter has it tattooed on her shoulder?" he asked.

10

The third part of John's dissertation was published by the
American Physical Society (2004, *Phys. Rev. Lett.* 09, 18 65–
88) and was cited with sufficient frequency to be included in
an online list of most important papers. Amy's mosaics were
exhibited by the Stern-Whitehall gallery in San Francisco, a
show that was favorably reviewed in *California Spectrum*. Fred
Marsh, hitherto unnamed, who drove the red Alfa Romeo
sports car and who was already rich at thirty-five (beachfront
property), was introduced to Heidi Egret at a gallery reception
in Berkeley and two weeks later they were living together at
his place.

The tattoo on Heidi's shoulder did—and still does—look
like the Greek letter psi, ψ, the symbol for the wave function in

Schrödinger's equations. The tattoo also looks like a pitchfork and like Poseidon's trident because, in fact, they all look alike. So much for the tattoo. As for Heidi's great-grandmother and whether she was the woman who spent fifteen or twenty days with Schrödinger in that snow-covered chalet, that's far less clear. It's as if nature had rigged the game so that the more precisely we get to know one part, the tattoo, the less certain we will be about the other, the great-grandmother. Indeed, in 1927 Heisenberg published a paper (*Zeitschrift für Physik* 43, 172–98) neatly defining this problem which has since become known as Heisenberg's uncertainty principle.

We know all we need to know about the tattoo. "It means I'm a follower of Neptune, you know, the sea god," Heidi explained. "I used to do a lot of surfing—Wadell Creek, Santa Cruz, places like that."

They were sitting in a café in Berkeley—Heidi and Fred and John and Amy. It was a clear sunny day and the view over the bay was spectacular.

"Does your mother have a tattoo like that?" John asked her.

"I don't remember any," Heidi said. Her mother had died when Heidi was eight. Heidi's father later remarried but was killed in a foggy car crash on California Route 101 when Heidi was fourteen. She was brought up by her stepmother, with whom she became quite close, but when Heidi was seventeen her stepmother married again and Heidi ran off to a life on the beach, surfing. That's when she got the tattoo. "In Santa Clara," she added.

"I learn something new about her every day," Fred said, smiling. He was wearing a silk jersey and a large expensive wristwatch and had his arm on the back of her chair.

"So it's just a tattoo of Neptune's trident," said Amy. "That's all?"

"And a good luck charm," Heidi told her. "It was engraved on a silver pendent that my grandmother gave me, my mother's mother, but I lost it."

"It won't get lost now," Fred said, patting her shoulder.

The grandmother had come from Ireland to spend a year with Heidi and her father right after Heidi's mother died. "And before she went back she gave me the pendent, her mother's, I think," Heidi said. "She's buried someplace in Ireland. I don't know where."

Amy Bellacqua and John Artopoulos married on September 18, 2004. Amy has been able to cut down on her waitressing and now works almost full time on her mosaics, and John works as a postdoc. The probabilities suggest they're living somewhere near Fermi Lab, around Batavia, Illinois. Or maybe they're living in Cambridge and he's working with Arkani-Hamed at Harvard. But Amy and John are together, that's certain.

GRAND MASTER AWARD

In addition to giving Nebula Awards each year, SFWA also presents the Damon Knight Grand Master Award to a living author for a lifetime of achievement in science fiction and/or fantasy. In accordance with SFWA's by-laws, the incumbent president nominates a candidate, normally after consulting with previous presidents and the board of directors. The nomination is then voted upon by the SFWA's officers.

Previous Grand Masters are Robert A. Heinlein (1974), Jack Williamson (1975), Clifford D. Simak (1976), L. Sprague de Camp (1978), Fritz Leiber (1980), André Norton (1983), Sir Arthur C. Clarke (1985), Isaac Asimov (1986), Alfred Bester (1987), Ray Bradbury (1988), Lester del Rey (1990), Frederik Pohl (1992), Damon Knight (1994), A. E. van Vogt (1995), Jack Vance (1996), Poul Anderson (1997), Hal Clement (Harry Stubbs) (1998), Brian W. Aldiss (1999), Philip José Farmer (2000), Ursula K. LeGuin (2002), Robert Silverberg (2003), Anne McCaffrey (2004), and Harlan Ellison (2005).

The 2006 Grand Master went to James Gunn, who is not only one of the premier writers in the field but a pioneer in teaching science fiction at the university level and bringing the field to acceptance by the academic community.

John Kessel, himself one of the field's best writers, gives well-deserved tribute to James Gunn.

JAMES GUNN, GRAND MASTER

JOHN KESSEL

In the history of science fiction, only one person has served as president of both SFWA, the international organization of professional science fiction and fantasy writers, and SFRA (Science Fiction Research Association), the organization of professional scholars and critics of science fiction. That person is James Gunn.

I first met James Gunn when I showed up in his office at the University of Kansas in August 1972, a newly minted graduate student fresh from an eleven-hundred-mile drive from upstate New York. On that first afternoon I foisted off on him my quite awful undergraduate honors thesis on Samuel Delany. He was gracious and patient. I was to come into his office a lot of times over the next nine years as I, at a glacial pace, pursued both a Ph.D. in English and a career as an SF writer. He was always gracious and patient.

I had driven that eleven hundred miles because of James Gunn. I wanted to write science fiction, and study literature. At that time, aside from Jack Williamson, he was just about the only working SF writer who also was a working teacher and scholar in a major university. He taught one of the few US university courses on the genre: his class Science Fiction and the Popular Media drew huge numbers of students, sometimes more than one hundred a semester. Much of the structure of the class shows up in Gunn's Pilgrim Award–winning history of the field, *Alternate Worlds*. Eventually I became Gunn's graduate assistant in that course.

It was only over the time I was at KU that I came to realize how his career represented, in some ways, the main thread of the development of science fiction. As a boy, he shook hands with H. G. Wells. In the late 1940s he sold fiction to John W. Campbell and throughout the 1950s he was a regular in Horace Gold's *Galaxy*, becoming a mainstay of the movement toward "sociological science fiction." He was one of the first people ever to study science fiction in the academy, writing a master's thesis on SF, portions of which were published in *Dynamic Science Fiction* in 1953. His first novel was a collaboration with Jack Williamson that the *New York Times* said read "like a collaboration between Asimov and Heinlein."

Over the last sixty years he has published over one hundred short stories and twenty-six books, among them *The Joy Makers*, *The Immortals*, *The Listeners*, and *Kampus*. *The Immortals* was adapted into a movie and served as the basis of a TV series. In his fiction Gunn brings a literary sensibility to traditional SF materials. *The Listeners* parallels a search for extraterrestrial intelligence with the difficulty of communication between human beings, realized movingly in the breaking relationship between a scientist in charge of a project listening for messages from space, and his wife, waiting at home for some contact with a husband who is so caught up in the pressures of his work, and his desire for contact with aliens who may or may not exist, that he is unable to touch her, or let her touch him.

In his career as historian, editor, and scholar, Jim Gunn has worked tirelessly for the acceptance of science fiction as a legitimate academic field of study. In the late 1960s and early 1970s he filmed interviews with and lectures by Isaac Asimov,

Harlan Ellison, Damon Knight, John Brunner, Theodore Sturgeon, John W. Campbell, Gordon Dickson, and Harry Harrison. In 1983 he received the Hugo Award for his nonfiction book *Isaac Asimov: The Foundations of Science Fiction*. In 1992 he received the Eaton Award for lifetime achievement as a science fiction scholar and critic. At Kansas in the 1970s he started and ran the Intensive English Institute on the Teaching of Science Fiction. This grew into the Center for the Study of Science Fiction, which annually administers and awards the Theodore Sturgeon Memorial Award for short fiction and the John W. Campbell Award for best SF novel.

His five-volume anthology *The Road to Science Fiction* is the best historical anthology of SF ever put together. His instructional book *The Science of Science Fiction Writing* is the result of a career's worth of experience in the classroom and in the practical world of publishing. It is a significant addition to the small shelf of works about SF writing from the inside, and Gunn's knowledge and craftmanship shine in every page.

It is as a writing teacher and a mentor that Jim Gunn means the most to me. No one knows more about how science fiction is and has been done. Writers as notable as Pat Cadigan and Bradley Denton have been his students, and I count it as one of my great honors to have sat in his classrooms at the University of Kansas back in the 1970s. I don't write a word today that is not influenced by his teaching.

While I worked for and with him he brought many writers to campus, giving me the opportunity to meet Ben and Barbara Bova, Gordon Dickson, Brian Aldiss, Samuel Delany, John Brunner, Fred Pohl, Theodore Sturgeon, and, more than once, Harlan Ellison. He directed my M.A. thesis, a collection of SF short stories. He served on the committee for my Ph.D. dissertation, another collection of SF stories.

Ours was not always an easy relationship. Jim pushed me to think more and emote less. He told me that stories are not written, they are rewritten. Coming out of the 1960s and the

New Wave, I wanted to reduce the differences between SF and mainstream writing. Jim insisted that the differences were vital, that to give them up was to sell out SF's birthright. Strangely, I was to hear the same arguments, almost word for word, from Bruce Sterling in 1985, and I have come to understand and appreciate them—though I'm afraid, Jim, we are never going to come to a meeting of the minds over the virtues of Tom Godwin's "The Cold Equations."

His office door was always open. When I came by, I would often interrupt him writing on his red IBM Selectric typewriter. He would turn around and give me, patiently, whatever time I needed, then calmly go back to work. We would argue about the nature of plotting, about character identification, about the triumphant Campbellian vision of the future of the human race. Looking back on it, I cringe to think of how much trivia I brought to him, when he had so much work to do. I know today how hard it is to get writing done and be a full-time academic. He did it, seemingly effortlessly.

Through all this, he never blew his own horn. He became, and is still, my role model. I wanted his job, and in some ways, I got it. I only hope that I treat the students who come into my office at North Carolina State with the respect that he gave me, long before anyone could ever have known that I might earn it.

On a number of occasions he invited me into his home, on the west side of Lawrence, at that time very much the edge of town. Outside his back door was a prairie with horses wandering around it. Sometimes they would come to the wire fence and stick their heads over into his backyard.

I imagine those horses are long gone.

Lots of things are gone. Barry Malzberg once commented on a photo that appears on page 193 of Gunn's *Alternate Worlds*, of a banquet table at the 1955 Worldcon in Cleveland. Seated at the table are Mildred Clingerman, Mark Clifton, Judith Merril, Frank Riley and family, and Jim Gunn, looking as young, dapper, and handsome as Kevin McCarthy from *Invasion of the Body Snatchers*.

All gone now, but Jim. His has been a life devoted to science fiction. He may not tell you what it has meant to him, but I just needed to tell you what he has meant to me.

Congratulations, Jim, and thanks.

THE LISTENERS

JAMES GUNN

As representative of the fiction that won him the 2007 Grand Master Award, James Gunn has selected his novelette "The Listeners." This work served as the opening chapter in his later novel of the same name, a book that was praised by Paul Shuck, president of the SETI League thusly: "*The Listeners* has done more for SETI [the Search for Extraterrestrial Intelligence] than anything else ever published."

Jim Gunn explains the genesis of "The Listeners":

After a decade when there never had been a day when I wasn't working on some story or novel, I accepted a position as the first administrative assistant to the chancellor for university relations at the University of Kansas. Those were the turbulent 1960s, and between learning my job and trying to explain student unrest to the various university publics, I had no time for writing. The Joy Makers, The Immortals, *and* Future Imperfect *were published between 1961 and 1964, but they had been written in the 1950s.*

By the middle of the 1960s I was feeling serious withdrawal symptoms, and I resolved to take the month's paid vacation that I was due. I prepared for that month—August after the end of the summer session and before the beginning of the fall semester—for months ahead so that when the time came I wouldn't have to think or do research;

I could sit down and write. Beginning in 1966, I wrote the second and third novellas that completed The Burning *(and published them in* If *and* Galaxy*), the second chapter of what later became* Kampus, *and the novelette I called "The Listeners."*

"The Listeners" was inspired by Walter Sullivan's We Are Not Alone. *Sullivan was the long-time science editor of the* New York Times. *He had attended a seminal conference of scientists in Washington, DC, along with many of the people who were being attracted to the idea of listening for messages from the stars—what now is called SETI, the Search for Extraterrestrial Intelligence—including Frank Drake and Carl Sagan. His book described the fascination people have displayed over the centuries about the possibility of life on other worlds, and various proposals for communicating with aliens. The availability of radio telescopes had led to recent discussions among such scientists as Guiseppe Cocconi and Philip Morrison about the possibility of picking up signals from space, and Cocconi had written a letter to Sir Bernard Lovell proposing that some time on the Jodrell Bank radio telescope be devoted to a search for signals from space.*

Sullivan's book was fascinating, and included a good deal of material that later found its way into my novel, but what stimulated my writer's instinct was the concept of a project that might have to be pursued for a century without results. What kind of need would produce that kind of dedication, I pondered, and what kind of people would it enlist—and have to enlist if it were to continue? I wrote "The Listeners," which in the novel is the chapter called "Robert MacDonald." My then literary agent thought it was overwritten for its audience, had too many foreign-language quotations, and anyway, he wrote, I should make my hero a young man fighting against the tyranny of tired old men. Another agent didn't care for it enough to take me on as a client, but when Galaxy *announced that it was going back to monthly publication (and, I realized, would need more material) I sent it to Fred Pohl and he wrote back saying that he'd be happy to publish it if I'd include translations of the foreign-language quotes. The following year Donald Wollheim included it in his* World's Best Science Fiction *anthology.*

In the next few years (I was working on other projects as well), I wrote five more chapters and saw all but the final chapter published in Fantasy & Science Fiction *and* Galaxy. *Meanwhile Charles Scribner's Sons had decided to develop a science fiction line under editor Norbert Slepyan, and one of the novels he signed up was* The Listeners. *He asked me once if I was going to add anything to the six chapters and I said I was planning on broadening the perspective to include some of the materials that were being gathered by the computer to aid in its recognition (and translation) of alien communications, as well as the beginnings of artificial intelligence (observant readers may watch it happen).*

The novel was published in hardcover in 1972 as "a novel" (not a science fiction novel). The same year it became a selection of the Science Fiction Book Club. The following year it was published by Signet Books and a decade later it was reprinted by Del Rey Books. It has been translated into Italian, German, Polish, Japanese, and Chinese. Three decades have passed since the novel was published, and more than a fourth of the century-long project. SETI projects on both coasts are still hard at work, trying to pick up messages from the stars, and they continue—without positive results. If the novel has any claims to vision, its insight may be found in its evaluation of human desire and persistence in the face of continuing discouragement. But we are approaching the period when the novel begins, and maybe the signal we all have been awaiting—that we are not alone—will soon be received.

If it is, if our search is rewarded, maybe The Listeners *will have played a part in it, and the book that started in 1966 in a hot August sleeping porch, in a college town in eastern Kansas, will have made a difference. After all, one of the SETI project directors told me recently that* The Listeners *had done more to turn people on to the search than any other book. My thanks go to Walter Sullivan's* We Are Not Alone. *I hope the title is right.*

THE LISTENERS

JAMES GUNN

T he voices babbled.

MacDonald heard them and knew that there was meaning in them, that they were trying to communicate and that he could understand them and respond to them if he could only concentrate on what they were saying, but he couldn't bring himself to make the effort.

"Back behind everything, lurking like a silent shadow behind the closed door, is the question we can never answer except positively: Is there anybody there?"

That was Bob Adams, eternally the devil's advocate, looking querulously at the others around the conference table. His round face was sweating, although the mahogany-paneled room was cool.

Saunders puffed hard on his pipe. "But that's true of all science. The image of the scientist eliminating all negative possibilities is ridiculous. Can't be done. So he goes ahead on faith and statistical probability."

MacDonald watched the smoke rise above Saunders' head in clouds and wisps until it wavered in the draft from the air duct, thinned out, disappeared. He could not see it, but the odor reached his nostrils. It was an aromatic blend easily distinguishable from the flatter smell of the cigarettes being smoked by Adams and some of the others.

Wasn't this their task? MacDonald wondered. To detect the thin smoke of life that drifts through the universe, to separate one trace from another, molecule by molecule, and then force them to reverse their entropic paths into their ordered and meaningful original form.

All the king's horses, and all the king's men . . . Life itself is impossible, he thought, but men exist by reversing entropy.

Down the long table cluttered with overflowing ash trays and coffee cups and doodled scratch pads, Olsen said, "We always knew it would be a long search. Not years but centuries. The computers must have sufficient data, and that means bits of information approximating the number of molecules in the universe. Let's not chicken out now."

> *"If seven maids with seven mops*
> *Swept it for half a year,*
> *Do you suppose," the Walrus said,*
> *"That they could get it clear?"*

". . . Ridiculous," someone was saying, and then Adams broke in. "It's easy for you to talk about centuries when you've been here only three years. Wait until you've been at it for ten years, like I have. Or Mac here who has been on the Project for twenty years and head of it for fifteen."

"What's the use of arguing about something we can't know anything about?" Sonnenborn said reasonably. "We have to base our position on probabilities. Shklovskii and Sagan estimated that there are more than one thousand million habitable planets in our galaxy alone. Von Hoerner estimated that one in three million have advanced societies in orbit around them; Sagan said one in one hundred thousand. Either way it's good odds that there's somebody there—three hundred or ten thousand in our segment of the universe. Our job is to listen in the right place or in the right way or understand what we hear."

Adams turned to MacDonald. "What do you say, Mac?"

"I say these basic discussions are good for us," MacDonald said mildly, "and we need to keep reminding ourselves what it is we're doing, or we'll get swallowed in a quicksand of data. I also say that it's time now to get down to the business at hand—what observations do we make tonight and the rest of the week before our next staff meeting?"

Saunders began, "I think we should make a methodical sweep of the entire galactic lens, listening on all wavelengths—"

"We've done that a hundred times," said Sonnenborn.

"Not with my new filter—"

"Tau Ceti still is the most likely," said Olsen. "Let's really give it a hearing—"

MacDonald heard Adams grumbling, half to himself, "If there is anybody, and they are trying to communicate, some amateur is going to pick it up on his ham set, decipher it on his James Bond coderule, and leave us sitting here on one hundred million dollars of equipment with egg all over our faces—"

"And don't forget," MacDonald said, "tomorrow is Saturday night and Maria and I will be expecting you all at our place at eight for the customary beer and bull. Those who have more to say can save it for then."

MacDonald did not feel as jovial as he tried to sound. He did not know whether he could stand another Saturday night session of drink and discussion and dissension about the Project. This was one of his low periods when everything seemed to pile up on top of him, and he could not get out from under, or tell anybody how he felt. No matter how he felt, the Saturday nights were good for the morale of the others.

Pues no es posible que esté continuo el arco armado
ni la condición y flaqueza humana se pueda sustenar
sin alguna lícita recreación.

Within the Project, morale was always a problem. Besides, it was good for Maria. She did not get out enough. She needed to see people. And then . . .

And then maybe Adams was right. Maybe nobody was there. Maybe nobody was sending signals because there was nobody to send signals. Maybe man was alone in the universe. Alone with God. Or alone with himself, whichever was worse.

Maybe all the money was being wasted, and the effort, and the preparation—all the intelligence and education and ideas being drained away into an endlessly empty cavern.

> *Habe nun, ach! Philosophie,*
> *Juristerei und Medizin,*
> *Und leider auch Theologie*
> *Durchaus studiert, mit heissem Bemühn.*
> *Da steh' ich nun, ich armer Tor!*
> *Und bin so klug als wie zuvor;*
> *Heisse Magister, heisse Doktor gar,*
> *Und ziehe schon an die zehen Jahr*
> *Herauf, herab und quer und krumm*
> *Meine Schüler an der Nase herum—*
> *Und sehe, dass wir nichts wissen können*

Poor fool. Why me? MacDonald thought. Could not some other lead them better, not by the nose but by his real wisdom? Perhaps all he was good for was the Saturday night parties. Perhaps it was time for a change.

He shook himself. It was the endless waiting that wore him down, the waiting for something that did not happen, and the Congressional hearings were coming up again. What could he say that he had not said before? How could he justify a project that already had gone on for nearly fifty years without results and might go on for centuries more?

"Gentlemen," he said briskly, "to our listening posts."

By the time he had settled himself at his disordered desk, Lily was standing beside him.

"Here's last night's computer analysis," she said, putting down in front of him a thin folder. "Reynolds says there's nothing there, but you always want to see it anyway. Here's the transcription of last year's Congressional hearings." A thick binder went on top of the folder. "The correspondence and the actual appropriation measure are in another file if you want them."

MacDonald shook his head.

"There's a form letter from NASA establishing the ground rules for this year's budget and a personal letter from Ted Wartinian saying that conditions are really tight and some cuts look inevitable. In fact, he says there's a possibility the Project might be scrubbed."

Lily glanced at him. "Not a chance," MacDonald said confidently.

"There's a few applications for employment. Not as many as we used to get. The letters from school children I answered myself. And there's the usual nut letters from people who've been receiving messages from outer space, and from one who's had a ride in a UFO. That's what he called it—not a saucer or anything. A feature writer wants to interview you and some others for an article on the Project. I think he's with us. And another one who sounds as if he wants to do an exposé."

MacDonald listened patiently. Lily was a wonder. She could handle everything in the office as well as he could. In fact, things might run smoother if he were not around to take up her time.

"They've both sent some questions for you to answer. And Joe wants to talk to you."

"Joe?"

"One of the janitors."

"What does he want?" They couldn't afford to lose a janitor. Good janitors were harder to find than astronomers, harder
even than electronicians.

"He says he has to talk to you, but I've heard from some of
the lunchroom staff that he's been complaining about getting
messages on his—on his—"

"Yes?"

"On his false teeth."

MacDonald sighed. "Pacify him somehow, will you, Lily?
If I talk to him we might lose a janitor."

"I'll do my best. And Mrs. MacDonald called. Said it
wasn't important and you needn't call back."

"Call her," MacDonald said. "And, Lily—you're coming to
the party tomorrow night, aren't you?"

"What would I be doing at a party with all the brains?"

"We want you to come. Maria asked particularly. It isn't all
shop talk, you know. And there are never enough women. You
might strike it off with one of the young bachelors."

"At my age, Mr. MacDonald? You're just trying to get rid
of me."

"Never."

"I'll get Mrs. MacDonald." Lily turned at the door. "I'll
think about the party."

MacDonald shuffled through the papers. Down at the bottom was the only one he was interested in—the computer analysis of last night's listening. But he kept it there, on the bottom, as
a reward for going through the others. Ted was really worried.
Move over, Ted. And then the writers. He supposed he would
have to work them in somehow. At least it was part of the fallout
to locating the Project in Puerto Rico. Nobody just dropped in.
And the questions. Two of them caught his attention.

How did you come to be named Project Director? That
was the friendly one. What are your qualifications to be Director? That was the other. How would he answer them? Could
he answer them at all?

Finally he reached the computer analysis, and it was just like those for the rest of the week, and the week before that, and the months and the years before that. No significant correlations. Noise. There were a few peaks of reception—at the twenty-one-centimeter line, for instance—but these were merely concentrated noise. Radiating clouds of hydrogen, as the Little Ear functioned like an ordinary radio telescope.

At least the Project showed some results. It was feeding star survey data tapes into the international pool. Fallout. Of a process that had no other product except negatives.

Maybe the equipment wasn't sensitive enough. Maybe. They could beef it up some more. At least it might be a successful ploy with the Committee, some progress to present, if only in the hardware. You don't stand still. You spend more money or they cut you back—or off.

Note: Saunders—plans to increase sensitivity.

Maybe the equipment wasn't discriminating enough. But they had used up a generation of ingenuity canceling out background noise, and in its occasional checks the Big Ear indicated that they were doing adequately on terrestrial noise, at least.

Note: Adams—new discrimination gimmick.

Maybe the computer wasn't recognizing a signal when it had one fed into it. Perhaps it wasn't sophisticated enough to perceive certain subtle relationships. . . . And yet sophisticated codes had been broken in seconds. And the Project was asking it to distinguish only where a signal existed, whether the reception was random noise or had some element of the unrandom. At this level it wasn't even being asked to note the influence of consciousness.

Note: ask computer—is it missing something? Ridiculous? Ask Olsen.

Maybe they shouldn't be searching the radio spectrum at all. Maybe radio was a peculiarity of man's civilization. Maybe others had never had it or had passed it by and now had more sophisticated means of communication. Lasers, for instance.

Telepathy, or what might pass for it with man. Maybe gamma rays, as Morrison suggested years before Ozma.

Well, maybe. But if it were so, somebody else would have to listen for those. He had neither the equipment nor the background nor the working lifetime left to tackle something new.

And maybe Adams was right.

He buzzed Lily. "Have you reached Mrs. MacDonald?"

"The telephone hasn't answered—"

Unreasoned panic . . .

"—Oh, here she is now, Mr. MacDonald, Mrs. MacDonald."

"Hello, darling, I was alarmed when you didn't answer."

That had been foolish, he thought, and even more foolish to mention it.

Her voice was sleepy. "I must have been dozing." Even drowsy, it was an exciting voice, gentle, a little husky, that speeded MacDonald's pulse. "What did you want?"

"You called me," MacDonald said.

"Did I? I've forgotten."

"Glad you're resting. You didn't sleep well last night."

"I took some pills."

"How many?"

"Just the two you left out."

"Good girl. I'll see you in a couple of hours. Go back to sleep. Sorry I woke you."

But her voice wasn't sleepy anymore. "You won't have to go back tonight, will you? We'll have the evening together?"

"We'll see," he promised.

But he knew he would have to return.

MacDonald paused outside the long, low concrete building that housed the offices and laboratories and computers. It was twilight. The sun had descended below the green hills, but orange and purpling wisps of cirrus trailed down the western sky.

Between MacDonald and the sky was a giant dish held aloft by skeletal metal fingers—held high as if to catch the stardust that drifted down at night from the Milky Way.

> Go and catch a falling star,
> Get with child a mandrake root,
> Tell me where all past years are,
> Or who cleft the Devil's foot;
> Teach me to hear mermaids singing,
> Or to keep off envy's stinging,
> And find
> What wind
> Serves to advance an honest mind.

Then the dish began to turn, noiselessly, incredibly, and to tip. And it was not a dish anymore but an ear, a listening ear cupped by the surrounding hills to overhear the whispering universe.

Perhaps this was what kept them at their jobs, MacDonald thought. In spite of all disappointments, in spite of all vain efforts, perhaps it was this massive machinery, as sensitive as their fingertips, that kept them struggling with the unfathomable. When they grew weary at their electronic listening posts, when their eyes grew dim with looking at unrevealing dials and studying uneventful graphs, they could step outside their concrete cells and renew their dull spirits in communion with the giant mechanism they commanded, the silent, sensing instrument in which the smallest packets of energy, the smallest waves of matter, were detected in their headlong, eternal flight across the universe. It was the stethoscope with which they took the pulse of the all and noted the birth and death of stars, the probe with which, here on an insignificant planet of an undistinguished star on the edge of its galaxy, they explored the infinite.

Or perhaps it was not just the reality but the imagery, like poetry, that soothed their doubting souls, the bowl held up to catch Donne's falling star, the ear cocked to hear the shout from the other side of the universe that faded to an indistinguishable murmur by the time it reached them. And one thousand miles above them was the giant, five-mile-in-diameter network, the largest radio telescope ever built, that men had cast into the heavens to catch the stars.

If they had the Big Ear for more than an occasional reference check, MacDonald thought practically, then they might get some results. But he knew the radio astronomers would never relinquish time to the frivolity of listening for signals that never came. It was only because of the Big Ear that the Project had inherited the Little Ear. There had been talk recently about a larger net, twenty miles in diameter. Perhaps when it was done, if it were done, the Project might inherit time on the Big Ear.

If they could endure until then, MacDonald thought, if they could steer their fragile vessel of faith between the Scylla of self-doubt and the Charybdis of Congressional appropriations.

The images were not all favorable. There were others that went boomp in the night. There was the image, for instance, of man listening, listening, listening to the silent stars, listening for an eternity, listening for signals that would never come, because—the ultimate horror—man was alone in the universe, a cosmic accident of self-awareness that needed and would never receive the comfort of companionship. To be alone, to be all alone, would be like being all alone on earth, with no one to talk to, ever—like being alone inside a bone prison, with no way to get out, no way to communicate with anyone outside, no way to know if anyone was outside. . . .

Perhaps that, in the end, was what kept them going—to stave off the terrors of the night. While they listened there was hope; to give up now would be to admit final defeat. Some said they should never have started; then they never would have the problem of surrender. Some of the new religions said that. The Solitarians, for one. There is nobody there; we are the one, the only created intelligence in the universe. Let us glory in our uniqueness. But the older religions encouraged the Project to continue. Why would God have created the myriads of other stars and other planets if He had not intended them for living creatures; why should man only be created in His image? Let us find out, they said. Let us communicate with them. What revelations have they had? What saviors have redeemed them?

> These are the words which I spake unto you, while I was yet with you, that all things must be fulfilled, which were written in the law of Moses, and in the prophets, and in the psalms, concerning me. . . . Thus it is written, and thus it behooved Christ to suffer, and to rise from the dead the third day: and that repentance and remission of sins should be preached in his name among all nations, beginning at Jerusalem. And we are witnesses of these things.
>
> And, behold, I send the promise of my Father upon you: but tarry ye in the city of Jerusalem, until ye be endued with power from on high.

Dusk had turned to night. The sky had turned to black. The stars had been born again. The listening had begun. MacDonald made his way to his car in the parking lot behind the building, coasted until he was behind the hill, and turned on the motor for the long drive home.

The hacienda was dark. It had that empty feeling about it that MacDonald knew so well, the feeling it had for him when Maria went to visit friends in Mexico City. But it was not empty now. Maria was here.

He opened the door and flicked on the hall light. "Maria?" He walked down the tiled hall, not too fast, not too slow.

"¿Querida?" He turned on the living room light as he passed. He continued down the hall, past the dining room, the guest room, the study, the kitchen. He reached the dark doorway to the bedroom. "Maria Chavez?"

He turned on the bedroom light, low. She was asleep, her face peaceful, her dark hair scattered across the pillow. She lay on her side, her legs drawn up under the covers.

> Men che dramma
> Di sangue m'e rimaso, che no tremi;
> Conosco i segni dell'antica fiamma.

MacDonald looked down at her, comparing her features one by one with those he had fixed in his memory.

Even now, with those dark, expressive eyes closed, she was the most beautiful woman he had ever seen. What glories they had known! He renewed his spirit in the warmth of his remembrances, recalling moments with loving details.

> C'estce dequoy j'ay le plus de peur que la peur.

He sat down upon the edge of the bed and leaned over to kiss her upon the cheek and then upon her upthrust shoulder where the gown had slipped down. She did not waken. He shook her shoulder gently. "Maria!" She turned upon her back, straightening. She sighed, and her eyes came open, staring blankly. "It is Robby," MacDonald said, dropping unconsciously into a faint brogue.

Her eyes came alive and her lips smiled sleepily. "Robby. You're home."

"Yo te amo," he murmured, and kissed her. As he pulled himself away, he said, "I'll start dinner. Wake up and get dressed. I'll see you in half an hour. Or sooner."

"Sooner," she said.

He turned and went to the kitchen. There was romaine lettuce in the refrigerator, and as he rummaged further, some thin slices of veal. He prepared Caesar salad and veal scaloppine, doing it all quickly, expertly. He liked to cook. The salad was ready, and the lemon juice, tarragon, white wine, and a minute later, the beef bouillon had been added to the browned veal when Maria appeared.

She stood in the doorway, slim, lithe, lovely, and sniffed the air. "I smell something delicious."

It was a joke. When Maria cooked, she cooked Mexican, something peppery that burned all the way into the stomach and lay there like a banked furnace. When MacDonald cooked, it was something exotic—French, perhaps, or Italian, or Chinese. But whoever cooked, the other had to appreciate it or take over all the cooking for a week.

MacDonald filled their wine glasses. "A la très-bonne, à la très-belle," he said, "qui fait ma joie et ma santé."

"To the Project," Maria said. "May there be a signal received tonight."

MacDonald shook his head. One should not mention what one desires too much. "Tonight there is only us."

Afterward there were only the two of them, as there had been now for twenty years. And she was as alive and as urgent, as filled with love and laughter, as when they first had been together.

At last the urgency was replaced by a vast ease and contentment in which for a time the thought of the Project faded into something remote which one day he would return to and finish. "Maria," he said.

"Robby?"

"Yo te amo, corazón."

"Yo te amo, Robby."

Gradually then, as he waited beside her for her breathing to slow, the Project returned. When he thought she was asleep, he got up and began to dress in the dark.

"Robby?" Her voice was awake and frightened.

"¿Querida?"

"You are going again?"

"I didn't want to wake you."

"Do you have to go?"

"It's my job."

"Just this once. Stay with me tonight."

He turned on the light. In the dimness he could see that her face was concerned but not hysterical. "Rast ich, so rost ich. Besides, I would feel ashamed."

"I understand. Go, then. Come home soon."

He put out two pills on the little shelf in the bathroom and put the others away again.

The headquarters building was busiest at night when the radio noise of the sun was least and listening to the stars was best. Girls bustled down the halls with coffee pots, and men stood near the water fountain, talking earnestly.

MacDonald went into the control room. Adams was at the control panel; Montaleone was the technician. Adams looked up, pointed to his earphones with a gesture of futility, and shrugged. MacDonald nodded at him, nodded at Montaleone, and glanced at the graph. It looked random to him.

Adams leaned past him to point out a couple of peaks. "These might be something." He had removed the earphones.

"Odds," MacDonald said.

"Suppose you're right. The computer hasn't sounded any alarms."

"After a few years of looking at these things, you get the feel of them. You begin to think like a computer."

"Or you get oppressed by failure."

"There's that."

The room was shiny and efficient, glass and metal and plastic, all smooth and sterile; and it smelled like electricity. Mac-

Donald knew that electricity had no smell, but that was the way he thought of it. Perhaps it was the ozone that smelled or warm insulation or oil. Whatever it was, it wasn't worth the time to find out, and MacDonald didn't really want to know. He would rather think of it as the smell of electricity. Perhaps that was why he was a failure as a scientist. "A scientist is a man who wants to know why," his teachers always had told him.

MacDonald leaned over the control panel and flicked a switch. A thin, hissing noise filled the room. It was something like air escaping from an inner tube—a susurration of surreptitious sibilants from subterranean sessions of seething serpents.

He turned a knob and the sound became what someone— Tennyson—had called "the murmuring of innumerable bees." Again, and it became Matthew Arnold's

> . . . *melancholy, long withdrawing roar*
> *Retreating, to the breath*
> *Of the night wind, down the vast edges drear*
> *And naked shingles of the world.*

He turned the knob once more, and the sound was a babble of distant voices, some shouting, some screaming, some conversing calmly, some whispering—all of them trying beyond desperation to communicate, and everything just below the level of intelligibility. If he closed his eyes, MacDonald could almost see their faces, pressed against a distant screen, distorted with the awful effort to make themselves heard and understood.

But they all insisted on speaking at once. MacDonald wanted to shout at them. "Silence, everybody! All but you—there, with the purple antenna. One at a time and we'll listen to all of you if it takes a hundred years or a hundred lifetimes."

"Sometimes," Adams said, "I think it was a mistake to put in the speaker system. You begin to anthropomorphize. After a while you begin to hear things. Sometimes you even get messages. I don't listen to the voices anymore. I used to wake up in the night with someone whispering to me. I was just on the verge of getting the message that would solve everything, and I would wake up." He flicked off the switch.

"Maybe somebody will get the message," MacDonald said. "That's what the audio frequency translation is intended to do. To keep the attention focused. It can mesmerize and it can torment, but these are the conditions out of which spring inspiration."

"Also madness," Adams said. "You've got to be able to continue."

"Yes." MacDonald picked up the earphones Adams had put down and held one of them to his ear.

"Tico-tico, tico-tico," it sang. "They're listening in Puerto Rico. Listening for words that never come. Tico-tico, tico-tico. They're listening in Puerto Rico. Can it be the stars are stricken dumb?"

MacDonald put the earphones down and smiled. "Maybe there's inspiration in that, too."

"At least it takes my mind off the futility."

"Maybe off the job, too? Do you really want to find anyone out there?"

"Why else would I be here? But there are times when I wonder if we would be better off not knowing."

"We all think that sometimes," MacDonald said.

In his office he attacked the stack of papers and letters again. When he had worked his way to the bottom, he sighed and got up, stretching. He wondered if he would feel better, less frustrated, less uncertain, if he were working on the Problem instead of just working so somebody else could work on the Problem. But somebody had to do it. Somebody had to keep the Project going, personnel coming in, funds in the bank, bills paid, feathers smoothed.

Maybe it was more important that he do all the dirty little

work in the office. Of course it was routine. Of course Lily could do it as well as he. But it was important that he do it, that there be somebody in charge who believed in the Project—or who never let his doubts be known.

Like the Little Ear, he was a symbol—and it is by symbols men live—or refuse to let their despair overwhelm them.

The janitor was waiting for him in the outer office.

"Can I see you, Mr. MacDonald?" the janitor said.

"Of course, Joe," MacDonald said, locking the door of his office carefully behind him. "What is it?"

"It's my teeth, sir." The old man got to his feet and with a deft movement of his tongue and mouth dropped his teeth into his hand.

MacDonald stared at them with a twinge of revulsion. There was nothing wrong with them. They were a carefully constructed pair of false teeth, but they looked too real. Mac-Donald always had shuddered away from those things which seemed to be what they were not, as if there were some treachery in them.

"They talk to me, Mr. MacDonald," the janitor mumbled, staring at the teeth in his hand with what seemed like suspicion. "In the glass beside my bed at night, they whisper to me. About things far off, like. Messages like."

MacDonald stared at the janitor. It was a strange word for the old man to use, and hard to say without teeth. Still, the word had been "messages." But why should it be strange? He could have picked it up around the offices or the laboratories. It would be odd, indeed, if he had not picked up something about what was going on. Of course: messages.

"I've heard of that sort of thing happening," MacDonald said. "False teeth accidentally constructed into a kind of crystal set, that pick up radio waves. Particularly near a powerful station. And we have a lot of stray frequencies floating around, what with the antennas and all. Tell you what, Joe. We'll make an appointment with the Project dentist to fix your teeth so that they don't bother you. Any small alteration should do it."

"Thank you, Mr. MacDonald," the old man said. He fitted his teeth back into his mouth. "You're a great man, Mr. Mac-Donald."

MacDonald drove the ten dark miles to the hacienda with a vague feeling of unease, as if he had done something during the day or left something undone that should have been other-wise.

But the house was dark when he drove up in front, not empty-dark as it had seemed to him a few hours before, but friendly-dark. Maria was asleep, breathing peacefully.

The house was brilliant with lighted windows that cast long fingers into the night, probing the dark hills, and the sound of many voices stirred echoes until the countryside itself seemed alive.

"Come in, Lily," MacDonald said at the door, and was re-minded of a winter scene when a Lily had met the gentlemen at the door and helped them off with their overcoats. But that was another Lily and another occasion and another place and somebody else's imagination. "I'm glad you decided to come."

He had a can of beer in his hand, and he waved it in the general direction of the major center of noisemaking. "There's beer in the living room and something more potent in the study—190-proof grain alcohol, to be precise. Be careful with that. It will sneak up on you. But—nunc est bibendum!"

"Where's Mrs. MacDonald?" Lily asked.

"Back there, somewhere." MacDonald waved again. "The men, and a few brave women, are in the study. The women, and a few brave men, are in the living room. The kitchen is common territory. Take your choice."

"I really shouldn't have come," Lily said. "I offered to spell Mr. Saunders in the control room, but he said I hadn't been checked out. It isn't as if the computer couldn't handle it all alone, and I know enough to call somebody if anything unexpected should happen."

"Shall I tell you something, Lily?" MacDonald said. "The computer could do it alone. And you and the computer could do it better than any of us, including me. But if the men ever feel that they are unnecessary, they would feel more useless than ever. They would give up. And they mustn't do that."

"Oh, Mac!" Lily said.

"They mustn't do that. Because one of them is going to come up with the inspiration that solves it all. Not me. One of them. We'll send somebody to relieve Charley before the evening is over."

Wer immer strebens sich bemüht,
Den können wir erlösen.

Lily sighed. "Okay, boss."

"And enjoy yourself!"

"Okay, boss, okay."

"Find a man, Lily," MacDonald muttered. And then he, too, turned toward the living room, for Lily had been the last who might come.

He listened for a moment at the doorway, sipping slowly from the warming can.

"—work more on gamma rays—"

"Who's got the money to build a generator? Since nobody's built one yet, we don't even know what it might cost."

"—gamma-ray sources should be a million times more rare than radio sources at twenty-one centimeters—"

"That's what Cocconi said nearly fifty years ago. The same arguments. Always the same arguments."

"If they're right, they're right."

"But the hydrogen-emission line is so uniquely logical. As

Morrison said to Cocconi—and Cocconi, if you remember, agreed—it represents a logical, prearranged rendezvous point. 'A unique, objective standard of frequency, which must be known to every observer of the universe,' was the way they put it."

"—but the noise level—"

MacDonald smiled and moved on to the kitchen for a cold can of beer.

"—Bracewell's 'automated messengers'?" a voice asked querulously.

"What about them?"

"Why aren't we looking for them?"

"The point of Bracewell's messengers is that they make themselves known to us!"

"Maybe there's something wrong with ours. After a few million years in orbit—"

"—laser beams make more sense."

"And get lost in all that star shine?"

"As Schwartz and Townes pointed out, all you have to do is select a wavelength of light that is absorbed by stellar atmospheres. Put a narrow laser beam in the center of one of the calcium absorption lines—"

In the study they were talking about quantum noise.

"Quantum noise favors low frequencies."

"But the noise itself sets a lower limit on those frequencies."

"Drake calculated the most favorable frequencies, considering the noise level, lie between 3.2 and 8.1 centimeters."

"Drake! Drake! What did he know? We've had nearly fifty years' experience on him. Fifty years of technological advance. Fifty years ago we could send radio messages one thousand light-years and laser signals ten light-years. Today those figures are ten thousand and five hundred at least."

"What if nobody's there?" Adams said gloomily.

Ich bin der Geist der stets vernient.

"Short-pulse it, like Oliver suggested. One hundred million billion watts in a ten-billionth of a second would smear across the entire radio spectrum. Here, Mac, fill this, will you?"

And MacDonald wandered away through the clustering guests toward the bar.

"And I told Charley," said a woman to two other women in the corner, "if I had a dime for every dirty diaper I've changed, I sure wouldn't be sitting here in Puerto Rico—"

"—neutrinos," said somebody.

"Nuts," said somebody else, as MacDonald poured grain alcohol carefully into the glass and filled it with orange juice, "the only really logical medium is Q waves."

"I know—the waves we haven't discovered yet but are going to discover about ten years from now. Only here it is nearly fifty years after Morrison suggested it, and we still haven't discovered them."

MacDonald wended his way back across the room.

"It's the night work that gets me," said someone's wife. "The kids up all day, and then he wants me there to greet him when he gets home at dawn. Brother!"

"Or what if everybody's listening?" Adams said gloomily. "Maybe everybody's sitting there, listening, just the way we are, because it's so much cheaper than sending."

"Here you are," MacDonald said.

"But don't you suppose somebody would have thought of that by this time and begun to send?"

"Double-think it all the way through and figure what just occurred to you would have occurred to everybody else, so you might as well listen. Think about it—everybody sitting around, listening. If there is anybody. Either way it makes the skin creep."

"All right, then, we ought to send something."

"What would you send?"

"I'd have to think about it. Prime numbers, maybe."

"Think some more. What if a civilization weren't mathematical?"

"Idiot! How would they build an antenna?"

"Maybe they'd rule-of-thumb it, like a ham. Or maybe they have built-in antennae."

"And maybe you have built-in antennae and don't know it."

MacDonald's can of beer was empty. He wandered back toward the kitchen again.

"—insist on equal time with the Big Ear. Even if nobody's sending we could pick up the normal electronic commerce of a civilization tens of light-years away. The problem would be deciphering, not hearing."

"They're picking it up now, when they're studying the relatively close systems. Ask for a tape and work out your program."

"All right, I will. Just give me a chance to work up a request—"

MacDonald found himself beside Maria. He put his arm around her waist and pulled her close. "All right?" he said.

"All right."

Her face was tired, though, MacDonald thought. He dreaded the notion that she might be growing older, that she was entering middle age. He could face it for himself. He could feel the years piling up inside his bones. He still thought of himself, inside, as twenty, but he knew that he was forty-seven, and mostly he was glad that he had found happiness and love and peace and serenity. He even was willing to pay the price in youthful exuberance and belief in his personal immortality. But not Maria!

> *Nel mezzo del cammin di nostra vita*
> *Mi ritrovai per una selva oscura,*
> *Che la diritta via era smarrita.*

"Sure?"

She nodded.

He leaned close to her ear. "I wish it was just the two of us, as usual."

"I, too."

"I'm going to leave in a little while—"

"Must you?"

"I must relieve Saunders. He's on duty. Give him an opportunity to celebrate a little with the others."

"Can't you send somebody else?"

"Who?" MacDonald gestured with good-humored futility at all the clusters of people held together by bonds of ordered sounds shared consecutively. "It's a good party. No one will miss me."

"I will."

"Of course, querida."

"You are their mother, father, priest, all in one," Maria said. "You worry about them too much."

"I must keep them together. What else am I good for?"

"For much more."

MacDonald hugged her with one arm.

"Look at Mac and Maria, will you?" said someone who was having trouble with his consonants. "What goddamned devotion!"

MacDonald smiled and suffered himself to be pounded on the back while he protected Maria in front of him. "I'll see you later," he said.

As he passed the living room someone was saying, "Like Edie said, we ought to look at the long-chain molecules in carbonaceous chondrites. No telling how far they've traveled—or been sent—or what messages might be coded in the molecules."

He closed the front door behind him, and the noise dropped to a roar and then a mutter. He stopped for a moment at the door of the car and looked up at the sky.

E quindi uscimmo a riveder le stelle.

The noise from the hacienda reminded him of something—the speakers in the control room. All those voices talking, talking, talking, and from here he could not understand a thing.

Somewhere there was an idea if he could only concentrate on it hard enough. But he had drunk one beer too many—or perhaps one too few.

After the long hours of listening to the voices, MacDonald always felt a little crazy, but tonight it was worse than usual. Perhaps it was all the conversation before, or the beers, or something else—some deeper concern that would not surface.

Tico-tico, tico-tico . . .

Even if they could pick up a message, they still would likely be dead and gone before any exchange could take place even with the nearest likely star. What kind of mad dedication could sustain such perseverance?

They're listening in Puerto Rico. . . .

Religion could. At least once it did, during the era of cathedral building in Europe, the cathedrals that took centuries to build.

"What are you doing, fellow?"

"I'm working for ten francs a day."

"And what are you doing?"

"I'm laying stone."

"And you—what are you doing?"

"I am building a cathedral."

They were building cathedrals, most of them. Most of them had that religious mania about their mission that would sustain them through a lifetime of labors in which no progress could be seen.

Listening for words that never come . . .

The mere layers of stone and those who worked for pay alone eliminated themselves in time and left only those who kept alive in themselves the concept, the dream.

But they had to be a little mad to begin with.

Can it be the stars are stricken dumb?

Tonight he had heard the voices nearly all night long. They kept trying to tell him something, something urgent, something he should do, but he could not quite make out the words. There was only the babble of distant voices, urgent and unintelligible.

Tico-tico, tico-tic . . .

He had wanted to shout "Shut up!" to the universe. "One at a time!" "You first!" But of course there was no way to do that. Or had he tried? Had he shouted?

They're listening with ears this big!

Had he dozed at the console with the voices mumbling in his ears, or had he only thought he dozed? Or had he only dreamed he waked? Or dreamed he dreamed?

Listening for thoughts just like their own.

There was madness to it all, but perhaps it was a divine madness, a creative madness. And is not that madness that which sustains man in his terrible self-knowledge, the driving madness which demands reason of a casual universe, the awful aloneness which seeks among the stars for companionship?

Can it be that we are all alone?

The ringing of the telephone half penetrated through the mists of mesmerization. He picked up the handset, half expecting it would be the universe calling, perhaps with a clipped British accent, "Hello there, Man. Hello. Hello. I say, we seem to have a bad connection, what? Just wanted you to know that we're here. Are you there? Are you listening? Message on the way. May not get there for a couple of centuries. Do be around to answer, will you? That's a good being. Righto. . . ."

Only it wasn't. It was the familiar American voice of Charley Saunders saying, "Mac, there's been an accident. Olsen is on his way to relieve you, but I think you'd better leave now. It's Maria."

Leave it. Leave it all. What does it matter? But leave the controls on automatic; the computer can take care of it all. Maria! Get in the car. Start it. Don't fumble! That's it. Go. Go. Car passing. Must be Olsen. No matter.

What kind of accident? Why didn't I ask? What does it matter what kind of accident? Maria. Nothing could have happened. Nothing serious. Not with all those people around. Nil desperandum. And yet—why did Charley call if it was not serious? Must be serious. I must be prepared for something bad, something that will shake the world, that will tear my insides.

I must not break up in front of them. Why not? Why must I appear infallible? Why must I always be cheerful, imperturbable, my faith unshaken? Why me? If there is something bad, if something impossibly bad has happened to Maria, what will matter? Ever? Why didn't I ask Charley what it was? Why? The bad can wait; it will get no worse for being unknown.

What does the universe care for my agony? I am nothing. My feelings are nothing to anyone but me. My only possible meaning to the universe is the Project. Only this slim potential links me with eternity. My love and my agony are me, but the significance of my life or death are the Project.

By the time he reached the hacienda, MacDonald was breathing evenly. His emotions were under control. Dawn had grayed the eastern sky. It was a customary hour for Project personnel to be returning home.

Saunders met him at the door. "Dr. Lessenden is here. He's with Maria."

The odor of stale smoke and the memory of babble still lingered in the air, but someone had been busy. The party remains had been cleaned up. No doubt they all had pitched in. They were good people.

"Betty found her in the bathroom off your bedroom. She wouldn't have been there except the others were occupied. I blame myself. I shouldn't have let you relieve me. Maybe if you had been here—But I knew you wanted it that way."

"No one's to blame. She was alone a great deal," MacDonald said. "What happened?"

"Didn't I tell you? Her wrists. Slashed with a razor. Both of them. Betty found her in the bathtub. Like pink lemonade, she said."

A fist tightened inside MacDonald's gut and then slowly relaxed. Yes, it had been that. He had known it, hadn't he? He had known it would happen ever since the sleeping pills, even though he had kept telling himself, as she had told him, that the overdose had been an accident.

Or had he known? He knew only that Saunders' news had been no surprise.

Then they were at the bedroom door, and Maria was lying under a blanket on the bed, scarcely making it mound over her body, and her arms were on top of the blankets, palms up, bandages like white paint across the olive perfection of her arms, now, MacDonald reminded himself, no longer perfection but marred with ugly red lips that spoke to him of hidden misery and untold sorrow and a life that was a lie. . . .

Dr. Lessenden looked up, sweat trickling down from his hairline. "The bleeding is stopped, but she's lost a good deal of blood. I've got to take her to the hospital for a transfusion. The ambulance should be here any minute."

MacDonald looked at Maria's face. It was paler than he had ever seen it. It looked almost waxen, as if it were already arranged for all time on a satin pillow. "Her chances are fifty-fifty," Lessenden said in answer to his unspoken question.

And then the attendants brushed their way past him with their litter.

"Betty found this on her dressing table," Saunders said. He handed MacDonald a slip of paper folded once.

MacDonald unfolded it:

Je m'en vay chercher un grand Peut=être.

Everyone was surprised to see MacDonald at the office.
They did not say anything, and he did not volunteer the information that he could not bear to sit at home, among the remembrances, and wait for word to come. But they asked him
about Maria, and he said, "Dr. Lessenden is hopeful. She's still
unconscious. Apparently will be for some time. The doctor
said I might as well wait here as at the hospital. I think I made
them nervous. They're hopeful. Maria's still unconscious. . . ."

O lente, lente currite, noctis equi!

The stars move still, time runs, the clock will strike. . . .
Finally MacDonald was alone. He pulled out paper and
pencil and worked for a long time on the statement, and then
he balled it up and threw it into the wastebasket, scribbled a
single sentence on another sheet of paper, and called Lily.

"Send this!"

She glanced at it. "No, Mac."

"Send it!"

"But—"

"It's not an impulse. I've thought it over carefully. Send it."

Slowly she left, holding the piece of paper gingerly in her
fingertips. MacDonald pushed the papers around on his desk,
waiting for the telephone to ring. But without knocking, un-
announced, Saunders came through the door first.

"You can't do this, Mac," Saunders said.

MacDonald sighed. "Lily told you. I would fire that girl if
she weren't so loyal."

"Of course she told me. This isn't just you. It affects the
whole Project."

"That's what I'm thinking about."

"I think I know what you're going through, Mac—" Saunders stopped. "No, of course I don't know what you're going

through. It must be hell. But don't desert us. Think of the Project!"

"That's what I'm thinking about. I'm a failure, Charley. Everything I touch—ashes."

"You're the best of us."

"A poor linguist? An indifferent engineer? I have no qualifications for this job, Charley. You need someone with ideas to head the Project, someone dynamic, someone who can lead, someone with—charisma."

A few minutes later he went over it all again with Olsen. When he came to the qualifications part, all Olsen could say was, "You give a good party, Mac."

It was Adams, the skeptic, who affected him most. "Mac, you're what I believe in instead of God."

Sonnenborn said, "You are the Project. If you go, it all falls apart. It's over."

"It seems like it, always, but it never happens to those things that have life in them. The Project was here before I came. It will be here after I leave. It must be longer lived than any of us, because we are for the years and it is for the centuries."

After Sonnenborn, MacDonald told Lily wearily, "No more, Lily."

None of them had had the courage to mention Maria, but MacDonald considered that failure, too. She had tried to communicate with him a month ago when she took the pills, and he had been unable to understand. How could he riddle the stars when he couldn't even understand those closest to him? Now he had to pay.

What would Maria want? He knew what she wanted, but if she lived, he could not let her pay that price. Too long she had been there when he wanted her, waiting like a doll put away on a shelf for him to return and take her down, so that he could have the strength to continue.

And somehow the agony had built up inside her, the

dreadful progress of the years, most dread of all to a beautiful woman growing old, alone, too much alone. He had been selfish. He had kept her to himself. He had not wanted children to mar the perfection of their being together.

Perfection for him; less than that for her.

Perhaps it was not too late for them if she lived. And if she died—he would not have the heart to go on with work to which, he knew now, he could contribute nothing.

And finally the call came. "She's going to be all right, Mac," Lessenden said. And after a moment, "Mac, I said—"

"I heard."

"She wants to see you."

"I'll be there."

"She said to give you a message. 'Tell Robby I've been a little crazy in the head. I'll be better now. That "great perhaps" looks too certain from here. And tell him not to be crazy in the head too.'"

MacDonald put down the telephone and walked through the doorway and through the outer office, a feeling in his chest as if it were going to burst. "She's going to be all right," he threw over his shoulder at Lily.

"Oh, Mac—"

In the hall, Joe the janitor stopped him. "Mr. MacDonald—"

MacDonald stopped. "Been to the dentist yet, Joe?"

"No, sir, not yet, but it's not—"

"Don't go. I'd like to put a tape recorder beside your bed for a while, Joe. Who knows?"

"Thank you, sir. But it's—They say you're leaving, Mr. MacDonald."

"Somebody else will do it."

"You don't understand. Don't go, Mr. MacDonald!"

"Why not, Joe?"

"You're the one who cares."

MacDonald had been about to move on, but that stopped him.

Ful wys is he that can himselven knowe!

He turned and went back to the office. "Have you got that sheet of paper, Lily?"

"Yes, sir."

"Have you sent it?"

"No, sir."

"Bad girl. Give it to me."

He read the sentence on the paper once more: I have great confidence in the goals and ultimate success of the Project, but for personal reasons I must submit my resignation.

He studied it for a moment.

A dwarf standing on the shoulder of a giant may see farther than the giant himself.

And he tore it up.

HOWL'S MOVING CASTLE

Instead of reprinting the script of the motion picture, we asked Diana Wynne Jones, author of the original novel, *Howl's Moving Castle*, to share her experience of seeing her novel turn into a very successful movie.

In her own words:

Diana Wynne Jones was born in London shortly before the outbreak of World War II, whereupon the world went mad and frightening, which accounts for her writing the kind of books she does. She was evacuated first to Wales and then to a large house in the English Lake District belonging to the secretary of John Ruskin. There she managed (age five) to rub out a large pile of Ruskin's flower drawings and had encounters, neither of them pleasant, with the writers Arthur Ransome and Beatrix Potter. Having found that writers were real people, she decided to be one herself and, despite serious dyslexia, began writing from the age of eight onwards.

After a lunatic sojourn in York, her family moved to a small town in Essex, where there were two self-confessed witches and the rest of the inhabitants did folk dancing, threw pots, did hand weaving, or were just plain mad. She went to school in the neighboring town of Saffron Walden and then went up to Oxford in 1953, where she attended the lectures of both C. S. Lewis and J. R. R. Tolkien.

After that she married the medievalist J. A. Burrow and went on living in Oxford, where her three sons were born.

As soon as they were at school, she started to write in earnest and went on writing when the family moved to Bristol, despite the fact that her books showed an alarming tendency to come true—for instance, after writing The Lives of Christopher Chant, *she found she had been walking around with a broken neck. She has now published over forty books. She still lives in Bristol with her husband and her cat. She has five grandchildren, most of whom read her books.*

BOOK TO FILM

DIANA WYNNE JONES

I t was always at a remove, except for rare instances. Late in the last century, Studio Ghibli suddenly negotiated with my agent for permission to make an animated film of *Howl's Moving Castle*. The first I heard of it was through the grapevine, to which I was connected by a very thin tendril, and I didn't really believe it. I had been a devoted admirer of Miyazaki for years before that. I had watched pirated versions of his movies at SF conventions whenever I could and I knew the man was a genius. So it seemed too good to be true that this mighty man actually wanted to use my book.

But it was true. Presently I signed a huge contract that said Miyazaki could have both characters and plot to do what he liked with and—basically—I was to keep out of it. I gathered, again through my tendril of grapevine, that Miyazaki had had endless problems with the writer of *Kiki's Delivery Service* and didn't want to repeat them with me. So I was very careful not even to ask things for the next completely silent year.

Then, again suddenly, I was told that a team from Studio Ghibli would be with me for tea next week. I made a cake, a British cake. Japanese cakes are kind of pink with baked beans embedded in them and not many Japanese like them, but I knew they liked our kind of cake better. This cake, as it turned out, was the main success of a very strange meeting.

They arrived, preceded by a formidable Japanese courier, who looked like a kind of Scottish toreador in a wide hat and wore two watches, one gold, one platinum. The rest were normal. Among them were the producer, the director, the interpreter, the script writer—who had a bad cold and looked as if she was hating every minute—and, I think, a designer. All of them were incredibly sharp and intelligent. They proceeded to pepper me with questions, mostly about what places they could use for background scenery. It was all made more difficult by the courier, whose English was many times better than that of the interpreter and who insisted on acting as interpreter, too. So questions came twice in different forms. And my problem was that I had made all the places in the book *up*.

In the end I suggested that they go and look at Dulverton and at Exmoor above it. But the courier wouldn't hear of that because he had booked them through to Cardiff. So they went away, presumably to Cardiff, and that was that for nearly three years.

After this interval, my tendril suddenly became active and stated—with what truth I know not—that Miyazaki had scrapped what this team had produced and sacked all of them except the producer, and was doing film and script himself. I do know that his was the major hand in the finished movie and that he went to Alsace for his background—well, I never believed that Cardiff was right anyway.

Nothing then for another couple of years. Then the tendril produced a picture of the moving castle and complained about the studio's secrecy. And some months after that, I and my family were invited to a private viewing of the finished film in Bristol, where I live, and then to meet Miyazaki himself at dinner afterward. This was very exciting indeed.

I will say straight away that I *loved* the film and was fascinated by the way my book had been altered. I still think, and my family also thought, that Miyazaki's changes had messed up the plot, but this does not change my admiration of the superb animation. Some of the war scenes are spectacular.

Miyazaki and I were both children during World War II, and I am intrigued by our different reactions to this. My reaction is seldom to put a war actually in a book: the war heralded in my *Howl's Moving Castle* takes place between that book and its sequel, whereas Miyazaki has it squarely *in there*, quite terrifyingly. I deal with the aftermath, Miyazaki with the present terror. Similarly, I kept picking up seeds of the film in my book: the scarecrow is mine, but more functional in the book, and so are Calcifer and the dog. But Miyazaki cut out the excursion to another world—Wales, indeed—in order to make his animation larger and more universal. That meant losing the second fire demon, which I still think is a pity, because the Witch of the Waste had to become a bemused old crone, but these are mere observations, not complaints.

I still find myself laughing at the memory of the Witch and old Sophie gasping their way up that enormous flight of steps (and that was in the book, too, except that Sophie climbs them alone, twice).

Meeting Miyazaki afterward was a true pleasure. He really is a genius.

But no one told me that the screenplay was around on its own—no reason to, I suppose, since I didn't write it—and it came as a real surprise to hear that it had won a Nebula Award. Who did write it, by the way?

Editor's Note: The screenplay of Howl's Moving Castle was written by Hayao Miyazaki, Cindy Davis Hewitt, and Donald H. Hewitt.

SEEKER

BY JACK MCDEVITT

Jack McDevitt is a Philadelphia native. He has been, among other things, a naval officer, an English teacher, a customs officer, and a Philadelphia taxi driver.

He started writing novels after Terry Carr invited him to contribute to the Ace Specials series in 1985. His most recent books are *Cauldron*, his fourteenth novel, and *Outbound*, a collection. In 2004, his novel *Omega* received the John W. Campbell Memorial Award. He won the first UPC Science Fiction Award, an international competition. And he is also the recipient of the Phoenix and SESFA Awards for his body of work.

He is married to the former Maureen McAdams of Philadelphia. McDevitt and his wife live in Brunswick, Georgia.

About *Seeker*, Jack McDevitt writes:

When I was about eight, an aunt gave me a copy of Richard Halliburton's Book of Marvels. *I immediately fell in love with it. It introduced me to the ancient world, and especially to its Seven Wonders: gardens and temples and statues and even a lighthouse.*

But each new wonder, shortly after it was introduced, turned out to be, at best, badly weathered. Usually it was missing altogether.

And then there was Atlantis. I tried to imagine how it

would have felt to be on the beach at Wildwood when the place started to sink and the waves began rolling in. I was so intrigued by the idea that I enlisted a librarian and we went to the source, Plato.

Nobody else in the ancient world ever mentioned a sea-borne civilization that had sunk beneath the sea. The librarian and I tracked the Atlantis comments down. He describes it in "Timaeus" and "Critias" as conducting wars against European enemies. If a reader is looking for advanced technologies, or a civilization ahead of its time, he will look in vain. I was probably the only little kid on the planet who got mad at Plato.

But the Seven Wonders and Atlantis and, for that matter, Mu and Lemuria combined to impress on me a sense of things lost. I'm sure it's no coincidence that Priscilla Hutchins, the heroine of my Academy novels, spends a sizable chunk of her time trying to reconstruct long-dead alien civilizations; and that Alex Benedict, my other series character, is an antiquarian in the far future who specializes in solving mysteries produced by artifacts from human history.

Atlantis lives again, in a different form, in Seeker. The Margolians abandoned a theocratic North America in the twenty-sixth century, headed for a destination, as one of them said, "so far that even God won't be able to find us." Nobody ever heard of them again. And eventually they became so remote in time that their very existence was transformed into the stuff of legend.

It was, I guess, inevitable that Alex and Chase would eventually pick up the trail.

EXCERPTED FROM *SEEKER*

JACK MCDEVITT

I was tempted to send a message to Alex, suggesting if he was determined to proceed with the hunt for the *Falcon* and its logs, he'd be the obvious person to do it since he had experience dealing with the Ashiyyur. The problem was that I knew how he'd respond: You're already there, Chase. Pull up your socks and go talk to them. See what you can find out.

So I bit the bullet. I sent a message telling him what I knew, and that if I could find out who had the *Falcon* I would proceed to Xiala. I also told him I was underpaid.

Then I linked through to the Mute embassy and was surprised when a young man answered the call. I figured they'd want a human face up front, but I'd expected an avatar. The guy on the circuit felt real, and when I flat-out asked him if it were so he said yes. "I think," he added with a laugh, "that we want to impress everyone that there's really nothing to fear." He grinned. "Now, Ms. Kolpath, what can I do for you?"

He had the unlikely name Ralf, and when I told him I needed some information, he invited me to go ahead. He was graceful, amiable, well-spoken. Auburn hair, brown eyes, good smile. Maybe thirty. A good choice for the up-front guy.

When I finished explaining he shook his head. "No," he said. "I wouldn't know anything about that. Wait, though. Let me check." He looked through a series of data tables, nodded at a couple of them, and tapped the screen. "How about that?" he said. "Here it is. The *Falcon*, right?"

"That's correct."

He read off the date and time of transfer. And the recipient. Which was another foundation.

"Good," I said. "Is there a way I can get access to the ship?" I went into my research-project routine.

"I really have no idea," he said. "I can tell you where it is. Or at least where it was shipped. After that you'll have to deal with them."

"Okay," I said. "Where is it?"

"It was delivered to the Provno Museum of Alien Life Forms. On Borkarat."

"Borkarat?"

"Yes. Do you have a travel document?"

He was talking about authorization from the Confederacy to enter Mute space. "No," I said.

"Get one. There's an office on the station. Then check in with our travel people. We have an office too. You'll have to file an application with us as well. It may take a few days."

I hung around the orbiter for two weeks thinking all kinds of angry thoughts about Alex, before the documentation was completed and my transport vessel arrived. Curious thing: There'd been an assumption when we'd first encountered the Mutes that a species that used telepathy in lieu of speech would be unable to lie, would never have known the nature of deceit. But of course they turned out to be no more truthful than we are. Not when they discovered humans couldn't penetrate them.

I'd kept Alex informed. I pointed out it would be expensive to take the connecting flight to Xiala. I would be on board the *Diponga*, or, as the station people called it, the *Dipsy-Doodle*. I also let him know I wasn't happy with the fact this was becoming a crusade. I suggested if he wanted to call a halt, I wouldn't resist. And I'd wait for his answer before going any farther.

His response was pretty much what I expected. He sat at my desk, looking serene, with the snow-covered forest visible through the windows, and told me how well I was doing, and how fortunate he was to have an employee with such persistence. "Most people would have simply given up, Chase," he said.

Most people were brighter than I was.

I thought about signing up for the Hennessey Foundation's seminar on How to Control Psychological Responses When Communicating with Ashiyyureans. But it was hard to see that it would be helpful if they didn't have an actual Mute come into the conference room. Anyhow, it seemed cowardly.

So when everything was in order, I boarded the *Dipsy-Doodle,* along with eight other human passengers. They settled us in the ship's common room, and an older man in a gray uniform inscribed with arcane symbols over his left-hand pocket—Mute Transport, I guessed—welcomed us on board, and told us his name was Frank and he'd be traveling with us and anything he could do to make things more comfortable we should just ask. We would be leaving in about an hour. He explained that the flight to Xiala would take approximately four standard days. And were there any questions?

My fellow passengers looked like business types. None was especially young, and none seemed very concerned. I was surprised, though, that all were human. Were there no Mutes returning home?

Afterward, Frank showed us to our compartments, and asked if, after settling in, we would all return to the common room. At 1900 hours. And thank you very much.

I stowed my gear. Four days to Xiala. Then it would be another four days to Borkarat, which was halfway across Mute space. I began to wonder if I wanted to look at something else in the way of career employment.

When we rejoined Frank, he talked about procedures for a few minutes, how the meal schedule would run, use of washroom facilities, and so on. Then he explained that the captain wanted to introduce himself.

On cue, the door to the bridge opened and the first Mute I had ever seen in person walked into the room. It had gray mottled skin, recessed eyes under heavy ridges, arms too long for the body, and the overall appearance of something that needed more sunlight. It wore a uniform similar to Frank's.

I had expected, judging from everything I'd heard, to feel a rush of horror. Accompanied by the knowledge that my thoughts lay exposed. But none of that happened. I would not have wanted to meet the captain on Bridge Street at night. But not because it, he, had a fearsome appearance. (He did appear to be a male, but he didn't look as if he were ready to try me with his hors d'oeuvres.) Rather, there was something about him that was revolting, like a spider, or insects in general. Yet the captain certainly bore no resemblance to a bug. I think it was connected with the fact that his skin glistened.

"Good evening, ladies and gentlemen," he said, speaking through a voice box. "I'm Captain Japuhr. Frank and I are pleased to have you on board the *Diponga*. Or, as Frank and the people at the station insist on calling it, the *Dipsy-Doodle*." The pronunciation wasn't quite right. It sounded more like *Dawdle*. "We hope you enjoy your flight, and we want you to know if there's anything we can do, please don't hesitate to tell us." He nodded at Frank, and Frank smiled.

Every hair I owned stood at attention. And I thought, He knows exactly what I'm feeling. He picks up the revulsion. And, as if to confirm my worst fears, the captain looked my way and nodded. It wasn't a human nod, it was rather a lowering of the whole head and neck, probably because he didn't have the structural flexibility to do it the way you or I would.

But I understood the gesture. He was saying hello. He understood my reaction, but he was not going to take offense.

That was a good thing. But what would happen when I was away from the captain and dealing with ordinary run-of-the-mill street-level Mutes?

What had I gotten myself into?

While I was worrying myself sick, Captain Japuhr came closer. Our eyes connected, his red and serene and a bit too large, and mine—. Well, I felt caught in somebody's sights. At that moment, while I swam against the tide, thinking no, you have no idea, you can't read me, his lips parted in an attempt to smile. "It's all right, Ms. Kolpath," he said to me. "Everyone goes through this in the beginning."

It was the only time I saw his fangs.

During the flight, the captain, for the most part, confined himself to the bridge and to his quarters, which were located immediately aft the bridge, and separated from the area accessible to the passengers. My fellow travelers explained that the Ashiyyur—nobody used the term Mute on shipboard—were conscious of our visceral reaction to them, and in fact they had their own visceral reaction to deal with. They were repulsed by us too. So they sensibly tried to defuse the situation as much as they were able.

Frank explained there were no Ashiyyurean passengers for much the same reason. Flights were always reserved for one species or the other. I asked whether that also applied to him. Had he made flights with alien passengers?

"No," he said. "It's against the rules."

We were about twelve hours out when we made our jump. One of the passengers got briefly ill. But the reaction passed, and she had her color back a few minutes after transition was complete. Frank informed us that we were going to arrive at Xiala sixteen hours ahead of schedule. That would mean a nineteen-hour layover at the station before I could catch my connecting flight. "I was looking at the passenger list," Frank said. "You'll be traveling on the *Komar*, and you'll be the only human passenger."

"Okay," I said. I'd suspected that might happen.

"Have you traveled before in the Assemblage?" That was the closest approximation in Standard of the Mutes' term for their section of the Orion Arm. I should add here that they have a looser political organization than the human worlds do. There is a central council, but it is strictly a deliberative body. It has no executive authority. Worlds, and groups of worlds, operate independently. On the other hand, we've learned the hard way how quickly and effectively they can unite in a common cause.

"No," I said. "This is my first time."

He let me see that he disapproved. "You should have someone with you."

I shrugged. "Nobody was available, Frank. Why? Will I be in physical danger?"

"Oh, no," he said. "Nothing like that. But you'll be a long time without seeing anybody else."

"It won't be the first time I've been alone."

"I didn't mean you'd be alone. You'll have company." He jiggled his hands, indicating there was no help for it now. "And I don't want to give you the wrong impression. I think you'll find your fellow travelers willing to help if you need it." More hesitation. "May I ask where you're headed? Are you going anywhere from Borkarat?"

"No," I said.

"When will you be coming back?"

"As soon as my business is completed."

"Good. I'm sure you'll be fine."

The first night I stayed up until midmorning. Everybody did. We partied and had a good time. And when we'd all had a bit too much to drink, the captain came out, and the atmosphere did not change.

When finally I retired to my cabin, I was in a rare good humor. I hadn't thought much about Captain Japuhr during the previous few hours, but when I killed the lights and pulled the sheets up, I began to wonder about the range of Mute abilities. (Think Ashiyyur, I told myself.) My quarters were removed from the bridge and his connecting cabin by at least thirty meters. Moreover, he was almost certainly asleep. But if he was not, I wondered, was he capable of picking up my thoughts at that moment? Was I exposed?

In the morning I asked Frank. Depends on the individual, he said. "Some can read you several rooms away. Although they all find humans tougher than their own kind."

And was the capability passive? Or was there an active component? Did they simply read minds? Or could they inject thought as well?

There were about five of us in the common room, eating breakfast, and Frank passed the question around to Joe Klaymoor. Joe was in his seventies, gray, small, and I would have thought introverted, but I could never make myself believe an introvert would head for Mute country. Make it maybe reticent. And a good guy. He kept his sense of humor through the whole experience. Laughed it off. "I have nothing to hide," he said. "To my everlasting regret.

"It was a big philosophical issue for them at one time," he continued. "Same as the question we once had, whether our eyes emitted beams of some sort which allowed us to see. Or whether the outside world put out the beams. Like our eyes, the Ashiyyur are receivers only. They collect what gets sent their way. And not just thoughts. They get images, emotions, whatever's floating around at your conscious level." He looked momentarily uncomfortable. " 'Floating around' is probably an inadequate expression."

"What would be adequate?" asked one of the other

passengers, Mary DiPalma, who was a stage magician from London.

"Something along the lines of an undisciplined torrent. They'll tell you that the human psyche is chaotic."

Great. If that's really so, no wonder they think we're all idiots. "The conscious level," I said. "But not subconscious?"

"They say not," said Joe. He laid his head on the back of the chair. "They didn't settle the transmission/reception issue, by the way, until they encountered us."

"Really. How'd that happen?"

"They understood a lot of what we were thinking, although a fair amount of it was garbled because of the language problem. When they tried to send something, I gather we just stared back."

Somebody else, I don't recall who, asked about animals. Can they read animals too?

Joe nodded. "The higher creatures, to a degree."

"And pain?" asked Mary DiPalma.

"Oh, yes. Absolutely."

"That must be a problem for them."

Frank took a long breath. "What's the survival advantage in that?" he asked. "I'd expect that a creature that feels pain around it would not last long."

Joe thought it over. "Evolution happens along two tracks," he said. "One track is individually based, and the other assists survival of the species. Or at least, that's the way it was explained to me. It's not my field."

"Then they're not predators," I suggested.

One of the women laughed. "Not predators? You get a look at those bicuspids? And the eyes? They're hunters, no doubt about that."

"That's true," said Joe. "From what I understand, they don't make the connection with their natural prey. It also seems to be the case that they developed the telepathic capability relatively late. They're a much older species than we are, by the way."

"I wonder," said one of the guys, "if we'll develop psi abilities eventually."

One of the women drew herself up straighter. "I certainly hope not," she said.

Mary laughed. "I can already do it."

"Show me," said Larry, the youngest guy on the ship.

Mary turned to me. "Can you read his mind, Chase?"

"Oh, yes," I said.

Nobody seemed in a hurry to make port. Frank broke out drinks every evening, and we partied. Mary warned me that she still remembered her first flight into alien space, and how unnerving it had been. "But just relax and enjoy it," she said. "You'll never experience anything like it the rest of your life."

They were good times on the *Dipsy-Doodle*.

I should say up front that during my visit to Mute country, no Ashiyyurean mistreated me in any way, or was anything but courteous. Still, we were aware of the thing on the bridge, that it was different, not only physically, but in some spiritual way. And that sense of the other, however nonthreatening it might be, drove us together. Herd instinct in action.

I made several friends on that flight, people with whom I'm still in contact. Like Joe Klaymoor, a sociologist from Toxicon, studying the effects on a society of widespread telepathy. And Mary DiPalma, from ancient London. Mary showed me enough to make me believe in magic. And Tolman Edward, who represented a trading company. Tolman, like me, had never been in the Assemblage before. He was headed into the interior to try to straighten out a trade problem.

I've thought since that the entire effort, trying to chase down the *Falcon*, was worth it just for the few days I spent with them. It had all started with a drinking cup from an interstellar. I have another one on my desk as I write these words. The characters, once again, are unfamiliar. The eagle is replaced by a seven-pointed star with a halo. It belonged, not to the *Seeker*, but to the *Dipsy-Doodle*.

But it had to end. When Captain Japuhr came back to inform us that we would be docking in fourteen hours, we all felt as if something was being lost. I've been on a lot of flights, a lifetime's worth, but I've never known anything quite like it. He asked if we were comfortable, and if there was anything he could do. Then he withdrew.

Frank took me aside. "Have you figured out how you're going to get around?" he asked.

"How do you mean?"

"There'll be a language problem."

"Why?" I'd assumed I was dealing with mind readers, so communication should be easy.

"You think in Standard. They'll read images, but not the language. Even if you can get them to understand you, you still won't be able to understand them."

"What do you suggest?"

He opened a cabinet and took out a notebook. "This will help." He turned it on and spoke to it. "Help me, I'm lost, I have no idea where I am." A group of Mute words appeared on the screen. "Just show them this. They'll read it, and they can input an answer for you." He smiled. "Don't expect them to be wearing voice-boxes."

"How do I read the reply?"

It had a Mute keyboard. "They can poke in whatever they want to say. It will translate and put it on the display." He frowned at it. "It's not practical for long conversations, but it will help you order food and find your hotel."

"May I borrow it?"

"You can rent it."

"Absolutely," I said. It wasn't cheap, but I put it on Rainbow's account. "What about food? Will I have trouble?"

"Some of the major hotels can provide a menu for you. Don't try to eat the stuff the Ashiyyur do. Okay?"

I'd seen pictures of what they eat. There was no danger of that.

"One other thing, Chase. There'll always be somebody who can speak Standard at our service counter. We're also as close as your link. They'll be able to direct you where you want to go."

We disembarked that night at the Xiala orbiter, picked up our bags, and did a last round of goodbyes. Good luck and all that. Captain Japuhr came out to wish us farewell. Everybody shook hands and hugged. We clung together for a few steps as we moved out into a concourse filled with Mutes. They towered over us and they had six digits on each hand and they liked solemn clothing (except one female with a yellow hat that looked like a sombrero). They eyed us as if we were, as the old saying goes, from Bashubal. Frank lingered with us and told us we'd be fine and wished us luck. He seemed especially concerned about me. And then, finally, I was alone.

I've watched lovers walk out of my life twice, guys I was seriously attached to, and about whom I still have regrets. But I never watched anybody walk off with quite the same level of misgiving as on that occasion.

A female with two children passed me, and she moved to put herself between them and me as if I might be dangerous. I wondered if she—and they—picked up the sudden resentment I felt. What was the point of having telepathic abilities if empathy didn't come with them?

The concourse was almost empty, for which I was grateful. I wandered over to one of the portals and looked down. The sun was just rising over the curve of the planet. Directly below, it was still night over a major land mass. I could see a single big moon. It was setting in the west, and its soft glow illuminated a series of mountain peaks.

The service counter surprised me. The avatar was a duplicate of me. "How may I help you, Chase?" she asked.

She confirmed my booking to Borkarat. The ship would leave next afternoon. She recommended a hotel, made my reservation, and wished me a pleasant evening.

Actually, she looked pretty good.

Overall anatomical structure of the Mutes is similar to our own, at least as far as things like waste disposal are concerned. I suppose there are only so many ways an intelligent creature can function. There'll necessarily be gravity, so energy-source intake has to happen near the top of the anatomy, the processing functions midway, and elimination near the bottom of the working area. What I'm saying is that the rooms assigned to humans at the Gobul Hotel were Mute rooms. Everything was bigger, and I'll confess I found the toilet something of a challenge.

I took my first meal in the restaurant, in an effort to accustom myself to my hosts. And I sat there like an idiot convinced everyone was watching me, the real me, not simply the external shell that we're accustomed to putting on display. What was most difficult, I hated being there, thoroughly disliked being in their company, struggled to hold down my emotions, and knew that all of it was visible to any who cared to look. Joe Klaymoor tells me Mutes are able, to a degree, to shield their minds from each other. They are, he says, probably evolving into an entity that will eventually possess a single consciousness. But not yet. And he adds the scary possibility that we may go the same way.

One or two came over to introduce themselves, and I said hello through the notebook, but it was a clumsy business. They told me they had never seen a real human before, and I knew they were trying to be complimentary. But I felt like a show animal. They left after a couple of minutes. My food came and

I hurried through it, tried smiling at the surrounding Mutes who persisted in staring at me when they thought I wasn't looking. I was glad to get back to my room.

I thought about calling it off. Let Alex track down the *Falcon* himself.

Which he would do.

He wouldn't say anything to me, wouldn't criticize me, but I knew how he was. Send a boy—or a woman—to do a man's job.

I boarded the *Komar* in the morning. Direct flight to Borkarat, one of the major worlds of the Assemblage. It was eighty-six light-years from Xiala.

I had twenty-one fellow passengers, all Mutes. Most were in the common room when I made my entrance. Which is the right word. A young male saw me. Nobody else turned in my direction, but they all came to alert. Don't ask me how I knew. But I was suddenly aware they were all watching me through that single pair of eyes.

A kid buried his head in his mother's robe.

I could see right away this was going to be a thoroughly enjoyable flight. I smiled lamely at the young male. Mutes don't smile well. Maybe they don't need to. Some, who've lived among us, have picked it up, but they don't do it naturally, which is the reason it always scares the pants off you when they try.

Another aspect of spending time with Mutes is that they don't talk. You're in a room with more than twenty people, and they're all sitting quietly, looking at one another. And nobody is saying anything.

They tried to be sociable. They made gestures in my direction. Made eye contact with me. Several raised their hands in greeting.

After a few minutes, I did what I'd promised myself I

wouldn't: I ducked into my compartment and closed the door, wishing with all my heart I could close the door on my conscious mind. Outside, a short time later, hatches closed. I heard the engines come to life. And there was a knock at the door.

I opened up and looked at a Mute in the same gray uniform Frank had worn. He handed me a white card. It said, *Welcome aboard. Please belt in. We are ready to launch.* And then a second card: *Do you require assistance?*

I leaned forward and pointed at my forehead, like a dolt. I wanted him to know I was thinking. And I formed the word *No* in my mind. *No, thank you. I'm fine.*

Then I remembered he probably didn't understand Standard. He bowed.

I know there's a harness attached to my chair. I'll use that. I visualized myself secured by the harness.

He bowed again and walked away.

I am a little blue cookie box.

I hid in my cabin. Went out just long enough to use the washroom facilities, or grab my meals, which were okay. (I understood there were special preparations on board for me.) Four days wasn't terribly long. I could live with that.

We were about an hour into the flight when the knock came again. This time, though, it wasn't the attendant. It was a male, of indeterminate age, tall even for a Mute. Too tall for the passageway, forcing him to hunch down. He looked at me with stone cold eyes and I wondered whether he was reading my discomfort. He wore dull blue leggings and a loose shirt, an outfit not uncommon among the Mutes I'd seen, although they usually preferred robes.

I stood staring up at him. Then I heard a click, and an electronic voice said, "Hello. Are you all right?"

I tried to push everything out of my mind, save a return greeting. "Hello," I said. "Yes, I'm fine, thank you."

"Good. I know this sort of thing can be unsettling."

"No. I'm fine. No problem at all." And I thought about the logic of trying to lie to a mind reader.

"Can I be of assistance?"

"I think you just have been."

"Excellent." The voice was coming from an amulet. "May I point out that, whatever you may think, you are among friends."

Naked among friends. And I tried to pull that one back.

He hesitated. I began to understand he didn't want to let me see he could actually probe me.

I was trying to decide whether to invite him in. "I appreciate your concern," I said.

"Do not take any of this experience seriously. We will be together four days, more or less. At the end of which we will go our separate ways. So nothing you do here can harm you."

"You're right, of course."

"Would you like to join us? We would be very happy to make your acquaintance."

"Yes. Of course." He backed away, making room for me. I followed him, closing the door behind me. "My name is Chase."

"You would probably find mine unpronounceable. Call me—" I literally felt his presence in my head. "Call me Frank."

Had I been thinking about the flight attendant on the *Dipsy-Doodle*? "Okay, Frank." I extended my hand.

I passed my notebook around and the other passengers used it to ask questions. Where was I from? Had I been in the Assemblage before? Where was I headed? Why was I so afraid? (This last came from a child who had participated reluctantly, and who seemed almost as fearful as I was.)

Frank was quite good. "There is nothing that can pass

through your mind that we have not seen before," he said. "Except, perhaps," he added, "your squeamishness in our presence."

Don't hold back, big fella. Just let me have it.

Several of them poked one another and bobbed their heads in what must have been laughter.

I asked Frank whether it wasn't distracting to be constantly experiencing a flow of thought and emotions from others.

"I can't imagine life without it," he explained. "I'd be cut off." His red eyes focused on me. "Don't you feel isolated? Alone?"

Over the course of the trip, I learned that a blending of minds lends an extra dimension to what lovers feel for each other. Or friends. That telepathy facilitates a deeper communication. That no, there is not any evolution that any of the Ashiyyur are aware of toward a group mind. In fact they laughed when I relayed Joe's theory. "We are individuals, Chase," said one of the females, "because we can see so plainly the differences between ourselves and others."

"We can't hide from what we think," Frank told me on the second day. "Or what we feel. And we know that. My understanding is that humans are not always honest even with themselves. I can't understand how that could be, but it's a fascinating concept. On another subject, we're aware of your struggle against your coarser notions. But we all have them. So we think nothing of it. It is part of what we are, what you are, so we accept it.

"And by the way, there is no need to be embarrassed by your reflexive reaction to our appearance. We find you unappealing also." He stopped and looked around. I had by then picked up some of the nonverbal cues they used, and several signalled their displeasure at his statement. "I should amend that," he said, "to physically unappealing. But we are coming to know your interior, your psyche. And there we find that you are one of us."

Although Borkarat was not the Mute home world, it was influential. This was where policy toward humans was formulated and, when possible, sold to the various independent political units of the Assemblage. This was the place where representatives met. And from which, during the recurring periods of hostility with the Confederacy, action had been directed.

No shots had been fired between Mute and human warships for a few years, but the long conflict still simmered. Nobody really knew what it was about any longer. Neither side was interested in real estate belonging to the other. Neither side actively threatened anyone. And yet there it was, a living antipathy, drifting down the centuries. Politicians on both sides got support by promising the voters to be tough with the aliens. (I wondered how the Mutes could have politicians when their minds were more or less open to all.)

The term Assemblage was a misnomer. The loose group of Mute states, worlds, duchies, outposts, orbital cities, and whatever else, were more a social grouping than a formal political entity. But they could react in concert with stunning efficiency. Some observers argued they could already see the stirrings of a group mind.

I was relieved to get off the *Komar*. I stopped at the service desk, where another human avatar in my image presented herself and gave me directions to get to the museum at Provno.

The shuttle I wanted was marked with a lightning bolt designator. It was crowded and I had to push in. There was nothing more revelatory of the alien nature of Mute society than boarding that vehicle and watching the Mutes interract with each other, make way, stow their packages, move their children into seats, quiz each other over who gets the window, and do it all in absolute silence. Well, maybe not absolute. There were of course the sounds of rustling clothing, closing panels, and air escaping from cushions. Harnesses clicked down into place. But there was never a voice.

I had by then been more than a week in the exclusive company of Mutes, and I was learning to ignore the sense of being exposed to the public gaze. Just don't worry about it, I told myself. But I couldn't resist occasionally glancing over at a fellow passenger and picturing myself waving hello.

There was usually a physical response, a meeting of eyes, a lifting of the brow, something. Occasionally they even waved back.

I tried to think warm and fuzzy. And in fact, my reaction to these creatures, the primal fear and revulsion I'd felt in their presence, was diminishing every day. But as I sat on that shuttle, trying to read and comprehending nothing on the page, I was a long way from being comfortable.

We dropped into the atmosphere, descended through a twilit sky, ran into some turbulence and a storm, and finally sailed out of the clouds beneath a canopy of stars. Below, cities blazed with light.

A female flight attendant stopped by my seat. "We'll be landing in seven minutes," she said. I couldn't tell where the voice was coming from.

I spent the night at a hotel just off a river walk. Ashiyyurean architectural styles, at least on Borkarat, are subtly different from anything we've employed. Human structures, whatever their cultural tendencies, are static. They are symmetrical, and however eclectic the design, one always detects balance and proportion. Mute buildings, on the other hand, are a study in motion, in flow, in energy. The symmetry is missing. Seen from a distance, my hotel looked incomplete, as though part of it projected into another dimension.

I ate in the restaurant, surrounded by Mutes. And I'm

proud to say I held my own. Stayed at my table, worked my way casually through my meal, and never flinched when a nearby infant took one horrified look at me and tried to burrow into its mother's mammaries.

I wondered how early in life the telepathic capability began. Could a child in the womb communicate?

Two humans, male and female, showed up. They saw me and came over. You'd have thought we were the oldest of friends. At my invitation, they sat down and we exchanged trivia for the next hour. They were from St. Petersburg, one of the ancient terrestrial capitals.

I think I've mentioned that the Ashiyyur do not use spirits of any kind. I read somewhere that there are no comparable drugs for them, and they do not understand the human compulsion to drown our senses. So the glasses we raised to each other that night were tame, but we made promises that we'd get together back home. Amazing how close Andiquar and St. Petersburg became.

I slept well, except for waking in the middle of the night after an especially realistic sexual dream. And there I was again, wondering if the Mutes could pick up nocturnal stuff as well. Had I frightened the children on three floors? No wonder they didn't like having people around.

I thought about the couple I'd met at dinner. They were young, recently married. But I bet myself that tonight they were sleeping apart, and probably drumming up more emotional vibrations for any Mute antennas paying attention than a good old-fashioned romp would have. Muteworld is not a place for a honeymoon.

The Museum of Alien Life Forms was located on an expanse of parkland on Provno, in a long island chain in one of the southern seas. The parkland area is largely devoted to public buildings and historical preserves. Landscaped sections are

blocked off, often commemorating historical figures, sometimes simply devoted to providing quiet places for reflection.
There are streams and myriad small creatures that come beg-
ging for handouts from the visitors.

The architecture was hyperbolic, rooftops that surged like
ocean waves, angled spires, soaring stalks. Crowds wandered
through the area on long curved walkways that sometimes as-
cended to the upper levels. Everywhere there were leafy porti-
coes to which you could retreat simply to enjoy the play of
nature. Everything seemed light and fragile, as ethereal as the
sunlight.

Private vehicular traffic was banned in the parks. Visitors
could enter by aircab, although the bulk of traffic was handled
by an over-water maglev train. I'd never seen one before, and
I have no idea how they handled the engineering.

The museum stood between two similar but not quite
identical obelisks. It was made of white marble, and incorporated arcs and columns and rising walkways so that it was
reminiscent of one of those children's puzzles that you can take
apart and reassemble but always looks different. A moving
ramp took me up to the front entrance, where I came to a wall
engraved with Mute characters. I turned my translator loose
on it, and it told me that the museum had been founded on an
indeterminate date. (The translator wasn't good at converting
dates and times.) And that life forms from all over the galaxy
were welcome.

I went inside, while Mute children looked alternately at me
and the sign and gaped, while others just gaped and still others
drew back in alarm. But I smiled politely and pushed ahead.

You might expect that a museum devoted to offworld biologi-
cal systems would give you lots of holograms of the various life
forms in action. But it wasn't that way at all. Maybe there was
a sense that visitors could get the holograms at home. So what

they had were display cases and exhibits filled with stuffed skins and heads.

They'd probably been picked for shock value. Giant creatures with maws big enough to swallow a lander. Snakes that could have used me for a toothpick. Predators of all sizes and shapes, some fearsome beyond belief. And the prey, cute little furred creatures that could run fast. And damn well better.

There were plants capable of gobbling down a fair-sized technician, and multilimbed creatures that lived in the trees of Barinor, wherever that was, and stole children. I wondered why anybody would choose to live under such conditions. At least, with kids.

I'm happy to report there were no stuffed people. Maybe that was a concession to the fact that they occasionally had human visitors. They did have a couple of birds and lizards from Rimway, and a tiger from Earth. But the only human was an avatar, a bearded guy who looked like a Neanderthal. He even carried a spear. When I approached him, he grunted.

Best foot forward, I always say. I wondered how many Mute kids were getting their first impression of the human race from this guy.

He was guarding the Hall of the Humans, an entire wing dedicated to us. The only other known technological species. It was big, circular, with a vaulted ceiling three stories high. Display cases and tables supporting exhibits stood everywhere. There were primitive and modern weapons on display, representations of various deities, musical instruments, clothing from various cultures, a chess game in progress, and dishware. An alcove was fitted out to look like a business office. Many of the displays, where appropriate, were marked with a date and world of origin. There were headsets that allowed you to plug into the history of the various objects. And an array of books, all translations into basic Mute. I scanned them and found *The Republic*, Burnwell's *Last Days of the American State*, *Four Novels* by Hardy Boshear, and a ton of other work. On the whole, they didn't have a very representative collection. Most of the writers were modern, and there were desperately few classics.

And in the center of the room, on a dais, was my target. The *Falcon*. Mutes were queued up on a ramp, waiting their turns to enter the airlock. They were coming out the other side, through an exit that had been cut through the hull.

DEPARTMENT OF PLANETARY SURVEY was inscribed up near the bridge, along with its designator TIV114. And, of course, FALCON. Its navigation lights were on. That was good news because it meant the thing had power. I'd brought a small generator on the possibility I'd have to supply my own.

There were maybe forty Mutes in the hall, but none of them was moving. They were all looking straight ahead, pretending to examine the various displays at hand, but the fact they were frozen in place gave them away. One female, standing near a statue of one of the ancient gods, was watching me, and everyone there was sitting behind her eyes.

She raised a hand. Hello.

I smiled and switched my attention back to the *Falcon*, telling myself what lovely lines it had, and how I'd enjoy piloting it. I tried to keep my mind off the actual reason for my visit. Gradually my fellow visitors began moving again. As far as I could tell, not one ever turned for a surreptitious look.

I strolled among the displays, fingering the data chip I'd brought for the download.

There were guide stations where you could learn about humans. I used my translator and discovered that we were high on the evolutionary scale, but remained a step below the Ashiyyur. We thought of ourselves as sentient, the guide explained, and in a limited sense we were even though our primary mode of communication was yapping. Okay, yapping is my translation. They said "by making sounds or noise." Take your pick.

We were described as having some admirable traits. We were loyal, reasonably intelligent, compassionate, and could be friendly.

On the other hand we were known to be dishonest, vile, violent, licentious, treacherous, and hypocritical, and on the whole we ran a society that had lots of police and needed them.

Individuals tend to be docile, said the guide, and may usually be approached without fear. But when humans form groups their behavior changes and becomes more problematic. They are more likely to subscribe to a generally held view than to seek their own. Elsewhere: There seems to be a direct correlation between the size of a group and its inclination to consent or resort to violence or other questionable behavior, and/or the predilection of individuals to acquiesce when leaders suggest violent or simplistic solutions to perceived problems.

This is the collective reaction phenomenon.

Several of the books were described as providing an especially incisive view of human mental limitations. I was beginning to get annoyed.

I kept an eye on the *Falcon* as I circled the hall, trying to tamp my thoughts, wondering again about telepathic range. More Mutes came in, and while I was wandering among the exhibits looking as casual as possible, they joined the line.

Realizing the line was not going to go away, I took my place at the rear. There were about a dozen in front of me, including two younger ones, not quite adult, but not children either. Both female. I saw them react, saw one touch the other's elbow and pull her robe more tightly around her.

I'd had it by then. I tried to send a message. To all who were listening. People who need to feel superior by accident of birth usually turn out to be dummies. I didn't know how to visualize it, so I don't imagine much of it got through, but I felt better afterward.

The hatchway onto the bridge was open so I could see the instruments and the pilot's position. But a blue restraining cord was drawn across the entrance and a sign read DO NOT ENTER. There were two chairs, one for the pilot, one for a visitor or technician. I thought this is where they had been, Margaret Wescott at the controls, and Adam in the auxiliary seat. I looked through the viewport at the gray museum walls, and wondered what had been visible to them.

In front of the pilot's seat, and to its right, was the reader. I reached into my pocket and touched the chip.

The AI's name had been James.

I leaned over the cord, acutely conscious of the others around me. I would have liked a few minutes alone. "James," I said in a whisper, "are you there?"

There was no vocal reply, but a green lamp came on. I wasn't familiar with the *Falcon* instrument panel. Still, some aspects remain identical from ship to ship, and from one era to another. The green lamp always means the AI is up and running. First hurdle cleared. (I assumed they'd disconnected the voice so James wouldn't startle anyone.)

The cord was too high for me to get over, so I lifted it and went under, and proceeded directly to the reader, ignoring the stir behind me. I inserted the chip. "James," I said, "download the navigation logs. Any that are connected with Dr. Adam Wescott."

Another lamp came on. White. I heard the data transmission begin. I turned and smiled at the Mutes standing behind me. Hi. How you doing? Enjoying your visit? I tried to think how this was routine maintenance. Instead it occurred to me that the Mutes might suspect I was trying to steal the ship, that I was planning to take off with it, blast out of the hall, and head for Rimway. Trailing Mutes all the way. I could see the *Falcon* rising over Borkarat's towers, then accelerating for deep space. No matter how hard I tried, I couldn't get the image out of my mind.

No such scenario of course was even remotely possible. The museum had removed a bulkhead to admit the ship, and then replaced it. The engines were at least disengaged and probably missing. And there wouldn't have been any fuel anyhow.

The chip whirred and hummed while the data collected over more than a decade flowed through the system. I looked over the other instruments, the way a technician might, just doing a little maintenance, got to adjust the thrust control here.

More Mutes were crowding up to the guide rope to see what was going on. I imagined I could feel them inside my head, checking to see whether I was deranged. It occurred to me they might conclude this was the way inferior species behaved and think no more of it. And I wondered whether that had been my own thought, or whether it had arrived somehow from outside.

A couple of them moved away but others took their places. I watched the lights, waiting for the white lamp to change color, indicating the operation was complete.

I straightened the chairs. Looked out the portals. Checked the settings on the viewscreens. Straightened my blouse.

I wished I'd thought to bring a dust cloth.

I looked out the portals again. Two Mutes in blue uniforms were converging on the *Falcon*.

The lamp stayed white.

The crowd began to shuffle, to clear out of the way. I heard heavy footsteps. And of course no sound of a voice anywhere.

Then the authorities arrived. Both in uniform. Both looking severe. But then, with an Ashiyyurean, how could you tell? I tried to cut that idea off at the pass. Tried to transmit Almost done. Just be patient a moment more.

They stepped over the cord. One took my arm and pulled me away from the reader. I looked back. The lamp was still white.

They wanted me to go with them and I was in no position to decline. They half-carried me back out through the airlock, and through a gawking crowd that now made no effort to hide the fact that they were watching. We exited the hall, went down a ramp, across a lobby, and into a passageway.

I was helpless. I was projecting all the protests I could manage. But nothing worked. You couldn't talk to these guys. Couldn't use nonverbals. Couldn't even use the old charm.

They hauled me through double doors and into a corridor lined with offices. I realized I wasn't simply being ejected. We were headed into the rear of the museum.

The doors were made of dark glass, and Mute symbols were posted electronically beside them. One opened and I was ushered inside. It was an empty office. I saw an inner door, a couple of tables and three or four chairs. All standard Mute size. My guards released me and set me down.

They stayed with me, both standing, one near the door by which we'd entered, the other by the inner door. I wondered whether my chip had finished loading yet.

We waited about five minutes. I heard noises on the other side of the inner door. Then it opened. A female emerged, wearing clothing that resembled a workout suit. The color was off-white. The suit had a hood, but it lay back on her shoulders.

She looked at me, and then at my escorts. They seemed to be exchanging information. Finally the escorts got up and left the room. Apparently I was not considered a threat.

The female reached into a pocket, produced a translator on a cord, and draped it around her neck. "Hello, Chase," she said. "I'm Selotta Movia Kabis. You may call me Selotta."

Even under the circumstances, it was hard not to laugh. I gave my name and said hello.

She stared at me. "We are pleased you decided to visit us today."

"It's my pleasure," I said. "This is a lovely museum."

"Yes." She circled me and took a chair opposite. "May I ask what you were doing in the *Falcon*?"

No point lying. The translator wouldn't help her read my

thoughts, but I wondered whether she really needed it. "I was trying to download the navigation logs."

"And why were you doing that? The *Falcon* has been in the Human Hall as long as I've been here. It must be twenty-five years."

"It's been a long time," I agreed.

She concentrated on me. Made no effort to hide the fact she was in my head. "What's the *Seeker*?" she asked.

I told her. I described its connection with Margolia, and then explained what Margolia was.

"Nine thousand years?" she said.

"Yes."

"And you hope to find this place? Margolia?"

"We know that's a trifle optimistic. But we do hope to find the ship."

Gray lids came down over her eyes. And rose again. The irises were black and diamond-shaped. She considered me for a long moment. "Who knows?" she said, finally. "Find one and it might lead you to the other."

"As you can see," I said, "I need your help to get the information from the *Falcon*."

She sat quite still while she considered it. Then she seemed to come to a conclusion. The door to the passageway opened. I turned and saw one of the guards. Selotta motioned him forward. He had my chip in his right hand. I wondered if it might be possible to grab the chip and run.

"No," said Selotta. "That would not be a good idea."

He handed it to her, turned and left. She inspected it, switched on a lamp, and took a longer look. When she'd finished she turned those diamond eyes directly on me. I got the distinct feeling she thought she was talking to me. Suddenly she seemed surprised. She shook her head in a remarkably human gesture and tapped the translator. "It's hard to remember sometimes I have to speak."

"I guess," I said.

"I was asking whether you don't have some qualms about the possibility of a living civilization out there. Your own people, after nine thousand years. You have no way of knowing what you might find."

"I know."

"No offense intended, but humans tend to be unpredictable."

"Sometimes," I said. "We don't expect to find a living world. But if we could find the original settlement, we could retrieve some artifacts. They'd be quite valuable."

"I'm sure."

I waited, hoping she'd give me the chip and wish me godspeed.

"Perhaps we can make an arrangement."

"What did you have in mind?"

"You may have your chip."

"If—?"

"I will expect, if you find what you're looking for, a generous bequest."

"You want some of the artifacts?"

"I think that would be a reasonable arrangement. Yes, I will leave the details to your generosity. I believe I may safely do that." She got up.

"Thank you, Selotta. Yes. If we succeed I will see the museum is taken care of."

"Through me personally."

"Of course."

She made no move to hand over the chip. "Chase," she said, "I'm surprised you didn't come to us first."

I stood there trying to look as if attempted theft had been a rational course of action. "I'm sorry," I said. "I should have. To be honest, I didn't know whether you would allow it."

"Or try to grab everything for ourselves."

"I didn't say that."

"You thought it." She put the chip on the table top. "I'll look forward to hearing from you, Chase."

TOMORROW AND TOMORROW . . .

In "All Our Yesterdays . . ." Bud Webster cast a look back on the history of science fiction and fantasy. In "Quo Vadis?" Orson Scott Card surveyed the field's present situation and direction. Now Mike Resnick looks to the future of the field and finds new opportunities to be explored—and exploited.

Mike Resnick is the author of more than fifty science fiction novels, close to two hundred stories, and two screenplays, and the editor of almost fifty anthologies. He has won a Nebula, five Hugos, and other major awards in the USA, France, Spain, Poland, Japan, and Croatia. His work has been translated into twenty-two languages. In his spare time, he reports, he sleeps.

I HAVE SEEN THE FUTURE—
AND IT AIN'T GOT A LOT OF
DEAD TREES IN IT

MIKE RESNICK

Let me start by saying that I love books and magazines. I like the heft and feel of them. I grew up with the printed page. I can't remember ever having a house where most of the wall space wasn't covered by overflowing bookshelves. I don't especially like reading my science fiction off the computer screen.

But as a science fiction writer—and one who has to pay the bills with his science fiction—it's my job to look ahead and see what's coming, and whether I like it or not makes no difference. It is not a matter of Good or Bad, but rather of True or False. And the truth is that we're not going to be pulping as many forests in the future.

Twenty years ago, when the Internet was just taking off, just about every established science fiction writer was approached by start-up publishers. The pitch was always the same: give me something for free today and I'll make you rich tomorrow (or maybe next week, or possibly in seventeen years, or conceivably in . . .). Every one of them went belly-up.

Then Omni Online, which certainly had deep pockets (or at least could borrow from *Penthouse*'s), came along, and suddenly we had a paying market. It lasted long enough for Ellen Datlow to become the very first to win a Hugo for editing an electronic publication. But it didn't last a lot longer than that.

Then we had GalaxyOnline.com of sainted memory. My God, we writers loved it! Half a buck a word (if you wrote the minimum; it was a set amount). But it was a loss leader for a film and TV company that never made any films or TV shows, and it was gone within a year.

Then there was Scifi.com, which paid more than double the going rate of the digests, and lasted long enough to win Ellen Datlow another Hugo for editing another electronic magazine . . . but it, too, bit the dust.

So what's with the title to this article (I hear you ask)? All these places had high hopes and high pay rates, and they all wound up in publishing's graveyard.

What can I tell you? The first few settlers who tried to reach the West Coast didn't make it either.

But they paved the way for those who came after them.

The first success story came from an unlikely source: Fictionwise.com, which publishes only reprints. They started out in 2000 with a small handful of science fiction writers— Robert Silverberg, Nancy Kress, James Patrick Kelly, myself, just a few others. And they paid twice as much for a short fiction reprint as the average anthology paid. And we all thought: wow, how long has this been going on? It's like stealing!

And we never thought of it again—until later that same year, when the royalty checks came, and we realized that, hey, there are thousands of people out there who, when confronted by trillions of free words of drivel on the Internet, prefer to pay for reprints by known authors.

That was only eight years ago. These days Fictionwise.com has literally thousands of authors, including such heavyweights as Dan Brown, Stephen King, Robert Ludlum, Isaac Asimov, Robert A. Heinlein, and that whole crowd.

They proved you could sell literally billions of words of electronic reprints, many (in fact, in the beginning, most) of them science fiction. So it was only a matter of time before a major science fiction publisher took a look at the direction the world was heading and decided it was time to go electronic. As I write these words, the pioneer is Baen Books with Jim Baen's Universe, but I'm sure by the time you read this (maybe a year from now) others will have joined the parade.

And I wouldn't be surprised to see some of the major houses start publishing novel-length science fiction online as well.

Will they have any trouble getting writers?

Not a chance. The online magazines can pay three and four times what the print magazines can pay, and the book publishers can easily offer 30 to 40 percent royalties to the author, rather than the 10 to 12 percent most hardcovers pay and the 8 to 10 percent that usually goes for paperbacks.

How can this be?

Easy.

Let's take a print magazine. It sells, let us hypothesize, for $5.00, give or take a nickel.

What does it cost to get that magazine into your hands?

Well, first of all, the publisher has to buy the stories.

There's an office, which means an overhead.

There's paper for the magazines to be printed on.

There are color separations for the covers.

There is the cost of printing tens of thousands (formerly a couple of hundred thousand) of copies of the magazine.

There are shipping costs. The subscribers don't drive to the printing plant to pick their copies up. Neither do the distributors. Neither do the stores.

There are the distribution costs, both for the national and local distributors. They're good guys, but they don't place the magazines in the stores for free.

There are the stores themselves. If they sell a $5.00

magazine, most of them are going to want $1.75 or thereabouts for their trouble.

There are warehouse costs for those magazines that are neither sold nor pulped.

And a month later, every copy has vanished from the newsstands and bookstores, to be replaced by the next month's issue, and the publisher will never make another cent on that out-of-date issue.

Now let's take a look at how these expenses affect an electronic magazine.

There is no office expense and no overhead, because the editors work out of their houses.

There are no paper expenses, because the magazine doesn't appear on paper.

There are no color separations, because they simply post the artwork right on the screen.

There are no printing expenses, because the magazine is not printed.

There are no shipping costs, because the magazine is not shipped.

There are no national or local distribution costs, because they are not distributed. They're right there online, and they don't have to pay anyone to put the magazine in your physical proximity.

There is no cut for the bookstores, because the magazine is not sold in bookstores. Or newsstands. Or supermarkets. It's online. You pay the price, you get the magazine, and there are no middlemen. (You might think about that. When you pay $5.00 for a digest magazine, the publisher might wind up with about $1.85 of it—and that'll be his average only if he sells the entire print run, which never happens, or even comes close to happening these days. You pay $5.00 for an electronic magazine, and the publisher gets $5.00.)

There are no warehouse costs, because the magazine exists in electronic phosphors, not paper pages. They'll post the next issue in another month or two, but this one won't be through earning money, because it will always be available for anyone who wants it.

Do you begin to see where the print magazines are at a bit of a disadvantage?

Now it should be clear to you why electronic publishers can outbid the print publishers for the writers they want. The print magazines are paying authors, overhead, color separations, paper, printing, shipping, national distributors, local distributors, bookstores, and warehouses.

And the electronic publishers? They're paying . . . authors. Period.

So of course they can triple or quadruple what the print magazines pay. (I assume we don't have to go over the whole thing again with books. Just cut to the last sentence: So of course they can triple or quadruple the hardcover and paperback royalty rates.)

Ah, but is there an audience out there in the vast electronic wilderness? After all, buying *The Da Vinci Code* or *The Shining* or the Foundation trilogy from Fictionwise.com is one thing, but will computer users go for new science fiction? (The obvious answer is: Certainly they will. An electronic story has already won the Nebula, and another one has just been nominated for a Hugo the same week I am writing this. But those are voters, not masses of buyers, and you want numbers, right?)

Okay—numbers you want, numbers we got.

I'm a Luddite, especially in a forward-looking community like science fiction writers and fans. Last summer I didn't even know what the word "podcast" meant. Then the young man who runs a website called Escape Pod, one of many such sites, bought reprint rights to some of my stories. I didn't give it another thought until he mentioned, a few months later, that the story of mine he had run most recently had received twenty-two thousand hits in its first month online.

Twenty-two thousand hits? The issue of the science fiction

magazine it had appeared in had only sold 18,500 copies. More people heard my story online (or on their iPods) than read it.

I was sure it had to be an aberration. So when my next story, which was not a traditional science fiction story, but had been sold to a young adult anthology, came out, I waited two weeks and then asked how it was doing.

Fourteen thousand hits. In two weeks. For me. Not for Kevin Anderson or Anne McCaffrey or Robert Jordan or someone else who lives on the bestseller list.

That's when I knew beyond any doubt that the world was changing, that the readers are still out there in quantity, but they're not necessarily browsing the bookstores or the news-stands anymore.

No sea change ever happens smoothly, especially not in as hidebound, old-fashioned, and unimaginative a business as publishing. Some of the start-ups that look good today may be dead by the time you read this. But if so, others will take their place. There are thirty-seven holes in the dike, and traditional publishers have only ten (figurative) fingers.

Like I said, I still love the feel of a book, the smell of an old pulp, the pleasure I get just from browsing a bookstore.

But I also can see the future coming at full speed, and I don't think anything's going to stop it. Certainly not me. I may not like reading electronic pages, but I'm editing an electronic prozine, and I'm selling to every podcaster I can find, and more than two hundred of my books and stories have been sold as electronic reprints.

I'm not happy with electronic publishing. I probably never will be. But I'd be a hell of a lot less happy if I was left behind.

THE ANDRÉ NORTON AWARD

MAGIC OR MADNESS

BY JUSTINE LARBALESTIER

The André Norton Award for Best Young Adult Science Fiction honors the memory of one of the field's most prolific and most beloved authors, André Norton. Equally adept in science fiction or fantasy, she was a major force in developing both genres for young readers.

The 2007 André Norton Award winner is Justine Larbalestier, for her novel *Magic or Madness*. She lives in Sydney and, she says, travels too much. In addition to the Magic or Madness trilogy, Larbalestier has written *Ultimate Fairy Book* and the nonfiction *Battle of the Sexes in Science Fiction*. She has also edited the scholarly anthology *Daughter of Earth*.

She writes:

Magic or Madness arose out of my desperate desire for a quicker way to get between Sydney (where I am from) and New York City (my husband's home). A way that did not involve twenty-four hours of taxis, airports, and planes. What if, I thought to myself, there were a door between there and here? Which led to other thoughts, like, Would you still get jet lag (or, rather, door lag) as you traveled between the two? Who would make such a door? How? And what kind of a world would have that kind of magic?

The book (and trilogy—Magic or Madness is the first of three) was also shaped by my exasperation with a certain kind of fantasy novel. The kind that usually has a scene like this:

"I am in trouble!" quoth the hero. "Fortunately I have a magic pill of trouble-destroying properties! I will swallow it! All will be well."

I couldn't swallow it. I have never been able to swallow it. I wanted to write about a world where magic wasn't there to fix every problem the hero (or author) encounters; a book where, indeed, magic is the problem.

Quite a nasty problem, actually. As the title suggests, the choice is between magic or madness. If you're born with magic but don't use it, you go mad. Not merely eccentric, but must-be-locked-up-because-dangerous mad. Yet if you use your magic, you shorten your life span. Most magic wielders don't make it much past thirty. In the Magic or Madness trilogy magic is not a blessing, it's a curse.

Make 'em suffer, after all, is an excellent prescription for page-turning novels and one at the heart of a great many young adult novels. That, and a set of questions centered around not just identity (learning who you are) but also questions of place (learning your world, literally and meta-physically). One of the many pleasures of writing for young adults is being free to explore such questions without having to send in an envoy from another planet to investigate this one. All teenagers are envoys from another planet.

On this planet right now it's an extraordinary time for young adult literature. Not only has the audience expanded hugely in the last ten years (thank you, J. K. Rowling), but so, too, has the quality and quantity of the work, not to mention the support of publishers, booksellers, librarians, readers, and other YA writers. Bliss it is in this dawn to be alive, but to be a young adult writer is very heaven.

Throughout each calendar year the members of SFWA recommend novels and stories for the annual Nebula Awards. The editor of the *Nebula Awards Report* collects these recommendations and publishes them in the SFWA *Forum*. Near the end of the year the *NAR* editor tallies the endorsements, draws up a preliminary ballot, and sends it to all active SFWA members. Each novel and story has a one-year eligibility period from its date of publication. If the work fails to make the preliminary ballot during that year it is dropped from further Nebula consideration.

The *NAR* editor then compiles a final ballot listing the five novels, novellas, novelettes, and short stories that garnered the most votes on the preliminary ballot. For purposes of the Nebula Award, a novel is defined as consisting of 40,000 words or more; a novella is 17,500 to 39,999 words; a novelette is 7,500 to 17,499 words; and a short story is 7,499 words or fewer.

SFWA also appoints a novel jury and a short-fiction jury to supplement the final ballot's five nominees with a sixth choice in cases where a presumably worthy work was neglected by the membership at large. Thus, the appearance of extra finalists in any category may stem either from a jury selection or a tie vote in the preliminary balloting.

Founded in 1965 by Damon Knight, the Science Fiction Writers of America began with a charter membership of seventy-eight authors. Today the organization has more than a thousand members and its name has been augmented to Science Fiction and Fantasy Writers of America.

Early in his tenure as SFWA's first secretary-treasurer, Lloyd Biggle Jr., proposed that the organization periodically select and publish the year's best stories. This idea quickly evolved into the elaborate balloting process, an annual awards banquet, and a series of Nebula anthologies, the latest of which you now hold in your hands. Judith Ann Lawrence designed the Nebula trophy from a sketch by Kate Wilhelm. It is a block of Lucite containing polished rock crystal and a representation of a spiral galaxy made of metallic glitter. The trophies are handmade, and no two are exactly alike.

1965

Best Novel: *Dune* by Frank Herbert
Best Novella (tie): "The Saliva Tree" by Brian W. Aldiss
"He Who Shapes" by Roger Zelazny
Best Novelette: "The Doors of His Face, the Lamps of His Mouth" by Roger Zelazny
Best Short Story: " 'Repent, Harlequin!' Said the Ticktockman" by Harlan Ellison

1966

Best Novel (tie): *Flowers for Algernon* by Daniel Keyes
Babel-17 by Samuel R. Delany
Best Novella: "The Last Castle" by Jack Vance
Best Novelette: "Call Him Lord" by Gordon R. Dickson
Best Short Story: "The Secret Place" by Richard McKenna

1967

Best Novel: *The Einstein Intersection* by Samuel R. Delany
Best Novella: "Behold the Man" by Michael Moorcock
Best Novelette: "Gonna Roll the Bones" by Fritz Leiber
Best Short Story: "Aye, and Gomorrah" by Samuel R. Delany

1968

Best Novel: *Rite of Passage* by Alexei Panshin
Best Novella: "Dragonrider" by Anne McCaffrey
Best Novelette: "Mother to the World" by Richard Wilson
Best Short Story: "The Planners" by Kate Wilhelm

1969

Best Novel: *The Left Hand of Darkness* by Ursula K. LeGuin
Best Novella: "A Boy and His Dog" by Harlan Ellison
Best Novelette: "Time Considered as a Helix of Semi-Precious Stones" by Samuel R. Delany
Best Short Story: "Passengers" by Robert Silverberg

1970

Best Novel: *Ringworld* by Larry Niven
Best Novella: "Ill Met in Lankhmar" by Fritz Leiber
Best Novelette: "Slow Sculpture" by Theodore Sturgeon
Best Short Story: No Award

1971

Best Novel: *A Time of Changes* by Robert Silverberg
Best Novella: "The Missing Man" by Katherine MacLean
Best Novelette: "The Queen of Air and Darkness" by Poul Anderson
Best Short Story: "Good News from the Vatican" by Robert Silverberg

1972

Best Novel: *The Gods Themselves* by Isaac Asimov
Best Novella: "A Meeting with Medusa" by Arthur C. Clarke

Best Novelette: "Goat Song" by Poul Anderson
Best Short Story: "When It Changed" by Joanna Russ

1973

Best Novel: *Rendezvous with Rama* by Arthur C. Clarke
Best Novella: "The Death of Doctor Island" by Gene Wolfe
Best Novelette: "Of Mist, and Grass, and Sand" by Vonda N. McIntyre
Best Short Story: "Love Is the Plan, the Plan Is Death" by James Tiptree Jr.
Best Dramatic Presentation: *Soylent Green* screenplay by Samuel R. Greenberg (based on the novel *Make Room! Make Room!* by Harry Harrison)

1974

Best Novel: *The Dispossessed* by Ursula K. LeGuin
Best Novella: "Born with the Dead" by Robert Silverberg
Best Novelette: "If the Stars Are Gods" by Gordon Eklund and Gregory Benford
Best Short Story: "The Day Before the Revolution" by Ursula K. LeGuin
Best Dramatic Presentation: *Sleeper* by Woody Allen
Grand Master: Robert A. Heinlein

1975

Best Novel: *The Forever War* by Joe Haldeman
Best Novella: "Home Is the Hangman" by Roger Zelazny
Best Novelette: "San Diego Lightfoot Sue" by Tom Reamy
Best Short Story: "Catch that Zeppelin!" by Fritz Leiber
Best Dramatic Writing: Mel Brooks and Gene Wilder for *Young Frankenstein*
Grand Master: Jack Williamson

1976

Best Novel: *Man Plus* by Frederik Pohl

Best Novella: "Houston, Houston, Do You Read?" by James Tiptree Jr.

Best Novelette: "The Bicentennial Man" by Isaac Asimov

Best Short Story: "A Crowd of Shadows" by Charles L. Grant

Grand Master: Clifford D. Simak

1977

Best Novel: *Gateway* by Frederik Pohl

Best Novella: "Stardance" by Spider and Jeanne Robinson

Best Novelette: "The Screwfly Solution" by Racoona Sheldon

Best Short Story: "Jeffty Is Five" by Harlan Ellison

Special Award: *Star Wars*

1978

Best Novel: *Dreamsnake* by Vonda N. McIntyre

Best Novella: "The Persistence of Vision" by John Varley

Best Novelette: "A Glow of Candles, a Unicorn's Eye" by Charles L. Grant

Best Short Story: "Stone" by Edward Bryant

Grand Master: L. Sprague de Camp

1979

Best Novel: *The Fountains of Paradise* by Arthur C. Clarke

Best Novella: "Enemy Mine" by Barry Longyear

Best Novelette: "Sandkings" by George R. R. Martin

Best Short Story: "giANTS" by Edward Bryant

1980

Best Novel: *Timescape* by Gregory Benford
Best Novella: "The Unicorn Tapestry" by Suzy McKee
   Charnas
Best Novelette: "The Ugly Chickens" by Howard
   Waldrop
Best Short Story: "Grotto of the Dancing Deer" by
   Clifford D. Simak
Grand Master: Fritz Leiber

1981

Best Novel: *The Claw of the Conciliator* by Gene Wolfe
Best Novella: "The Saturn Game" by Poul Anderson
Best Novelette: "The Quickening" by Michael Bishop
Best Short Story: "The Bone Flute" by Lisa Tuttle
   (declined by the author)

1982

Best Novel: *No Enemy but Time* by Michael Bishop
Best Novella: "Another Orphan" by John Kessel
Best Novelette: "Fire Watch" by Connie Willis
Best Short Story: "A Letter from the Clearys" by Connie
   Willis

1983

Best Novel: *Startide Rising* by David Brin
Best Novella: "Hardfought" by Greg Bear
Best Novelette: "Blood Music" by Greg Bear
Best Short Story: "The Peacemaker" by Gardner Dozois
Grand Master: André Norton

1984

Best Novel: *Neuromancer* by William Gibson
Best Novella: "PRESS ENTER■" by John Varley

Best Novelette: "Bloodchild" by Octavia E. Butler
Best Short Story: "Morning Child" by Gardner Dozois

1985

Best Novel: *Ender's Game* by Orson Scott Card
Best Novella: "Sailing to Byzantium" by Robert
    Silverberg
Best Novelette: "Portraits of His Children" by
    George R. R. Martin
Best Short Story: "Out of All Them Bright Stars" by
    Nancy Kress
Grand Master: Arthur C. Clarke

1986

Best Novel: *Speaker for the Dead* by Orson Scott Card
Best Novella: "R & R" by Lucius Shepard
Best Novelette: "The Girl Who Fell into the Sky" by
    Kate Wilhelm
Best Short Story: "Tangents" by Greg Bear
Grand Master: Isaac Asimov

1987

Best Novel: *The Falling Woman* by Pat Murphy
Best Novella: "The Blind Geometer" by Kim Stanley
    Robinson
Best Novelette: "Rachel in Love" by Pat Murphy
Best Short Story: "Forever Yours, Anna" by Kate
    Wilhelm
Grand Master: Alfred Bester

1988

Best Novel: *Falling Free* by Lois McMaster Bujold
Best Novella: "The Last of the Winnebagos" by Connie
    Willis

Best Novelette: "Schrodinger's Kitten" by George Alec
    Effinger
Best Short Story: "Bible Stories for Adults, No. 17: The
    Deluge" by James Morrow
Grand Master: Ray Bradbury

1989

Best Novel: *The Healer's War* by Elizabeth Ann Scarborough
Best Novella: "The Mountains of Mourning" by Lois
    McMaster Bujold
Best Novelette: "At the Rialto" by Connie Willis
Best Short Story: "Ripples in the Dirac Sea" by Geoffrey
    A. Landis

1990

Best Novel: *Tehanu: The Last Book of Earthsea* by Ursula
    K. LeGuin
Best Novella: "The Hemingway Hoax" by Joe
    Haldeman
Best Novelette: "Tower of Babylon" by Ted Chang
Best Short Story: "Bears Discover Fire" by Terry Bisson
Grand Master: Lester del Rey

1991

Best Novel: *Stations of the Tide* by Michael Swanwick
Best Novella: "Beggars in Spain" by Nancy Kress
Best Novelette: "Guide Dog" by Mike Conner
Best Short Story: "Ma Qui" by Alan Brennert

1992

Best Novel: *Doomsday Book* by Connie Willis
Best Novella: "City of Truth" by James Morrow
Best Novelette: "Danny Goes to Mars" by Pamela
    Sargent

Best Short Story: "Even the Queen" by Connie Willis
Grand Master: Frederik Pohl

1993

Best Novel: *Red Mars* by Kim Stanley Robinson
Best Novella: "The Night We Burned Road Dog" by
Jack Cady
Best Novelette: "Georgia on My Mind" by Charles
Sheffield
Best Short Story: "Graves" by Joe Haldeman

1994

Best Novel: *Moving Mars* by Greg Bear
Best Novella: "Seven Views of Olduvai Gorge" by Mike
Resnick
Best Novelette: "The Martian Child" by David Gerrold
Best Short Story: "A Defense of the Social Contracts" by
Martha Soukup
Grand Master: Damon Knight
Author Emeritus: Emil Petaja

1995

Best Novel: *The Terminal Experiment* by Robert J. Sawyer
Best Novella: "Last Summer at Mars Hill" by Elizabeth
Hand
Best Novelette: "Solitude" by Ursula K. LeGuin
Best Short Story: "Death and the Librarian" by Esther
M. Friesner
Grand Master: A. E. van Vogt
Author Emeritus: Wilson "Bob" Tucker

1996

Best Novel: *Slow River* by Nicola Griffith
Best Novella: "Da Vinci Rising" by Jack Dann

Best Novelette: "Lifeboat on a Burning Sea" by Bruce
Holland Rogers
Best Short Story: "A Birthday" by Esther M. Friesner
Grand Master: Jack Vance
Author Emeritus: Judith Merril

1997

Best Novel: *The Moon and the Sun* by Vonda N.
McIntyre
Best Novella: "Abandon in Place" by Jerry Oltion
Best Novelette: "The Flowers of Aulit Prison" by Nancy
Kress
Best Short Story: "Sister Emily's Lightship" by Jane
Yolen
Grand Master: Poul Anderson
Author Emeritus: Nelson Slade Bond

1998

Best Novel: *Forever Peace* by Joe Haldeman
Best Novella: "Reading the Bones" by Sheila Finch
Best Novelette: "Lost Girls" by Jane Yolen
Best Short Story: "Thirteen Ways to Water" by Bruce
Holland Rogers
Bradbury Award: J. Michael Straczynski
Grand Master: Hal Clement (Harry Stubbs)
Author Emeritus: William Tenn (Philip Klass)

1999

Best Novel: *Parable of the Talents* by Octavia E. Butler
Best Novella: "Story of Your Life" by Ted Chiang
Best Novelette: "Mars Is No Place for Children" by
Mary A. Turzillo
Best Short Story: "The Cost of Doing Business" by
Leslie What

Best Script: *The Sixth Sense* by M. Night Shyamalan
Grand Master: Brian W. Aldiss
Author Emeritus: Daniel Keyes

2000

Best Novel: *Darwin's Radio* by Greg Bear
Best Novella: "Goddesses" by Linda Nagata
Best Novelette: "Daddy's World" by Walter Jon
  Williams
Best Short Story: "macs" by Terry Bisson
Best Script: *Galaxy Quest* by Robert Gordon and David
  Howard
Bradbury Award: Yuri Rasovsky and Harlan Ellison
Grand Master: Philip José Farmer
Author Emeritus: Robert Sheckley

2001

Best Novel: *The Quantum Rose* by Catherine Asaro
Best Novella: "The Ultimate Earth" by Jack Williamson
Best Novelette: "Louise's Ghost" by Kelly Link
Best Short Story: "The Cure for Everything" by Severna
  Park
Best Script: *Crouching Tiger, Hidden Dragon* by James
  Schamus, Kuo Jung Tsai, and Hui-Ling Wang (from
  the book by Du Lu Wang)
President's Award: Betty Ballantine

2002

Best Novel: *American Gods* by Neil Gaiman
Best Novella: "Bronte's Egg" by Richard Chwedyk
Best Novelette: "Hell Is the Absence of God" by Ted
  Chiang
Best Short Story: "Creature" by Carol Emshwiller
Best Script: *The Lord of the Rings: The Fellowship of the
  Ring* by Fran Walsh, Philippa Boyens, and Peter

Jackson (based on *The Lord of the Rings* by J. R. R. Tolkien)

Grand Master: Ursula K. LeGuin

Author Emeritus: Katherine MacLean

2003

Best Novel: *The Speed of Dark* by Elizabeth Moon

Best Novella: "Caroline" by Neil Gaiman

Best Novelette: "The Empire of Ice Cream" by Jeffrey Ford

Best Short Story: "What I Didn't See" by Karen Joy Fowler

Best Script: *The Lord of the Rings: The Two Towers* by Fran Walsh, Philippa Boyens, Stephen Sinclair, and Peter Jackson (based on *The Lord of the Rings* by J. R. R. Tolkien)

Grand Master: Robert Silverberg

Author Emeritus: Charles L. Harness

2004

Best Novel: *Paladin of Souls* by Lois McMaster Bujold

Best Novella: "The Green Leopard Plague" by Walter Jon Williams

Best Novelette: "Basement Magic" by Ellen Klages

Best Short Story: "Coming to Terms" by Eileen Gunn

Best Script: *The Lord of the Rings: The Return of the King* by Fran Walsh, Philippa Boyens, and Peter Jackson (based on *The Lord of the Rings* by J. R. R. Tolkien)

Grand Master: Anne McCaffrey

2005

Best Novel: *Camouflage* by Joe Haldeman

Best Novella: "Magic for Beginners" by Kelly Link

Best Novelette: "The Faery Handbag" by Kelly Link

Best Short Story: "I Live with You" by Carol Emshwiller
Best Script: *Serenity* by Joss Whedon
André Norton Award: *Valiant: A Modern Tale of Faerie* by
    Holly Black
Grand Master: Harlan Ellison
Author Emeritus: William F. Nolan

THE AUTHORS EMERITI

The Author Emeritus Award is SFWA's way of recognizing writers who have made significant contributions to the field of science fiction and fantasy. The award is decided by the board of directors through discussion and consensus.

The Authors Emeriti are:

Emil Petaja	(1994)
Wilson "Bob" Tucker	(1995)
Judith Merril	(1996)
Nelson Slade Bond	(1997)
William Tenn (Philip Klass)	(1998)
Daniel Keyes	(1999)
Robert Sheckley	(2000)
Katherine MacLean	(2002)
Charles L. Harness	(2003)
William F. Nolan	(2005)
D. G. Compton	(2006)